ALISTAIR MACLEAN

Fear is the Key

HarperCollins*Publishers*

HarperCollins*Publishers*
1 London Bridge Street,
London SE1 9GF

This paperback edition 2019
1

Previously published in paperback by HarperCollins*Publishers* 2004
and by Fontana 1963

First published in Great Britain by Collins 1961

Copyright © HarperCollins*Publishers* 1961

Alistair MacLean asserts the moral right to
be identified as the author of this work

ISBN: 978-0-00-833742-1

This novel is entirely a work of fiction.
The names, characters and incidents portrayed in it are
the work of the author's imagination. Any resemblance to
actual persons, living or dead, events or localities is
entirely coincidental.

Typeset in Meridien by Palimpsest Book Production Limited,
Falkirk, Stirlingshire

Printed and bound in Great Britain by
CPI Group (UK) Ltd, Croydon CR0 4YY

All rights reserved. No part of this publication may be
reproduced, stored in a retrieval system, or transmitted,
in any form or by any means, electronic, mechanical,
photocopying, recording or otherwise, without the prior
permission of the publishers.

This book is sold subject to the condition that it shall not,
by way of trade or otherwise, be lent, re-sold, hired out or
otherwise circulated without the publisher's prior consent
in any form of binding or cover other than that in which it
is published and without a similar condition including this
condition being imposed on the subsequent purchaser.

MIX
Paper from
responsible sources
FSC™ C007454

This book is produced from independently certified FSC™ paper
to ensure responsible forest management.

For more information visit: www.harpercollins.co.uk/green

To W. A. Murray

FOREWORD

The Second World War changed everything, including how authors became authors. Case in point: a boy was born in Scotland, in 1922, and raised in Daviot, which was a tiny village southeast of Inverness, near the remote northern tip of the British mainland, closer to Oslo in Norway than London in England. In the 1920s and 30s such settlements almost certainly had no electricity or running water. They were not reached by the infant BBC's wireless service. The boy had three brothers, but otherwise saw no one except a handful of neighbors. Adding to his isolation, his father was a minister in the Church of Scotland, and the family spoke only Gaelic at home, until the boy was six, when he started to learn English as a second language. Historical precedent suggested such a boy would go on to live his whole life within a ten-mile radius, perhaps working a rural white-collar job, perhaps as a land agent or country solicitor. Eventually the BBC's long-wave Home

Service would have become scratchily audible, and ghostly black and white television would have arrived decades later, when the boy was already middle aged. Such would have been his life.

But Hitler invaded Poland in 1939, and the isolated boy turned 18 in 1940, and joined the Royal Navy in 1941. Immediately he was plunged into the company of random strangers from all over the British Isles and the world, all locked cheek-by-jowl together in a desperate rough-and-tumble bid for survival and victory. He saw deadly danger in the North Atlantic and on Arctic convoys, including the famous PQ 17, and in the Mediterranean, and in the Far East, where ultimately his combat role was pre-empted by the atom bombs and the Japanese surrender, no doubt to his great relief, but where he saw horrors of a different kind, ferrying home the sick and skeletal survivors of Japanese prison camps. Like millions of others, the boy came out of this five-year crucible a 24-year-old man, his horizons radically expanded, his experiences increased many thousandfold, and like many of the demobilized, his nature perturbed by an inchoate restlessness, and his future dependent on a vague, unasked question: well, now what?

The man was Alistair MacLean, and he became a schoolteacher. But the restlessness nagged at him. He wanted more. He began writing short stories, and in 1954, the year I was born, he won a newspaper competition. Legend has it the prize was a hundred pounds, which if true was an enormous sum of money – half of what my dad earned that year, as a junior but determinedly white-collar civil servant. The story was a maritime tale. The competition win was followed by a commission from the Glasgow publisher Collins, to write a novel, with a thousand-pound advance – another enormous sum. That novel was *HMS Ulysses*, which drew on MacLean's own experiences on the Murmansk convoys. It was an immediate and significant success. It was followed by *The Guns of Navarone* and *South by Java Head*, both also set during the war, and both also huge sellers. After three books MacLean was comfortably established as one of the world's biggest-selling fiction writers.

His next three books were different, in one important way – they were set postwar. In the first half of the 1950s, British popular culture was utterly dominated by war stories, very understandably, given the depths of the recent dangers and the immensity of the recent triumph. Churchill was prime minister again. On the page and the screen, brave pilots bombed from low levels, and plucky POWs escaped through sandy tunnels, and charging destroyers smashed through towering waves. The first movie I ever saw was *The Dam Busters*. The second was *Reach for the Sky*. A Saturday morning double bill, up at Villa Cross, for nine-pence. Comic books were full of lantern-jawed privates, fighting through Normandy.

But it had to stop. At some point we had to move on. Merely a question of timing. It was a fraught decision. A delicate psychological balance. The Suez crisis of 1956 was a humiliation that rubbed our noses in our much-diminished power and status. The temptation to keep on revisiting past glories was huge. But the present was happening, and the future was almost upon us. MacLean adapted better than most, perhaps because – as his books show – he was notably non-ideological. He wasn't a Colonel Blimp, living in the past. He had a healthy cynicism about the present, and no great hopes for the future. He had no political position. As a result he was able to nimbly unmoor himself from 1939–1945 in narrative terms, but crucially he was smart enough to bring with him the tropes and memes he had developed while writing about those years. The result was his second trio of novels, books four, five and six, which I think surely represent the absolute plateau of his talent and achievement. They are the perfect MacLeans. Some will argue that the hot streak continued another five years (the Ian Stuart pen name being then unknown) and I would agree that book seven, *The Golden Rendezvous*, and book nine, *When Eight Bells Toll*, are almost-perfect MacLeans, glorious and solid in every possible way, but, in my view, slightly backward-looking, slightly over-reliant on muscle memory, not quite able to overcome the Perfect Three's gravitational pull.

The first of the Perfect Three was MacLean's fourth novel, *The Last Frontier*. Its backstory was rooted in wartime events, and its characters were war-weary and war-experienced, but its setting was explicitly contemporary late-1950s, in communist Hungary, with the recent uprising still fresh in the memory. True to Maclean's non-ideological nature, the book contains an astonishingly humane and sympathetic understanding of Soviet feelings and paranoia. Its characters are compelling and multi-dimensional, and in some cases genuinely and affectingly tragic. By any standard it's one of the great postwar thrillers.

Next up was *Night Without End*. It's set when commercial transatlantic air travel was just beginning to change from a pipe dream to a roaring, thrashing reality. In terms of structure, it's a classic locked-room mystery, but set on the polar icecap. An airliner crashes near a remote research station. The scientists rescue the survivors. One of them is clearly a murderer. Various clocks start ticking. It firms up MacLean's instinctive facility with character types. He knew what we wanted from the hero. He knew we wanted a talented and uncompromising sidekick. Overall it's a total success. Weather has never been done better.

The last of the Perfect Three is *Fear is the Key*, the volume you're holding right now. It has everything. Its melancholy opening harks back to those millions of unspoken demob questions: what now? Some young veterans knew they could never settle down, nine to five. They started cockamamie charter airlines, or rag-tag air cargo operations, using war-surplus planes. John Talbot – this book's hero and first-person narrator – did just that, in partnership with his brother. It didn't end well. Read on, to find out how justice is served. Along the way you'll enjoy every single one of MacLean's signature strengths, all present and correct and in perfect working order – the silent but preternaturally skilled boatman, the stolid and reliable family chauffeur, who we know will play a minor role in saving the day, the dramatic physical infrastructure, the constant presence of the sea, its sound and smell, its depths and dangers. Plus an opening with an amazing first reveal. Above all you'll enjoy the easy and natural grip of a born storyteller. It feels like coming back to a place you had a good time before.

Lee Child

PROLOGUE

May 3rd, 1958.

If you could call a ten by six wooden box mounted on a four-wheel trailer an office, then I was sitting in my office. I'd been sitting there for four hours, the earphones were beginning to hurt and the darkness was coming in from the swamps and the sea. But if I had to sit there all night, then I was going to do just that: those earphones were the most important thing in the world. They were the only remaining contact between me and all the world held for me.

Peter should have been within radio range three hours ago. It was a long haul north from Barranquilla, but we'd made that haul a score of times before. Our three DCs were old but as mechanically perfect as unceasing care and meticulous attention could make them. Pete was a fine pilot, Barry a crack navigator, the West Caribbean forecast had been good and it was far too early in the season for hurricanes.

There was no conceivable reason why they shouldn't have been on the air hours ago. As it was, they must have already passed the point of nearest approach and be drawing away to the north, towards Tampa, their destination. Could they have disobeyed my instructions to make the long dog-leg by the Yucatan Strait and flown the direct route over Cuba instead? All sorts of unpleasant things could happen to planes flying over war-torn Cuba those days. It seemed unlikely, and when I thought of the cargo they were carrying it seemed impossible. Where any element of risk was concerned, Pete was even more cautious and far-seeing than myself.

Over in the corner of my office on wheels a radio was playing softly. It was tuned in to some English-speaking station and for the second time that evening some hill-billy guitar-player was singing softly of the death of mother or wife or sweetheart, I wasn't sure which. 'My Red Rose Has Turned to White' it was called. Red for life and white for death. Red and white – the colours of the three planes of our Trans-Carib Air Charter service. I was glad when the song stopped.

There was nothing much else in the office. A desk, two chairs, a filing cabinet and the big RCA receiver-transmitter powered by a heavy TRS cable that ran through the hole in the door and snaked across the grass and mud and one corner of the tarmac to the main terminal buildings. And there was a mirror. Elizabeth had put that up the only time she'd ever been here and I'd never got around to taking it down.

I looked in the mirror and that was a mistake. Black hair, black brows, dark blue eyes and a white strained haggard face to remind me how desperately worried I was. As if I needed reminding. I looked away and stared out of the window.

That was hardly any better. The only advantage was that I could no longer see myself. I certainly couldn't see anything else. Even at the best of times there was little enough to see through that window, just the ten empty desolate miles of flat swampland stretching from the Stanley Field airport to Belize, but now that the Honduras rainy season had begun, only that morning, the tiny tidal waves of water rolling endlessly down the single sheet of glass and the torn and lowering and ragged hurrying clouds driving their slanting rain into the parched and steaming earth turned the world beyond the window into a grey and misty nothingness.

I tapped out our call sign. The same result as the last five hundred times I'd tapped it. Silence. I altered the waveband to check that reception was still OK, heard a swift succession of voices, static, singing, music, and homed back on our own frequency again.

The most important flight the Trans-Carib Air Charter Co. had ever made and I had to be stuck here in our tiny sub-office waiting endlessly for the spare carburettor that never came. And until I got it

3

that red and white DC parked not fifty yards away on the apron was about as useful to me right then as a pair of sun-glasses.

They'd have got off from Barranquilla, I was certain of that. I'd had the first news three days ago, the day I'd arrived here, and the coded cable had made no mention of any possible trouble. Everything highly secret, only three permanent civil servants knew anything about it, Lloyd's willing to carry the risk even although at one of the biggest premiums ever. Even the news, received in a radio report, of an attempted *coup d'état* yesterday by pro-dictatorship elements to try to prevent the election of the Liberal Lleras hadn't concerned me too much, for although all military planes and internal services had been grounded, foreign airlines had been excluded: with the state of Colombia's economy they couldn't afford to offend even the poorest foreigners, and we just about qualified for that title.

But I'd taken no chances. I'd cabled Pete to take Elizabeth and John with him. If the wrong elements did get in on May 4th – that was tomorrow – and found out what we'd done, the Trans-Carib Air Charter Co. would be for the high jump. But fast. Besides, on the fabulous fee that was being offered for this one freight haul to Tampa . . .

The phones crackled in my ears. Static, weak, but bang on frequency. As if someone was trying to tune in. I fumbled for the volume switch, turned it to maximum, adjusted the band-switch a hair-line on either side and listened as I'd never listened before. But nothing. No voices, no morse call sign, just nothing. I eased off one of the earphones and reached for a packet of cigarettes.

The radio was still on. For the third time that evening and less than fifteen minutes since I'd heard it last, someone was again singing 'My Red Rose Has Turned to White.'

I couldn't stand it any longer. I tore off the phones, crossed to the radio, switched it off with a jerk that almost broke the knob and reached for the bottle under my desk. I poured myself a stiff one, then replaced the headphones.

'CQR calling CQS. CQR calling CQS. Can you hear me? Can you hear me? Over.'

The whisky splashed across the desk, the glass fell and broke with a tinkering crash on the wooden floor as I grabbed for the transmitter switch and mouthpiece.

'CQS here, CQS here!' I shouted. 'Pete, is that you, Pete? Over.'

'Me. On course, on time. Sorry for the delay.' The voice was faint and faraway, but even the flat metallic tone of the speaker couldn't rob it of its tightness, its anger.

'I've been sitting here for hours.' My own anger sounded through my relief, and I was no sooner conscious of it than ashamed of it. 'What's gone wrong, Pete?'

'This has gone wrong. Some joker knew what we had aboard. Or maybe he just didn't like us.

5

He put a squib behind the radio. The detonator went off, the primer went off, but the charge – gelignite or TNT or whatever – failed to explode. Almost wrecked the radio – luckily Barry was carrying a full box of spares. He's only just managed to fix it.'

My face was wet and my hands were shaking. So, when I spoke again, was my voice.

'You mean someone planted a bomb? Someone tried to blow the crate apart?'

'Just that.'

'Anyone – anyone hurt?' I dreaded the answer.

'Relax, brother. Only the radio.'

'Thank God for that. Let's hope that's the end of it.'

'Not to worry. Besides, we have a watchdog now. A US Army Air Force plane has been with us for the past thirty minutes. Barranquilla must have radioed for an escort to see us in.' Peter laughed dryly. 'After all, the Americans have a fair interest in this cargo we have aboard.'

'What kind of plane?' I was puzzled, it took a pretty good flier to move two or three hundred miles out into the Gulf of Mexico and pick up an incoming plane without any radio directional bearing. 'Were you warned of this?'

'No. But not to worry – he's genuine, all right. We've just been talking to him. Knows all about us and our cargo. It's an old Mustang, fitted with long-range tanks – a jet fighter couldn't stay up all this time.'

'I see.' That was me, worrying about nothing, as usual. 'What's your course?'

'040 dead.'

'Position?'

He said something which I couldn't catch. Reception was deteriorating, static increasing.'

'Repeat, please?'

'Barry's just working it out. He's been too busy repairing the radio to navigate.' A pause. 'He says two minutes.'

'Let me talk to Elizabeth.'

'Wilco.'

Another pause, then the voice that was more to me than all the world. 'Hallo, darling. Sorry we've given you such a fright.' That was Elizabeth. Sorry she'd given *me* a fright: never a word of herself.

'Are you all right? I mean, are you sure you're –'

'Of course.' Her voice, too, was faint and far-away, but the gaiety and the courage and the laughter would have come through to me had she been ten thousand miles away. 'And we're almost there. I can see the light of land ahead.' A moment's silence, then very softly, the faintest whisper of sound. 'I love you, darling.'

'Truly?'

'Always, always, always.'

I leaned back happily in my chair, relaxed and at ease at last, then jerked forwards, on my feet, half-crouched over the transmitter as there came a sudden exclamation from Elizabeth and then the harsh, urgent shout from Pete.

'He's diving on us! The bastard's diving on us and he's opened fire. All his guns! He's coming straight –'

The voice choked off in a bubbling, choking moan, a moan pierced and shattered by a high-pitched feminine cry of agony and in the same instant of time there came to me the staccato thunderous crash of exploding cannon-shells that jarred the earphones on my head. Two seconds it lasted, if that. Then there was no more sound of gunfire, no more moaning, no more crying. Nothing.

Two seconds. Only two seconds. Two seconds to take from me all this life held dear for me, two seconds to leave me alone in an empty and desolate and meaningless world.

My red rose had turned to white.

May 3rd, 1958.

ONE

I don't quite know what I had expected the man behind the raised polished mahogany desk to look like. Subconsciously, I suppose, I'd looked for him to match up with those misconceptions formed by reading and film-going – in the far-off days when I had had time for such things – that had been as extensive as they had been hopelessly unselective. The only permissible variation in the appearances of the county court judges in the southeastern United States, I had come to believe, was in weight – some were dried-up, lean and stringy, others triple-jowled and built to match – but beyond that any departure from the norm was unthinkable. The judge was invariably an elderly man: his uniform was a crumpled white suit, off-white shirt, bootlace necktie and, on the back of his head, a panama with coloured band: the face was usually red, the nose purplish, the drooping tips of the silver-white Mark Twain moustache stained with bourbon or mint-juleps or whatever it was they

9

drank in those parts; the expression was usually aloof, the bearing aristocratic, the moral principles high and the intelligence only moderate.

Judge Mollison was a big disappointment. He didn't match up with any of the specifications except perhaps the moral principles, and those weren't visible. He was young, clean-shaven, impeccably dressed in a well-cut light grey tropical worsted suit and ultra-conservative tie and, as for the mint-juleps, I doubt if he'd ever as much as looked at a bar except to wonder how he might close it. He looked benign, and wasn't: he looked intelligent, and was. He was highly intelligent, and sharp as a needle. And he'd pinned me now with this sharp needle of his intelligence and was watching me wriggle with a disinterested expression that I didn't much care for.

'Come, come,' he murmured gently. 'We are waiting for an answer, Mr – ah – Chrysler.' He didn't actually say that he didn't believe that my name was Chrysler, but if any of the spectators on the benches missed his meaning they should have stayed at home. Certainly the bunch of round-eyed schoolgirls, courageously collecting credit marks for their civics course by venturing into this atmosphere of sin and vice and iniquity, didn't miss it: neither did the sad-eyed dark-blonde girl sitting quietly on the front bench and even the big black ape-like character sitting three benches behind her seemed to get it. At least the broken nose beneath the negligible clearance between eyebrows and

10

hairline seemed to twitch. Maybe it was just the flies. The court-room was full of them. I thought sourly that if appearances were in any way a reflection of character he ought to be in the box while I was below watching him. I turned back to the judge.

'That's the third time you've had trouble in remembering my name, Judge.' I said reproachfully. 'By and by some of the more intelligent citizens listening here are going to catch on. You want to be more careful, my friend.'

'I am not your friend.' Judge Mollison's voice was precise and legal and he sounded as if he meant it. 'And this is not a trial. There are no jurors to influence. This is only a hearing, Mr – ah – Chrysler.'

'Chrysler. Not ah-Chrysler. But you're going to make damned certain that there will be a trial, won't you, Judge?'

'You would be advised to mind both your language and your manners,' the judge said sharply. 'Don't forget I have the power to remand you in gaol – indefinitely. Once again, your passport. Where is it?'

'I don't know. Lost, I suppose.'

'Where?'

'If I knew that it wouldn't be lost.'

'We are aware of that,' the judge said dryly. 'But if we could localize the area we could notify the appropriate police stations where it might have been handed in. When did you first notice you no longer had your passport and where were you at the time?'

'Three days ago – and you know as well as I do where I was at the time. Sitting in the dining-room of the La Contessa Motel, eating my dinner and minding my own business when Wild Bill Hickock here and his posse jumped me.' I gestured at the diminutive alpaca-coated sheriff sitting in a cane-bottomed chair in front of the judge's bench and thought that there could be no height barriers for the law enforcement officers of Marble Springs: the sheriff and his elevator shoes together couldn't have topped five feet four. Like the judge, the sheriff was a big disappointment to me. While I had hardly expected a Wild West lawman complete with Frontier Colt I had looked for something like either badge or gun. But no badge, no gun. None that I could see. The only gun in sight in the court-house was a short-barrelled Colt revolver stuck in the holster of the police officer who stood behind and a couple of feet to the right of me.

'They didn't jump you,' Judge Mollison was saying patiently. 'They were looking for a prisoner who had escaped from the nearby camp of one of our state convict road forces. Marble Springs is a small town and strangers easily identifiable. You are a stranger. It was natural –'

'Natural!' I interrupted. 'Look, Judge, I've been talking to the gaoler. He says the convict escaped at six o'clock in the afternoon. The Lone Ranger here picks me up at eight. Was I supposed to have escaped, sawed off my irons, had a bath, shampoo, manicure and shave, had a tailor measure and fit a suit for me, bought underclothes, shirt and shoes –'

'Such things have happened before,' the judge interrupted. 'A desperate man, with a gun or club –'

'—and grown my hair three inches longer all in the space of two hours?' I finished.

'It was dark in there, Judge—' the sheriff began, but Mollison waved him to silence.

'You objected to being questioned and searched. Why?'

'As I said I was minding my own business. I was in a respectable restaurant, giving offence to no one. And where I come from a man doesn't require a state permit to enable him to breathe and walk around.'

'He doesn't here either,' the judge said patiently. 'All they wanted was a driver's licence, insurance card, social security card, old letters, any means of identification. You could have complied with their request.'

'I was willing to.'

'Then why this?' The judge nodded down at the sheriff. I followed his glance. Even when I'd first seen him in the La Contessa the sheriff had struck me as being something less than good-looking and I had to admit that the large plasters on his forehead and across the chin and the corner of the mouth did nothing to improve him.

'What else do you expect?' I shrugged. 'When big boys start playing games little boys should stay home with Mother.' The sheriff was halfway out of his seat, eyes narrowed and ivory-knuckled fists gripping the cane arms of his chair, but the judge waved him back impatiently. 'The two gorillas he had with him started roughing me up. It was self-defence.'

'If they assaulted you,' the judge asked acidly, 'how do you account for the fact that one of the officers is still in hospital with damaged knee ligaments and the other has a fractured cheekbone, while you are still unmarked?'

'Out of training, Judge. The state of Florida should spend more money on teaching its law officers to look after themselves. Maybe if they ate fewer hamburgers and drank less beer –'

'Be silent!' There was a brief interval while the judge seemed to be regaining control of himself, and I looked round the court again. The schoolgirls were still goggle-eyed, this beat anything they'd ever had in their civics classes before: the dark-blonde in the front seat was looking at me with a curious half-puzzled expression on her face, as if she were trying to work out something: behind her, his gaze lost in infinity, the man with the broken nose chewed on the stump of a dead cigar with machine-like regularity: the court reporter seemed asleep: the attendant at the door surveyed the scene with an Olympian detachment: beyond him, through the open door,

I could see the harsh glare of the late afternoon sun on the dusty white street and beyond that again, glimpsed through a straggling grove of palmettos, the twinkling ripple of sunlight reflecting off the green water of the Gulf of Mexico . . . The judge seemed to have recovered his composure.

'We have established,' he said heavily, 'that you are truculent, intransigent, insolent and a man of violence. You also carry a gun – a small-bore Lilliput, I believe it is called. I could already commit you for contempt of court, for assaulting and obstructing constables of the law in the course of the performance of their duties and for being in illegal possession of a lethal weapon. But I won't.' He paused for a moment, then went on: 'We will have much more serious charges to prefer against you.'

The court reporter opened one eye for a moment, thought better of it and appeared to go to sleep again. The man with the broken nose removed his cigar, examined it, replaced it and resumed his methodical champing. I said nothing.

'Where were you before you came here?' the judge asked abruptly.

'St Catherine.'

'I didn't mean that, but – well, how did you arrive here from St Catherine?'

'By car.'

'Describe it – and the driver.'

'Green saloon – sedan, you'd call it. Middle-aged

15

businessman and his wife. He was grey, she was blonde.'

'That's all you can remember?' Mollison asked politely.

'That's all.'

'I suppose you realize that description would fit a million couples and their cars?'

'You know how it is,' I shrugged. 'When you're not expecting to be questioned on what you've seen you don't bother –'

'Quite, quite.' He could be very acid, this judge. 'Out of state car, of course?'

'Yes. But not of course.'

'Newly arrived in our country and already you know how to identify licence plates of –'

'He said he came from Philadelphia. I believe that's out of state.'

The court reporter cleared his throat. The judge quelled him with a cold stare, then turned back to me.

'And you came to St Catherine from –'

'Miami.'

'Same car, of course?'

'No. Bus.'

The judge looked at the clerk of the court, who shook his head slightly, then turned back to me. His expression was less than friendly.

'You're not only a fluent and barefaced liar, Chrysler' – he'd dropped the 'Mister' so I assumed the time for courtesies was past – 'but a careless one. There's no bus service from Miami to

St Catherine. You stayed the previous night in Miami?'

I nodded.

'In a hotel,' he went on. 'But, of course, you will have forgotten the name of that hotel?'

'Well, as a matter of fact –'

'Spare us.' The judge held up his hand. 'Your effrontery passes all limits and this court will no longer be trifled with. We have heard enough. Cars, buses, St Catherine, hotels, Miami – lies, all lies. You've never been in Miami in your life. Why do you think we kept you on remand for three days?'

'You tell me,' I encouraged him.

'I shall. To make extensive inquiries. We've checked with the immigration authorities and every airline flying into Miami. Your name wasn't on any passenger or aliens list, and no one answering to your description was seen that day. You would not be easily overlooked.'

I knew what he meant, all right. I had the reddest hair and the blackest eyebrows I'd ever seen on anyone and the combination was rather startling. I'd got used to it myself, but I had to admit it took a bit of getting used to. And when you added to that a permanent limp and a scar that ran from the corner of my right brow to the lobe of my right ear – well, when it came to identification, I was the answer to the policeman's prayer.

'As far as we can discover,' the judge went on coldly, 'you've spoken the truth once. Only

17

once.' He broke off to look at the youth who had just opened the door leading to some chambers in the rear, and lifted his eyebrows in fractional interrogation. No impatience: no irritation: all very calm: Judge Mollison was no pushover.

'This just came for you, sir,' the boy said nervously. He showed an envelope. 'Radio message. I thought –'

'Bring it here.' The judge glanced at the envelope, nodded at no one in particular, then turned back to me.

'As I say, you told the truth just once. You said you had come here from Havana. You did indeed. You left this behind you there, In the police station where you were being held for interrogation and trial.' He reached into a drawer and held up a small book, blue and gold and white. 'Recognize it?'

'A British passport,' I said calmly. 'I haven't got telescopic eyes but I assume that it must be mine otherwise you wouldn't be making such a song and dance about it. If you had it all the time, then why –?'

'We were merely trying to discover the degree of your mendacity, which is pretty well complete, and your trustworthiness, which does not appear to exist.' He looked at me curiously. 'Surely you must know what this means: if we have the passport, we have much else besides. You appear unmoved. You're a very cool customer, Chrysler, or very dangerous: or can it be that you are just very stupid?'

18

'What do you want me to do?' I asked. 'Faint?'

'Our police and immigration authorities happen, for the moment at least, to be on very good terms with their Cuban colleagues.' He might never have heard my interjection. 'Our cables to Havana have produced much more than this passport: they have produced much interesting information.'

'Your name is not Chrysler, it's Ford. You have spent two and a half years in the West Indies, and are well known to the authorities in all of the principal islands.'

'Fame, Judge. When you've as many friends –'

'Notoriety. Served three minor prison sentences in two years.' Judge Mollison was skimming through a paper he had in his hand. 'No known means of support except three months working as consultant to a Havana salvage and diving firm.' He looked up at me. 'And in what – ah – capacity did you serve this firm?'

'I told 'em how deep the water was.'

He regarded me thoughtfully then returned to his paper.

'Associate of criminals and smugglers,' he went on. 'Chiefly of criminals known to be engaged in the stealing and smuggling of precious stones and metal. Known to have fomented, or attempted to foment, labour troubles in Nassau and Manzanillo, for ends suspected to be other than political. Deported from San Juan, Haiti and Venezuela. Declared *persona non grata* in Jamaica and refused landing permit in Nassau, Bahamas.' He broke off

19

and looked at me. 'A British subject – and not even welcome in British territories.'

'Sheer prejudice, Judge.'

'You have, of course, made an illegal entry into the United States.' Judge Mollison was a difficult man to knock off his stride. 'How, I don't pretend to know – it happens constantly in those parts. Probably by Key West and a landing at night somewhere between Port Charlotte and here. It doesn't matter. And so now, in addition to assaulting officers of the law and carrying a gun without declaring it or possessing a licence for it, you can be charged with illegal entry. A man with your record could collect a stiff sentence for those, Ford.'

'However, you won't. Not here, at least. I have consulted with the state immigration authorities and they agree with me that what best meets the case is deportation: we wish no part of any person like you. We understand from the Cuban authorities that you broke custody while being held on a charge of inciting violence among dockworkers and on a further alleged charge of attempted shooting of the policeman who arrested you. Such offences carry heavy penalties in Cuba. The first charge is not an extraditable offence and on the second we have had no demand from the competent authorities. However, as I say, we intend to work not under extradition laws but deportation laws – and we're deporting you to Havana. The proper authorities will be there to meet your plane when it lands tomorrow morning.'

20

I stood still and said nothing. The court-room was very quiet. Presently I cleared my throat and said, 'Judge, I think that's downright unkind of you.'

'It depends on the point of view,' he said indifferently. He rose to go, caught sight of the envelope the youth had brought in and said: 'No, wait a moment,' and sat down again, slitting open the envelope. He smiled bleakly at me as he extracted the flimsy sheets of paper.

'We thought we would ask Interpol to find out what was known about you in your own country, although I hardly think now there will be any further useful information. We have all we want . . . No, no, I thought not, nothing fresh here, not known . . . no longer listed. Wait a minute though!' The calm leisured voice rose to a sudden shout that brought the somnolent reporter jack-in-the-box bolt upright and sent him scurrying after note-book and pen that had spilled over the floor. 'Wait a minute!'

He turned back to the first page of the cable.

'37b Rue Paul-Valéry, Paris,' he read rapidly. 'Your request received, etc. etc. Regret inform you no criminal listed in rotary card index under name of John Chrysler. Could be any of four others under alias, but unlikely: identification impossible without cephalic index and fingerprints.

'Remarkable resemblance from your description to the late John Montague Talbot. Reasons for your request and demand for urgency unknown but

21

enclosed please find summarized copy of salient features of Talbot's life. Regret unable to help you further, etc.

'John Montague Talbot. Height 5 feet 11 inches, weight 185 lb, deep red hair parted far over on left side, deep blue eyes, heavy black brows, knife scar above right eye, aquiline nose, exceptionally even teeth. Carries left shoulder perceptibly higher than right owing to fairly severe limp.'

The judge looked at me and I looked out the door: I had to admit the description was not at all bad.

'Date of birth unknown, probably early 1920s. Place of birth unknown. No record of war career. Graduated Manchester University 1948 with B.Sc. in engineering. Employed for three years by Siebe, Gorman & Co.' He broke off, looked sharply at me. 'Who are Siebe, Gorman & Co?'

'Never heard of them.'

'Of course not. But I have. Very well-known European engineering firm specializing, among other things, in all types of diving equipment. Ties in rather neatly with your employment with a salvage and diving firm in Havana, doesn't it?' He obviously didn't expect an answer, for he carried on reading at once.

'Specialized in salvage and deep-water recovery. Left Siebe Gorman, joined Dutch salvage firm from which dismissed after eighteen months following inquiries into whereabouts of two missing 28-lb ingots worth 60,000 dollars salvaged by

22

firm in Bombay Harbour from the wreck of the ammunition and treasure ship *Fort Strikene* which blew up there 14th April, 1944. Returned England, joined Portsmouth salvage and diving firm, associated with "Corners" Moran, notorious jewellery thief, during salvage work on the *Nantucket Light* which sank off the Lizard, June 1955, carrying valuable cargo diamonds from Amsterdam to New York. Salvaged jewels to the value of 80,000 dollars were found to be missing. Talbot and Moran traced to London, arrested, escaped from police wagon when Talbot shot police officer with small concealed automatic. Police officer subsequently died.'

I was leaning far forward now, my hands gripped tightly on the edge of the box. Every eye was on me but I had eyes only for the judge. There wasn't a sound to be heard in that stuffy courtroom except the drowsy murmur of flies high up near the ceiling and the soft sighing of a big overhead fan.

'Talbot and Moran finally traced to riverside rubber warehouse.' Judge Mollison was reading slowly now, almost haltingly, as if he had to take time to appreciate the significance of what he was saying. 'Surrounded, ignored order to surrender. For two hours resisted all attempts by police armed with guns and tear-gas bombs to overcome them. Following explosion, entire warehouse swept by uncontrollable fire of great intensity. All exits guarded but no attempt at escape. Both men perished in fire. Twenty-four hours later firemen found no trace of Moran – believed to have been almost completely incinerated. Talbot's charred remains positively identified by ruby ring worn on left hand, brass buckles of shoes and German 4.25 automatic which he was known to carry habitually . . .'

The judge's voice trailed off and he sat in silence several moments. He looked at me, wonderingly, as if unable to credit what he saw, blinked, then slowly swivelled his gaze until he was looking at the little man in the cane chair.

'A 4.25 mm gun, Sheriff? Have you any idea –?'

'I do.' The sheriff's face was cold and mean and hard and his voice exactly matched his expression. 'What we call a .21 automatic, and as far as I know there's only one of that kind made – a German "Lilliput."'

'Which was what the prisoner was carrying when you arrested him.' It was a statement, not a question. '*And* he's wearing a ruby ring on his left hand.' The judge shook his head again, then looked at me for a long, long moment: you could see the disbelief was slowly giving way to inescapable conviction. 'The leopard – the criminal leopard – never changes his spots. Wanted for murder – perhaps two murders: who knows what you did to your accomplice in that warehouse? It was his body they found, not yours?'

The court was hushed and shocked and still: a falling pin would have had the lot airborne.

'A cop-killer.' The sheriff licked his lips, looked

24

up at Mollison and repeated the words in a whisper. 'A cop-killer. He'll swing for that in England, won't he, Judge?'

The judge was on balance again.

'It's not within the jurisdiction of this court to –'

'Water!' The voice was mine, and even to my own ears it sounded no more than a croak. I was bent over the side of the box, swaying slightly, propped up by one hand while I mopped my face with a handkerchief held in the other. I'd had plenty of time to figure it out and I think I looked the way I think I ought to have looked. At least, I hoped I did. 'I – I think I'm going to pass out. Is there – is there no water?'

'Water?' The judge sounded half-impatient, half-sympathetic. 'I'm afraid there's no –'

'Over there,' I gasped. I waved weakly to a spot on the other side of the officer who was guarding me. 'Please!'

The policeman turned away – I'd have been astonished if he hadn't – and as he turned I pivoted on both toes and brought my left arm whipping across just below waist level – three inches higher and that studded and heavily brass-buckled belt he wore around his middle would have left me needing a new pair of knuckles. His explosive grunt of agony was still echoing through the shocked stillness of the court-room when I spun him round as he started to fall, snatched the heavy Colt from his holster and was waving it gently around the room even before the policeman had struck the side of the box and slid, coughing and gasping painfully for air, to the wooden floor.

I took in the whole scene with one swift sweeping glance. The man with the nose was staring at me with an expression as near amazement as his primitive features could register, his mouth fallen open, the mangled stub of his cigar clinging impossibly to the corner of his lower lip. The girl with the dark-blonde hair was bent forward, wide-eyed, her hand to her face, her thumb under her chin and her fore-finger crooked across her mouth. The judge was no longer a judge, he was a waxen effigy of himself, as motionless in his chair as if he had just come from the sculptor's hands. The clerk, the reporter, the door attendant were as rigid as the judge, while the group of school-girls and the elderly spinster in charge were as goggle-eyed as ever, but the curiosity had gone from their faces and fear stepped in to take its place: the teenager nearest to me had her eyebrows arched high up into her forehead and her lips were trembling, she looked as if she were going to start weeping or screaming any moment. I hoped, vaguely, that it wasn't going to be screaming, then an instant later I realized that it didn't matter for there was likely going to be a great deal of noise in the very near future indeed. The sheriff hadn't been so unarmed as I had supposed: he was reaching for his gun.

His draw was not quite the clean swift blurring action to which the cinema of my youth had accustomed me. The long flapping tails of his alpaca coat impeded his hand and he was further hindered by the arm of his cane chair. Fully four seconds elapsed before he reached the butt of his gun.

'Don't do it, Sheriff!' I said quickly. 'This cannon in my hand is pointing right at you.'

But the little man's courage, or foolhardiness, seemed to be in inverse proportion to his size. You could tell by his eyes, by the lips ever so slightly drawn back over the tightly clamped tobacco-stained teeth, that there was going to be no stopping him. Except in the only possible way. At the full stretch of my arm I raised the revolver until the barrel was level with my eyes – this business of dead-eye Dan snap-shooting from the hip is strictly for the birds – and as the sheriff's hand came clear of the folds of his jacket I squeezed the trigger. The reverberating boom of that heavy Colt, magnified many times by the confining walls of that small court-house, quite obliterated any other sound. Whether the sheriff cried out or the bullet struck his hand or the gun in his hand no one could say: all we could be sure of was what we saw, and that was the sheriff's right arm and whole right side jerking convulsively and the gun spinning backwards to land on a table inches from the note-book of the startled reporter.

Already my Colt was lined up on the man at the door.

'Come and join us, friend,' I invited. 'You look as

27

if you might be having ideas about fetching help.'
I waited till he was halfway down the aisle then
whirled round quickly as I heard a scuffling noise
behind me.

There had been no need for haste. The policeman was on his feet, but that was all that could
be said for him. He was bent almost double, one
hand clutching his midriff, the knuckles of the
other all but brushing the floor: he was whooping
violently, gasping for the breath to ease the pain
in his body. Then he slowly straightened to a
crouched stooping position, and there was no fear
in his face, only hurt and anger and shame and a
do-or-die determination.

'Call off your watchdog, Sheriff,' I said curtly.
'He's liable to get hurt real bad next time.'

The sheriff glared at me venomously and spat
out one single unprintable word. He was hunched
in his chair, left hand tightly gripping his right
wrist: he gave every impression of a man too
preoccupied with his own hurt to worry about
any damage to others.

'Give me that gun!' the policeman demanded
hoarsely. His throat seemed to be constricted, he
had difficulty in forcing out even those few words.
He had taken one lurching step forward and was
no more than six feet away. He was only a kid,
hardly a day over twenty-one.

'Judge!' I said urgently.

'Don't do it, Donnelly!' Judge Mollison had
shaken off the first numbing shock. *'Don't do it!*

28

That man's a killer. He's got nothing to lose by killing again. Stay where you are.'

'Give me that gun.' Judge Mollison might have been talking to himself for all the effect his words had had. Donnelly's voice was wooden, unemotional, the voice of a man whose decision lies so far behind that it is no longer a decision but the sole obsessive reason for his existence.

'Stay where you are, sonny,' I said quietly. 'Like the judge said, I have nothing to lose. Take another step forward and I'm going to shoot you in the thigh. Have you any idea what a soft-nosed low-velocity lead bullet does, Donnelly? If it gets your thigh-bone it'll smash it so badly that you'll be like me and walk with a limp for the rest of your life: if it gets the femoral artery you'll like as not bleed to death before – you fool!'

For the second time the court-room shook to the sharp crack and the hollow reverberations of the Colt. Donnelly was on the floor, both hands gripped round his lower thigh, staring up at me with an expression compounded of incomprehension and dazed disbelief.

'We've all got to learn some time,' I said flatly. I glanced at the doorway, the shots were bound to have attracted attention, but there was no one there. Not that I was anxious on this point: apart from the two constables – both of them temporarily unfit for duty – who had jumped me at the La Contessa, the sheriff and Donnelly constituted the entire police force of Marble Springs.

But even so, delay was as foolish as it was dangerous.

'You won't get far, Talbot!' The sheriff's thin-lipped mouth twisted itself into exaggerated movements as he spoke through tightly clenched teeth. 'Within five minutes of you leaving, every law officer in the county will be looking for you: within fifteen minutes the call will be state-wide.' He broke off, wincing, as a spasm of pain twisted his face, and when he looked at me again his expression wasn't pretty. 'The call's going out for a murderer, Talbot, an armed murderer: they'll have orders to shoot on sight and shoot to kill.'

'Look, now, Sheriff—' the judge began, but got no further.

'Sorry, Judge. He's mine.' The sheriff looked down at the policeman lying groaning on the floor. 'The moment he took that gun he stopped being your business . . . You better get going, Talbot: you won't have far to run.'

'Shoot to kill, eh?' I said thoughtfully. I looked round the court. 'No, no, not the gentlemen – they might start getting death or glory ideas about having medals pinned on them . . .'

'What the hell you talking about?' the sheriff demanded.

'Nor the young ladies of the high school. Hysteria . . .' I murmured. I shook my head then looked at the girl with the dark-blonde hair. 'Sorry, miss, it'll have to be you.'

'What – what do you mean?' Maybe she was

scared, maybe she was just acting scared. 'What do you want?'

'You. You heard what the Lone Ranger said – as soon as the cops see me they're going to start shooting at everything in sight. But they wouldn't shoot at a girl, especially not at one as good looking as you. I'm in a jam, miss, and I need an insurance policy. You're it. Come on.'

'Damn it, Talbot, you can't do that!' Judge Mollison sounded hoarse, frightened. 'An innocent girl. You'd put her life in danger –'

'Not me,' I pointed out. 'If anybody's going to put her life in danger it'll be the friends of the sheriff here.'

'But – but Miss Ruthven is my guest. I – I invited her here this afternoon to –'

'Contravention of the rules of the old southern hospitality. I know. Emily Post would have something to say about this.' I caught her by the arm, pulled her none too gently to her feet and outside into the aisle. 'Hurry up, miss, we haven't –'

I dropped her arm and took one long step up the aisle, clubbed pistol already reversed and swinging. For some time now I'd had my eye on the broken-nosed character three seats behind the girl and the play and shift of expression across the broken land-scape of his Neanderthalic features as he struggled to arrive at and finally make a decision couldn't have been more clearly indicated by ringing bells and coloured lights.

He was almost vertical and halfway out into the

aisle, with his right hand reaching deep under the lapel of his coat when the butt end of my Colt caught his right elbow. The impact jarred even my arm so I could only guess what it did to his: quite a lot, if his anguished howl and sudden collapse back into the bench were any criterion. Maybe I'd misjudged the man, maybe he'd only been reaching for another cigar; that would teach him not to carry a cigar-case under his left armpit.

He was still making a great deal of noise when I hobbled my way swiftly up the aisle, pulled the girl out into the porch, slammed the door and locked it. That would only give me ten seconds, fifteen at the most, but it was all I needed. I grabbed the girl's hand and ran down the path to the street.

There were two cars parked by the kerb. One, an open Chevrolet without any official markings, was the police car in which the sheriff, Donnelly and I had arrived at the court, the other, presumably Judge Mollison's, a low-built Studebaker Hawk. The judge's looked to be the faster car of the two, but most of these American cars had automatic drive controls with which I was quite unfamiliar: I didn't know how to drive a Studebaker and the time it would take me to find out could be fatal. On the other hand, I *did* know how to operate the automatic drive on a Chevrolet. On the way up to the court-house I'd sat up front beside the sheriff, who drove, and I hadn't missed a move he made.

'Get in!' I nodded my head in the direction of the police car. 'Fast!'

I saw her open the door out of a corner of an eye while I spared a few moments for the Studebaker. The quickest and most effective way of immobilizing any car is by smashing its distributor. I spent three or four seconds hunting for the bonnet catch before I gave it up and turned my attention to the front tyre nearest me. Had it been a tubeless tyre and had I been carrying my usual automatic, the small calibre steel-jacketed bullet might have failed to make more than a tiny hole, no sooner made than sealed: as it was, the mushrooming Colt bullet split the sidewall wide open and the Studebaker settled with a heavy bump.

The girl was already seated in the Chevrolet. Without bothering to open the door I vaulted over the side into the driving-seat, took one swift glance at the dashboard, grabbed the white plastic handbag the girl held in her lap, broke the catch and ripped the material in my hurry to open it, and emptied the contents on the seat beside me. The car keys were on the top of the pile, which meant she'd shoved them right to the bottom of her bag. I'd have taken long odds that she was good and scared, but longer odds still that she wasn't terrified.

'I suppose you thought that was clever?' I switched on the motor, pressed the automatic drive button, released the handbrake and gunned the motor so savagely that the rear tyres spun and whined furiously on the loose gravel before getting traction.

'Try anything like that again and you'll be sorry. Regard that as a promise.'

I am a fairly experienced driver and where road-holding and handling are concerned I am no admirer of American cars: but when it came to straightforward acceleration those big V-8 engines could make the average British and European sports models look silly. The Chevrolet leapt forward as if it had been fitted with a rocket-assisted take-off – I suspected that being a police car it might have had a hotted-up engine – and when I'd straightened it up and had time for a fast look in the mirror we were a hundred yards away from the court-house: I had time only for a glimpse of the judge and the sheriff running out on to the road, staring after the Chevrolet, before a sharp right-angle bend came sweeping towards us: a quick twist of the wheel to the right, a four-wheel drift, the back end breaking away, another twist of the wheel to the left and then, still accelerating, we were clear of the town limits and heading into the open country.

TWO

We were heading almost due north along the highway, a white and dusty ribbon of road built up several feet above the level of the surrounding land. Away to our left the Gulf of Mexico glittered and twinkled like an opalescent emerald under the broiling sun. Between the road and the sea was a flat uninteresting belt of low mangrove coast, to our right swampy forests not of palms or palmettos as I would have expected to find in those parts but pine, and disheartened-looking scrub pine at that.

I wasn't enjoying the ride. I was pushing the Chev along as fast as I dared, and the soft swinging suspension gave me no feeling of security at all. I had no sun-glasses, and even though the sun was not directly in my face the savage glare of sub-tropical light off that road was harsh and hurtful to the eyes. It was an open car, but the windscreen was so big and deeply curved that we got almost no cooling benefit at all from the wind whistling by our ears at over eighty miles an hour. Back in the court-room, the shade temperature had been close on a hundred: what it was out here in the open I couldn't even begin to guess. But it was hot, furnace hot: I wasn't enjoying the ride.

Neither was the girl beside me. She hadn't even bothered to replace the stuff I'd emptied out of her bag, just sat there with her hands clasped tightly together. Now and again, as we took a fast corner, she reached out to grab the upper edge of the door but otherwise she'd made no movement since we'd left Marble Springs except to tie a white bandanna over her fair hair. She didn't once look at me, I didn't even know what colour her eyes were. And she certainly didn't once speak to me. Once or twice I glanced at her and each time she was staring straight ahead, lips compressed, face pale, a faint red patch burning high up in her left cheek. She was still scared, maybe more scared than ever. Maybe she was wondering what was going to happen to her. I was wondering about that myself.

Eight miles and eight minutes out of Marble Springs the expected happened. Somebody certainly seemed to have thought and moved even faster.

The expected was a road-block. It came at a point where some enterprising firm had built up the land to the right of the road with crushed stones and coral, asphalted it and built a filling station and drivers' pull-up. Right across the road a car had been drawn up, a big black police car – if the two pivoting searchlights and the big red 'STOP' light were not enough, the eight-inch white-lettered 'POLICE' sign would have removed all doubt. To the left, just beyond the nose of the police car, the land dropped sharply four or five feet into a ditch that lifted only slowly to the mangrove coast beyond: there was no escape that way. To the right, where the road widened and angled into the courtyard of the filling station, a vertically upright line of black corrugated fifty-gallon oil drums completely blocked the space between the police car and the first of the line of petrol pumps that paralleled the road.

All this I saw in the four or five seconds it took me to bring the shuddering skidding Chevrolet down from 70 to 30 mph, the high-pitched scream in our ears token of the black smoke trail of melted rubber that we were leaving on the white road behind us. I saw, too, the policemen, one crouched behind the bonnet of the police car, a second with his head and right arm just visible above the boot: both of them carried revolvers. A third policeman was standing upright and almost completely hidden behind the nearest petrol pump, but there was nothing hidden about his gun, that most lethal of all close-quarters weapons, a whipper, a sawn-off shotgun firing 20-gauge medium-lead shot.

I was down to 20 mph now, not more than forty yards distant from the block. The policemen, guns levelled on my head, were rising up and moving out into the open when out of the corner of my eye I caught a glimpse of the girl reaching for the handle of the door and half-turning away from me as she gathered herself for the leap out of the car. I said nothing, just leaned across, grabbed her arm, jerked her towards me with a savage force that made her gasp with pain and, in the same instant that I transferred my grip to her shoulders and held her half against half in front of me so that the police dared not shoot, jammed my foot flat down on the accelerator.

'You madman! You'll kill us!' For a split second of time she stared at the row of fifty-gallon drums rushing up to meet us, the terror in her face accurately reflecting the terror in her voice, then turned away with a cry and buried her face in my coat, the nails of her hands digging into my upper arms.

We hit the second drum from the left fair and square with the centre of our fender. Subconsciously, I tightened my grip on the girl and the steering wheel and braced myself for the numbing shattering shock, the stunning impact that would crush me against the steering-wheel or pitch me through the windscreen as the 500-lb dead weight of that drum sheared the chassis retaining bolts and smashed the engine back into the driving compartment. But there was no such convulsive shock, just a screeching of metal and a great hollow reverberating clang as the fender lifted the drum clear off the road, a moment of shock when I thought the drum would be carried over the bonnet of the car to smash the windscreen and pin us to the seat. With my free hand I jerked the wheel violently to the left and the cartwheeling drum bounced across the nearside wing and vanished from sight as I regained the road, jerked the wheel in the opposite direction and straightened out. The oil drum had been empty. And not a shot had been fired.

Slowly the girl lifted her head, stared over my shoulder at the road-block dwindling in the distance, than stared at me. Her hands were still gripping both my shoulders, but she was completely unaware of it.

'You're mad.' I could hardly catch the husky whisper through the crescendo roar of the engine. 'You're mad, you must be. Crazy mad.' Maybe she hadn't been terrified earlier on, but she was now.

'Move over, lady,' I requested. 'You're blocking my view.'

She moved, perhaps six inches, but her eyes, sick with fear, were still on me. She was trembling violently.

'You're mad,' she repeated. 'Please, *please* let me out.'

'I'm not mad.' I was paying as much attention to my rear mirror as to the road ahead. 'I think a little, Miss Ruthven, and I'm observant. They couldn't have had more than a couple of minutes to prepare that road-block – and it takes more than a couple of minutes to bring six full drums out of

39

store and manhandle them into position. The drum I hit had its filling hole turned towards me – and there was no bung. It had to be empty. And as for letting you out – well, I'm afraid I can't spare the time. Take a look behind you.'

She looked.

'They're – they're coming after us!'

'What did you expect them to do – go into the restaurant and have a cup of coffee?'

The road was closer to the sea, now, and winding to follow the indentations of the coast. Traffic was fairly light, but enough to hold me back from overtaking on some blind corners, and the police car behind was steadily gaining on me: the driver knew his car better than I did mine, and the road he obviously knew like the back of his hand. Ten minutes from the road-block he had crept up to within a hundred and fifty yards of us.

The girl had been watching the pursuing car for the past few minutes. Now she turned and stared at me. She made an effort to keep her voice steady, and almost succeeded.

'What's – what's going to happen now?'

'Anything,' I said briefly. 'They'll likely play rough. I don't think they can be any too pleased with what happened back there.' Even as I finished speaking there came, in quick succession, two or three whip-like cracks clearly audible above the whine of the tyres and the roar of the engine. A glance at the girl's face told me I didn't need to spell out what was happening. She knew all right.

'Get down,' I ordered. 'That's it, right down on the floor. Your head, too. Whether it's bullets or a crash, your best chance is down there.'

When she was crouched so low that all I could see was her shoulders and the back of her blonde head I eased the revolver out of my pocket, abruptly removed my foot from the accelerator, grabbed for the handbrake and hauled hard.

With no tell-tale warning from the foot-operated braking lights, the slowing down of the Chevrolet was as unexpected as it was abrupt, and the screech of tyres and violent slewing of the pursuing police car showed that the driver had been caught completely off balance. I loosed off one quick shot and as I did the windscreen in front of me shattered and starred as a bullet went clear through the centre of it: I fired a second time, and the police car skidded wildly and finished up almost broadside across the road, the nearside front wheel into the ditch on the right-hand side of the road. It was the sort of uncontrollable skid that might have come from a front tyre blowout.

Certainly no harm had come to the policemen inside, within a couple of seconds of hitting the ditch all three were out on the road, squeezing off shots after us as fast as they could pull the triggers: but we were already a hundred, a hundred and fifty yards away and for all the value of revolvers and riot guns in distance work of this kind they

41

might as well have been throwing stones at us. In a few seconds we rounded a curve and they were lost to sight.

'All right,' I said. 'The war's over. You can get up, Miss Ruthven.'

She straightened and pushed herself back on the seat. Some dark-blonde hair had fallen forward over her face, so she took off her bandanna, fixed her hair and pulled the bandanna on again. Women, I thought: if they fell over a cliff and thought there was company waiting at the bottom, they'd comb their hair on the way down.

When she'd finished tying the knot under her chin she said in a subdued voice, without looking at me: 'Thank you for making me get down. I – I might have been killed there.'

'You might,' I agreed indifferently. 'But I was thinking about myself, lady, not you. Your continued good health is very closely bound up with mine. Without a real live insurance policy beside me they'd use anything from a hand grenade to a 14-inch naval gun to stop me.'

'They were trying to hit us then, they were trying to kill us.' The tremor was back in her voice again as she nodded at the bullet hole in the screen. 'I was sitting in line with that.'

'So you were. Chance in a thousand. They must have had orders not to fire indiscriminately, but maybe they were so mad at what happened back at the road-block that they forgot their orders. Likely that they were after one of our rear tyres. Hard to

42

shoot well from a fast-moving car. Or maybe they just can't shoot well anyway.'

Approaching traffic was still light, maybe two or three cars to the mile, but even that was too much for my peace of mind. Most of the cars were filled with family groups, out-of-state vacationers, and like all vacationers they were not only curious about everything they saw but obviously had the time and the inclination to indulge their curiosity. Every other car slowed down as it approached us and in my rear-view mirror I saw the stop lights of three or four of them come on as the driver tramped on the brakes and the occupants twisted round in their seats. Hollywood and a thousand TV films had made a bullet-scarred windscreen an object readily identifiable by millions.

This was disturbing enough. Worse still was the near certainty that any minute now every local radio station within a hundred miles would be broadcasting the news of what had happened back at the Marble Springs court-house, together with a complete description of the Chevrolet, myself and the blonde girl beside me. The chances were that at least half of those cars approaching me had their radios tuned in to one of those local stations with their interminable record programmes MC'd by disc jockeys with fixations about guitar and hill-billy country music. The inevitable news flash, then all it needed was for one of those cars to be driven by a halfwit out to show his wife and children what a hero he really was all the time although they had never suspected it.

I picked up the girl's still-empty handbag, stuck my right hand inside it, made a fist and smashed away the centre of the laminated safety plate glass. The hole was now a hundred times bigger than before, but not nearly so conspicuous: in those days of stressed and curved glass, mysteriously shattered windscreens were not so unknown as to give rise to much comment: a flying pebble, a sudden change of temperature, even a loud enough sound at a critical frequency – any of those could blow out a screen.

But it wasn't enough. I knew it wasn't enough, and when an excited fast-talking voice broke into the soap opera on the Chev's radio and gave a concise if highly-coloured account of my escape, warning all highway users to look out for and report the Chev, I knew that I would have to abandon the car, and at once. It was too hot, and on this, the only main north-south route, the chances of escaping detection just didn't exist. I had to have a new car, and had to have it fast.

I got one almost at once. We had been passing through one of those new towns which mushroom by the score along the seaboards of Florida when I heard the flash, and less than two hundred yards beyond the limits we came to a lay-by on the shore side of the road. There were three cars there, and obviously they had been travelling in company for through a gap in the trees and low scrub that curved round the lay-by I could see a group of seven or eight people picking their way down to the shore, about three hundred yards away: they were carrying with them a barbecue grill, a cooking stove and luncheon baskets: they looked as if they intended making a stay.

I jumped out of the Chev, taking the girl with me, and quickly checked all three cars. Two were convertibles, a third a sports car and all were open. There were no ignition keys in any of the locks, but the sports car owner, as many do, had a spare set in a cubby-hole by the steering column, hidden only by a folded chamois cloth.

I could have just driven off leaving the police car there, but that would have been stupid. As long as the Chev's whereabouts remained unknown, the search would be concentrated exclusively on it and little attention would be paid to the common car thief who had taken the other: but if the Chev were found in the lay-by then the state-wide search would immediately be switched to the sports car.

Thirty seconds later I had the Chev back at the limits of the new town, slowing down as I came to the first of the all-but-completed split-levels on the shore side of the road. There was no one around, and I didn't hesitate: I turned in on the concrete drive of the first house, drove straight in under the open tip-up door of the garage, shut off the engine and quickly closed the garage door.

When we emerged from the garage two or three minutes later anyone looking for us would have looked a second or third time before getting suspicious. By coincidence, the girl had been wearing a short-sleeved green blouse of exactly the same shade of colour as my suit, a fact that had been repeated twice over the radio. A fast check point and a dead giveaway. But now the blouse had gone and the white sun-top she'd on beneath it was worn by so many girls that blazing summer afternoon that she'd subtly merged her identity with those of a thousand other women: her blouse was tucked inside my coat, my coat was inside out over my arm with only the grey lining showing and my necktie was in my pocket. I'd taken the bandanna from her, wrapped it kerchief-wise over my head, the loose ends of the knot hanging down the right-hand side, in front, all but obscuring my scar. The red hair showing at the temples was still a giveaway and while, by the time I had finished smearing it with her moistened mascara pencil, it didn't look like any hair I had ever seen, at least it didn't look red.

Under the blouse and coat I carried the gun.

Walking slowly so as to minimize my limp, we reached the sports car in three minutes. This, too, like the one we'd just tucked away in the garage, was a Chevrolet, with the same engine as the other, but there the resemblance ended. It was a plastic-bodied two-seater, I'd driven one in Europe, and I knew that the claims for 120 mph were founded on fact.

I waited till a heavy gravel truck came grinding

past from the north, started the Corvette's engine under the sound of its passing – the group of people I'd seen earlier were on the shoreline now but they might just have heard the distinctive note of this car's engine and might just have been suspicious – made a fast U-turn and took off after the truck. I noticed the startled expression on the girl's face as we drove off in the direction from which we'd just come.

'I know. Go on, say it, I'm crazy. Only I'm not crazy. The next road-block won't be so very far to the north now, and it'll be no hurried makeshift affair like the last time, it'll stop a fifty-ton tank. Maybe they'll guess that I'll guess that, maybe they'll conclude that I'll leave this road and make for the side-roads and dirt-tracks in the swamp-lands to the east there. Anyway, that's what I'd figure in their place. Good country for going to ground. So we'll just go south. They won't fig-ure on that. And then we'll hide up for a few hours.'

'Hide up? Where? Where can you hide up?' I didn't answer her question and she went on: 'Let me go, please! You – you're quite safe now. You must be. You must be sure of yourself or you wouldn't be heading this way. Please!'

'Don't be silly,' I said wearily. 'Let you go – and within ten minutes every cop in the state will know what kind of car I'm driving and where I'm heading! You must think I'm crazy.'

'But you can't trust me,' she persisted. I hadn't

shot anybody in twenty minutes, she wasn't scared any longer, at least not too scared to work things out. 'How do you know I won't make signs at people, or shout out when you do nothing about it, like at traffic lights, or – or hit you when you're not looking? How do you know –?'

'That cop, Donnelly,' I said apropos of nothing. 'I wonder if the doctors got to him in time.'

She got the point. The colour that had come back to her face drained out of it again. But she had the best kind of courage, or maybe the worst kind, the kind that gets you into trouble.

'My father is a sick man, Mr Talbot.' It was the first time she'd used my name, and I appreciated the 'Mister'. 'I'm terribly afraid of what will happen to him when he hears this. He – well, he has a very bad heart and –'

'And I have a wife and four starving kiddies,' I interrupted. 'We can wipe each other's tears away. Be quiet.'

She said nothing, not even when I pulled up at a drugstore a few moments later, went inside and made a short phone call. She was with me, far enough away not to hear what I was saying but near enough to see the shape of the gun under my folded coat. On the way out I bought cigarettes. The clerk looked at me, then at the Corvette roadster parked outside.

'Hot day for driving, mister. Come far?'

'Only from Chilicoote Lake.' I'd seen the turn-off sign three or four miles to the north. My efforts at an American accent made me wince. 'Fishing.'

'Fishing, eh?' The tone was neutral enough, which was more than could be said for the half-leer in his eyes as he looked over the girl by my side, but my Sir Galahad instincts were in abeyance that afternoon so I let it pass. 'Catch anything?'

'Some.' I had no idea what fish if any were in the local lakes and, when I came to think of it, it seemed unlikely that anyone should take off for those shallow swampy lakes when the whole of the Gulf of Mexico lay at his front door. 'Lost 'em, though.' My voice sharpened in remembered anger. 'Just put the basket down on the road for a moment when some crazy idiot comes past doing eighty. Knocked basket and fish to hell and breakfast. And so much dust on those side roads I couldn't even catch his number.'

'You get 'em everywhere.' His eyes suddenly focused on a point a hundred miles away, then he said quickly: 'What kind of car, mister?'

'Blue Chev. Broken windscreen. Why, what's the matter?'

'"What's the matter?" he asks. Do you mean to tell me you haven't – Did you see the guy drivin' it?'

'No. Too fast. Just that he had a lot of red hair, but –'

'Red hair. Chilicoote Lake. Brother!' He turned and ran for the phone.

We went out into the sunshine. The girl said: 'You don't miss much, do you? How – how can you be so cool? He might have recognized –'

'Get into the car. Recognized me? He was too busy looking at you. When they made that sun-top I guess they ran out of material but just decided to go ahead and finish it off anyway.'

We got in and drove off. Four miles farther on we came to the place I had noticed on the way up. It was a palm-shaded parking-lot between the road and the shore, and a big sign hung under a temporary wooden archway. 'Codell Construction Company' it read, then, underneath, in bigger lettering, 'Sidewalk Superintendents: Drive Right In.'

I drove right in. There were fifteen, maybe twenty cars already parked inside, some people sitting on the benches provided, but most of them still in the seats of their cars. They were all watching the construction of foundations designed to take a seaward extension of a new town. Four big draglines, caterpillar-mounted power shovels, were crawling slowly, ponderously around, tearing up underwater coral rock from the bay bottom, building up a solid wide foundation, then crawling out on the pier just constructed and tearing up more coral rock. One was building a wide strip straight out to sea: this would be the new street of the community. Two others were making small piers at right angles to the main one – those would be for house lots, each house with its own private landing-stage. A fourth was making a big loop to the north, curving back into land again. A yacht harbour, probably. It was a fascinating process to watch, this making of a town out of the bottom of the sea, only I was in no mood to be fascinated.

I parked the car between a couple of empty convertibles, opened the pack of cigarettes I'd just bought and lit one. The girl half-turned in her seat and was staring at me incredulously.

'Is this the place you meant when you said we'd go somewhere to hide up?'

'This is it,' I assured her.

'You're going to stay here?'

'What's it look like to you?'

'With all those people around? Where everyone can see you? Twenty yards off the road where every passing police patrol –'

'See what I mean? Everyone would think the same as you. This is the last place any hunted man in his senses would think of coming. So it's the ideal place. So here we stay.'

'You can't stay here for ever,' she said steadily.

'No,' I agreed. 'Just till it gets dark. Move closer, Miss Ruthven, real close. A man fleeing for his life, Miss Ruthven. What picture does that conjure up? An exhausted wild-eyed individual crashing through the high timber or plunging up to his arm-pits through some of the choicer Florida swamps. Certainly not sitting in the sunshine getting all close and confidential with a pretty girl. Nothing in the world less calculated to arouse suspicion, is there? Move over, lady.'

'I wish I had a gun in my hand,' she said quietly.

'I don't doubt it. Move over.'

She moved. I felt the uncontrollable shudder of revulsion as her bare shoulder touched mine. I tried to imagine how I would feel if I were a pretty young girl in the company of a murderer, but it was too difficult, I wasn't a girl, I wasn't even particularly young or good-looking, so I gave it up, showed her the gun under the coat lying over my knees, and sat back to enjoy the light on-shore breeze that tempered the sunlight filtering through the fronds of the rustling palm trees. But it didn't look as if the sunlight would be with us too long, that sea breeze being pulled in by the sun-scorched land was laden with moisture and already the tiny white scraps of cloud that had been drifting across the sky were building and thickening up into grey cumulus. I didn't like that much. I wanted to have the excuse to keep wearing the bandanna on my head.

Maybe ten minutes after we arrived a black police car came along the highway, from the south. I watched in the rear-view mirror as it slowed down and two policemen put their heads out to give the parking-lot a quick once-over. But their scrutiny was as cursory as it was swift, you could see they didn't really expect to see anything interesting, and the car pulled away before its speed had dropped to walking pace.

The hope in the girl's eyes – they were grey and cool and clear, I could see now – died out like a snuffed candleflame, the rounding and drooping of her sunburned shoulders unmistakable.

Half an hour later the hope was back. Two motor-cycle cops, helmeted, gauntleted, very tough and very competent, swept in under the archway in perfect unison, stopped in perfect unison and killed their motors on the same instant. For a few seconds they sat there, high gleaming boots astride on the ground, then they dismounted, kicked down the rests and started moving round the cars. One of them had his revolver in his hand.

They started at the car nearest the entrance, with only a quick glance for the car itself but a long penetrating wordless stare for the occupants. They weren't doing any explaining and they weren't doing any apologizing: they looked like cops might look if they had heard that another cop had been shot. And was dying. Or dead.

Suddenly they skipped two or three cars and came straight at us. At least, that seemed to be their intention, but they skirted us and headed for a Ford to the left and ahead of us. As they passed by, I felt the girl stiffening, saw her taking a quick deep breath.

'Don't do it!' I flung an arm around her and grabbed her tight. The breath she'd meant for the warning shout was expelled in a gasp of pain. The policeman nearest turned round and saw the girl's face buried between my shoulder and neck and looked away again. Having seen what he thought he'd seen he made a remark to his companion that wasn't as *sotto voce* as it might have been and might have called for action in normal circumstances. But the circumstances weren't normal. I let it go.

When I released the girl her face was red practically all the way down to the sun-top. Pressed in against my neck she hadn't been getting much air but I think it was the policeman's remark that was responsible for most of the colour. Her eyes were wild. For the first time she'd stopped being scared and was fighting mad.

'I'm going to turn you in.' Her voice was soft, implacable. 'Give yourself up.'

The policeman had checked the Ford. The driver had been dressed in a green jacket the same colour as mine, with a panama hat jammed far down on his head: I'd seen him as he'd driven in, his hair was black and his tanned face moustached and chubby. But the police hadn't moved on. They were no more than five yards away, but the tearing and growling of the big draglines covered our soft voices.

'Don't be a fool,' I said quietly. 'I have a gun.'

'And there's only one bullet in it.'

She was right. Two slugs gone in the courthouse, one blowing out the tyre in the judge's Studebaker, and two when the police car was chasing us.

'Quite the little counter, aren't we?' I murmured. 'You'll have plenty of time to practise counting in hospital after the surgeons have fixed you up. If they can fix you up.'

She looked at me, her lips parted, and said nothing.

'One little slug, but what an awful mess it can make.' I brought the gun forward under the coat, pressed it against her. 'You heard me telling that fool Donnelly what a soft lead slug can do. This barrel is against your hipbone. Do you realize what that means?' My voice was very low now, very menacing. 'It'll shatter that bone beyond repair. It means you'll never walk again, Miss Ruthven. You'll never run or dance or swim or sit a horse again. All the rest of your life you'll have to drag that beautiful body of yours about on a pair of crutches. Or in a bath chair. And in pain all the time. All the days of your life . . . Still going to shout to the cops?'

She said nothing at first, her face was empty of colour, even her lips were pale.

'Do you believe me?' I asked softly.

'I believe you.'

'So?'

'So I'm going to call them,' she said simply. 'Maybe you'll cripple me – but they'll surely get you. And then you can never kill again. I have to do it.'

'Your noble sentiments do you credit, Miss Ruthven.' The jeer in my voice was no reflection of the thoughts in my mind. She was going to do what I wouldn't have done.

'Go and call them. Watch them die.'

She stared at me. 'What – what do you mean? You've only one bullet –'

'And it's no longer for you. First squawk out of you, lady, and that cop with the gun in his hand gets it. He gets it right through the middle of the chest. I'm pretty good with one of these Colts – you saw how I shot the gun out of the sheriff's hands. But I'm taking no chances. Through the chest. Then I hold up the other cop – there'll be no trouble about that, his own gun is still buttoned down, he knows I'm a killer and he doesn't know my gun will be empty – take his gun, wing him with it and go off.' I smiled. 'I don't think anyone will try to stop me.'

'But – but I'll tell him your gun's empty. I'll tell –'

'You come first, lady. An elbow in the solar plexus and you won't be able to tell anybody anything for the next five minutes.'

There was a long silence, the cops were still there, then she said in a small voice: 'You'd do it, wouldn't you?'

'There's only one way to find out the answer to that one.'

'I hate you.' There was no expression in her voice, the clear grey eyes were dark with despair and defeat. 'I never thought I could hate anyone so much. It – it scares me.'

'Stay scared and stay alive.' I watched the police-men finish their tour of the parking-lot, walk slowly back to their motor bikes and ride away.

The late afternoon wore slowly on. The dragliners growled and crunched and crawled their implac-able way out towards the sea. The sidewalk super-intendents came and went, but mostly went and soon there were only a couple of cars left in the parking-lot, ours and the Ford belonging to the man in the green coat. And then the steadily darkening cumulus sky reached its final ominous indigo colour and the rain came.

It came with the violence of all sub-tropical storms, and before I could get the unaccustomed hood up my thin cotton shirt was wet as if I had been in the sea. When I'd wound up the side-screens and looked in the mirror, I saw that my face was streaked with black lines from temple to chin – the mascara on my hair had almost washed out. I scrubbed as clean as I could with my handkerchief, then looked at my watch. With the dark cloud obscuring the sky from horizon to horizon, evening had come before its time. Already the cars swishing by on the highway had their sidelights on, although it was still more day than night. I started the engine.

'You were going to wait until it was dark.' The girl sounded startled. Maybe she'd been expecting more cops, smarter cops to come along.

'I was,' I admitted. 'But by this time Mr Chas Brooks is going to be doing a song and dance act a few miles back on the highway. His language will be colourful.'

'Mr Chas Brooks?' From her tone, I wondered if she really thought I was crazy.

'Of Pittsburg, California.' I tapped the licence tag on the steering column. 'A long way to come to have your car hijacked.' I lifted my eyes to the machine-gun symphony of the heavy rain drumming on the canvas roof. 'You don't think he'll still be grilling and barbecuing down on the beach in this little lot, do you?'

I pulled out through the makeshift archway and turned right on the highway. When she spoke this time I knew she really did think I was crazy.

'Marble Springs.' A pause, then: 'You're going back there?' It was a question and statement both.

'Right. To the motel – La Contessa. Where the cops picked me up. I left some stuff there and I want to collect it.'

This time she said nothing. Maybe she thought 'crazy' a completely inadequate word.

I pulled off the bandanna – in the deepening dusk that white gleam on my head was more conspicuous than my red hair – and went on: 'Last place they'll ever think to find me. I'm going to spend the night there, maybe several nights until I find me a boat out. So are you.' I ignored the involuntary exclamation. 'That's the phone call I made back at the drug store. I asked if Room 14 was vacant, they said yes, so I said I'd take it, friends who'd passed through had recommended it as having the nicest view in the motel. In point of fact it has the nicest view. It's also the most private room, at the seaward end of a long block, it's right beside the closet where they put my case away when the cops pinched me and it has a nice private little garage where I can stow this machine away and no one will ever ask a question.'

A mile passed, two miles, three and she said nothing. She'd put her green blouse back on, but it was a lacy scrap of nothing, she'd got just as wet as I had when I was trying to fix the roof, and she was having repeated bouts of shivering. The rain had made the air cool. We were approaching the outskirts of Marble Springs when she spoke.

'You can't do it. How can you? You've got to check in or sign a book or pick up keys or have to go to the restaurant. You can't just –'

'Yes, I can. I asked them to have the place opened up ready for us, keys in the garage and room doors, and that we'd check in later: I said we'd come a long way since dawn, that we were bushed and that we'd appreciate room service for meals and a little privacy.' I cleared my throat. 'I told the receptionist we were a honeymoon couple. She seemed to understand our request for privacy.'

We were there before she could find an answer. I turned in through an ornate lilac-painted gateway and drew up near the reception hallway in the central block, parking the car directly under a powerful floodlamp which threw such black shadows that my red hair would be all but invisible under the car roof. Over by the entrance stood a negro dressed in a lilac, blue and gold-buttoned uniform that had been designed by a colour-blind man wearing smoked glasses. I called him across.

'Room 14?' I asked. 'Which way, please?'

'Mr Brooks?' I nodded, and he went on: 'I've left all the keys ready. Down this way.'

'Thank you.' I looked at him. Grey and bent and thin and the faded old eyes the clouded mirrors of a thousand sorrows and defeats. 'What's your name?'

'Charles, sir.'

'I want some whisky, Charles.' I passed money across. 'Scotch not bourbon. And some brandy. Can you?'

'Right away, sir.'

'Thanks.' I let in the gear, drove down the block to No. 14. It was at the end of a narrow peninsula between the gulf to the left and a kidney-shaped swimming pool to the right. The garage door was open and I drove straight in, switched off the car lights, closed the sliding door in the near-darkness, then switched on the overhead light.

At the inner end of the left-hand wall a single door led off the garage. We went through this, into a kitchenette, neat, hygienic and superbly equipped if all you wanted was a cup of coffee and had all night to make it. A door led off this into the bed-sitting-room. Lilac carpet, lilac drapes, lilac bedspread, lilac lamp-shades, lilac seatcovers, the same excruciating motif wherever you looked. Somebody had liked lilac. Two doors off this room: to the left, let into the same wall as the kitchen door, the door to the bathroom: at the far end, the door leading into the corridor.

I was in the corridor within ten seconds of arriving in the room, dragging the girl after me. The closet was no more than six feet away, unlocked, and my bag still where it had been left. I carried it back to the room, unlocked it and was about to start throwing stuff on the bed when a knock came to the door.

'That will be Charles,' I murmured. 'Open the door, stand well back, take the bottles, tell him to keep the change. Don't try to whisper, make signs or any clever little jumps out into the middle of the corridor. I'll be watching you from the crack of the bathroom door and my gun will be lined up on your back.'

She didn't try any of those things. I think she was too cold, miserable and exhausted by the accumulated tension of the day to try anything. The old man handed over the bottles, took the change with a surprised murmur of thanks and closed the door softly behind him.

'You're frozen and shivering,' I said abruptly. 'I don't want my insurance policy to go catching pneumonia.' I fetched a couple of glasses. 'Some brandy, Miss Ruthven, then a hot bath. Maybe you'll find something dry in my case.'

'You're very kind,' she said bitterly. 'But I'll take the brandy.'

'No bath, huh?'

'No.' A hesitant pause, a glint in her eyes more imagined than seen, and I knew I'd been mistaken in imagining her to be too worn out to try anything. 'Yes, that too.'

'Right.' I waited till she'd finished her glass, dumped my case on the bathroom floor and stood to let her pass. 'Don't be all night. I'm hungry.'

The door closed and the key clicked in the lock. There came the sound of water running into the bath, then all the unmistakable soaping and splashing sounds of someone having a bath. All meant to lull any suspicions. Then came the sound of someone towelling themselves, and when, a minute or two later, there came the furious gurgling of water running out of the waste pipe, I eased myself off the door, passed through the two kitchen doors and outside garage door just in time to see the bathroom window open and a little cloud of steam come rushing out. I caught her arm as she lowered herself to the ground, stifled the frightened gasp with my free hand, and led her back inside.

I closed the kitchen door and looked at her. She looked fresh and scrubbed and clean and had one of my white shirts tucked into the waistband of her dirndl. She had tears of mortification in her eyes and defeat in her face, but for all that it was a face worth looking at. Despite our long hours in the car together it was the first time I had really looked at it.

She had wonderful hair, thick and gleaming and parted in the middle and of the same wheat colour and worn in the same braids as that often seen in girls from the East Baltic states or what used to be the Baltic states. But she would never win a Miss America contest, she had too much character in her face for that, she wouldn't even have been in the running for Miss Marble Springs. The face was slightly Slavonic, the cheekbones too high and wide, the mouth too full, the still grey eyes set too far apart and the nose definitely retroussé. A mobile and intelligent face, a face, I guessed, that could move easily into sympathy and kindness and humour and laughter, when the weariness was gone and the fear taken away. In the days before I had given up the dream of my own slippers and my own fireside, this was the face that would have fitted the dream. She was the sort of person who would wear well, the sort of person who would still be part of you long after the synthetic chromium polished blondes from the production lines of the glamour factory had you climbing up the walls.

I was just standing there, feeling a little sorry for her and feeling a little sorry for myself, when I felt a cold draught on the back of my neck. It came from the direction of the bathroom door and ten seconds ago that bathroom door had been closed and locked. But it wasn't now.

THREE

It didn't require the sudden widening of the girl's eyes to tell me that I wasn't imagining that cold draught on the back of my neck. A cloud of steam from the overheated bathroom drifted past my right ear, a little bit too much to have escaped through the keyhole of a locked door. About a thousand times too much. I turned slowly, keeping my hands well away from my sides. Maybe I would try something clever later. But not now.

The first thing I noticed was the gun in his hands, and it wasn't the sort of gun a beginner carries around with him. A big dull black German Mauser 7.63. One of those economical guns; the bullet goes clear through three people at once.

The second thing I noticed was that the bathroom doorway seemed to have shrunk since I'd seen it last. His shoulders didn't quite touch both sides of the doorway, but that was only because it was a wide doorway. His hat certainly touched the lintel.

The third thing I noticed was the kind of hat he wore and the colour of the jacket. A panama hat, a green jacket. It was our friend and neighbour from the Ford that had been parked beside us earlier that afternoon.

He reached behind him with his left hand and softly closed the bathroom door.

'You shouldn't leave windows open. Let me have your gun.' His voice was quiet and deep, but there was nothing stagy or menacing about it, you could see it was the way he normally spoke.

'Gun?' I tried to look baffled.

'Look, Talbot,' he said pleasantly. 'I suspect we're both what you might call professionals. I suggest we cut the unnecessary dialogue. Gun. The thing you're carrying in your right coat pocket there. With the finger and thumb of the left hand. So. Now drop it on the carpet. Thank you.'

I kicked the gun across to him without being told. I didn't want him to think I wasn't a professional too.

'Now sit down,' he said. He smiled at me, and I could see now that his face wasn't chubby, unless you could call a lump of rock chubby. It was just broad and looked as if you could bounce a two by four off it without achieving very much. The narrow black moustache and the thin, almost Grecian nose looked out of place, as incongruous, almost, as the laughter lines round the eyes and on either side of the mouth. I didn't place much store on the laughter lines, maybe he only practised

65

smiling when he was beating someone over the head with a gun.

'You recognized me in the parking-lot?' I asked.

'No.' He broke open the Colt with his left hand, ejected the remaining shell, closed the gun and with a careless flick of his wrist sent it spinning ten feet to land smack in the waste-paper basket. He looked as if he could do this sort of thing ten times out of ten, everything this man tried would always come off: if he was as good as this with his left hand, what could he do with his right? 'I'd never seen you before this afternoon, I'd never even heard of you when first I saw you in the lot,' he continued. 'But I'd seen and heard of this young lady here a hundred times. You're a Limey, or you'd have heard of her too. Maybe you have, but don't know who you got there, you wouldn't be the first person to be fooled by her. No make-up, no accent, hair in kid's plaits. And you only look and behave like that either if you've given up competing – or there's no one left to compete against.' He looked at the girl and smiled again. 'For Mary Blair Ruthven there's no competition left. When you're as socially acceptable as she is, and your old man is who he is, then you can dispense with your Bryn Mawr accent and the Antonio hairdo. That's for those who need them.'

'And her old man?'

'Such ignorance. Blair Ruthven. General Blair Ruthven. You've heard of the Four Hundred – well, he's the guy that keeps the register. You've

66

heard of the *Mayflower* – it was old Ruthven's ancestors who gave the Pilgrims permission to land. And, excepting maybe Paul Getty, he's the richest oil man in the United States.'

I made no comment, there didn't seem to be any that would meet the case. I wondered what he'd say if I told him of my pipe-dream of slippers, a fire and a multimillion heiress. Instead I said: 'And you had your radio switched on in the parking-lot. I hear it. And then a news flash.'

'That's it,' he agreed cheerfully.

'Who are you?' It was Mary Blair speaking for the first time since he'd entered and that was what being in the top 1 per cent of the Four Hundred did for you. You didn't swoon, you didn't murmur 'Thank God' in a broken voice, you didn't burst into tears and fling your arms round your rescuer's neck, you just gave him a nice friendly smile which showed he was your equal even if you know quite well he wasn't and said: 'Who are you?'

'Jablonsky, miss. Herman Jablonsky.'

'I suppose you came over in the *Mayflower* too,' I said sourly. I looked consideringly at the girl. 'Millions and millions of dollars, eh? That's a lot of money to be walking around. Anyway, that explains away Valentino.'

'Valentino?' You could see she still thought I was crazy.

'The broken-faced gorilla behind you in the court-room. If your old man shows as much judgement in picking oil wells as he does in picking

67

bodyguards, you're going to be on relief pretty soon.'

'He's not my usual—' She bit her lip, and something like a shadow of pain touched those clear grey eyes. 'Mr Jablonsky, I owe you a great deal.'

Jablonsky smiled again and said nothing. He fished out a pack of cigarettes, tapped the bottom, extracted one with his teeth, bent back a cardboard match in a paper folder, then threw cigarettes and matches across to me. That's how the high-class boys operated today. Civilized, courteous, observing all the little niceties, they'd have made the hoodlums of the thirties feel slightly ill. Which made a man like Jablonsky all the more dangerous: like an iceberg, seven-eighths of his lethal menace was out of sight. The old-time hoodlums couldn't even have begun to cope with him.

'I take it you are prepared to use that gun,' Mary Blair went on. She wasn't as cool and composed as she appeared and sounded; I could see a pulse beating in her neck and it was going like a racing car. 'I mean, this man can't do anything to me now?'

'Nary a thing,' Jablonsky assured her.

'Thank you.' A little sigh escaped her, as if it wasn't until that moment that she really believed her terror was over, that there was nothing more to fear. She moved across the room. 'I'll phone the police.'

'No,' Jablonsky said quietly.

She broke step. 'I beg your pardon?'

'I said "No",' Jablonsky murmured. 'No phone, no police, I think we'll leave the law out of it.'

'What on earth do you mean?' Again I could see a couple of red spots burning high up in her cheeks. The last time I'd seen those it had been fear that had put them there, this time it looked like the first stirrings of anger. When your old man had lost count of the number of oil wells he owned, people didn't cross your path very often. 'We must have the police,' she went on, speaking slowly and patiently like someone explaining something to a child. This man is a criminal. A wanted criminal. And a murderer. He killed a man in London.'

'And in Marble Springs,' Jablonsky said quietly. 'Patrolman Donnelly died at five-forty this afternoon.'

'Donnelly – died?' Her voice was a whisper. 'Are you sure?'

'Six o'clock news-cast. Got it just before I tailed you out of the parking-lot. Surgeons, transfusion, the lot. He died.'

'How horrible!' She looked at me, but it was no more than a flickering glance, she couldn't bear the sight of me. 'And – and you say, "Don't bring the police." What do you mean?'

'What I say,' the big man said equably. 'No law.'

'Mr Jablonsky has ideas of his own, Miss Ruthven,' I said dryly.

'The result of your trial is a foregone conclusion,' Jablonsky said to me tonelessly. 'For a man with three weeks to live, you take things pretty coolly. Don't touch that phone, miss!'

'You wouldn't shoot me.' She was already across the room. '*You're* no murderer.'

'I wouldn't shoot you,' he agreed. 'I don't have to.' He reached her in three long strides – he could move as quickly and softly as a cat – took the phone from her, caught her arm and led her back to the chair beside me. She tried to struggle free but Jablonsky didn't even notice it.

'You don't want law, eh?' I asked thoughtfully. 'Kind of cramps your style a little bit, friend.'

'Meaning I don't want company?' he murmured. 'Meaning maybe I would be awful reluctant to fire this gun?'

'Meaning just that.'

'I wouldn't gamble on it,' he smiled.

I gambled on it. I had my feet gathered under me and my hands on the arms of the chair. The back of my chair was solidly against the wall and I took off in a dive that was almost parallel to the floor, arrowing on for a spot about six inches below his breastbone.

I never got there. I'd wondered what he could do with his right hand and now I found out. With his right hand he could change his gun over to his left, whip a sap from his coat pocket and hit a diving man over the head faster than anyone I'd ever known. He'd been expecting something

70

like that from me, sure: but it was still quite a performance.

By and by someone threw cold water over me and I sat up with a groan and tried to clutch the top of my head. With both hands tied behind your back it's impossible to clutch the top of your head. So I let my head look after itself, climbed shakily to my feet by pressing my bound hands against the wall at my back and staggered over to the nearest chair. I looked at Jablonsky, and he was busy screwing a perforated black metal cylinder on to the barrel of the Mauser. He looked at me and smiled. He was always smiling.

'I might not be so lucky a second time,' he said diffidently.

I scowled.

'Miss Ruthven,' he went on. '*I'm* going to use the phone.'

'Why tell me?' She was picking up my manners and they didn't suit her at all.

'Because I'm going to phone your father. I want you to tell me his number. It won't be listed.'

'Why should you phone him?'

'There's a reward out for our friend here,' Jablonsky replied obliquely. 'It was announced right after the news-cast of Donnelly's death. The state will pay five thousand dollars for any information leading to the arrest of John Montague Talbot.' He smiled at me. 'Montague, eh? Well, I believe I prefer it to Cecil.'

'Get on with it,' I said coldly.

'They must have declared open season on Mr Talbot,' Jablonsky said. 'They want him dead or alive and don't much care which . . . And General Ruthven has offered to double that reward.'

'Ten thousand dollars?' I asked.

'Ten thousand.'

'Piker,' I growled.

'At the last count old man Ruthven was worth 285 million dollars. He might,' Jablonsky agreed judiciously, 'have offered more. A total of fifteen thousand. What's fifteen thousand?'

'Go on,' said the girl. There was a glint in those grey eyes now.

'He can have his daughter back for fifty thousand bucks,' Jablonsky said coolly.

'Fifty thousand!' Her voice was almost a gasp. If she'd been as poor as me she would have gasped.

Jablonsky nodded. 'Plus, of course, the fifteen thousand I'll collect for turning Talbot in as any good citizen should.'

'Who are you?' the girl demanded shakily. She didn't look as if she could take much more of this. 'What are you?'

'I'm a guy that wants, let me see – yes, sixty-five thousand bucks.'

'But this is blackmail!'

'Blackmail?' Jablonsky lifted an eyebrow. 'You want to read up on some law, girlie. In its strict legal sense, blackmail is hush-money – a tribute paid to buy immunity, money extorted by the threat of telling everyone what a heel the

72

blackmailee is. Had General Ruthven anything to hide? I doubt it. Or you might just say that blackmail is demanding money with menaces. Where's the menace? I'm not menacing you. If your old man doesn't pay up I'll just walk away and leave you to Talbot here. Who can blame me? I'm scared of Talbot. He's a dangerous man. He's a killer.'

'But – but then you would get nothing.'

'I'd get it,' Jablonsky said comfortably. I tried to imagine this character flustered or unsure of himself: it was impossible. 'Only a threat. Your old man wouldn't dare gamble I wouldn't do it. He'll pay, all right.'

'Kidnapping is a federal offence—' the girl began slowly.

'So it is,' Jablonsky agreed cheerfully. 'The hot chair or the gas chamber. That's for Talbot. He kidnapped you. All I'm doing is talking about leaving you. No kidnapping there.' His voice hardened. 'What hotel is your father staying at?'

'He's not at any hotel.' Her voice was flat and toneless and she'd given up. 'He's out on the X 13.'

'Talk sense,' Jablonsky said curtly.

'X 13 is one of his oil rigs. It's out in the gulf, twelve, maybe fifteen miles from here. I don't know.'

'Out in the gulf. You mean one of those floating platforms for drilling for oil? I thought they were all up off the bayou country off Louisiana.'

'They're all round now – off Mississippi, Alabama

and Florida. Dad's got one right down near Key West. And they don't float, they – oh, what does it matter? He's on X 13.'

'No phone, huh?'

'Yes. A submarine cable. And a radio from the shore office.'

'No radio. Too public. The phone – just ask the operator for the X 13, huh?'

She nodded without speaking, and Jablonsky crossed to the phone, asked the motel switchboard girl for the exchange, asked for the X 13 and stood there waiting, whistling in a peculiarly tuneless fashion until a sudden thought occurred to him.

'How does your father commute between the rig and shore?'

'Boat or helicopter. Usually helicopter.'

'What hotel does he stay at when he's ashore?'

'Not a hotel. Just an ordinary family house. He's got a permanent lease on a place about two miles south of Marble Springs.'

Jablonsky nodded and resumed his whistling. His eyes appeared to be gazing at a remote point in the ceiling, but when I moved a foot a couple of experimental inches those eyes were on me instantly. Mary Ruthven had seen both the movement of my foot and the immediate switch of Jablonsky's glance, and for a fleeting moment her eyes caught mine. There was no sympathy in it, but I stretched my imagination a little and thought I detected a flicker of fellow-feeling. We were in the same boat and it was sinking fast.

The whistling had stopped. I could hear an indistinguishable crackle of sound then Jablonsky said: 'I want to speak to General Ruthven. Urgently. It's about – say that again? I see. I see.'

He depressed the receiver and looked at Mary Ruthven.

'Your father left the X 13 at 4 p.m., and hasn't returned. They say he won't be back until they've found you. Blood, it would appear, is thicker than oil. Makes things all the easier for me.' He got through to the new number he'd been given from the oil rig and asked for the general again. He got him almost at once and didn't waste a word.

'General Blair Ruthven . . . I've got news for you, General. Good news and bad. I've got your daughter here. That's the good news. The bad news is that it'll cost you fifty thousand bucks to get her back.' Jablonsky broke off and listened, spinning the Mauser gently round his forefinger, smiling as always. 'No, General, I am not John Talbot. But Talbot's with me right now. I've persuaded him that keeping father and daughter apart any longer is downright inhuman. You know Talbot, General, or you know of him. It took a lot of persuading. Fifty thousand bucks' worth of persuading.'

The smile suddenly vanished from Jablonsky's face leaving it bleak and cold and hard. The real Jablonsky. His voice, when he spoke, was softer and deeper than ever and gently reproving as to an erring child.

'General, do you know what? I just heard a

75

funny little click. The sort of funny little click you hear on a line when some smart-alec nosey picks up an extension and starts flapping his ears or when somebody cuts in a tape recorder. I don't want any eavesdroppers. No records of private conversations. Neither do you. Not if you ever want to see your daughter again . . . ah, that's better. And General, don't get any funny ideas about telling someone to get through to the cops on another line to ask them to trace this call. We'll be gone from wherever we are in exactly two minutes from now. What's your answer? Make it quickly, now.'

Another brief pause, then Jablonsky laughed pleasantly.

'Threatening you, General? Blackmail, General? Kidnapping, General? Don't be so silly, General. There's no law that says that a man can't run away from a vicious killer, is there? Even if that vicious killer happens to have a kidnappee with him. I'll just walk out and leave them together. Tell me, are you bargaining for your daughter's life, General? Is she worth no more to you than less than one-fiftieth of one per cent of all you own? Is that all her value to a doting father? She's listening in to all this, General. I wonder what she might think of you, eh? Willing to sacrifice her life for an old shoe-button – for that's all fifty thousand bucks is to you . . . Sure, sure you can speak to her.' He beckoned to the girl, who ran across the room and snatched the phone from his hand.

'Daddy? Daddy! . . . Yes, yes, it's me, of course it's me. Oh, Daddy, I never thought –'

'Right, that'll do.' Jablonsky laid his big square brown hand across the mouthpiece and took the phone from her. 'Satisfied, General Blair? The genuine article, huh?' There was a short silence, then Jablonsky smiled broadly. 'Thank you, General Blair. I'm not worrying about any guarantee. The word of General Ruthven has always been guarantee enough.' He listened a moment, and when he spoke again the sardonic glint in his eyes as he looked at Mary Ruthven gave the lie to the sincerity in his voice. 'Besides, you know quite well that if you welshed on that money and had a house full of cops, your daughter would never speak to you again . . . No need to worry about my not coming. There's every reason why I should. Fifty thousand, to be exact.'

He hung up. 'On your feet, Talbot. We have an appointment with high society.'

'Yes.' I sat where I was. 'And then you turn me over to the law and collect your fifteen thousand?'

'Sure. Why not?'

'I could give you twenty thousand reasons.'

'Yeah?' He looked at me speculatively. 'Got 'em on you?'

'Don't be stupid. Give me a week, or perhaps –'

'Bird-in-the-hand Jablonsky, pal, that's me. Get going. Looks like being a nice night's work.'

He cut my bonds and we went out through the garage. Jablonsky had a hand on the girl's wrist and a gun about thirty inches from my back. I couldn't see it, but I didn't have to. I knew it was there.

Night had come. The wind was rising, from the north-west, and it carried with it the wild harsh smell of the sea and a cold slanting rain that splattered loudly against the rustling dripping fronds of the palms and bounced at an angle off the asphalt pavement at our feet. It was less than a hundred yards to where Jablonsky had left his Ford outside the central block of the motel, but that hundred yards made us good and wet. The parking-lot, in that rain, was deserted, but even Jablonsky had backed his car into the darkest corner. He would. He opened both offside doors of the Ford, then went and stood by the rear door.

'You first, lady. Other side. You're driving, Talbot.' He banged my door shut as I got in behind the wheel, slid into the back seat and closed his own door. He let me feel the Mauser, hard, against the back of my neck in case my memory was failing me.

'Turn south on the highway.'

I managed to press the proper buttons, eased through the deserted motel courtyard and turned right. Jablonsky said to the girl: 'Your old man's place is just off the main highway? Right?'

'Yes.'

'Any other way of getting there? Back streets? Side roads?'

'Yes, you can go round the town and –'

'So. We'll go straight through. I'm figuring the same way as Talbot figured when he came to the La Contessa – no one will be looking for him within fifty miles of Marble Springs.'

We drove through the town in silence. The roads were almost deserted and there weren't half a dozen pedestrians to be seen. I caught the red both times at the only two sets of traffic lights in Marble Springs, and both times the Mauser came to rest on the back of my head. By and by we were clear of the town and the rain sheeting down in a torrential cascade that drummed thunderously on the roof and hood of the car. It was like driving under a waterfall and the windscreen-wipers weren't built for driving under waterfalls. I had to slow down to twenty and even so I was all but blind whenever the headlights of an approaching car spread their whitely-diffused glare over the streaming glass of the windscreen, a blindness which became complete with the spraying wall of water that thudded solidly against screen and offside of the body as the approaching cars swept by with the sibilant whisper of wet rubber on wet roads and a bow-wave that a destroyer captain would have been proud to own.

Mary Ruthven peered into the alternating glare and gloom with her forehead pressed against the windscreen. She probably knew the road well, but she didn't know it tonight. A north-bound truck growled by at the wrong moment and she almost missed the turn-off.

79

'There it is!' She grabbed my forearm so hard that the Ford skidded for a moment on to the shoulder of the road before I could bring it under control. I caught a glimpse through the rain of a dimly phosphorescent glow on the left and was fifty yards beyond before I stopped. The road was too narrow for a U-turn so I backed and filled until we were heading the other way, crawled up to the illuminated opening in first and turned in slowly. I should have hated to turn in there quickly. As it was, I managed to pull up a few feet short of a six-barred white-painted metal gate that would have stopped a bulldozer.

The gate appeared to be at the end of an almost flat-roofed tunnel. On the left was a seven-foot high white limestone wall, maybe twenty feet long. On the right was a white lodge with an oak door and chintz-covered windows looking out on to the tunnel. Lodge and wall were joined by a shallowly curved roof. I couldn't see what the roof was made of. I wasn't interested in it anyway: I was too busy looking at the man who had come through the lodge door even before I had braked to a stop.

He was the dowager's dream of a chauffeur. He was perfect. He was immaculate. He was a poem in maroon. Even his gleaming riding boots looked maroon. The flaring Bedford cord breeches, the high-buttoned tunic, the gloves perfectly folded under one epaulette, even the peak of the cap were all of the same perfect shade. He took his cap off.

His hair wasn't maroon. It was thick and black and gleaming and parted on the right. He had a smooth brown face and dark eyes set well apart, just like his shoulders. A poem, but no pansy. He was as big as I was, and a whole lot better looking.

Mary Ruthven had the window wound down, and the chauffeur bent to look at her, one sinewy brown hand resting on the edge of the door. When he saw who it was the brown face broke into a wide smile and if the relief and gladness in his eyes weren't genuine he was the best actor-chauffeur I'd ever known.

'It *is* you, Miss Mary.' The voice was deep, educated and unmistakably English: when you'd two hundred and eighty-five million bucks it didn't cost but pennies extra to hire a home-grown shepherd to look after your flock of imported Rolls-Royces. English chauffeurs were class. 'I'm delighted to see you back, ma'am. Are you all right?'

'I'm delighted to be back, Simon.' For a brief moment her hand lay over his and squeezed it. She let her breath go in what was half-sigh, half-shudder, and added: 'I'm all right. How is Daddy?'

'The general has been worried stiff, Miss Mary. But he'll be all right now. They told me to expect you. I'll let them know right away.' He half-turned, wheeled, craned forward and peered into the back of the car. His body perceptibly stiffened.

'Yeah, it's a gun,' Jablonsky said comfortably from the rear seat. 'Just holding it, sonny – gets kinda uncomfortable sitting down with a gun in

81

your hip pocket. Haven't you found that yourself?'
I looked and, sure enough, I could see the slight
bulge on the chauffeur's right hip. 'Spoils the cut
of the Little Lord Fauntleroy suit, don't it, though?'
Jablonsky went on. 'And don't get any funny ideas
about using yours. The time for that's past. Besides,
you might hit Talbot. That's him behind the wheel.
Fifteen thousand dollars on the hoof and I want to
deliver him in prime condition.'

'I don't know what you're talking about, sir.'
The chauffeur's face had darkened, his voice was
barely civil. 'I'll ring the house.' He turned away,
went into the small lobby behind the door, lifted
the phone and pressed a button, and as he did so
the heavy gate swung open silently, smoothly, of
its own accord.

'All we need now is a moat and a portcullis,'
Jablonsky murmured as we began to move forward. 'Looks after his 285 million, does the old
general. Electrified fences, patrols, dogs, the lot,
eh, lady?'

She didn't answer. We were moving past a big
four-car garage attached to the lodge. It was a
carport-type garage without doors and I could see
I had been right about the Rolls-Royces. There
were two of them, one sand-brown and beige, the
other gun-metal blue. There was also a Cadillac.
That would be for the groceries. Jablonsky was
speaking again.

'Old Fancy-pants back there. The Limey. Where'd
you pick that sissy up?'

'I'd like to see you say that to him without that gun in your hand,' the girl said quietly. 'He's been with us for three years now. Nine months ago three masked men crashed our car with only Kennedy and myself in it. They all carried guns. One's dead, the other two are still in prison.'

'A lucky sissy,' Jablonsky grunted and relapsed into silence.

The asphalt drive-way up to the house was narrow, long, winding and thickly wooded on both sides. The small evergreen leaves of live oak and long dripping grey festoons of Spanish moss reached out and brushed the roof and sidescreens of the car. Suddenly the trees receded on both sides from the beams of the headlamps, giving way to strategically placed clumps of palms and palmettos, and there, behind a stepped granite balustrade wall and a gravel terrace, lay the general's house.

Built as an ordinary family house, the girl had said. Built for a family of about fifty. It was enormous. It was an old white ante-bellum-type house, so Colonial that it creaked, with a huge pillared two-storey porch, a curiously double-angled roof of a type I'd never seen before and enough glass to keep an active window-cleaner in year-round employment. Over the entrance of the lower porch were two more lights, big old-fashioned coach lamps each with a powerful electric bulb inside. Below the lamps stood the reception committee.

I hadn't expected the reception committee. Subconsciously, I suppose, I had expected the old high-class routine of being welcomed by the butler and deferentially and ceremoniously conducted to the library where the general would be sipping his Scotch before a crackling pine fire. Which was pretty silly, when you come to think of it. When you're expecting a daughter back from the dead and the door-bell rings, you don't just keep on sipping whisky. Not if you're halfway human. The chauffeur had warned them: hence the committee.

The butler was there too. He came down the steps of the porch carrying a huge golf umbrella out into the heavy rain. He didn't look like any butler I'd ever seen. His coat was far too tight round his upper arms, shoulders and chest in a fashion that used to be popular among prohibition gangsters and his face did nothing to dispel the impression. He looked first cousin to Valentino, the bodyguard back in the court-room. Or maybe even more closely related. He even had the same broken nose. The general had a weird taste in butlers, especially when you considered his choice of chauffeur.

But the butler seemed courteous enough. At least I thought he was until he saw who it was behind the driving-wheel and then he made a smart about turn, went round the front of the car and escorted Mary Ruthven to the shelter of the porch where she ran forward and threw her arms round her father's neck. Jablonsky and I had to make it alone. We got wet, but no one seemed worried.

By this time the girl had become disentangled from her father. I had a good look at him. He was an immensely tall old coot, thin but not too thin, in a silver-white linen suit. The colour of the suit was a perfect match for the hair. He had a long lean craggy Lincolnesque face, but just how craggy it was impossible to say for almost half of it was hidden behind a luxuriant white moustache and beard. He didn't look like any big business magnate I'd ever come across, but with 285 million dollars he didn't have to. He looked like the way I'd expected a southern judge to look and didn't.

'Come in, gentlemen,' he said courteously. I wondered if he included me among the three other men standing in the shadows in the porch. It seemed unlikely, but I went in all the same. I hadn't much option. Not only was Jablonsky's Mauser jammed into the small of my back but another man who'd just stepped out of the shadow also carried a gun. We trooped across a huge, wide, chandelier-lit, tessellated-tile floored hall, down a broad passage and into a large room. I'd been right about the room anyway. It was a library, it did have a blazing pine fire and the slightly oily smell of fine leather-bound books mingled very pleasantly with the aroma of expensive Coronas and a high-class Scotch. I noticed there was nobody there smoking cigars. The walls that weren't covered with book-shelves were panelled in polished elm. Chairs and settees were in dark gold leather and moquette, and the curtains of shot gold. A bronze-coloured carpet flowed over the floor from wall to wall and with a strong enough draught the nap on it would have waved and undulated like a wind-rippled field of summer corn. As it was, the chair castors were so deeply sunk in it as to be almost invisible.

'Scotch, Mr – ah –?' the general asked Jablonsky.

'Jablonsky. I don't mind, General. While I'm standing. And while I'm waiting.'

'Waiting for what, Mr Jablonsky?' General Ruthven had a quiet pleasant voice with very little inflection in it. With 285 million bucks you don't have to shout to make yourself heard.

'Ain't you the little kidder, now?' Jablonsky was as quiet, as unruffled as the general. 'For the little paper, General, with your name signed at the bottom. For the fifty thousand iron men.'

'Of course.' The general seemed faintly surprised that Jablonsky should think it necessary to remind him of the agreement. He crossed to the dressed-stone mantelpiece, pulled a yellow bank slip from under a paper-weight. 'I have it here, just the payee's name to be filled in.' I thought a slight smile touched his mouth but under all that foliage it was difficult to be sure. 'And you needn't worry about my phoning the bank with instructions not to honour this cheque. Such is not my way of doing business.'

'I know it's not, General.'

'And my daughter is worth infinitely more to me than this. I must thank you, sir, for bringing her back.'

'Yeah.' Jablonsky took the cheque, glanced casually at it, then looked at the general, a speculative glint in his eyes.

'Your pen slipped, General,' he drawled. 'I asked for fifty thousand. You got seventy thousand here.'

'Correct.' Ruthven inclined his head and glanced at me. 'I had offered ten thousand dollars for information about this man here. I also feel that I'm morally bound to make good the five thousand offered by the authorities. It's so much easier to make out one lump-sum cheque to one person, don't you agree?'

'And the extra five thousand?'

'For your trouble and the pleasure it will give me to hand this man over to the authorities personally.' Again I couldn't be sure whether or not he smiled. 'I can afford to indulge those whims, you know.'

'Your pleasure is my pleasure, General. I'll be on my way, then. Sure you can handle this fellow? He's tough, fast, tricky as they come.'

'I have people who can handle him.' It was plain that the general wasn't referring to the butler and another uniformed servant hovering in the background. He pressed a bell, and when some sort of footman came to the door, said: 'Ask Mr Vyland and Mr Royale to come in, will you, Fletcher?'

'Why don't you ask them yourself, General?' To my way of thinking I was the central figure in that little group, but they hadn't even asked me to speak, so I thought it was time to say something. I bent down to the bowl of artificial flowers on the table by the fire, and pulled up a fine-meshed microphone. 'This room's bugged. A hundred gets one your friends have heard every word that's been said. For a millionaire and high society flier, Ruthven, you have some strange habits.' I broke off and looked at the trio who had just come through the doorway. 'And even stranger friends.'

Which wasn't quite an accurate statement. The first man in looked perfectly at home in that luxurious setting. He was of medium height, medium build, dressed in a perfectly cut dinner suit and smoking a cigar as long as your arm. That was the expensive smell I'd picked up as soon as I had come into the library. He was in his early fifties, with black hair touched by grey at the temples: his neat clipped moustache was jet black. His face was smooth and unlined and deeply sunburnt. He was Hollywood's ideal of a man to play the part of a top executive, smooth, urbane and competent to a degree. It was only when he came closer and you saw his eyes and the set of the planes of his face that you realized that here was a toughness, both physical and mental, and a hardness that you would never see around a movie set. A man to watch.

The second man was more off-beat. It was hard to put a finger on the quality that made him so. He was dressed in a soft grey flannel suit, white shirt, and grey tie of the same shade as the suit. He was slightly below medium height, broadly built, with a pale face and smooth slicked hair almost the same colour as Mary Ruthven's. It wasn't until you looked again and again that you saw what made him off-beat, it wasn't anything he had, it was something he didn't have. He had the most expressionless face, the emptiest eyes I had even seen in any man.

Off-beat was no description for the man who brought up the rear. He belonged in that library the way Mozart would have belonged in a rock and roll club. He was only twenty-one or -two, tall, skinny, with a dead-white face and coal-black eyes. The eyes were never still, they moved restlessly from side to side as if it hurt them to be still, flickering from one face to another like a will-o'-the-wisp on an autumn evening. I didn't notice what he wore, all I saw was his face. The face of a hophead, a junky, an advanced dope addict. Take away his white powder for even twenty-four hours and he'd be screaming his head off as all the devils in hell closed in on him.

'Come in, Mr Vyland.' The general was speaking to the man with the cigar and I wished for the tenth time that old Ruthven's expression wasn't so hard to read. He nodded in my direction. 'This is Talbot, the wanted man. And this is Mr Jablonsky, the man who brought him back.'

'Glad to meet you, Mr Jablonsky.' Vyland smiled in a friendly fashion and put his hand out. 'I'm the general's chief production engineer.' Sure, he was the general's chief production engineer, that made me President of the United States. Vyland nodded at the man in the grey suit. 'This is Mr Royale, Mr Jablonsky.'

'Mr Jablonsky! Mr Jablonsky!' The words weren't spoken, they were hissed by the tall thin boy with the staring eyes. His hand dived under the lapel of his jacket and I had to admit he was fast. The gun trembled in his hand. He swore, three unprintable words in succession, and the eyes were glazed and mad. 'I've waited two long years for this, you – Damn you, Royale! Why did –?'

'There's a young lady here, Larry.' I could have sworn that Royale's hand hadn't reached under his coat, or for his hip pocket, but there had been no mistaking the flash of dulled metal in his hand, the sharp crack of the barrel on Larry's wrist and the clatter of the boy's gun bouncing off a brass-topped table. As an example of sleight-of-hand conjuring, I'd never seen anything to beat it.

'We know Mr Jablonsky,' Royale was continuing. His voice was curiously musical and soothing and soft. 'At least, Larry and I know. Don't we, Larry? Larry did six months once on a narcotics charge. It was Jablonsky that sent him up.'

'Jablonsky sent—' the general began.

'Jablonsky.' Royale smiled and nodded at the big man. 'Detective-Lieutenant Herman Jablonsky, of New York Homicide.'

FOUR

It was one of those silences. It went on and on and on. Pregnant, they call it. It didn't worry me much, I was for the high jump anyway. It was the general who spoke first and his voice and face were stiff and cold as he looked at the man in the dinner suit.

'What is the explanation of this outrageous conduct, Vyland?' he demanded. 'You bring into this house a man who is apparently not only a narcotics addict and carries a gun, but who also served a prison sentence. As for the presence of a police officer, someone might care to inform me –'

'Relax, General. You can drop the front.' It was Royale who spoke, his voice quiet and soothing as before and curiously devoid of any trace of insolence. 'I wasn't quite accurate. Ex-Detective-Lieutenant, I should have said. Brightest boy in the bureau in his day, first narcotics, then homicide, more arrests and more convictions for arrests than

91

any other police officer in the eastern states. But your foot slipped, didn't it, Jablonsky?'

Jablonsky said nothing and his face showed nothing, but it didn't mean he wasn't thinking plenty. My face showed nothing, but I was thinking plenty. I was thinking how I could try to get away. The servants had vanished at a wave of the hand from the general and, for the moment, everyone seemed to have lost interest in me. I turned my head casually. I was wrong, there was someone who hadn't lost interest in me. Valentino, my court-room acquaintance, was standing in the passageway just outside the open door, and the interest he was taking in me more than made up for the lack of interest in the library. I was pleased to see that he was carrying his right arm in a sling. His left thumb was hooked in the side pocket of his coat, and although he might have had a big thumb it wasn't big enough to make all that bulge in his pocket. He would just love to see me trying to get away.

'Jablonsky here was the central figure in the biggest police scandal to hit New York since the war,' Royale was saying. 'All of a sudden there were a lot of murders – important murders – in his parish, and Jablonsky boobed on the lot. Everyone knew a protection gang was behind the killings. Everybody except Jablonsky. All Jablonsky knew was that he was getting ten grand a stiff to look in every direction but the right one. But he had even more enemies inside the force than outside, and they nailed him. Eighteen months ago it was, and he had the headlines to himself for an entire week. Don't you remember, Mr Vyland?'

'Now I do,' Vyland nodded. 'Sixty thousand tucked away and they never laid a finger on a cent. Three years he got, wasn't it?'

'And out in eighteen months,' Royale finished. 'Jumped the wall; Jablonsky?'

'Good conduct remission,' Jablonsky said calmly. 'A respectable citizen again. Which is more than could be said for you, Royale. You employing this man, General?'

'I fail to see —'

'Because if you are, it'll cost you a hundred bucks more than you think. A hundred bucks is the price Royale usually charges his employers for a wreath for his victims. A very fancy wreath. Or has the price gone up, Royale? And who are you putting the finger on this time?'

Nobody said anything. Jablonsky had the floor.

'Royale here is listed in the police files of half the states in the Union, General. Nobody's ever pinned anything on him yet, but they know all about him. No.1 remover in the United States, not furniture but people. He charges high, but he's good and there's never any comeback. A freelance, and his services are in terrific demand by all sorts of people you'd never dream of, not only because he never fails to give satisfaction but also because of the fact that it's a point of Royale's code that he'll never touch a man who has employed him. An awful lot of people sleep an awful lot easier, General, just because they know they're on Royale's list of untouchables.' Jablonsky rubbed a bristly chin with a hand the size of a shovel. 'I wonder who he could be after this time, General? Could it even be yourself, do you think?'

For the first time the general registered emotion. Not even the beard and moustache could hide a narrowing of the eyes, a tightening of the lips and a slight but perceptible draining of colour from the cheeks. He wet his lips, slowly, and looked at Vyland.

'Did you know anything of this? What truth is there –?'

'Jablonsky's just shooting off the top of his mouth,' Vyland interjected smoothly. 'Let's get them into another room, General. We must talk.'

Ruthven nodded, his face still pale, and Vyland glanced at Royale. Royale smiled and said without inflection: 'All right, you two, out. Leave that gun there, Jablonsky.'

'And if I don't?'

'You haven't cashed that cheque yet,' Royale said obliquely. They'd been listening, all right.

Jablonsky put his gun on the table. Royale himself didn't have a gun in his hand. With the speed he could move at it would have been quite superfluous anyway. The hophead, Larry, came up behind me and dug his pistol barrel in my kidney with a force that made me grunt in pain. Nobody said anything, so I said: 'Do that again, hophead, and it'll take a dentist a whole day to repair your face.' So he did it again, twice as painfully as before, and when I swung round he was too quick for me and caught me with the barrel of his gun high up on the face and raked the sight down my cheek. Then he stood off, four feet away, gun pointed at my lower stomach and those crazy eyes jumping all over the place, a wicked smile on his face inviting me to jump him. I mopped some of the blood off my face and turned and went out the door.

Valentino was waiting for me, gun in hand and heavy boots on his feet, and by the time Royale came leisurely out of the library, closed the door behind him and stopped Valentino with a single word, I couldn't walk. There's nothing wrong with my thigh, it's carried me around for years, but it's not made of oak and Valentino wore toe-plates on his boots. It just wasn't my lucky night. Jablonsky helped me off the floor into an adjacent room. I stopped at the doorway, looked back at the grinning Valentino and then at Larry, and I wrote them both down in my little black book.

We spent perhaps ten minutes in that room, Jablonsky and I sitting, the hophead pacing up and down with the gun in his hand and hoping I would twitch an eyebrow, Royale leaning negligently against a table, nobody saying anything, until by and by the butler came in and said the general wanted to see us. We all trooped out again. Valentino was still there, but I made it safely to the library. Maybe he'd hurt his toe, but I knew it wasn't that: Royale had told him once to lay off, and just once would be all that Royale would have to tell anybody anything.

A far from subtle change had taken place in the atmosphere since we'd left. The girl was sitting on a stool by the fire, head bent and the flickering light gleaming off her wheat-coloured braids, but Vyland and the general seemed easy and relaxed and confident and the latter was even smiling. A couple of newspapers were lying on the library table and I wondered sourly if those, with their big black banner headlines 'Wanted Killer Slays Constable, Wounds Sheriff' and the far from flattering pictures of myself had anything to do with their confidence. To emphasize the change in atmosphere, a footman came in with a tray of glasses, decanter and soda siphon. He was a young man, but moved with a peculiarly stiff leaden-footed gait and he laid the tray down on the table with so laborious a difficulty that you could almost hear his joints creak. His colour didn't look too good either. I looked away, glanced at him again and then indifferently away once more, hoping that the knowledge of what I suddenly knew didn't show in my face.

They'd read all the right books on etiquette, the footman and the butler knew exactly what to do. The footman brought in the drinks, the butler carried them around. He gave a sherry to the girl, whisky to each of the four men – Hophead was pointedly bypassed – and planted

96

himself in front of me. My gaze travelled from his hairy wrists to his broken nose to the general in the background. The general nodded, so I looked back at the silver tray again. Pride said no, the magnificent aroma of the amber liquid that had been poured from the triangular dimpled bottle said yes, but pride carried the heavy handicap of my hunger, soaked clothes and the beating I'd just had and the aroma won looking round. I took the glass and eyed the general over the rim. 'A last drink for the condemned man, eh, General?'

'Not condemned yet.' He lifted his glass. 'Your health, Talbot.'

'Very witty,' I sneered. 'What do they do in the state of Florida, General? Strap you over a cyanide bucket or just fry you in the hot seat?'

'Your health,' he repeated. 'You're not condemned, maybe you'll never be condemned. I have a proposition to put before you, Talbot.'

I lowered myself carefully into a chair. Valentino's boot must have mangled up one of the nerves in my leg, a thigh muscle was jumping uncontrollably. I waved at the papers lying on the library table.

'I take it you've read those, General. I take it you know all about what happened today, all about my record. What kind of proposition can a man like you possibly have to put to a man like me?'

'A very attractive one.' I imagined I saw a touch of red touch the high cheekbones but he spoke steadily enough. 'In exchange for a little service

I wish you to perform for me I offer you your life.'

'A fair offer. And the nature of this little service, General?'

'I am not at liberty to tell you at present. In about, perhaps – thirty-six hours, would you say, Vyland?'

'We should hear by then,' Vyland agreed. He was less and less like an engineer every time I looked at him. He took a puff at his Corona and looked at me. 'You agree to the general's proposition, then?'

'Don't be silly. What else can I do? And after the job, whatever it is?'

'You will be provided with papers and passport and sent to a certain South American country where you will have nothing to fear,' the general answered. 'I have the connections.' Like hell I would be given papers and a trip to South America: I would be given a pair of concrete socks and a vertical trip to the bottom of the Gulf of Mexico.

'And if I don't agree, then of course –'

'If you don't agree then they will all be overcome by a high sense of civic responsibility and turn you over to the cops,' Jablonsky interrupted sardonically. 'The whole set-up stinks to high heaven. Why should the general want you? – he can hire practically any man in the nation. Why, especially, should he hire a killer on the lam? What earthly use can you be to him? Why should he help a wanted murderer to evade justice?' He sipped his drink thoughtfully. 'General Blair Ruthven, the moral pillar of New England society, best-known and highest-minded do-gooder after the Rockefellers. It stinks. You're paddling in some dark and dirty water, General. Very dark, very dirty. And paddling right up to your neck. Lord knows what stakes *you* must be playing for. They must be fantastic.' He shook his head. 'This I would never have believed.'

'I have never willingly or knowingly done a dishonest thing in my life,' the general said steadily.

'Jeez!' Jablonsky ejaculated. For a few seconds he was silent, then said suddenly: 'Well, thanks for the drink, General. Don't forget to sup with a long spoon. I'll take my hat and my cheque and be on my way. The Jablonsky retirement fund is in your debt.'

I didn't see who made the signal. Probably it came from Vyland. Again I didn't see how the gun got into Royale's hand. But I saw it there. So did Jablonsky. It was a tiny gun, a very flat automatic with a snub barrel, even smaller than the Lilliput the sheriff had taken from me. But Royale probably had the eye and the aim of a squirrel-hunter, and it was all he needed: a great big hole in the heart from a heavy Colt makes you no deader than a tiny little hole from a .22.

Jablonsky looked thoughtfully at the gun. 'You would rather I stayed, General?'

'Put that damn gun away,' the general snapped. 'Jablonsky's on our side. At least, I hope he's going

99

to be. Yes, I'd rather you stayed. But no one's going to make you if you don't want to.'

'And what's going to make me want to?' Jablonsky inquired of the company at large. 'Could it be that the general, who has never willingly done a dishonest thing in his life, is planning to hold up payment on that cheque? Or maybe just planning to tear it up altogether?'

It didn't need the general's suddenly averted eyes to confirm Jablonsky's guess. Vyland cut in smoothly: 'It'll only be for two days, Jablonsky, three at the most. After all, you are getting a great deal of money for very little. All we're asking you to do is to ride herd on Talbot here until he's done what we want him to do.'

Jablonsky nodded slowly. 'I see. Royale here wouldn't stoop to bodyguarding – he takes care of people in a rather more permanent way. The thug out in the passage there, the butler, our little friend Larry here – Talbot could eat 'em all before breakfast. You must need Talbot pretty badly, eh?'

'We require him,' Vyland said smoothly. 'And from what we've learnt from Miss Ruthven – and from what Royale knows of you – you can hold him. And your money's safe.'

'Uh-huh. And tell me, am I a prisoner looking after a prisoner, or am I free to come and go?'

'You heard what the general said,' Vyland answered. 'You're a free agent. But if you do go out make sure he's locked up or tied so that he can't break for it.'

'Seventy thousand bucks' worth of guarding, eh?' Jablonsky said grimly. 'He's safe as the gold in Fort Knox.' I caught Royale and Vyland exchanging a brief flicker of a glance as Jablonsky went on: 'But I'm kind of worried about that seventy thousand. I mean, if someone finds out Talbot is here, I won't get the seventy thousand. All I'll get, with my record, is ten years for obstructing the course of justice and giving aid and comfort to a wanted murderer.' He looked speculatively at Vyland and the general and went on softly: 'What guarantee have I that no one in this house will talk?'

'No one will talk,' Vyland said flatly.

'The chauffeur lives in the lodge, doesn't he?' Jablonsky said obliquely.

'Yes, he does.' Vyland spoke softly, thoughtfully. 'It might be a good idea to get rid of –'

'No!' the girl interrupted violently. She'd jumped to her feet, fists clenched by her sides.

'Under no circumstances,' General Ruthven said quietly. 'Kennedy remains. We are too much in his debt.'

Vyland's dark eyes narrowed for a moment and he looked at the general. But it was the girl who answered the unspoken query.

'Simon won't talk,' she said tonelessly. She moved towards the door: 'I'll go to see him.'

'Simon, eh?' Vyland scraped a thumb-nail against the corner of his moustache, and looked at her appraisingly. 'Simon Kennedy, chauffeur and general handyman.'

She retraced a few steps, stopped in front of Vyland and looked at him steadily, tiredly. You could just see the fifteen generations stretching back to the *Mayflower* and every one of the 285 million bucks was showing. She said distinctly: 'I think you are the most utterly hateful man I have ever known,' and walked out, closing the door behind her.

'My daughter is overwrought,' the general said hastily. 'She –'

'Forget it, General.' Vyland's voice was as urbane as ever, but he looked a bit overwrought himself. 'Royale, you might show Jablonsky and Talbot their quarters for tonight. East end of the new wing – the rooms are being fixed now.'

Royale nodded, but Jablonsky held up his hand. 'This job Talbot is going to do for you – is it in this house?'

General Ruthven glanced at Vyland, then shook his head.

'Then where?' Jablonsky demanded. 'If this guy is taken out of here and anybody within a hundred miles spots him, we've had it. Particularly, it would be goodbye to my money. I think I'm entitled to a little reassurance on this point, General.'

Again the swift interchange of looks between the general and Vyland, again the latter's all but imperceptible nod.

'I think we can tell you that,' the general said.

'The job's on the X 13, my oil rig out in the gulf.' He smiled faintly. 'Fifteen miles from here and well out in the gulf. No passers-by to see him there, Mr Jablonsky.'

Jablonsky nodded, as though for the moment satisfied, and said no more. I stared at the ground. I didn't dare to look up. Royale said softly: 'Let's be on our way.'

I finished my drink and got up. The heavy library door opened outwards into the passage and Royale, gun in hand, stood to one side to let me pass through first. He should have known better. Or maybe my limp deceived him. People thought my limp slowed me up, but people were wrong.

Valentino had disappeared. I went through the doorway, slowed up and moved to one side round the edge of the door as if I were waiting for Royale to catch up and show me where to go, then whirled round and smashed the sole of my right foot against the door with all the speed and power I could muster.

Royale got nailed neatly between door and jamb. Had it been his head that was caught it would have been curtains. As it was, it caught his shoulders but even so it was enough to make him grunt in agony and send the gun spinning out of his hand to fall a couple of yards down the passage. I dived for it, I scooped it up by the barrel, swung round, still crouched, as I heard the quick step behind me. The butt of the automatic caught the diving Royale

103

somewhere on the face, I couldn't be sure where, but it sounded like a four-pound axe sinking into the bole of a pine. He was unconscious before he hit me – but he did hit me. An axe won't stop a falling pine. It took only a couple of seconds to push him off and change my grip to the butt of the pistol, but two seconds would always be enough and more than enough for a man like Jablonsky.

His foot caught my gun-hand and the gun landed twenty feet away. I launched myself for his legs but he moved to one side with the speed of a fly-weight, lifted his knee and sent me crashing against the open door. And then it was too late, for he had the Mauser in his hand and it was pointing between my eyes.

I climbed slowly to my feet, not trying anything. The general and Vyland, the latter with a gun in his hand, came crowding through the open door, then relaxed when they saw Jablonsky with the gun on me. Vyland bent down and helped a now-moaning Royale to a sitting position. Royale had a long, heavily bleeding cut above his left eye and and tomorrow he'd have a duck's egg bruise there. After maybe half a minute he shook his head to clear it, wiped blood away with the back of his hand and looked slowly round till his eyes found mine. I'd been mistaken. I'd thought his the emptiest, the most expressionless eyes I'd ever seen, but I'd been mistaken. I looked in them and I could almost smell the moist freshly-turned earth of an open grave.

'I can see that you gents really do need me around,' Jablonsky said jovially. 'I never thought anyone would try that stuff with Royale and live to talk about it. But we learn.' He dug into a side pocket and brought out a set of very slender blued-steel cuffs and slipped them expertly on my wrists. 'A souvenir of the bad old days,' he explained apologetically. 'Would there happen to be another pair and some wire or chain round the house?'

'It might be arranged,' Vyland said almost mechanically. He still couldn't credit what had happened to his infallible hatchet-man.

'Fine.' Jablonsky grinned down at Royale. 'You don't need to lock your door tonight. I'll keep Talbot out of your hair.' Royale transferred his sombre, evil stare from my face to Jablonsky's and his expression didn't alter any that I could see. I fancied perhaps Royale was beginning to have ideas about a double grave.

The butler took us upstairs and along a narrow passage to the back of the big house, took a key from his pocket, unlocked the door and ushered us in. It was just another bedroom, sparsely but expensively furnished, with a wash-basin in one corner and a modern mahogany bed in the middle of the right wall. To the left was a communicating door to another bedroom. The butler took a second key from his pocket and unlocked this door also. It gave on to another room, the mirror image of the first, except for the bed, which was an old-fashioned iron-railed effort. It looked as if it had been made with girders left over from the Key West bridge. It looked solid. It looked as if it were going to be my bed.

We went back into the other room. Jablonsky stretched out his hand. 'The keys, please.'

The butler hesitated, peered uncertainly at him, then shrugged, handed over the keys and turned to leave. Jablonsky said pleasantly: 'This Mauser I'm holding here, friend – want that I should bounce it off your head two three times?'

'I'm afraid I don't understand, sir.'

' "Sir", hey? That's good. I wouldn't have expected them to have books on buttling in Alcatraz. The other key, my friend. The one leading to the passage from Talbot's room.'

The butler scowled, handed over a third key, and left. Whatever buttling book he'd read he'd skipped the section on closing doors, but it was a stout door and it stood up to it. Jablonsky grinned, locked the door with an ostentatious click, pulled the curtains, checked rapidly that there were no peep-holes in the walls and crossed back to where I stood. Five or six times he smacked a massive fist into a massive palm, kicked the wall and knocked over an armchair with a thud that shook the room. Then he said, not too softly, not too loudly: 'Get up when you're ready, friend. That's just a little warning, shall we say, not to try any further tricks like you tried on Royale. Just move one finger and you'll think the Chrysler building fell on top of you.'

I didn't move a finger. Neither did Jablonsky. There was a complete silence inside the room. We listened hard. The silence in the passageway outside was not complete. With his flat feet and adenoidal, broken-nosed breathing, the butler was completely miscast as the Last of the Mohicans and he was a good twenty feet away by the time the thick carpet absorbed the last of his creaking footfalls.

Jablonsky took out a key, softly opened the handcuffs, pocketed them and shook my hand as if he meant to break every finger I had. I felt like it, too, but for all that my grin was as big, as delighted as his own. We lit cigarettes and started on the two rooms with toothpicks, looking for bugs and listening devices.

The place was loaded with them.

Exactly twenty-four hours later I climbed into the sports car that had been left empty, but with the ignition key in the lock, four hundred yards away from the entrance lodge to the general's house. It was a Chevrolet Corvette – the same car that I'd stolen the previous afternoon when I'd been holding Mary Ruthven hostage.

The rain yesterday had vanished, completely. The sky had been blue and cloudless all day long – and for me it had been a very long day indeed. Lying fully dressed and handcuffed to the rails of an iron bed for twelve hours while the temperature in a closed-window south-facing room rises to a hundred in the shade – well, the heat and the somnolent inactivity would have been just right for a Galapagos tortoise. It left me as limp as a shot rabbit. They'd kept me there all day, Jablonsky bringing me food and parading me shortly after dinner before the general, Vyland and Royale to let them see how good a watch-dog he was and that I was still relatively intact. Relatively was the word: to increase the effect I'd redoubled my limp and had sticking plaster crossed over cheek and chin.

Royale needed no such adventitious aids to advertise the fact that he had been in the wars. I doubt if they made sticking plaster wide enough to cover the enormous bruise he had on his forehead. His right eye was the same bluish-purple as the bruise, and completely shut. I'd done a good job on Royale: and I knew, for all the empty remote expression that was back in his face and one good eye, that he'd never rest until he'd done a better job on me. A permanent job.

The night air was cool and sweet and full of the smell of the salt air. I had the hood down and as I travelled south I leaned far back and to one side to let the freshness drive away the last of the cobwebs from my dopy mind. It wasn't just the heat that had made my mind sluggish, I had slept so long during that sticky afternoon that I was overslept and paying for it: but then, I wasn't going to get much sleep that coming night. Once or twice I thought of Jablonsky, that big black smiling man with the engaging grin, sitting back in his upstairs room diligently and solemnly guarding my empty bedroom with all three keys in his pocket. I felt in my own pocket and they were still there, the duplicates that Jablonsky had had cut that morning when he had taken the air in the direction of Marble Springs. Jablonsky had been busy that morning.

I forgot about Jablonsky. He could take better care of himself than any man I'd ever known. I had enough troubles of my own coming up that night.

The last traces of the brilliant red sunset had just vanished over the wine-dark gulf to the west and the stars were standing clear in the high and windless sky when I saw a green-shaded lantern on the right of the road. I passed it, then a second, then at the third I turned sharp right and ran the Corvette down on to a little stone jetty, switching off my headlights even before I coasted to a standstill beside a tall, bulky man with a tiny pencil flash in his hand.

He took my arm – he had to, I was blind from staring into the glaring white pool of light cast by the Corvette's headlamps – and led me wordlessly down a flight of wooden steps to a floating landing jetty and across this to a long dark shape that lay rocking gently by the side of the jetty. I was seeing better already, and I managed to grab a stay and jump down into the boat without a helping hand. A squat, short man rose to greet me.

'Mr Talbot?'

'Yes. Captain Zaimis, isn't it?'

'John.' The little man chuckled and explained in his lilting accent: 'My boys would laugh at me. "Captain Zaimis", they would say. "And how is the *Queen Mary* or the *United States* today?" they would say. And so on. The children of today.' The little man sighed in mock sorrow. 'Ah, well, I suppose "John" is good enough for the captain of the little *Matapan*.'

I glanced over his shoulder and had a look at the children. They were, as yet, no more than dark blurs against a slightly less dark skyline, but there was little enough to let me see that they averaged about six feet and were built in proportion. Nor was the *Matapan* so little: she was at least forty feet long, twin-masted, with curious athwartships and fore-and-aft rails just above the height of a tall man's head. Both men and vessel were Greek: the crew were Greeks to a man and if the *Matapan* wasn't entirely Grecian, she had at least been built by Greek shipwrights who had come to and settled down in Florida just for the express purpose of building those sponge ships. With its slender graceful curves and upswept bows Homer would have had no trouble in identifying it as a direct lineal descendant of the galleys that had roamed the sunlit Aegean and the Levant countless centuries ago. I felt a sudden sense of gratitude and security that I was aboard such a vessel, accompanied by such men.

'A fine night for the job in hand,' I said.

'Perhaps. Perhaps not.' The humour had left his voice. 'I don't think so. It is not the night that John Zaimis would have chosen.'

I didn't point out that choice didn't enter into the matter. I said: 'Too clear, is that it?'

'Not that.' He turned away for a moment, gave some orders in what could only have been Greek, and men started moving about the deck, unhitching ropes from the bollards on the landing stage. He turned back to me. 'Excuse me if I speak to them in our old tongue. Those three boys are not yet six months in this country. My own boys, they will not dive. A hard life, they say, too hard a life. So we have to bring the young men from Greece . . . I don't like the weather, Mr Talbot. It is too fine a night.'

'That's what I said.'

'No.' He shook his head vigorously. 'Too fine. The air is too still, and the little breeze it comes from the north-west? That is bad. Tonight the sun was a flame in the sky. That is bad. You feel the little waves that are rocking the *Matapan*? When the weather is good the little waves they slap against the hull every three seconds, maybe four. Tonight?' He shrugged. 'Twelve seconds, maybe every fifteen. For forty years I have sailed out of Tarpon Springs. I know the waters here, Mr Talbot, I would be lying if I say any man knows them better. A big storm comes.'

'A big storm, eh?' When it came to big storms

111

I didn't fancy myself very much. 'Hurricane warning out?'

'No.'

'Do you always get those signs before a hurricane?' Captain Zaimis wasn't going to cheer me up, somebody had to try.

'Not always, Mr Talbot. Once, maybe fifteen years ago, there was a storm warning but none of the signs. Not one. The fishermen from the South Caicos went out. Fifty drowned. But when it is September and the signs are there, then the big storm comes. Every time it comes.'

Nobody was going to cheer me up tonight. 'When will it come?' I asked.

'Eight hours, forty-eight hours, I do not know.' He pointed due west, the source of the long slow oily swell. 'But it comes from there . . . You will find your rubber suit below, Mr Talbot.'

Two hours and thirteen miles later we were uncomfortably nearer that still-distant storm. We had travelled at full speed, but full speed on the *Matapan* was nothing to write home about. Almost a month ago two civilian engineers, sworn to secrecy, had bypassed the exhaust of the *Matapan's* engine to an underwater cylinder with a curiously arranged system of baffle plates. They'd done a fine job, the exhaust level of the *Matapan* was no more than a throaty whisper, but back pressure had cut the thrust output in half. But it was fast enough. It got there. It got there too fast for me, and the farther out we went into the starlit gulf the longer and deeper became the troughs between the swells, the more convinced I was of the hopelessness of what I had set out to do. But someone had to do it and I was the man who had picked the joker.

There was no moon that night. By and by, even the stars began to go out. Cirrus clouds in long grey sheets began to fill the sky. Then the rain came, not heavy, but cold and penetrating, and John Zaimis gave me a tarpaulin for shelter – there was a cabin on the *Matapan*, but I had no wish to go below.

I must have dozed off, lulled by the motion of the boat, for the next I knew the rain had stopped spattering on the tarpaulin and someone was shaking my shoulder. It was the skipper, and he was saying softly: 'There she is, Mr Talbot. The X 13.'

I stood up, using a mast to support myself – the swell was becoming really unpleasant now – and followed the direction of his pointing hand. Not that he needed to point, even at the distance of a mile the X 13 seemed to fill the entire sky.

I looked at it, looked away, then looked back again. It was still there. I'd lost more than most, I didn't have a great deal to live for, but I did have a little, so I stood there and wished myself ten thousand miles away.

I was scared. If this was the end of the road, I wished to God I'd never set foot on it.

FIVE

I'd heard of those off-shore rigs before. I'd even had one of them described to me by a man who designed them, but I'd never seen one before and now that I did I realized that the description I'd had had been on the same level as my imaginative capacity to clothe with flesh the bare bones of facts and statistics.

I looked at the X 13 and I just didn't believe it.

It was enormous. It was angular and ungainly as was no other structure I'd ever seen before. And, above all, it was unreal, a weird combination of Jules Verne and some of the fancier flights of space fiction.

At first glance, in the fleeting patches of dim starlight, it looked like a forest of huge factory chimneys sticking up out of the sea. Halfway up their height those chimneys were all joined by a deep and massive platform through the sides of which those chimneys penetrated. And, at the very right hand side, built on the platform itself and

114

reaching up into the sky, mysterious and fragile in the spiderlike tracery of its slenderly interwoven girders, twice the height of the chimneys and outlined against the night sky in its fairy-like festoon of white and coloured operating and aircraft warning lights, was the oil-drilling derrick itself.

I'm not one of those characters who go about pinching themselves to convince themselves that things are real, but if I were I would never have had a better opportunity or reason to pinch than right then. To see that weird Martian structure suddenly thrusting itself up out of the sea would have had the most hardened topers in the country screaming to climb aboard the water wagon.

The chimneys, I knew, were massive tubular metal legs of almost unbelievable strength, each one capable of supporting a weight of several hundred tons, and on this rig I could count no less than fourteen of those legs, seven on each side, and there must have been a stretch of four hundred feet between the outer ones at the ends. And the astonishing thing was that this huge platform was mobile: it had been towed there with the platform deep-sunk in the sea and the legs thrusting high up almost to the level of the top of the derrick: arrived at the right spot, those legs had dropped right down to the floor of the sea – and then the whole huge platform and derrick, maybe four or five thousand tons in all and powered by huge engines, had risen dripping from the sea till it was safe beyond the reach of even the highest of the hurricane-lashed waves of the Gulf of Mexico.

All this I had known; but knowing and seeing weren't the same things at all.

A hand touched my arm and I jumped. I had quite forgotten where I was.

'What do you think of him, Mr Talbot?' It was the skipper. 'You like, eh?'

'Yes. It's nice. How much did this little toy cost? Any idea?'

'Four million dollars.' Zaimis shrugged. 'Maybe four and a half.'

'A fair investment,' I conceded. 'Four million dollars.'

'Eight,' Zaimis corrected. 'A man cannot just come and start drilling, Mr Talbot. First he buy the land under the sea, five thousand acres, three million dollars. Then to drill a well – just one well, maybe two miles deep – it cost perhaps three-quarters of a million. If he's lucky.'

Eight million dollars. And not an investment either. A gamble. Geologists could be wrong, they were more often wrong than right. General Blair Ruthven, a man with eight million dollars to throw away: what colossal prize could a man like that, with a reputation like his, be working for if he was prepared, as he so obviously was prepared, to step outside the law? There was only one way of finding out. I shivered and turned to Zaimis.

'You can get in close? Real close, I mean?'

'All the way.' He pointed to the near side of

the vast structure. 'You have seen the ship tied up alongside?'

I hadn't but I could see her now, a lean dark shape maybe two hundred and fifty feet long, completely dwarfed by the massive rig, the tips of her masts reaching no more than halfway up to the platform deck of the oil rig. I looked back at Zaimis.

'Is that going to queer our pitch, John?'

'Get in our way, you mean? No. We make a wide curve and approach from the south.'

He touched the rudder and the *Matapan* swung away to port, heading to bypass the X 13 to the south: to have gone to the north, the right, would have brought the *Matapan* under the glare of the arc and floodlights that illuminated the big working platform round the derrick. Even at a mile we could clearly see men moving around the derrick and the subdued hum of powerful machinery, like that of diesel compressors, came at us clearly over the darkened waters. So much, at least, was in our favour; it had not occurred to me that work on those mobile rigs would go on twenty-four hours a day but at least the clamour of their operations would drown out the throaty whisper of the *Matapan*'s engines.

The boat had begun to corkscrew violently. We were quartering to the south-west, taking that long, deepening swell on our starboard bow and water was beginning to break over the sides of the boat. And I was getting wet. I crouched under a tarpaulin near the rudder, lit a last cigarette under cover and looked at the skipper.

'That ship out there, John. What chances of it moving away?'

'I don't know. Not much, I think. It is a supply and power ship. It brings out food and drink and mud for the drills and thousands of gallons of oil. Look closely, Mr Talbot. It is a kind of small tanker. Now it brings oil for the big machines, and perhaps electricity from its dynamos. Later, when the strike comes, it takes oil away.'

I peered out under a corner of the tarpaulin. It did look, as John said, a kind of small tanker. I had seen the same type of ship years ago in the war; the high, raised, bare centre-deck and after accommodation and engine-room of the inshore fleet oiler. But what interested me more right then was John's statement that it was there most of the time.

'I want to go aboard that ship, John. Can do?' I didn't want to go aboard, but I knew I had to. The idea of a vessel more or less permanently moored there had never occurred to me: now that I knew it to be a fact it was suddenly the most important factor in my considerations.

'But – but I was told you wanted to go aboard the rig itself, Mr Talbot.'

'Yes. Perhaps. But later. Can you manage the ship?'

'I can try.' Captain Zaimis sounded grim. 'It is a bad night, Mr Talbot.'

118

He was telling me. I thought it was a terrible night. But I said nothing. Still angling south-west, we were passing directly opposite the middle of one of the long sides of the rig and I could see that the massive steel columns supporting the derrick platform were not so symmetrically arranged as I had imagined. Between the fourth and fifth of the huge legs, on either side, was a gap of perhaps a hundred and fifty feet and here the platform was scooped out to a much lower level than the main deck. On this lower level the thin spindly cigar-shaped outline of a crane reached up as high as the topmost level of the columns: the ship was moored directly below this cut-out well-deck, spanning the gap and a couple of steel pillars on either side of the gap.

Five minutes later the skipper changed course until we were heading due west again, in a direction that would have taken us clear to the south of the rig, but we had hardly time to get accustomed to the comparative comfort of heading straight into the swell when he put the helm over again, and headed north-west. We steered straight in, as it seemed, for the most southerly leg on the landward side of the rig, passing within forty feet of the bow of the ship moored alongside, scraped by the leg with only feet to spare and so found ourselves directly under the massive platform of the oil rig.

One of the young Greeks, a black-haired bronzed boy by the name of Andrew, was busy in the bows, and as we passed right under the platform and came abreast of the second pillar from the south on the seaward side he called softly to John and at the same time threw a lifebelt, attached to a coil of light rope, as far as he could to one side. As he did so John cut the engine to the merest whisper, and the *Matapan*, urged by the swell, drifted slowly back past one side of the pillar while the lifebelt came back on the other, so passing the light line completely round the pillar. Andrew picked up the lifebelt with a boat-hook and started pulling in the grass line which had been bent on to a heavier manila: within a minute the *Matapan* was securely moored to the pillar, with the engine just ticking over sufficiently to give her enough way to take the strain of the rope so that she wouldn't snag too heavily in the steadily deepening swell. Nobody had heard us, nobody had seen us: not, at least, as far as we could tell.

'You will be very quick,' John said softly, anxiously. 'I do not know how long we shall be able to wait. I smell the storm.'

He was anxious. I was anxious. We were all anxious. But all he had to do was to sit in that boat. Nobody was going to beat his head in or tie rocks to him and throw him into the Gulf of Mexico.

'You've got nothing to worry about,' I said reassuringly. Nor had he, compared to me. 'Half an hour.' I stripped off my overcoat, snapped the vulcanized neck and wrist cuffs of the tanned twill and rubber suit I was wearing beneath it, slipped an oxygen apparatus over my shoulders, tightened the straps, took the nose and eye piece in one hand and coat, pants and hat under the other arm and stepped gingerly over the side into the rubber raft the crew had already slipped over the side.

Andrew sat at the after end of this flimsy contraption, holding a line in his hand, and, as soon as I'd settled, let go his grip on the gunwale of the *Matapan*. The drift of the swell carried us quickly under the gloomy mass of the platform, Andrew paying out the line as we went. Paddling a rubber dinghy in a swell is difficult enough, paddling it in a specific direction against such a swell all but impossible: it would be a hundred times easier to regain the *Matapan* by hauling ourselves back hand over hand.

At a whispered word from me Andrew checked the rope and took a turn. We were now close up to the side of the ship, but still in deep shadow: the ship lay close in to the massive legs, but the platform overhung those legs, and so ourselves, by a good dozen feet, so that the angled light from the floodlights by the crane on the well-deck above barely succeeded in touching the faraway side – the port side – of the upper deck of the ship. All the rest of the vessel lay shrouded in deep darkness except for a patch of light that fell on the fo'c'sle from a rectangular gap high up in the overhang of the platform. Through this hole was suspended the vertical gangway, a zig-zag set of caged-in metal steps like a fire-escape, which, I supposed, could be raised or lowered, with the ebb and flow of the tide.

The conditions might have been made for me.

The ship was low in the water, the ribbed oil tanks standing high but the gunwale only at waist level. I took a pencil light from my coat and went aboard.

I moved right for'ard in the darkness. Apart from a glimmer from the accommodation aft there was no light at all on board, not even navigation or riding lights: the Christmas tree illuminations of the oil derrick made those superfluous.

There were deep sliding vertical doors giving to the raised fo'c'sle. I pulled the head and foot bolts on one of these, waited for a slight roll of the ship to help and eased the door back a crack, enough for my head, arm and light. Barrels, paint drums, ropes, wood, heavy chains – it was some sort of bosun's store. There was nothing there for me. I eased the door back, slid in the bolts and left.

I made my way aft over the tanks. There were raised trapdoors with large clips which stuck out at all angles, there were fore-and-aft and athwart-ships pipes of every conceivable size and at every conceivable height, there were valves, big wheels for turning those valves and nasty knobbly venti-lators, and I don't think I missed one of all of those, with my head, kneecaps or shins, on the way aft. It was like hacking your way through a virgin jungle. A metal virgin jungle. But I made it, and I made it with the sure knowledge that there wasn't a trap or hatch on that deck able to take anything larger than a human being.

There was nothing for me in the stern either. Most of the deck space and superstructure there was given over to cabins: the one big coach-type hatch was glassed in and had a couple of skylights open. I used the flash. Engines. That ruled that hatch out. And the whole of the upper deck.

Andrew was waiting patiently in the dinghy. I felt, rather than saw, his inquiring look and shook my head. Not that I had to shake my head. When he saw me clamping on my rubber skull-cap and oxygen mask that was all the answer he needed. He helped me make fast a life-line round the waist, and it took the two of us a whole minute: the rubber raft was pitching and bouncing about so much that we had one hand for ourselves and only one for the job.

With the closed oxygen circuit the safe maximum depth I could get was about twenty-five feet. The oiler drew perhaps fifteen, so I had plenty in hand. The underwater search for a wire, or for something suspended from a wire, proved far easier than I had anticipated, for even at fifteen feet the effect of the surface swell motion was almost negligible. Andrew paid out, slackened and tightened the life-line to adjust to my every underwater movement as if he had been doing this sort of thing all his working life, which indeed he had. I covered the entire submerged length of the oiler twice, keeping close to the bilge keels on either side, examining every foot of the way with a powerful underwater flash. Halfway along the second sweep I saw a huge moray eel, which writhed out of the darkness beyond the beam of the torch and thrust its head with its evil unwinking eyes and vicious poisonous teeth right up against the glass of the flashlight: I clicked the beam on and off a couple of times and he was gone. But that was all I saw.

I felt tired when I got back to the rubber dinghy and hauled myself aboard. I felt tired because fifteen minutes' hard swimming in an oxygen outfit would make anybody tired: but I knew too well if I'd found what I'd been looking for tiredness would never have touched me. I'd banked heavily on finding what I'd been looking for in on or under that ship. I felt let down.

I felt tired and low and dispirited and cold. I wished I could smoke. I thought of a crackling wood fire, of steaming coffee and a long long nightcap. I thought of Herman Jablonsky sleeping peacefully in his big mahogany bed back in the general's house. I stripped off mask and cylinder, kicked the flippers off my feet, pulled on a pair of shoes with numbed and fumbling fingers, flung my pants, coat and hat up on the deck of the oiler and dragged myself up after them. Three minutes later, dressed in my outer clothes and dripping like a blanket that's just been hauled from a wash-boiler, I was on my way up the enclosed gangway to the well-deck of the oil rig a hundred feet above my head.

Drifting grey cloud had washed the last of the starlight out of the sky, but that didn't help me any. I'd thought the overhead lamp illuminating the gangway had been weak, but it hadn't, it had only been distant. By the time I was ten feet from the underside of the platform it was a searchlight. And if they kept a gangway watch? Did I tell them I was the Second Engineer from the oiler and was suffering from insomnia? Did I stand there and spin a plausible story while the moisture dripping down under my pants from the diving-suit formed a pool of water under my feet and my vis-à-vis examined with interest the ruched high-necked glistening rubber where my collar and tie ought to have been? I had no gun, and I was prepared to believe that anyone in any way associated with General Ruthven and Vyland pulled on his shoulder holster before his socks when he got up in the morning: certainly everyone I'd met so far had been a walking armoury. And if a gun were pulled on me? Did I start running down a hundred and thirty steps while someone picked me off at their leisure? Of course I didn't have to run, the fire-escape gangway was only enclosed on three sides, but the fourth opened seawards and I wouldn't bounce far off that maze of valves and pipes on the oiler below. I concluded that any halfway intelligent man would have gone straight back down.

I went right on up.

There was no one there. The gangway emerged in an alcove closed off on three sides – by the railed platform edge on one side, by high steel walls on the other two. The fourth side gave directly on to the well-deck where the crane was. What little I could see of this well was brightly illuminated and I could hear the clank of machinery and the voices of men not thirty feet away. It didn't seem like a good idea to wander straight out into their midst so I looked for another way out. I found it at once, a set of steel rungs built into one of the twelve-foot high steel bulkheads by my side.

I went up those, flattening myself out as I went over the top, crawled a few yards then stood up behind the shelter of one of the huge pillars. I could see the whole panorama of the oil rig now.

A hundred yards away, on the larger raised platform, to the north, was the derrick itself, looking more massive than ever, with control cabins at its base and men moving around: under the surface of that platform, I supposed, would be the power-generating machinery, the living accommodation. The smaller platform to the south, the one on which I stood, was almost completely bare with a semi-circular extension reaching out over the sea to the south. The purpose of this large cleared space baffled me for a moment and then something clicked in my memory: Mary Ruthven had said that the general normally commuted between oil-rig and shore in his helicopter. The helicopter would need a landing-ground. This was it.

On the well-deck between the two platforms, almost at my feet, men were moving large barrels with the aid of a tracked crane, trundling them into a brightly-lit opening half-way along the high bulkhead on the northern platform. Oil would be piped aboard, so those barrels could only be 'Mud', a chemical mixture of barites used for forcing down under pressure the cement that formed the outer casing of the drill hole. There was a whole series of those big storage sheds, most of them open, extending right across the width of the rig. There, if anywhere, would be what I was looking for.

I crossed to the far side of the south platform, found another set of rungs and dropped down to the well-deck. There was nothing to be gained by caution or stealth now; apart from the fact that they would only excite suspicion, the time factor was becoming all-important: with the weather steadily worsening – the wind now seemed twice as strong as it had been half an hour previously and it wasn't just a factor of the height – Captain Zaimis would be climbing up the mast. Perhaps he might even be forced to take off without me. But there was no future in that thought and certainly none for me. I put it out of my mind and crossed to the first of the storage bays.

The door was held on a heavy steel latch, unlocked. I opened the latch, pushed back the door and passed inside. It was pitch dark, but my torch found the light switch right away. I pressed it and looked around.

The bay was perhaps a hundred feet long. Stacked in nearly empty racks on both sides were three or four dozen screwed pipes almost as long as the bay itself. Round each pipe, near the end, were deep gouge marks as if some heavy metal claws had bitten into it. Sections of the drill pipe. And nothing else. I switched off the light, went out, pulled shut the door and felt a heavy hand on my shoulder.

'Would you be looking for something, my friend?' It was a deep rough no-nonsense voice, as Irish as a sprig of shamrock.

I turned slowly, but not too slowly, pulling the lapels of my coat together with both hands as if to ward off the wind and the thin cold rain that was beginning to sift across the deck, glittering palely through the beams of the arc-lamps then vanishing into the darkness again. He was a short stocky man, middle-aged, with a battered face that could be kindly or truculent as the needs of the moment demanded. At that moment, the balance of expression was tipped on the side of truculence. But not much. I decided to risk it.

'As a matter of fact, I am.' Far from trying to conceal my British accent, I exaggerated it. A marked high-class English accent in the States excites no suspicion other than the charitable one that you may be slightly wrong in the head. 'The field foreman told me to inquire for the – ah – roustabout foreman. Are you he?'

'Golly!' he said. I felt that it should have been 'begorrah' but the grammatical masterpiece had floored him. You could see his mind clambering on to its feet again. 'Mr Jerrold sent you to look for me, he?'

'Yes, indeed. Miserable night, isn't it?' I pulled my hat-brim lower. 'I certainly don't envy you fellows –'

'If you was looking for me,' he interrupted, 'why were you poking about in there?'

'Ah, yes. Well, I could see you were busy and as he thought he had lost it in there, I thought perhaps I –'

'Who had lost what where?' He breathed deeply, patience on a monument.

'The general. General Ruthven. His brief-case, with very important private papers – and very urgent. He'd been making a tour of inspection yesterday – let me see, now, it would have been early afternoon – when he received the dastardly news –'

'He what?'

'When he heard his daughter had been kidnapped. He went straight for his helicopter, forgetting all about the brief-case and –'

'I get you. Important, huh?'

'Very. General Ruthven says he'd put it down just inside some doorway. It's big, morocco, marked C. C. F. in gold letters.'

'C.C.F.? I thought you said it was the general's?'

'The general's papers. He'd borrowed my case. I'm

Farnborough, his private confidential secretary.' It was very long odds indeed against one of the scores of roustabouts foremen employed by the general knowing the real name of his secretary, C. C. Farnborough.

'C.C., eh?' All suspicions and truculence now vanished. He grinned hugely. 'Not Claude Cecil by any chance?'

'One of my names does happen to be Claude,' I said quietly. 'I don't think it's funny.'

I had read the Irishman rightly. He was instantly contrite.

'Sorry, Mr Farnborough. Talkin' outa turn. No offence. Want that me and my boys help you look?'

'I'd be awfully obliged.'

'If it's there we'll have it in five minutes.'

He walked away, issued orders to his gang of men. But I had no interest in the result of the search, my sole remaining interest lay in getting off that platform with all speed. There would be no brief-case there and there would be nothing else there. The foreman's gang were sliding doors open with the abandon of men who have nothing to conceal. I didn't even bother glancing inside any of the bays, the fact that doors could be opened without unlocking and were being opened indiscriminately in the presence of a total stranger was proof for me that there was nothing to be concealed. And apart from the fact that there were far too many men there to swear to secrecy,

130

it stood out a mile that that genial Irishman was not the type to get mixed up in any criminal activities. Some people are like that, you know it the moment you see and speak to them. The roustabout foreman was one of those.

I could have slipped away and down the gangway while the search was still going on but that would have been stupid. The search for the missing brief-case would be nothing compared to the all-out search that would then start for C. C. Farnborough. They might assume I had fallen over the side. Powerful searchlights could pick up the *Matapan* in a matter of minutes. And even were I aboard the *Matapan* I didn't want to leave the vicinity of the rig. Not yet. And above all I didn't want the news to get back ashore that an intruder disguised as, or at least claiming to be, the general's secretary had been prowling around the X 13.

What to do when the search was over? The foreman would expect me to go back to the derrick side, where the accommodation and offices were, presumably to report failure of a mission to Mr Jerrold. Once I left for there my retreat to the gangway would be cut off. And so far it hadn't occurred to the foreman to ask how I had arrived aboard the rig. He was bound to know that there had been no helicopter or boat out to the rig in hours. Which argued the fact that I must have been aboard for hours. And if I had been aboard for hours why had I delayed so long in starting this so very urgent search for the missing brief-case?

The search, as far as I could see, was over. Doors were being banged shut and the foreman was starting back towards me when a bulkhead phone rang. He moved towards it. I moved into the darkest patch of shadow I could see and buttoned my coat right up to the neck. That, at least, wouldn't excite suspicion: the wind was strong now, the cold rain driving across the well-deck at an angle of almost forty-five degrees.

The foreman hung up and crossed over to where I was standing. 'Sorry, Mr Farnborough, no luck. You sure he left it here?'

'Certain, Mr – ah –'

'Curran. Joe Curran. Well, it's not here now. And we can't look any more.' He hunched deeper into his black glistening oilskin. 'Gotta go and start yo-yo-ing that damn pipe.'

'Oh, yes,' I said politely.

He grinned and explained: 'The drill. Gotta haul it up and change it.'

'On a night like this and in a wind like this? And it must take some time.'

'It takes some time. Six hours if we're lucky. That damned drill's two and half miles straight down, Mr Farnborough.'

I made the proper noises of astonishment instead of the noises of relief I felt like making. Mr Curran working on the derrick for the next six hours in this weather would have more to worry about than stray secretaries.

He made to go. Already his men had filed past

132

and climbed up a companionway to the north platform. 'Coming, Mr Farnborough?'

'Not yet.' I smiled wanly. 'I think I'll go and sit in the shelter of the gangway for a few minutes and work out what I'm going to tell the general.' I had an inspiration. 'You see, he only phoned up about five minutes ago. You know what he's like. Lord knows what I'm going to tell him.'

'Yeah. It's tough.' The words meant nothing, already his mind was on the recovery of the drill. 'Be seein' you.'

'Yes. Thank you.' I watched him out of sight and two minutes later I was back aboard the rubber dinghy: another two minutes and we had been hauled back to the *Matapan*.

'You have been far too long, Mr Talbot,' Captain Zaimis scolded. His small agitated figure gave the impression of hopping around in the darkness although it would have taken a monkey to hop around that pitching heaving sponge-boat without falling overboard with the first hop. The engine note was much louder now: not only had the skipper been forced to increase engine revolutions to keep a certain amount of slack on the rope tying the *Matapan* to the pillar, but the vessel was now pitching so wildly that almost every time the bows plunged deep into the sea the underwater exhaust beneath the stern came clear in a brief but carrying crackle of sound.

'You have been successful, no?' Captain Zaimis called in my ear.

'No.'

'So. It is sad. But no matter. We must leave at once.'

'Ten minutes, John. Just another ten minutes. It's terribly important.'

'No. We must leave at once.' He started to call the order to cast off to the young Greek sitting in the bows when I caught his arm.

'Are you afraid, Captain Zaimis?' Despicable, but I was desperate.

'I am beginning to be afraid,' he said with dignity. 'All wise men know when it is time to be afraid and I hope I am not a fool, Mr Talbot. There are times when a man is selfish if he is not afraid. I have six children, Mr Talbot.'

'And I have three.' I hadn't even one, not any more. I wasn't even married, not any more. For a long moment we stood there, clinging on to the mast while the *Matapan* pitched and corkscrewed wickedly in that almost impenetrable darkness under the cavernous shadow of the oil rig, but apart from the thin whistling of the rain-laden wind in the rigging, it was a long silent moment. I changed my tactics. 'The lives of men depend upon this, Captain Zaimis. Do not ask me how I know but I know. Would you have it said that men died because Captain Zaimis would not wait ten minutes?'

There was a long pause, the rain hissed whitely into the heaving blackness of the sea beneath us, then he said: 'Ten minutes. No more.'

I slipped off shoes and outer clothing, made sure the life-line was securely tied to my waist just above the weights, slipped on the oxygen mask and stumbled forward to the bows, again thinking, for no reason at all, of big Herman Jablonsky sleeping the sleep of the just in his mahogany bed. I watched until a particularly big swell came along, waited until it had passed under and the bows were deep in the water, stepped off into the sea and grabbed for the rope that moored the *Matapan* to the pillar.

I went out towards the pillar hand over hand – it couldn't have been more than twenty feet away – but even with the rope to help me I got a pretty severe hammering and without the oxygen mask I don't know how much water I would have swallowed. I collided with the pillar before I realized I was near it, let go the rope and tried to grab the pillar. Why, I don't know. I might as well have tried to put my arms round a railway petrol tanker for the diameter was about the same. I grabbed the rope again before I was swept away and worked my way round to the left towards the seaward side of the massive steel leg. It wasn't easy. Every time the *Matapan*'s bows rose with the swell the rope tightened and jammed my clutching hand immovably against the metal, but just so long as I didn't lose any fingers I was beyond caring.

When my back was squarely to the swell I released the rope, spread out my arms and legs, thrust myself below water and started to descend that pillar something in the fashion of a Sinhalese boy descending an enormous palm tree, Andrew paying out the line as skilfully as before. Ten feet, twenty, nothing: thirty, nothing: thirty-five, nothing. My heart was starting to pound irregularly and my head beginning to swim; I was well below the safe operating limit of that closed oxygen mask. Quickly I half-swam, half-clawed my way up and came to rest about fifteen feet below the surface clinging to that enormous pillar like a cat halfway up a tree and unable to get down.

Five of Captain Zaimis's ten minutes were gone. My time was almost run out. And yet it *had* to be that oil rig, it simply had to be. The general himself had said so, and there had been no need to tell anything but the truth to a man with no chance of escape: and if that weren't enough, the memory of that stiff, creaking, leaden-footed man who'd brought the tray of drinks into the general's room carried with it complete conviction.

But there was nothing on the ship alongside, nor was there anything under it. I would have sworn to that. There was nothing on the oil rig itself: I would have sworn to that too. And if it wasn't on the platform, then it was under the platform, and if it was under the platform it was attached to a wire or chain. And that wire or chain must be attached, underwater, to one of those supporting legs.

I tried to think as quickly and clearly as I could. Which of those fourteen legs would they use? Almost certainly I could eliminate right away the eight legs that supported the derrick platform. Too much activity there, too many lights, too many eyes, too many dangling lines to catch the hundreds of fish attracted by the powerful overhead lights, too much danger altogether. So it had to be the helicopter platform under which the *Matapan* was rolling and plunging at the end of her mooring rope. To narrow it still farther – I had to narrow it, to localize the search by gambling on the probable and ignoring the possible and almost equally probable, there were only minutes left – it was more likely that what I sought was on the seaward side, where I was now, than on the landward side where there was always danger from ships mooring there.

The middle pillar of the seaward three, the one to which the *Matapan* was moored, I had already investigated. Which of the remaining two to try was settled at once by the fact that my life-line was passed round the left-hand side of the pillar. To have worked my way round three-quarters of the circumference would have taken too long. I rose to the surface, gave two tugs to indicate that I would want more slack, placed both feet against the metal, pushed off hard and struck out for the corner pillar.

I almost didn't make it. I saw now why Captain Zaimis was so worried – and he'd a forty-foot boat and forty horse-power to cope with the power of the wind and the sea and that steadily growing, deepening swell that was already breaking white on the tops. All I had was myself and I could have done with more. The heavy weights round my waist didn't help me any, it took me a hundred yards of frantic thrashing and gasping to cover the fifteen yards that lay between the two pillars, and closed oxygen sets aren't designed for the kind of gasping I was doing. But I made it. Just.

Once more on the seaward side and pinned against the pillar by the pressure of the swell I started crabbing my way down below the surface. This time it was easy, for right away, by chance, my hand found a broad, deeply- and sharply-cut series of slightly curved grooves in the metal extending vertically downwards. I am no engineer, but I knew this must be the worm that engaged against the big motor-driven pinion which would be required to raise and lower those pillars. There must have been one on the last pillar also, but I'd missed it.

It was like going down a cliff with a series of rungs cut in the rock-face. I paused every other foot or so, reaching out on both sides, but there was nothing, no projection, no wire, just the smooth rather slimy surface. Steadily, painstakingly, I forced myself downwards, increasingly more conscious of the gripping pressure of the water, the difficulty of breathing. Somewhere close on forty feet I called it a day. Damaging my ear-drums or lungs or getting nitrogen into the bloodstream wasn't going to help anyone. I gave up. I went up.

Just below the surface I stopped to have a rest

and clear my head. I felt bitterly disappointed, I had banked more heavily than I knew on this last chance. Wearily, I laid my head against the pillar and thought with a bleak hopelessness that I would have to start all over again. And I had no idea in the world where to start. I felt tired, dead tired. And then, in a moment, the tiredness left me as if it had never been.

That great steel pillar was alive with sound. There could be no doubt about it, instead of being silent and dead and full of water, it was alive with sound.

I ripped off my rubber helmet, coughed and gagged and spluttered as some water found its way in under the oxygen mask, then pressed my ear hard against the cold steel.

The pillar reverberated with a deep resonant vibration that jarred the side of my head. Water-filled pillars don't reverberate with sound, not with sound of any kind. But this one did, beyond all question. It wasn't water that was in that pillar, it was air. Air! All at once I identified that peculiar sound I was hearing; I should have identified it immediately. That rhythmical rising and falling of sound as a motor accelerated and slowed, accelerated and slowed, was a sound that had for many years been part and parcel of my professional life. It was an air compressor, and a big one at that, hard at work inside the pillar. An air compressor deep down below water level inside one of the support legs of a mobile rig standing far out in the Gulf of

139

Mexico. It didn't make sense, it didn't make any kind of sense at all. I leant my forehead against the metal, and it seemed as if the shuddering, jarring vibration was an insistent clamorous voice trying to tell me something, something of urgency and vital importance, if only I could listen. I listened. For half a minute, perhaps a minute, I listened, and all of a sudden it made the very best kind of sense there was. It was the answer I would never have dreamed of, it was the answer to many things. It took me time to guess this might be the answer, it took me time to realize this must be the answer, but when I did realize it I was left with no doubts in the world.

I gave three sharp tugs on the rope and within a minute was back aboard the *Matapan*. I was hauled aboard as quickly and with as little ceremony as if I had been a sack of coals and I was still stripping off oxygen cylinder and mask when Captain Zaimis barked for the mooring rope to be slipped, gunned the engine, scraped by the mooring pillar and put the rudder hard over. The *Matapan* yawed and rolled wickedly as she came broadside on to the troughs, shipping solid seas and flying clouds of spray over the starboard side, and then, stern to the wind and steady on course, headed for shore.

Ten minutes later, when I'd peeled off the diving-suit, dried off, dressed in shore clothes and was just finishing my second glass of brandy, Captain Zaimis came down to the cabin. He was smiling, whether with satisfaction or relief I couldn't guess, and seemed to regard all danger as being past: and true enough, riding before the sea, the *Matapan* was now almost rock-steady. He poured himself a thimble of brandy and spoke for the first time since I'd been dragged aboard.

'You were successful, no?'

'Yes.' I thought the curt affirmative a bit ungracious. 'Thanks to you, Captain Zaimis.'

He beamed. 'You are kind, Mr Talbot, and I am delighted. But not thanks to me but to our good friend here who watches over us, over all those who gather sponges, over all who go to sea.' He struck a match and put a light to a wick in an oil-filled boat-shaped pottery dish which stood in front of a glassed-in portrait of St Nicholas.

I looked sourly at him. I respected his piety and appreciated his sentiments but I thought he was a bit late in striking the matches.

SIX

It was exactly two o'clock in the morning when Captain Zaimis skilfully eased the *Matapan* alongside the wooden jetty from which we had left. The sky was black now, the night so dark that it was scarcely possible to distinguish land from sea and the rain was a drumfire of sound on the roof of the cabin. But I had to go and go at once. I had to get back inside the house without being observed, I had to have a long conference with Jablonsky, and I had to get my clothes dry: my luggage was still in La Contessa, I'd only the one suit, and I had to have it dry before morning. I couldn't bank on not seeing anyone until evening, as I'd done the previous day. The general had said that he'd let me know what job it was he had in mind inside thirty-six hours: the thirty-six hours would be up at eight o'clock this morning. I borrowed a long oilskin to keep off the worst of the rain, put it on over my own raincoat – the oilskin was a couple of sizes too small, it felt as if I were wearing a strait-jacket – shook hands all round, thanked them for what they had done for me and left.

At a quarter past two, after making a brief stop at a call-box, I parked the Corvette in the side turning where I'd found it and squelched along the road in the direction of the drive leading up to the general's house. There were no sidewalks on the road, the kind of people who lived on this exclusive stretch of sea frontage didn't have any need of sidewalks, and the gutters were swollen little rivers with the muddy water spilling over the uppers of my shoes. I wondered how I was going to get my shoes dry in time for the morning.

I passed the lodge where the chauffeur lived – or where I presumed he lived – and passed by the driveway also. The enclosed tunnel was brightly lit and clambering over the top of that six-barred gate in that blaze of light wouldn't have been a very clever thing to do. And for all I knew the top bar might be set to work some electrically operated warning bell if sufficient weight were brought to bear. I wouldn't have put anything beyond the lot who lived in that house.

Thirty yards beyond the drive I squeezed through an all but imperceptible gap in the magnificent eight-foot hedge that fronted the general's estate. Less than two yards behind the edge was an equally magnificent eight-foot wall, hospitably topped with huge chunks of broken glass set in cement. Neither the hedge concealing the wall, nor the wall designed to discourage those too shy to enter by the main

143

driveway was, I had learnt from Jablonsky, peculiar to the general's estate. All the neighbours had money enough and importance enough to make the protection of their privacy a matter of considerable consequence, and this set-up was common to most of them. The rope dangling from the gnarled branch of the big live oak on the other side of the wall was where I had left it. Badly hampered by the binding constriction of the oilskin I waddled rather than walked up that wall, swung to earth on the other side, clambered up the oak, unfastened the rope and thrust it under an exposed root. I didn't expect to have to use that rope again, but one never knew: what I did know was that I didn't want any of Vyland's playmates finding it.

What *was* peculiar to the general's estate was the fence about twenty feet beyond the wall. It was a five-stranded affair, and the top three were barbed. The sensible person, obviously, pushed up the second lowest plain wire, pushed down the bottom one, stooped and passed through. But what I knew, thanks to Jablonsky, and what the sensible person didn't, was that pressure on either of the two lower wires operated a warning bell, so I climbed laboriously over the top three wires, to the sound of much ripping and tearing, and lowered myself down on the other side. Andrew wasn't going to have much farther use for his oilskin by the time he got it back. If he ever got it back.

Under the closely packed trees the darkness was

144

almost absolute. I had a pencil flash but I didn't dare use it, I had to trust to luck and instinct to circle the big kitchen garden that lay to the left of the house and so reach the fire-escape at the back. I had about two hundred yards to go and I didn't expect to make it in under a quarter of an hour.

I walked as old Broken-nose, the butler, had fancied he walked when he crept away from our bedroom door after leaving Jablonsky and myself there. I had the advantages of normal arches to my feet and no adenoids worth talking about. I walked with both arms outstretched before me, and it wasn't until my face collided with a tree trunk that I learned not to walk with my arms outspread as well as outstretched. I couldn't do anything about the dripping clammy Spanish moss that kept wrapping itself about my face but I could do something about the hundreds of twigs and broken branches that littered the ground. I didn't walk, I shuffled. I didn't lift my feet, I slid each one forward slowly and carefully, brushing aside whatever lay in my path, and not allowing any weight to come on the leading foot until I had made good and certain that there was nothing under that foot that would snap or creak when my weight was transferred to it. Although I do say it, I was pretty silent.

It was as well that I was. Ten minutes after leaving the fence, when I was seriously beginning to wonder whether I had angled off in the wrong direction, suddenly, through the trees and the curtain of rain dripping steadily from the oaks, I thought I saw a tiny glimmer of light. A flicker, then gone. I might have imagined it, but I don't have that kind of imagination. I knew I didn't, so I slowed down still more, pulling my hat-brim down and coat collar up so that no faintest sheen of paleness might betray my face. You couldn't have heard the rustle of my heavy oilskin three feet away.

I cursed the Spanish moss. It wrapped its long clammy tendrils round my face, it made me blink and shut my eyes at the very moments when shutting my eyes might have been the last thing I ever did, and it obscured my vision to a degree where I felt like dropping to my hands and knees and crawling forward on all fours. I might even have done that, but I knew the crackling of the oilskin would give me away.

Then I saw the glimmer of light again. It was thirty feet away, no more, and it wasn't pointing in my direction, it was illuminating something on the ground. I took a couple of quick smooth steps forward, wanting to pinpoint the light source, and see the reason for its use, and then I discovered that my navigational sense in the darkness had been completely accurate. The kitchen garden was surrounded by a wire-netted wooden fence and halfway through my second step I walked right into it. The top rail cracked like the door to an abandoned dungeon.

There came a sudden exclamation, the dousing

of the light, a brief silence and then the torch flicked on again, the beam no longer pointing at the ground but reaching out for and searching the perimeter of the kitchen garden. Whoever held the torch was as nervous as a kitten, because whoever held the torch had more than a vague idea where the sound had come from and a steady careful sweep would have picked me up in three seconds. As it was the search consisted of a series of jittery probings and jerkings of the beam and I'd time to take a long smooth step backwards. Just one: there was no time for more. As far as it is possible to melt into a neighbouring oak tree, I melted into a neighbouring oak tree, I pressed against it as if I were trying to push it over and wished as I had never wished before: I wished I had a gun.

'Give me that flash.' The cold quiet voice was unmistakably Royale's. The torch beam wavered, steadied, then shone down on the ground again. 'Get on with it. Now!'

'But I heard something, Mr Royale!' It was Larry, his voice a high-pitched jittery whisper. 'Over there! I know I did.'

'Yeah, me too. It's all right.' With a voice like Royale's, with a voice with as much warmth in it as a champagne bucket, it was difficult to sound soothing, but he was doing his best. 'Woods are full of those noises in the dark. Hot day, cold rain at night, contraction, then all sorts of noises. Now hurry it up. Want to stay out in this damned rain all night?'

'Look, Mr Royale.' The whisper was more than earnest now, it was desperate. 'I didn't make a mistake, honest, I didn't! I heard –'

'Missed out on your shot of the white stuff, tonight?' Royale interrupted cruelly. The strain of even a moment's kindness had been too much for him. 'God, why did I have to be saddled with a junky like you. Shut up and work.'

Larry shut up. I wondered about what Royale had said, because I'd been wondering about it ever since I saw Larry. His behaviour, the fact that he was allowed to associate with Vyland and the general, the liberties he was permitted, above all his very presence there. Big criminal organizations working for big stakes – and if this bunch weren't working for big stakes I couldn't imagine who were – usually picked the members of their organization with as much care and forethought as a big corporation picks its top executives. More. A careless slip-up, a moment's indiscretion on the part of an executive won't ruin a big corporation but it can destroy a criminal set-up. Big crime is big business, and big criminals are big businessmen, running their illegal activities with all the meticulous care and administrative precision of their more law-abiding colleagues. If, most reluctantly, it was found necessary to remove rivals or such as offered menace to their security, the removal was entrusted to quiet polite people like Royale. But Larry was about as much use to them as a match in a powder magazine.

There were three of them in that corner of the kitchen garden, Royale, Larry and the butler, whose range of duties appeared to be wider than that normally expected of his profession in the better class English country houses. Larry and the butler were busy with spades. Digging, I thought at first, because Royale had the light hooded and even at ten yards in that rain it was difficult to see anything, but by and by, judging more by ear than by eye, I knew that they were filling in a hole in the ground. I grinned to myself in the darkness. I would have taken long odds that they were burying something very valuable indeed, something that would not be remaining there very long. A kitchen garden was hardly the ideal permanent hiding place for treasure trove.

Three minutes later they were finished. Someone drew a rake to and fro across the filled-in hole – I assumed that they must have been digging in a freshly turned vegetable patch and wanted to conceal the signs of their work – and then they all went off together to the gardening shed a few yards away and left their spades and rake there.

They came out again, talking softly, Royale in the lead with the torch in his hand. They passed through a wicker gate not fifteen feet from me, but by this time I'd withdrawn some yards into the wood and had the thick bole of an oak for cover. They went off together up the path that led to the front of the house and by and by the low murmur of voices faded and vanished. A bar of light fell across the porch as the front door opened, then there came the solid click of a heavy door closing on its latch. Then silence.

I didn't move. I stayed exactly where I was, breathing lightly and shallowly, not stirring an inch. The rain redoubled in violence, the thick foliage of the oak might have been a wisp of gauze for all the protection it afforded, but I didn't move. The rain trickled down inside oilskin and overcoat and ran down my back and legs. But I didn't move. It trickled down my front and into my shoes, but I didn't move. I could feel the tide rising up to my ankles, but I didn't move. I just stayed where I was, a human figure carved from ice, but colder. My hands were numb, my feet frozen and uncontrollable shivers shook my entire body every few seconds. I would have given the earth to move. But I didn't. Only my eyes moved.

Hearing was of little value to me now. With the high moan of the steadily increasing wind through the topmost swaying branches of the trees and the loud frenetic rustling of the rain driving through the leaves, you couldn't have heard a careless footfall ten feet away. But after three-quarters of an hour standing there motionless, eyes became perfectly accustomed to the dark and you could have spotted a careless movement ten yards away. And I spotted it.

A movement, that is, but not careless. Deliberate. I think it must have been a sudden furious flurry of wind and rain that finally broke the

150

patience of the shadow that now detached itself from the shelter of a nearby tree and moved away silently up towards the house. If I hadn't been watching, staring into the darkness with eyes sore and strained from staring, I would have missed it, for I certainly would have heard nothing. But I didn't miss it. A shadow moving with the sound-lessness of a shadow. A quiet deadly man. Royale. His words to Larry had been so much bluff for the benefit of any listener. Royale had heard a noise, all right, and the noise must have been just sufficiently off-beat to make him wonder if someone were there. Only enough to make him wonder. If Royale had been certain he'd have remained there all night waiting to strike. The strike of a fer-de-lance. I thought of myself going into that kitchen garden immediately after the three had left, getting a spade and starting to investigate, and I felt colder than ever. I could see myself bending over the hole, the unseen, unheard approach of Royale, and then the bullet, just one, a cupro-nickel jacketed .22 at the base of the skull.

But I had to go and get a spade and start investigating some time, and no better time than now. The rain was torrential, the night as dark as the tomb. In those conditions it was unlikely that Royale would return though I would have put nothing past that cunning and devious mind, but even if he did he would have been exposed to the bright lights inside and it would take him ten minutes, at least, to re-adapt his eyes to that almost total darkness before he would dare move around again. That he wouldn't move around with a torch was certain: if he thought there was still an intruder in the grounds, then he thought that intruder had seen the digging operations but had still made no move: and if he thought there was such a man, then he would assume him to be a careful and dangerous man to move in search of whom with a lighted torch in hand would be to ask for a bullet in the back. For Royale was not to know that the intruder had no gun.

I thought ten minutes would be enough to find out what I wanted, both because any burial of anything in a garden was bound to be temporary and because neither Larry nor the butler had struck me as people who would derive any pleasure from using a spade or who would dig an inch deeper than was absolutely necessary. I was right. I found a spade in the tool shed, located the freshly-raked earth with a pin-point of light from my pencil flash, and from the time I had passed through the wicker gate till I had cleared off the two or three inches of earth that covered some kind of white pine packing case, no more than five minutes had elapsed.

The packing case was lying at a slight angle in the ground and so heavy was the rain drumming down on my bent back and on top of the case that within a minute the lid of the case had been washed white and clean and free from the last stain of earth, the muddy water draining off to one side. I flashed the torch cautiously: no name, no marks, nothing to give any indication of the contents.

The case had a wood and rope handle at each end. I grabbed one of those, got both hands round it and heaved, but the case was over five feet long and seemed to be filled with bricks: even so I might have managed to move it, but the earth around the hole was so waterlogged and soft that my heels just gouged through it and into the hole itself.

I took my torch again, hooded it till the light it cast was smaller than a penny, and started quartering the surface of the packing case. No metal clasps. No heavy screws. As far as I could see, the only fastenings holding down the lid were a couple of nails at either end. I lifted the spade, dug a corner under one end of the lid. The nails creaked and squealed in protest as I forced them out of the wood, but I went on anyway and sprung the end of the lid clear. I lifted it a couple of feet and shone my flash inside.

Even in death Jablonsky was still smiling. The grin was lopsided and crooked, the way they had had to make Jablonsky himself lopsided and crooked in order to force him inside the narrow confines of that case, but it was still a smile. His face was calm and peaceful, and with the end of a pencil you could have covered that tiny hole between his eyes. It was the kind of hole that would have been made by the cupro-nickel jacketed bullet from a .22 automatic.

Twice that night, out on the gulf, I had thought of Jablonsky sleeping peacefully. He'd been asleep all right. He'd been asleep for hours, his skin was cold as marble.

I didn't bother going through the pockets of the dead man, Royale and Vyland would have done that already. Besides, I knew that Jablonsky had carried nothing incriminating on his person, nothing that could have pointed to the true reason for his presence there, nothing that could have put the finger on me.

I wiped the rain off the dead face, lowered the lid and hammered the nails softly home with the handle of the spade. I'd opened a hole in the ground and now I closed a grave. It was well for Royale that I did not meet him then.

I returned spade and rake to the tool shed and left the kitchen garden.

There were no lights at the back of the entrance lodge. I found one door and two ground-level windows – it was a single-storey building – and they were all locked. They would be. In that place everything would be locked, always.

But the garage wasn't. Nobody was going to be so crazy as to make off with a couple of Rolls-Royces, even if they could have got past the electrically operated gate, which they couldn't. The garage was fit match for the cars: the tool bench and equipment were the do-it-yourself devotee's dream.

I ruined a couple of perfectly good wood chisels,

but I had the catch slipped on one of the windows in a minute flat. It didn't seem likely that they had burglar alarms fitted to a lodge, especially as there hadn't even been an attempt made to fit half-circle thief-proof sash latches. But I took no chances, pulled the top window down and climbed in over it. When wiring a window the usual idea is to assume that the sneak-thief who breaks and enters is a slave to habit who pushes up the lower sash and crawls in under, apart from which the average electrician finds it much kinder on the shoulder muscles to wire at waist level instead of above the head. And in this case, I found, an average electrician had indeed been at work. The lodge was wired.

I didn't drop down on top of any startled sleeper in a bedroom or knock over a row of pots and pans in the kitchen for the sufficient reason that I'd picked a room with frosted windows and it seemed a fair bet that that might be the bathroom. And so it was.

Out in the passageway I flicked my pencil light up and down. The lodge had been designed – if that was the word – with simplicity. The passage directly joined the back and front doors. Two small rooms opened off either side of the passage: that was all.

The room at the back opposite the bathroom proved to be the kitchen. Nothing there. I moved up the small passageway as softly as the squelching of my shoes would permit, picked the door on the left, turned the handle with millimetric caution and moved soundlessly inside.

This was it. I closed the door behind me and moved softly in the direction of the deep regular breathing by the left hand wall. When I was about four feet away I switched on my pencil flash and shone it straight on the sleeper's closed eyes.

He didn't remain sleeping long, not with that concentrated beam on him. He woke as at the touch of a switch and half sat up in bed, propped on an elbow while a free hand tried to shade his dazzled eyes. I noticed that even when woken in the middle of the night he looked as if he'd just brushed that gleaming black hair ten seconds previously: I always woke up with mine looking like a half-dried mop, a replica of the current feminine urchin cut, the one achieved by a short-sighted lunatic armed with garden shears.

He didn't try anything. He looked a tough, capable, sensible fellow who knew when and when not to try anything, and he knew that now was not the time. Not when he was almost blind.

'There's a .32 behind this flash, Kennedy,' I said. 'Where's your gun?'

'What gun?' He didn't sound scared because he wasn't.

'Get up,' I ordered. The pyjamas, I was glad to see, weren't maroon. I might have picked them myself. 'Move over to the door.'

He moved. I reached under his pillow.

'This gun,' I said. A small grey automatic. I

didn't know the make. 'Back to your bed and sit on it.'

Torch transferred to my left hand and the gun in the right, I made a quick sweep of the room. Only one window, with deep velvet wine curtains closed right across. I went to the door, switched on the overhead light, glanced down at the gun and slipped off the safety catch. The click was loud, precise and sounded as if it meant business. Kennedy said: 'So you hadn't a gun.'

'I've got one now.'

'It's not loaded, friend.'

'Don't tell me,' I said wearily. 'You keep it under your pillow just so you can get oil stains all over the sheets? If this gun was empty you'd be at me like the Chatanooga Express. Whatever that is.'

I looked over the room. A friendly, masculine place, bare but comfortable, with a good carpet, not in the corn-belt class of the one in the general's library, a couple of armchairs, a damask-covered table, small settee and glassed-in wall cupboard. I crossed over to the cupboard, opened it and took out a bottle of whisky and a couple of glasses. I looked at Kennedy. 'With your permission, of course.'

'Funny man,' he said coldly.

I went ahead and poured myself a drink anyway. A big one. I needed it. It tasted just the way it ought to taste and all too seldom does. I watched Kennedy and he watched me.

'Who are you, friend?' he asked.

157

I'd forgotten that only about two inches of my face was visible. I turned down the collar of my oilskin and overcoat and took off my hat. My hat had become no better than a sponge, my hair was wet and plastered all over my head but for all that I don't suppose it was any less red than normal. The tightening of Kennedy's mouth, the suddenly still expressionless eyes told their own story.

'Talbot,' he said slowly. 'John Talbot. The killer.'

'That's me,' I agreed. 'The killer.'

He sat very still, watching me. I suppose a dozen different thoughts must have been running through his mind, but none of them showed, he had as much expression in his face as a wooden Indian. But the brown intelligent eyes gave him away: he could not quite mask the hostility, the cold anger that showed in their depths.

'What do you want, Talbot? What are you doing here?'

'You mean, why am I not high-tailing it for the tall timber?'

'Why have you come back? They've had you locked up in the house, God knows why, since Tuesday evening. You've escaped, but you didn't have to mow anyone down to escape or I would have heard of it. They probably don't even know you've been away or I'd have heard of that too. But you've been away. You've been out in a boat, I can smell the sea off you and that's a seaman's oilskin you've got on. You've been out for a long time, you couldn't be any wetter if you'd stood under a waterfall for half an hour. And then you came back. A killer, a wanted man. The whole set-up is screwy as hell.'

'Screwy as hell,' I agreed. The whisky was good, I was beginning to feel half-human for the first time in hours. A smart boy, this chauffeur, a boy who thought on his feet and thought fast. I went on: 'Almost as screwy a set-up as this weird bunch you're working for in this place.'

He said nothing, and I didn't see why he should. In his place I don't think I would have passed the time of day by discussing my employers with a passing murderer. I tried again.

'The general's daughter,' Miss Mary. She's pretty much of a tramp, isn't she?'

That got him. He was off the bed, eyes mad, fists balled into hard knots and was halfway towards me before he remembered the gun pointing straight at his chest. He said softly: 'I'd love you to say that again, Talbot – without that gun in your hand.'

'That's better,' I said approvingly. 'Signs of life at last. Committing yourself to a definite opinion, you know the old saw about actions speaking louder than words. If I'd just asked you what Mary Ruthven was like you'd just have clammed up or told me go jump in the lake. I don't think she's a tramp either. I know she's not. I think she's a nice kid, a very fine girl indeed.'

'Sure you do.' His voice was bitter, but I could see the first shadows of puzzlement touching his eyes. 'That's why you scared the life out of her that afternoon.'

'I'm sorry about that, sincerely sorry. But I had to do it, Kennedy, although not for the reasons that you or any of that murderous bunch up at the big house think.' I downed what was left of my whisky, looked at him for a long speculative moment, then tossed the gun across to him. 'Suppose we talk?'

It took him by surprise but he was quick, very quick. He fielded the gun neatly, looked at it, looked at me, hesitated, shrugged then smiled faintly. 'I don't suppose another couple of oil stains will do those sheets any harm.' He thrust the gun under the pillow, crossed to the table, poured himself a drink, filled up my glass and stood there waiting.

'I'm not taking the chance you might think I am,' I began. 'I heard Vyland trying to persuade the general and Mary to get rid of you. I gathered you were a potential danger to Vyland and the general and others I may not know of. From that I gathered you're not on the inside of what's going on. And you're bound to know there's something very strange indeed going on.'

He nodded. 'I'm only the chauffeur. And what did they say to Vyland?' From the way he spoke the name I gathered he regarded Vyland with something less than affection.

'They stuck in their heels and refused point-blank.'

He was pleased at that. He tried not to show it, but he was.

'It seems you did the Ruthven family a great service not so long ago,' I went on. 'Shot up a couple of thugs who tried to kidnap Mary.'

'I was lucky.' Where speed and violence were concerned, I guess, he'd always be lucky. 'I'm primarily a bodyguard, not a chauffeur. Miss Mary's a tempting bait for every hoodlum in the country who fancies a quick million. But I'm not the bodyguard any longer,' he ended abruptly.

'I've met your successor,' I nodded. 'Valentino. He couldn't guard an empty nursery.'

'Valentino?' He grinned. 'Al Grunther. But Valentino suits him better. You damaged his arm, so I heard.'

'He damaged my leg. It's black and blue and purple all over.' I eyed him speculatively. 'Forgotten that you're talking to a murderer, Kennedy?'

'You're no murderer,' he said flatly. There was a long pause, then he broke his gaze from me and stared down at the floor.

'Patrolman Donnelly, eh?' I asked.

He nodded without speaking.

'Donnelly is as fit as you are,' I said. 'Might take him some little time to wash the powder-stains out of his pants, but that's all the damage he suffered.'

'Rigged, eh?' he asked softly.

'You've read about me in the papers.' I waved a hand at the magazine stand in the corner. I was still front page news and the photograph was even worse than the previous one. 'The rest you'll have heard from Mary. Some of what you've heard and read is true, some of it just couldn't be less true.

'My name *is* John Talbot and I am, as they said in court, a salvage expert. I have been in all the places they mention, except Bombay, and for approximately the periods they mention. But I have never been engaged in any criminal activities of any kind. However, either Vyland or the general or both are very cagey birds indeed. They've sent cables to contacts in Holland, England and Venezuela – the general, of course, has oil interests in all three places – to check on my bonafides. They'll be satisfied. We've spent a long time preparing the groundwork for this.'

'How do you know they sent those cables?'

'Every overseas cable out of Marble Springs in the past two months has been vetted. The general – all cables are in his name – uses code, of course. Perfectly legal to do so. There's a little old man from Washington living a block away from the post office. He's a genius with codes: he says the general's is childish. From his point of view.'

I got up and started to walk around. The effects of the whisky were vanishing. I felt like a cold wet flounder.

'I had to get in on the inside. Up till now we've been working very much in the dark, but for reasons which would take too long to explain at present we knew that the general would jump at the chance of getting hold of a salvage expert. He did.'

'We?' Kennedy still had his reservations about me.

'Friends of mine. Don't worry, Kennedy, I've got all the law in the world behind me. I'm not in this for myself. To make the general take the bait we had to use the general's daughter. She knows nothing of what actually went on. Judge Mollison's pretty friendly with the family, so I got him to invite Mary along for a meal, suggesting that she drop in at the court-house first while she was waiting for him to clear up the last cases.'

'Judge Mollison's in on this?'

'He is. You've a phone there, and a phone book. Want to ring him?'

He shook his head.

'Mollison knows,' I continued, 'and about a dozen cops. All sworn to secrecy and they know that a word the wrong way and they're looking for a job. The only person outside the law who knows anything about it is the surgeon who is supposed to have operated on Donnelly and then signed his death certificate. He'd a kind of troublesome conscience, but I finally talked him into it.'

'All a phoney,' he murmured. 'Here's one that fell for it.'

'Everybody did. They were meant to. Phoney reports from Interpol and Cuba – with the full backing of the police concerned – blank rounds in the first two chambers of Donnelly's Colt, phoney

163

road blocks, phoney chases by the cops, phoney –'

'But – but the bullet in the windscreen?'

'I told her to duck. I put it there myself. Car and empty garage all laid on, and Jablonsky laid on too.'

'Mary was telling me about Jablonsky,' he said slowly. 'Mary', I noticed, not. 'Miss Mary'. Maybe it meant nothing, maybe it showed the way he habitually thought of her. '"A crooked cop", she said. Just another plant?'

'Just another plant. We've been working on this for over two years. Earlier on we wanted a man who knew the Caribbean backwards. Jablonsky was the man. Born and brought up in Cuba. Two years ago he was a cop, in New York homicide. It was Jablonsky who thought up the idea of rigging false charges against himself. It was smart: it not only accounted for the sudden disappearance of one of the best cops in the country, but it gave him the entrée into the wrong kind of society when the need arose. He'd been working with me in the Caribbean for the past eighteen months.'

'Taking a chance, wasn't he? I mean, Cuba is home from home for half the crooks in the States, and the chances –'

'He was disguised,' I said patiently. 'Beard, moustache, both home-grown, all his hair dyed, glasses, even his own mother wouldn't have known him.'

There was a long silence, then Kennedy put down his glass and looked steadily at me. 'What goes on, Talbot?'

164

'Sorry. You'll have to trust me. The less anyone knows the better. Mollison doesn't know, none of the lawmen know. They've had their orders.'

'It's that big?' he asked slowly.

'Big enough. Look, Kennedy, no questions. I'm asking you to help me. If you're not frightened for Mary's health, it's time you started to be. I don't think she knows a thing more about what goes on between Vyland and the general than you do, but I'm convinced she's in danger. Great danger. Of her life. I'm up against big boys playing for big stakes. To win those stakes they've already killed eight times. Eight times to my certain knowledge. If you get mixed up in this business I'd say the chances are more than even that you'll end up with a bullet in your back. And I'm asking you to get mixed up in it. I've no right to, but I'm doing it. What's it to be?'

Some of the colour had gone out of his brown face, but not much. He didn't like what I'd just said, but if his hands were trembling I couldn't notice.

'You're a clever man, Talbot,' he said slowly. 'Maybe too clever, I don't know. But you're clever enough not to have told me all this unless you were pretty certain I'd do it. Playing for big stakes, you said: I think I'd like to sit in.'

I didn't waste any time in thanking him or congratulating him. Sticking your neck in a running noose isn't a matter for congratulation. Instead I said: 'I want you to go with Mary. No matter where she goes I want you to go also. I'm almost certain that tomorrow morning – this coming morning, that is – we'll all be going out to the oil rig. Mary will almost certainly go along too. She'll have no option. You will go with her.'

He made to interrupt, but I held up my hand.

'I know, you've been taken off the job. Make some excuse to go up to the house tomorrow morning, early. See Mary. Tell her that Valentino is going to have a slight accident in the course of the morning and she –'

'What do you mean, he'll have an accident?'

'Don't worry,' I said grimly. 'He'll have his accident all right. He won't be able to look after himself, far less anybody else, for some time to come. Tell her that she is to insist on having you back. If she sticks out her neck and makes an issue of it she'll win. The general won't object, and I'm pretty sure Vyland won't either: it's only for a day, and after tomorrow the question of who looks after her won't worry him very much. Don't ask me how I know, because I don't. But I'm banking on it.' I paused. 'Anyway, Vyland will just think she's insisting on having you because he thinks she has, shall we say, a soft spot for you.' He kept his wooden Indian expression in place, so I went on: 'I don't know whether it's so and I don't care. I'm just telling you what I think Vyland thinks and why that should make him accept her suggestion – that, and the fact that he doesn't trust you and would rather have you out on the rig and under his eye anyway.'

'Very well.' I might have been suggesting that he come for a stroll. He was a cool customer, all right. 'I'll tell her and I'll play it the way you want.' He thought for a moment, then continued: 'You tell me I'm sticking my neck out. Maybe I am. Maybe I'm doing it of my own free will. At the same time, I think that the fact that I'm doing it at all entitles me to a little more honesty on your part.'

'Have I been dishonest?' I wasn't annoyed, I was just beginning to feel very tired indeed.

'Only in what you don't say. You tell me you want me so that I'll look after the general's daughter. Compared to what you're after, Talbot, Mary's safety doesn't matter a tuppenny damn to you. If it did you could have hidden her away when you had her the day before yesterday. But you didn't. You brought her back. You say she's in great danger. It was *you*, Talbot, who brought her back to this danger. OK, so you want me to keep an eye on her. But you want me for something else, too.'

I nodded. 'I do. I'm going into this with my hands tied. Literally. I'm going into this as a prisoner. I must have someone I can trust. I'm trusting you.'

'You can trust Jablonsky,' he said quietly.

'Jablonsky's dead.'

He stared at me without speaking. After a few moments he reached out for the bottle and splashed whisky into both our glasses. His mouth was a thin white line in the brown face.

'See that?' I pointed to my sodden shoes. 'That's the earth from Jablonsky's grave. I filled it in just before I came here, not fifteen minutes ago. They got him through the head with a small-bore automatic. They got him between the eyes. He was smiling, Kennedy. You don't smile when you see death coming to you. Jablonsky never saw it coming. He was murdered in his sleep.'

I gave him a brief account of what had happened since I'd left the house, including the trip in the Tarpon Springs sponge boat out to the X 13, up to the moment I had come here. When I was finished he said: 'Royale?'

'Royale.'

'You'll never be able to prove it.'

'I won't have to.' I said it almost without realizing what I was saying. 'Royale may never stand trial. Jablonsky was my best friend.'

He knew what I was saying, all right. He said softly: 'I'd just as soon you never came after me, Talbot.'

I drained my whisky. It was having no effect now. I felt old and tired and empty and dead. Then Kennedy spoke again.

'What are you going to do now?'

'Do? I'm going to borrow some dry shoes and socks and underwear from you. Then I'm going to go back up to the house, go to my room, dry my clothes off, handcuff myself to the bed and throw the keys away. They'll come for me in the morning.'

168

'You're crazy,' he whispered. 'Why do you think they killed Jablonsky?'

'I don't know,' I said wearily.

'You must know,' he said urgently. 'Why else should they kill him if they hadn't found out who he really was, what he was really doing? They killed him because they found out the double-cross. And if they found that out about him, they must have found it out about you. They'll be waiting for you up there in your room, Talbot. They'll know you'll be coming back, for they won't know you found Jablonsky. You'll get it through the head as you step over the threshold. Can't you see that, Talbot? For God's sake, man, can't you see it?'

'I saw it a long time ago. Maybe they know all about me. Maybe they don't. There's so much I don't know, Kennedy. But maybe they won't kill me. Maybe not yet.' I got to my feet. 'I'm going back on up.'

For a moment I thought he was going to use physical force to try to stop me but there must have been something in my face that made him change his mind. He put his hand on my arm.

'How much are they paying you for this, Talbot?'

'Pennies.'

'Reward?'

'None.'

'Then what in the name of God is the compulsion that will drive a man like you to crazy lengths like those?' His good-looking brown face

169

was twisted in anxiety and perplexity, he couldn't understand me.

I couldn't understand myself either. I said: 'I don't know . . . Yes, I do. I'll tell you someday.'

'You'll never live to tell anybody anything,' he said sombrely.

I picked up dry shoes and clothes, told him good night and left.

SEVEN

There was nobody waiting for me in my room up in the general's house. I unlocked the corridor door with the duplicate key Jablonsky had given me, eased it open with only a whisper of sound and passed inside. Nobody blasted my head off. The room was empty.

The heavy curtains were still drawn shut as I had left them, but I let the light switch be. There was a chance that they didn't know that I'd left the room that night but if anyone saw a light come on in the room of a man handcuffed to his bed they'd be up to investigate in nothing flat. Only Jablonsky could have switched it on and Jablonsky was dead.

I went over every square foot of floor and walls with my pencil flash. Nothing missing, nothing changed. If anyone had been here he'd left no trace of his visit. But then if anyone had been here I would have expected him to leave no trace.

There was a big wall heater near the communicating door to Jablonsky's room. I switched this on to full, undressed by its ruddy glow, towelled myself dry and hung trousers and coat over the back of a chair to dry off. I pulled on the underwear and socks I'd borrowed from Kennedy, stuffed my own rain-soaked underwear and socks into my sodden shoes, opened the curtains and windows and hurled them as far as I could into the dense undergrowth behind the house, where I'd already concealed oilskin and overcoat before climbing the fire-escape. I strained my ears but I couldn't even hear the sound the shoes made on landing. I felt pretty sure no one else could have heard anything either. The high moan of the wind, the drumming of that torrential rain smothered all sound at its source.

I took keys from the pocket of my already steaming jacket and crossed to the communicating door to Jablonsky's room. Maybe the reception committee was waiting there. I didn't much care.

There was no committee. The room was as empty as my own. I crossed to the corridor door and tried the handle. The door was locked.

The bed, as I expected, had been slept in. Sheets and blankets had been pulled back so far that most of them were on the floor. There were no signs of a struggle. There were no signs, even, of violence: not until I turned the pillow upside down.

The pillow was a mess, but nothing to what it would have been if death hadn't been instantaneous. The bullet must have passed clean through the skull, not what you would have expected

172

from a .22 but then Mr Royale used very fancy ammunition. I found the shell in the down of the pillow. Cupro-nickel. It wasn't like Royale to be so careless. I was going to look after that little piece of metal. I was going to treasure it like the Cullinan diamond. I found some adhesive in a drawer, pulled off a sock, taped the spent bullet under the second and third toes where there would be no direct pressure on it and where it wouldn't interfere with my walking. It would be safe there. The most thorough and conscientious search – should there be one – would miss it. Houdini went around for years with tiny steel instruments taped to the soles of his feet and no one ever thought to look.

Down on my hands and knees I levelled the torch along the nap of the carpet and squinted down the beam. It wasn't much of a carpet but it was enough, the two parallel indentations where Jablonsky's heels had dragged across it were unmistakable. I rose to my feet, examined the bed again, picked up a cushion that lay on the armchair and examined that. I couldn't see anything, but when I bent my head and sniffed there could be no doubt about it: the acrid odour of burnt powder clings to fabrics for days.

I crossed to the small table in the corner, poured three fingers of whisky into a glass and sat down to try to figure it all out.

The set-up just didn't begin to make any sense at all. Nothing jibed, nothing fitted. How had Royale

173

and whoever had been with him – for no one man could have carried Jablonsky out of that room by himself – managed to get in in the first place? Jablonsky had felt as secure in that house as a stray lamb in a starving wolf pack and I knew he would have locked the door. Somebody else could have had a key, of course, but the point was that Jablonsky invariably left his key in the lock and jammed it so that it couldn't be pushed out or turned from the other side – not unless enough force were used and noise made to wake him up a dozen times over.

Jablonsky had been shot when sleeping in bed. Jablonsky, I knew, had pyjamas and used them – but when I found him in the kitchen garden he'd been completely clothed. Why dress him? It didn't make sense, especially trying to dress a dead man weighing 240 lb didn't make sense. And why had there been no silencer fitted to the gun? I knew there hadn't been; with the pressure absorption of a silencer not even those special bullets would travel through a skull-bone twice, and, besides, he'd used a cushion to muffle the shot. Understandable enough, in a way: those rooms were in a remote wing of the house and with the help of a cushion and the background noise of the growing storm the chances were that the shot would not be heard in the other parts of the house. But the point was that I had been right next door and was bound to have heard it, unless I were deaf or dead, and as far as Royale had

174

known – or as far as I thought he had known – I had been asleep in the next room. Or had Royale known I was not in that room? Had he come to make a quick check, found I was gone, knew that it must have been Jablonsky that had let me go and killed Jablonsky there and then? It fitted with the facts: but it didn't fit with the smile on the dead man's face.

I went back into my own room, rearranged my steaming clothes on the back of the chair before the electric fire, then returned to Jablonsky's room. I took up my glass again and glanced at the whisky bottle. It was a five-gill flask, still three parts full. That was no help, what was missing wouldn't even have begun to affect Jablonsky's razor-edge vigilance. I'd seen Jablonsky dispose of an entire bottle of rum – he wasn't a whisky man – in an evening and the only apparent effect it had had on him was that he smiled even more than usual.

But Jablonsky would never smile again.

Sitting there alone in the near darkness, the only illumination the glow from the electric fire in the next room, I lifted my glass. A toast, a farewell, I don't know what you'd call it. It was for Jablonsky. I sipped it slowly, rolling the whisky over my tongue to savour to the full the rich bouquet and taste of a fine old Scotch; for the space of two or three seconds I sat very still indeed, then I put the glass down, rose, crossed quickly to the corner of the room, spat the Scotch into the wash-basin and rinsed my mouth out very carefully indeed.

It was Vyland who had provided the whisky. After Jablonsky had paraded me downstairs last night, Vyland had given him a sealed whisky bottle and glasses to take back to his room. Jablonsky had poured out a couple of drinks soon after we had gone upstairs and I'd actually had my glass in my hand when I remembered that drinking alcohol before breathing oxygen on a deep dive wasn't a very clever thing to do. Jablonsky had drained them both, then had maybe a couple more after I had left.

Royale and his friends didn't have to batter Jablonsky's door in with foreaxes, they had a key for the job, but even if they had used axes Jablonsky would never have heard them. There had been enough knockout drops in that bottle of whisky to put an elephant out for the count. He must have been just able to stagger as far as his bed before collapsing. I knew it was stupid, but I stood there in the silent dark reproaching myself bitterly for not having accepted that drink; it was a fairly subtle blending of a Mickey Finn and Scotch, but I think I would have got on to it straight away. But Jablonsky wasn't a whisky man, maybe he thought that was the way Scotch ought to taste.

And Royale, of course, had found two glasses with whisky dregs in them. That made me as unconscious as Jablonsky. But it hadn't been any part of their plan to kill me too.

I understood it all now, everything except the answer to the one question that really mattered:

why had they killed Jablonsky? I couldn't even begin to guess. And had they bothered looking in to check on me? I didn't think so. But I wouldn't have bet a pair of old bootlaces on it.

There was nothing to be gained by sitting and thinking about it, so I sat and thought about it for a couple of hours. By that time my clothes were dry, or as near dry as made no difference. The trousers, especially, were lined and wrinkled like a pair of elephant's legs, but then you couldn't expect an immaculate crease in the clothes of a man who is compelled to sleep in them. I dressed, all except for coat and tie, opened the window and was just on the point of throwing out the three duplicate keys for the room doors and the handcuff key to join the other stuff in the shrubbery below when I heard a soft tapping on the door of Jablonsky's room.

I only jumped about a foot, then I froze. I suppose I should have stood there with my mind racing but the truth was that with what I had been through that night and with all the inconclusive and futile thinking I'd been doing in the past two hours, my mind was in no condition to walk, far less race. I just stood there. Lot's wife had nothing on me. For a lifetime of ten seconds not a single intelligent thought came, just an impulse, one single overpowering impulse. To run. But I had no place to run to.

It was Royale, that quiet cold deadly man with the little gun. It was Royale, he was waiting outside that door and the little gun would be in his hand.

177

He knew I was out, all right. He'd checked. He knew I'd be back, because he knew that Jablonsky and I were in cahoots and that I hadn't gone to such extreme lengths to get myself into that household just to light out at the first opportunity that offered, and he'd guessed that I should have been back by this time. Maybe he'd even seen me coming back. Then why had he waited so long?

I could guess the answer to that one too. He knew I would have been expecting Jablonsky to be there when I returned. He would think that I would have figured that Jablonsky must have gone off on some private expedition of his own and that as I'd locked the door when I came back and left the key there Jablonsky wouldn't be able to use his own to get in. So he would knock. Softly. And after having waited two hours for my partner's return I would be so worried stiff by his continuing absence that I would rush to the door when the knock came. And then Royale would let me have one of those cupro-nickel bullets between the eyes. Because if they knew beyond doubt that Jablonsky and I were working together they would also know that I would never do for them what they wanted me to do and so I would be of no further use to them. So, a bullet between the eyes. Just the same way Jablonsky had got his.

And then I thought of Jablonsky, I thought of him lying out there jammed up in that cheap packing case, and I wasn't afraid any more. I didn't see that I'd much chance, but I wasn't afraid. I cat-footed through to Jablonsky's room, closed my hand round the neck of the whisky bottle, went as silently back into my own room and slid a key into the lock of the door opening on to the passage outside. The bolt slid back without even the whisper of a click and just at that moment the knocking came again, slightly louder this time and more sustained. Under cover of the sound I slid the door open a crack, raised the bottle over my head ready for throwing and stuck my head round the corner of the door.

The passage was only dimly lit by a single weak night-light at the other end of a long corridor, but it was enough. Enough to let me see that the figure in the passage had no gun in its hand. Enough to let me see that it wasn't Royale. It was Mary Ruthven. I lowered the whisky bottle and stepped back softly into my room.

Five seconds later I was at the door of Jablonsky's room. I said in my best imitation of Jablonsky's deep husky voice: 'Who's there?'

'Mary Ruthven. Let me in. Quickly. Please!'

I let her in. Quickly. I had no more desire than she had that she could be seen out in that passage. I kept behind the door as she came through, then closed it swiftly before the pale glimmer of light from outside gave her time to identify me.

'Mr Jablonsky.' Her voice was a quick, urgent, breathless, frightened whisper. 'I had to come to see you, I simply had. I thought I could never get away but Gunther dropped off to sleep and he may wake up at any moment and find that I'm –'

'Easy, easy,' I said. I'd lowered my voice to a whisper, it was easier to imitate Jablonsky that way, but even so it was one of the worst imitations I had ever heard. 'Why come to see me?'

'Because there was no one else I could turn to. You're not a killer, you're not even a crook, I don't care what they say you've done, you're not bad.' She was a sharp one, all right, her woman's insight or intuition or whatever had taken her far beyond what either Vyland or the general could see. 'You must help me – us – you simply must. We – we are in great trouble.'

'We?'

'Daddy and I.' A pause. 'I honestly don't know about my father, I honestly don't. Perhaps he's not in trouble. Maybe he's working with those – those evil men because he wants to. He comes and goes as he pleases. But – but it's so unlike him. Maybe he has to work with them. Oh, I don't know, I don't know. Perhaps they have power over him, some terrible hold, perhaps—' I caught the glint of fair hair as she shook her head. 'He – well, he was always so good and honourable and straight and – and everything, but now –'

'Easy.' I interrupted again. I couldn't keep this deception up much longer, if she hadn't been so scared, so worried, she'd have caught on right away. 'Facts, miss, if you please.'

I'd left the electric fire burning in my room, the

communicating door was open and I was pretty sure it was only a matter of time till she could see enough of my features to see that I wasn't Jablonsky – and that red thatch of mine was a dead giveaway. I turned my back to the glow of the fire.

'How can I begin?' she said. 'We seem to have lost all our freedom, or daddy has. Not in moving around, *he's* not a prisoner, but we never make decisions for ourselves, or, rather, Daddy makes mine for me and I think he has his made for him too. We're never allowed to be apart for any time. Daddy says I'm to write no letters unless he sees them, make no phone calls, never go anywhere except when that horrible man Gunther is with me. Even when I go to a friend's house, like Judge Mollison's, that creature is there all the time. Daddy says he's had kidnap threats about me recently. I don't believe it and if it were true Simon Kennedy – the chauffeur – is far better than Gunther. I never have a private moment to myself. When I'm out on the rig – the X 13 – I'm no prisoner, I just can't get off, but here my room windows are screwed into the wall and Gunther spends the night in the ante-room watching to see –'

The last three words took a long, long time to come out and trailed off into a shocked silence. In her excitement, her eagerness to unburden herself of all those things that had been worrying her for weeks, she had come close to me. And now her eyes were adjusted to the darkness. She started to shake. Her right hand began to move up slowly towards her mouth, the arm trembling all the time and jerking like the arm of a marionette, her mouth opened and her eyes widened and kept on widening until I could see white all the way round the pupils. And then she drew a long quavering breath. Prelude to a scream.

But the prelude was all that there was to it. In my business, you don't telegraph your signals. I'd one hand over her mouth and an arm round her before she'd even made up her mind what key to sing in. For several seconds, with surprising strength – or in the circumstances perhaps not so surprising – she struggled furiously, then sagged against me, limp as a shot rabbit. It took me by surprise, I'd thought the day when young ladies had passed out in moments of stress had vanished with the Edwardians. But perhaps I was underestimating the fearsome reputation I appeared to have built up for myself, perhaps I was underestimating the cumulative effect of the shock after a long night of nerving herself to take this last desperate chance, after weeks of endless strain. Whatever the reasons, she wasn't faking, she was out cold. I lifted her across to the bed, then for some obscure reason I had a revulsion of feeling, I couldn't bear to have her lie on that bed where Jablonsky had so recently been murdered, so I carried her through to the bed in my own room.

I've had a fairly extensive practical first-aid education, but I didn't know the first thing about bringing young ladies out of swoons. I had a vague feeling that to do anything might be dangerous, a feeling that accorded well enough with my ignorance of what to do, so I came to the conclusion that not only the best thing but the only thing to do was to let her come out of it by herself. But I didn't want her to come out of it unknown to me and start bringing the house down so I sat on the edge of the bed and kept the flash on her face, the beam just below the eyes so as not to dazzle her.

She wore a blue quilted silk dressing-gown over blue silk pyjamas. Her high-heeled slippers were blue, even the night-ribbon for holding those thick shining braids in place was of exactly the same colour. Her face, just then, was as pale as old ivory. Nothing would ever make it a beautiful face, but then I suppose that if it had been beautiful my heart wouldn't have chosen that moment to start doing handsprings, the first time it had shown any life at all, far less such extravagant activity, in three long and empty years. Her face seemed to fade and again I could see the fire and the slippers that I'd seen two nights ago and all that stood between us was 285 million dollars and the fact that I was the only man in the world the very sight of whom could make her collapse in terror. I put my dreams away.

She stirred and opened her eyes. I felt that the

technique I'd used with Kennedy – telling him that there was a gun behind my torch – might have unfortunate results in this case. So I caught one of the hands that were lying limply on the coverlet, bent forward and said softly, reprovingly: 'You silly young muggins, why did you go and do a daft thing like that?'

Luck or instinct or both had put me on the right track. Her eyes were wide, but not staring wide, and the fear that still showed there was touched with puzzlement. Murderers of a certain category don't hold your hand and speak reassuringly. Poisoners, yes: knife-plungers in the back, possibly: but not murderers with my reputation for pure violence.

'You're not going to try to scream again, are you?' I asked.

'No.' Her voice was husky. 'I – I'm sorry I was so stupid –'

'Right,' I said briskly. 'If you're feeling fit for it, we'll talk. We have to, and there's little time.'

'Can't you put the light on?' she begged.

'No light. Shines through curtains. We don't want any callers at this time –'

'There are shutters,' she interrupted. 'Wooden shutters. On every window in the house.'

Hawk-eye Talbot, that was me. I'd spent a whole day doing nothing but staring out the window and I'd never even seen them. I rose, closed and fastened the shutters, closed the communicating door to Jablonsky's room and switched on the light. She was sitting on the side of the bed now, hugging her arms as if she were cold.

'I'm hurt,' I announced. 'You can take one look at Jablonsky and tell right away, or so you think, that *he's* not a crook. But the longer you look at me the more convinced you are that I'm a murderer.' I held up a hand as she was about to speak. 'Sure, you got reasons. Excellent reasons. But they're wrong.' I hitched up a trouser leg and offered for her inspection a foot elegantly covered in a maroon sock and completely plain black shoe. 'Ever seen those before?'

She looked at them, just for a second, then switched her gaze to my face. 'Simon's,' she whispered. 'Those are Simon's.'

'Your chauffeur.' I didn't care much for this Simon business. 'He gave them to me a couple of hours ago. Of his own free will. It took me five minutes flat to convince him that I am *not* a murderer and far from what I appear to be. Are you willing to give me the same time?'

She nodded slowly without speaking.

It didn't even take three minutes. The fact that Kennedy had given me the OK was the battle more than half won as far as she was concerned. But I skipped the bit about finding Jablonsky. She wasn't ready for any shocks of that nature, not yet.

When I was finished she said, almost unbelievingly: 'So you knew about us all the time? About Daddy and me and our troubles and –'

'We've known about you for several months.

Not specifically about your trouble, though, nor you father's whatever that may be: all we knew was that General Blair Ruthven was mixed up in something that General Blair Ruthven had no right to be mixed up in. And don't ask me who "we" are or who I am, because I don't like refusing to answer questions and it's for your own sake anyway. What's your father scared of, Mary?'

'I – I don't know. I know he's frightened of Royale, but –'

'He's frightened of Royale. I'm frightened of Royale. We're all frightened of Royale. I'll take long odds that Vyland feeds him plenty of stories about Royale to keep him good and scared. But it's not that. Not primarily. He's frightened for your sake, too, but my guess is that those fears have only grown since he found out the kind of company he's keeping. What they're really like, I mean. I think he went into this with his eyes open and for his own ends, even if he didn't know what he was letting himself in for. Just how long have Vyland and you father been, shall we way, business associates?'

She thought a bit and she said: 'I can tell you that exactly. It started when we were on holiday with our yacht, the *Temptress*, in the West Indies late last April. We'd been in Kingston, Jamaica, when Daddy got word from Mummy's lawyers that she wanted a legal separation. You may have heard about it,' she went on miserably. 'I don't think there was a paper in North America that missed out on the story and some of them were pretty vicious about it.'

'You mean the general had been so long held up as the model citizen of the country and their marriage as the ideal family marriage?'

'Yes, something like that. They made a lovely target for all the yellow Press,' she said bitterly. 'I don't know what came over Mummy, we had all always got on so well together, but it just shows that children never know exactly how things were or are between their parents.'

'Children?'

'I was just speaking generally.' She sounded tired and dispirited and beaten, and she looked that way. And she was, or she would never have talked to a stranger of such things. 'As it happens, there's another girl. Jean, my young sister – she's ten years younger than I am. Daddy married late in life. Jean's with my mother. It looks as if she's going to stay with my mother, too. The lawyers are still working things out. There'll be no divorce, of course.' She smiled emptily. 'You don't know the New England Ruthvens, Mr Talbot, but if you did you'd know that there are certain words missing from their vocabulary. "Divorce" is one of them.'

'And your father has never made any attempts at reconciliation?'

'He went up to see her twice. It was no good. She doesn't – she doesn't even want to see me. She's gone away somewhere and apart from Daddy nobody quite knows where. When you have money

187

those things aren't too difficult to arrange.' It must have been the mention of the money that sent her thoughts off on a new tack for when she spoke again I could hear those 285 million dollars back in her voice and see the *Mayflower* in her face. 'I don't quite see how all our private family business concerns you, Mr Talbot.'

'Neither do I,' I agreed. It was as near as I came to an apology. 'Maybe I read the yellow Press, too. I'm only interested in it as far as the Vyland tie-up is concerned. It was at this moment that he stepped in?'

'About then. A week or two later. Daddy was pretty low, I suppose he was willing to listen to any proposal that would take his mind off his troubles, and – and –'

'And, of course, his business judgement was below par. Although it wouldn't have to be more than a fraction below to allow friend Vyland to get his foot stuck in the front door. From the cut of his moustache to the way he arranges his display handkerchief Vyland is everything a top-flight industrialist ought to be. He's read all the books about Wall Street, he hasn't missed his Saturday night at the cinema for years, he's got every last littlest trick off to perfection. I don't suppose Royale appeared on the scene until later?'

She nodded dumbly. She looked to me to be pretty close to tears. Tears can touch me, but not when I'm pushed for time. And I was desperately short of time now. I switched off the light, went to the window, pulled back one of the shutters and stared out. The wind was stronger than ever, the rain lashed against the glass and sent the water streaming down the pane in little hurrying rivers. But, more important still, the darkness in the east was lightening into grey, the dawn was in the sky. I turned away, closed the shutter, switched on the light and looked down at the weary girl.

'Think they'll be able to fly the helicopter out to the X 13 today?' I asked.

'Choppers can fly in practically any weather.' She stirred. 'Who says anybody's flying out there today?'

'I do,' I didn't elaborate. 'Now, perhaps, you'll tell me the truth of why you came here to see Jablonsky?'

'Tell you the truth –'

'You said he had a kind face. Maybe he has, maybe he hasn't, but as a reason it's rubbish.'

'I see. I'm not holding anything back, honestly I'm not. It's just that I'm so – so worried. I overheard something about him that made me think –'

'Get to the point,' I said roughly.

'You know the library's wired, I mean they've got listening devices plugged in –'

'I've heard of them,' I said patiently. 'I don't need a diagram.'

Colour touched the pale cheeks. 'I'm sorry. Well, I was next door in the office where the earphones are and I don't know why I just put them on.' I grinned: the idea of the biter bit appealed. 'Vyland and Royale were in the library. They were talking about Jablonsky.'

I wasn't grinning any more.

'They had him tailed this morning when he went into Marble Springs. It seems he went into a hardware store, why, they don't know.' I could have filled that part in: he'd gone to buy a rope, have duplicate keys cut and do quite a bit of telephoning. 'It seems he was there half an hour without coming out, then the tail went in after him. Jablonsky came out, but his shadower didn't. He'd disappeared.' She smiled faintly. 'It seems that Jablonsky must have attended to him.'

I didn't smile. I said quietly: 'How do they know this? The tail hasn't turned up, has he?'

'They had three tails on Jablonsky. He didn't catch on to the other two.'

I nodded wearily. 'And then?'

'Jablonsky went to the post office. I saw him going in myself when we – Daddy and I – were on our way to tell the police the story Daddy insisted I tell, about how you'd dumped me and I'd thumbed a lift home. Well, it seems Jablonsky picked up a pad of telegraph forms, went into the booth, wrote out and sent off a message. One of Vyland's men waited till he'd left then got the pad and took off the top message sheet – the one under the sheet Jablonsky had written on – and brought it back here. From what I could hear Vyland seemed to be working on this with some powder and lamps.'

So even Jablonsky could slip up. But in his place I would have done the same. Exactly the same. I would have assumed that if I'd disposed of a shadower that would be the lot. Vyland was clever, maybe he was going to be too clever for me. I said to the girl: 'Hear anything more?'

'A little, not much. I gather they made out most of what was written on the form, but they couldn't understand it, I think it must have been in code.' She broke off, wet her lips then went on gravely: 'But the address was in plain language, of course.'

'Of course.' I crossed the room and stared down at her. I knew the answer to my next question, but I had to ask her. 'And the address?'

'A Mr J. C. Curtin, Federal Bureau of Investigation. That – that was really why I came. I knew I had to warn Mr Jablonsky. I didn't hear any more, somebody came along the passage and I slipped out a side door, but I think he's in danger. I think he's in great danger, Mr Talbot.'

For the past fifteen minutes I'd been looking for a way to break the news to her, but now I gave up.

'You're too late.' I hadn't meant my voice to sound harsh and cold but that's the way it sounded. 'Jablonsky's dead. Murdered.'

They came for me at eight o'clock next morning, Royale and Valentino.

I was fully dressed except for my coat and I

191

was fastened to the bed-head by a single set of handcuffs – I'd thrown the key away together with Jablonsky's three duplicate keys after I'd locked all the doors.

There was no reason why they should search me and I hoped as I never hoped before that they wouldn't. After Mary had left, tear-stained, forlorn and having unwillingly promised me that no word of what had passed should be repeated to anyone, not even her father, I'd sat down and thought. All my thinking so far had been in a never-ending circle and I'd got so deep in the rut that I could hardly see daylight any more and just when my mental processes had been about to vanish completely into the darkness I'd had the first illuminating flash, in the dark gloom of my thinking a blindingly bright flash of intuition or common sense, that I'd had since I'd come to that house. I'd thought about it for another half-hour, then I'd got a sheet of thin paper and written a long message on one side, folded it twice until it was only a couple of inches wide, sealed it with tape and addressed it to Judge Mollison at his home address. Then I'd folded it in half lengthwise, slid it over the neck-band of my tie and turned my collar down over it until it was completely hidden. When they came for me I'd had less than an hour in bed and I hadn't slept at all.

But I pretended to be sound asleep when they came in. Somebody shook me roughly by the shoulder. I ignored it. He shook me again. I stirred.

He gave up the shaking as unprofitable and used the back of his hand across my face, not lightly. Enough was enough. I groaned, blinked my eyes painfully and propped myself up in bed, rubbing my forehead with my free hand.

'On your feet, Talbot.' Apart from the upper left-hand side of his face, a miniature sunset viewed through an indigo haze, Royale looked calm and smooth as ever, and fully rested: another dead man on his conscience wasn't going to rob him of much sleep. Valentino's arm, I was glad to see, was still in a sling: that was going to make my task of turning him into an ex-bodyguard all the easier.

'On your feet,' Royale repeated. 'How come only one handcuff?'

'Eh?' I shook my head from side to side and made a great play of being dazed and half-doped. 'What in hell's name did I have for dinner last night?'

'Dinner?' Royale smiled his pale quiet smile. 'You and your gaoler emptied that bottle between you. That's what you had for dinner.'

I nodded slowly. He was on safe ground as far as he knew his ground; if I'd been doped I'd have only the haziest recollection of what had happened immediately before I'd passed out. I scowled at him and nodded at the handcuffs: 'Unlock this damn thing, will you?'

'Why only one cuff?' Royale repeated gently.

'What does it matter if it's one cuff or twenty,' I said irritably. 'I can't remember. I seem to think

Jablonsky shoved me in here in a great hurry and could only find one. I think perhaps he didn't feel too good either.' I buried my face in my hands and drew them down hard as if to clear my head and eyes. Between my fingers I glimpsed Royale's slow nod of understanding and I knew I had it made: it was exactly what Jablonsky would have done; he'd have felt something coming over him and rushed in to secure me before he collapsed.

The cuff was unlocked and on the way through Jablonsky's room I glanced casually at the table. The whisky bottle was still there. Empty. Royale – or Vyland – didn't miss much.

We went out into the passage with Royale leading and Valentino bringing up the rear. I shortened my step abruptly and Valentino dug his gun into the small of my back. Nothing Valentino would do would ever be gently, but, for him, it was a comparatively gentle prod and my sharp exclamation of pain might have been justified if it had been about ten times as hard. I stopped in my tracks, Valentino bumped into me and Royale swung round. He'd done his conjuring act again and his deadly little toy gun was sitting snugly in the palm of his hand.

'What gives?' he asked coldly. No inflection, not the slightest raising of the pitch of voice. I hoped I lived to see the day when Royale was good and worried.

'This gives,' I said tightly. 'Keep your trained ape

out of my hair, Royale, or I'll take him apart. Gun or no guns.'

'Lay off him, Gunther,' Royale said quietly.

'Jeez, boss, I didn't hardly touch him.' Discounting the anthropoid brow, broken nose, pock-marks and scars, there wasn't much room left on Valentino's face for the shift and play of expression, but what little area remained appeared to indicate astonishment and a sharp sense of injustice. 'I just gave him a little tap –'

'Sure, I know.' Royale had already turned and was on his way. 'Just lay off him.'

Royale reached the head of the stairs first and was half a dozen steps down by the time I got there. Again I slowed abruptly, again Valentino bumped into me. I swung round, chopped the side of my hand against his gun-wrist and knocked the automatic to the ground. Valentino dived to pick it up with his left hand then roared in anguish as the heel of my right shoe stamped down and crushed his fingers between leather and metal. I didn't hear any bones break, but nothing so drastic was necessary – with both his hands out of commission Mary Ruthven was going to need a new bodyguard.

I made no attempt to stoop and pick up the gun. I made no attempt to move. I could hear Royale coming slowly up the stairs.

'Move well back from that gun,' he ordered. 'Both of you.'

We moved. Royale picked up the gun, stood to

one side and waved me down the stairs in front of him. I couldn't tell what he was thinking; for all the expression on his face he might just as well have been watching a leaf falling. He said nothing more, he didn't even bother to glance at Valentino's hand.

They were waiting for us in the library, the general, Vyland and Larry the junky. The general's expression, as usual, was hidden behind moustache and beard but there was a tinge of blood to his eyes and he seemed greyer than thirty-six hours ago: maybe it was just my imagination, everything looked bad to me that morning. Vyland was urbane and polished and smiling and tough as ever, freshly shaven, eyes clear, dressed in a beautifully cut charcoal-grey suit, white soft shirt and red tie. He was a dream. Larry was just Larry, white-faced, with the junky's staring eyes, pacing up and down behind the desk. But he didn't look quite so jerky as usual; he too, was smiling, so I concluded that he'd had a good breakfast, chiefly of heroin.

'Morning, Talbot.' It was Vyland speaking; the big-time crooks today find it just as easy to be civil to you as to snarl and beat you over the head and it pays off better. 'What was the noise, Royale?'

'Gunther.' Royale nodded indifferently at Valentino, who had just come in, left hand tucked tightly under his disabled right arm and moaning in pain. 'He rode Talbot too hard and Talbot didn't like it.'

'Go off and make a noise somewhere else,'

Vyland said coldly. The Good Samaritan touch. 'Feeling tough and tetchy this morning, hey, Talbot?' There was no longer even an attempt at keeping up the pretence that the general was the boss, or even had an equal say in what went on in his own house: he just stood quietly in the background, remote and dignified and in some way tragic. But maybe the tragedy was only in my own mind; I could be guessing wrongly about the general. I could be terribly wrong about him. Fatally wrong.

'Where's Jablonsky?' I demanded.

'Jablonsky?' Vyland raised a lazy eyebrow: George Raft couldn't have done it any better. 'What's Jablonsky to you, Talbot?'

'My gaoler,' I said briefly. 'Where is he?'

'You appear very anxious to know, Talbot?' He looked at me long and consideringly and I didn't like it at all. 'I've seen you before, Talbot. So has the general. I wish I could remember who it is you remind me of.'

'Donald Duck.' This was perilous ground indeed. 'Where is he?'

'He's left. Lammed out. With his seventy thousand bucks.'

'Lammed out' was a slip, but I let it pass. 'Where is he?'

'You are becoming boringly repetitious, my friend.' He snapped his fingers. 'Larry, the cables.'

Larry picked up some papers from the desk, handed them to Vyland, grinned at me wolfishly and resumed his pacing.

'The general and I are very careful people, Talbot,' Vyland went on. 'Some people might say highly suspicious. Same thing. We checked up on you. We checked in England, Holland and Venezuela.' He waved the papers. 'These came in this morning. They say you're all you claim to be, one of Europe's top salvage experts. So now we can go ahead and use you. So now we don't need Jablonsky any more. So we let him go this morning. With his cheque. He said he fancied a trip to Europe.'

Vyland was quiet, convincing, utterly sincere and could have talked his way past St Peter. I looked as I thought St Peter might have looked as he was in the process of being convinced, then I said a lot of things St Peter would never have said and finished up by snarling: 'The dirty lying double-crosser!'

'Jablonsky?' Again the George Raft touch with the eyebrows.

'Yes, Jablonsky. To think that I listened to that lying two-timer. To think I even spent five seconds listening to him. He promised me –'

'Well, what did he promise you?' Vyland asked softly.

'No harm now,' I scowled. 'He reckoned I was for the high jump here – and he reckoned that the charges that had had him dismissed from the New York police had been rigged. He thinks – or said he thought – he could prove it, if he was given the chance to investigate certain policemen and certain police files.' I swore again. 'And to think that I believed –'

'You're wandering, Talbot,' Vyland interrupted sharply. He was watching me very closely indeed. 'Get on.'

'He thought he could buy this chance – and at the same time have me help him while he helped me. He spent a couple of hours in our room trying to remember an old federal code and then he wrote a telegram to some agency offering to supply some very interesting information about General Ruthven in exchange for a chance to examine certain files. And I was mug enough to think he meant it!'

'You don't by any chance happen to remember the name of the man to whom this telegram was addressed?'

'No. I forget.'

'You better remember, Talbot. You may be buying yourself something very important to you – your life.'

I looked at him without expression, then stared at the floor. Finally I said without looking up: 'Catin, Cartin, Curtin – yes, that was it. Curtin. J. C. Curtin.'

'And all he offered was to give information if his own conditions were met. Is that it?'

'That's it.'

'Talbot, you've just bought yourself your life.'

Sure, I'd bought myself my life. I noticed Vyland didn't specify how long I would be allowed to hang on to my purchase. Twenty-four hours, if that. It all depended how the job went. But I didn't care. The satisfaction it had given me to stamp on Valentino's hand upstairs was nothing compared to the glow I felt now. They'd fallen for my story, they'd fallen for it hook, line and sinker. In the circumstances, with the cards dealt the right way, it had been inevitable that they should. And I'd dealt my cards just right. Judged from the standpoint of their limited awareness of the extent of my knowledge, it would have been impossible for me to have concocted such a story. They didn't and couldn't know that I knew Jablonsky to be dead, that they had him tailed yesterday and deciphered the telegram's address: for they didn't know that I had been in the kitchen garden during the previous night, that Mary had overheard their conversation in the library and that she had been to see me. Had they thought I had been an accomplice of Jablonsky's throughout, they'd have shot me out of hand. As it was, they wouldn't shoot me for some time yet. Not a long time. But perhaps long enough.

I saw Vyland and Royale exchange glances, a mere flicker, and the faint shrug of Vyland's shoulders. They were tough all right, those two, tough and cool and ruthless and calculating and dangerous. For the past twelve hours they must have lived with the knowledge or the possibility that Federal agents would be around their necks any moment but they had shown no awareness of pressure, no signs of strain. I wondered what they would have thought, how they would have reacted, had they known that Federal agents could have been on to them all of three months ago. But the time had not then been ripe. Nor was it yet.

'Well, gentlemen, is there any need for further delay?' It was the first time the general had spoken, and for all his calmness there was a harsh burred edge of strain beneath. 'Let's get it over with. The weather is deteriorating rapidly and there's a hurricane warning out. We should leave as soon as possible.'

He was right about the weather, except in the tense he used. It had deteriorated. Period. The wind was no longer a moan, it was a high sustained keening howl through the swaying oaks, accompanied by intermittent squally showers of brief duration but extraordinary intensity. There was much low cloud in the sky, steadily thickening. I'd glanced at the barometer in the hall, and it was creeping down towards 27, which promised something very unpleasant indeed. Whether the centre of the storm was going to hit or pass by us I didn't know: but if we stood in its path we'd have it in less than twelve hours. Probably much less.

'We're just leaving, General. Everything's set. Petersen is waiting for us down in the bay.' Petersen, I guessed, would be the helicopter pilot. 'A couple of fast trips and we should all be out there in an hour or so. Then Talbot here can get to work.'

'All?' asked the general. 'Who?'

'Yourself, myself, Royale, Talbot, Larry and, of course, your daughter.'

'Mary. Is it necessary?'

Vyland said nothing, he didn't even use the eyebrow routine again, he just looked steadily at the general. Five seconds, perhaps more, then the general's hands unclenched and his shoulders drooped a fraction of an inch. Picture without words.

There came the quick light tap of feminine footsteps from the passage inside and Mary Ruthven walked in through the open door. She was dressed in a lime-coloured two-piece costume with an open-necked green blouse beneath. She had shadows under her eyes, she looked pale and tired and I thought she was wonderful. Kennedy was behind her, but he remained respectfully in the passage, hat in hand, a rhapsody of maroon and shining high leather boots, his face set in the remote unseeing, unhearing expression of the perfectly trained family chauffeur. I started to move aimlessly towards the door, waiting for Mary to do what I'd told her less than two hours previously, just before she'd gone back to her own room.

'I'm going in to Marble Springs with Kennedy, Father,' Mary began without preamble. It was phrased as a statement of fact, but was in effect a request for permission.

'But – well, we're going to the rig, my dear,' her father said unhappily. 'You said last night –'

'I'm coming,' she said with a touch of impatience.

'But we can't all go to once. I'll come on the second trip. We won't be more than twenty minutes. Do you mind, Mr Vyland?' she asked sweetly.

'I'm afraid it's rather difficult, Miss Ruthven,' Vyland said urbanely. 'You see, Gunther has hurt himself –'

'Good!'

He worked his eyebrow again. 'Not so good for you, Miss Ruthven. You know how your father likes you to have protection when –'

'Kennedy used to be all the protection I ever needed,' she said coldly. 'He still is. What is more, I'm not going out to the rig with you and Royale and that – that creature there' – she left no doubt but that she meant Larry – 'unless Kennedy comes with me. And that's final. And I must go into Marble Springs. Now.'

I wondered when anyone had last talked to Vyland like that. But the veneer never even cracked.

'Why must you, Miss Ruthven?'

'There are some questions a gentleman never asks,' she said icily.

That floored him. He didn't know what she meant, the same as I wouldn't have known what she meant, and the net result was to leave him stranded. Every eye in the room was on the two of them, except mine: mine were on Kennedy's and his were on mine. I was near the door now, with my back turned to the company. It had been easy to slip out the piece of paper from under my collar and now I held it against my chest so that he could see Judge Mollison's name on it. His expression didn't alter and it would have taken a micrometer to measure his nod. But he was with me. Everything was fine – but for the chance that Royale might get me with a snapshot before I cleared the doorway.

And it was Royale who broke the tension in the room, giving Vyland an easy out. 'I'd like some fresh air, Mr Vyland. I could go along with them for the ride.'

I went out through that doorway the way a torpedo leaves its tube. Kennedy had his arm outstretched and I caught it: we crashed heavily to the floor and went rolling along the passageway together. Inside the first two seconds I had the letter stuck deep inside his tunic and we were still threshing about and belabouring each other on the shoulders and back and everywhere it didn't hurt very much when we heard the unmistakable flat click of a safety catch.

'Break it up, you two.'

We broke it up and I got to my feet under the steady menace of Royale's gun. Larry, too, was hopping around in the background, waving a revolver in his hand: had I been Vyland I wouldn't even have let him have a catapult in his hand.

'That was a good job of work, Kennedy,' Vyland was saying warmly. 'I won't forget it.'

'Thank you, sir,' Kennedy said woodenly. 'I don't like killers.'

'Neither do I, my boy, neither do I,' Vyland

said approvingly. He only employed them himself because he wanted to rehabilitate them. 'Very well, Miss Ruthven. Mr Royale will go along. But be as quick as you can.'

She swept by without a word to him or a glance at me. Her head was high. I still thought she was wonderful.

EIGHT

I hadn't enjoyed the helicopter trip out to the oil rig.

Planes I'm used to, I've flown my own, I once even owned a piece in a small charter airline, but helicopters are not for me. Not even in fine weather, and the weather that morning was indescribable. We swayed and rocked and plummeted and soared up again as if some drunk had us on the end of a giant yo-yo, and nine-tenths of the time we couldn't see where we were going because the wipers couldn't cope with the deluge of water that lashed against the windscreen: but Petersen was a fine pilot and we made it. We touched down on the landing-deck of the X 13 shortly after ten o'clock in the morning.

It took six men to hold the machine even reasonably steady while the general, Vyland, Larry and I shinned down the extension ladder. Petersen gunned his motor and took off just as the last of us reached the deck, and was lost in a blinding flurry of rain inside ten seconds. I wondered if I would ever see him again.

Out there on the exposed deck the wind was far stronger and much gustier than it had been on land and it was all that we could do to keep our balance on the slippery metal underfoot. Not that there was much chance of me falling, at least not backwards, not with Larry's cannon jabbing into the small of my back all the time. He was wearing the big-collared, big-lapelled, belted, epauletted and leather-buttoned coat that Hollywood had taught him was the correct rig of the day for this kind of weather, and he had the gun inside one of the deep pockets. I felt nervous. Larry didn't like me and would have counted a hole in his fine coat as a small price to pay for the privilege of pulling that trigger. I'd got right under Larry's skin like a burr under a saddle, and I meant to stay there. I rarely spoke to him, but when I did I never failed to refer to him as 'hophead' or 'junky' and to hope that his supplies of snow were coming along all right. On the way down to the helicopter that morning I'd inquired solicitously whether or not he'd remembered to pack his grip, and when he'd asked suspiciously what the unprintable I meant by that I explained that I was concerned that he might have forgotten to pack his syringe. It took Vyland and the general all the strength of their combined efforts to pull him off me. There is nothing more dangerous and unpredictable than a drug addict, just as there is nothing more pitiable:

but there was no pity in my heart then, Larry was the weakest link in the chain and I meant to keep sawing away at him until something snapped.

We staggered along against the wind till we came to a raised hatch-cover entrance which gave to a wide companionway leading to the deck below. A group of men awaited us here, and I had my collar turned up, hat-brim turned down and a handkerchief in my hand busy wiping the rain off my face, but I needn't have bothered: Joe Curran, the roustabout foreman I'd talked to ten hours previously, was not there. I tried to imagine what would have happened had he been there, or had he asked the general whether C. C. Farnborough, his private confidential secretary, had found the missing brief-case; but I gave it up, the strain on the imagination was too great. I'd probably just have borrowed Larry's gun and shot myself.

Two men came forward to meet us. General Ruthven did the honours: 'Martin Jerrold, our field foreman, Tom Harrison, our petroleum engineer. Gentlemen, this is John Smith, a specialist engineer flown out from England to help Mr Vyland in his research.' John Smith, I gathered, was the inspired choice of name for myself.

Both men made perfunctory noises of greeting. Larry prodded me in the back so I said I was delighted too, but they obviously had no interest at all in me. Both men looked worried and uneasy, and both men were doing their best to conceal the fact. But the general didn't miss it.

'Something bothering you, Harrison?' Out here on the rig it was obviously the policy for Vyland to keep very much in the background.

'Very much so, sir.' Harrison, a crew-cut youngster with heavy horn-rimmed spectacles, looked to me as if he should still be in college, but he must have been good to hold down the responsible job he did. He produced a small chart, spread it out and pointed with a carpenter's pencil. 'This chart's good, General Ruthven. It couldn't be better, and Pride and Honeywell are the best geological team in the business. But we're already twelve hundred feet overdue. We should have hit oil at least five hundred feet back. But there's not even a smell of gas yet. I can't even begin to explain it, sir.'

I could have explained it, but it was hardly the time.

'Those things happen, my boy,' the general said easily. I had to admire the old coot; I was beginning to have more than a fair idea of the almost inhuman strain he was labouring under, but the control, the self-possession were admirable. 'We're lucky if we make it two out of five. And no geologist would claim to be 100 per cent accurate, or even within shouting distance of it. Give it another thousand. The responsibility's mine.'

'Thank you, sir.' Harrison looked relieved, but there was still a certain uneasiness about him and the general was quick to get on to it.

'Still something worrying you, Harrison?'

'No, sir, of course not.' He was too quick, too

emphatic, he wasn't half the actor the old boy was. 'Nothing at all.'

'Hmm.' The general considered him thoughtfully, then looked at Jerrold. 'Something on your mind, too?'

'The weather, sir.'

'Of course.' The general nodded understandingly. 'Latest reports are that Hurricane Diane is going to hit Marble Springs fair and square. And that means the X 13. You don't have to ask me, Jerrold. You know that. You're the captain of this ship, I'm only a passenger. I don't like losing ten thousand dollars a day, but you must suspend drilling the moment you think it's right to.'

'It's not that, sir,' Jerrold said unhappily. He jerked a thumb over his shoulder. 'That experimental leg you're working on, sir – shouldn't it be lowered to give maximum stability?'

So the drilling crew did know there was something going on in that pillar I'd investigated the previous night. When I came to think of it, although it wasn't inevitable that they should know, it was advisable. So much easier to give the crew a specious explanation for the activities taking place there than to cordon off a section and raise suspicion and unwanted and possibly dangerous speculation. I wondered what sort of yarn had been spun to them. I was to find that out right away.

'Vyland?' The general had turned to the man by his side and raised a questioning eyebrow.

'I'll accept full responsibility, General Ruthven.'

He spoke in the quiet, precise, confident tones that a top-flight engineer might have employed, although it would have surprised me if he knew a nut from a bolt. But he could use reason, too, for he added: 'This storm is going to hit from the west and the maximum strain is going to be on the other, the landward, side. The effect on this side will merely be to lift it.' He made a deprecating gesture. 'It does seem rather pointless, doesn't it, to lower an additional leg just when the other legs on that same side will have far less strain than normal to carry? Besides, General, we are now so near the perfection of this technique which is going to revolutionize underwater drilling that it would be a crime to set it back, maybe several months, by lowering the leg and perhaps destroying all our delicate equipment.'

So that was the line. It was well done, I had to admit: the dedicated enthusiasm in his voice was so exactly right, without being in any way overdone.

'That's good enough for me,' Jerrold said. He turned back to the general. 'Coming across to your quarters, sir?'

'Later. To eat, but don't wait lunch for us. Order it for my stateroom, will you? Mr Smith here is keen to get to work right away.' Like hell I was.

We left them and made our way down a broad passage. Deep inside the platform here the sound of the wind and the rising waves crashing and

211

breaking against the pillars was completely inaudible. Perhaps some faint murmur of sound might have been heard if the air in that brightly-lit steel passage hadn't been filled with the hum of powerful generators: we appeared to be passing by some diesel engine room.

At the far end of the passage we turned left and walked almost to its far cul-de-sac limits before stopping outside a door on the right-hand side. On this door, printed in large white letters, was the legend: 'Drilling Research Project' followed, in letters scarcely less large, by the words: 'Private. Most Secret. Positively No Admittance'.

Vyland rapped on the door in a long code knock – I made a mental note of it: four shorts, two long, four shorts – waited till there came three long knocks from the inside, then knocked again, four times in rapid succession. Ten seconds later we had all passed through the door and it was double locked and bolted behind us. It made all the signs about 'Private' and 'No Admittance' seem rather superfluous.

Steel floor, steel bulkheads, steel ceiling, it was a black cheerless box of a room. At least, three sides of it formed a box – the bulkhead we'd just passed through, the blank bulkhead on the left and the one to the right, with a high grilled door in its centre. The fourth side was convex, bulging out into the room in an almost perfect semicircle, with a butterfly-clamped hatchway in its middle: the trunking, I felt certain, of the big steel pillar reaching down to the floor of the sea. On either side of the hatchway hung large drums with neatly coiled rubber tubes armoured in flexible steel. Below each drum, and bolted to the floor, was a large motor: the one on the right was, I knew, an air compressor – that's what I'd heard when I'd been out there during the night – and the one on the left probably a forced-suction water pump. As for the furnishings of the room, even the Spartans would have found it rugged: a deal table, two benches and a metal wall-rack.

There were two men in the room – the one who had opened the door and another sitting at the table, dead cigar in his mouth and a pack of greasy cards spread out on the table in front of him – and both cast in the same mould. It wasn't the fact that they were both shirt-sleeved and had leather holsters strapped across their chests and high up on their left sides that gave them close similarity, not even their evenly-matched height and weight and broad bulky shoulders. The sameness lay in their faces, hard expressionless faces with cold, still, watchful eyes. I'd seen men out of the same mould before, the top-notch professionals of the strong-arm underworld, all that Larry would have given his life to be and could never hope to be. They were so exactly the type of men I would have expected Vyland to employ that the presence of Larry was all the more mysterious indeed.

Vyland grunted a greeting and that was all the

213

time he wasted in the next ten minutes. He walked across to the wall-rack, reached down a long roll of canvas-backed paper that was wrapped round a wooden stick, unrolled it flat on the table and weighted the ends to keep them from curling up again. It was a large and highly complicated diagram, sixty inches long by about thirty in depth. He stood back and looked at me.

'Ever seen that before, Talbot?'

I bent over the table. The diagram represented a peculiar object shaped halfway between a cylinder and a cigar, about four times as long as its average width. It was flat on top, flat along the middle third of the bottom, then tapering slightly upwards towards either end. At least eighty per cent of it appeared to be given up to some kind of storage tanks – I could see the fuel lines leading to the tanks from a raised bridge-like structure superimposed on the top side. This same bridge housed the beginnings of a vertical cylindrical chamber which ran clear through the body of the machine, passed out through the bottom, angled sharply left and entered an oval-shaped chamber suspended beneath the body of the cigar. On either side of this oval chamber and attached to the underside of the cigar were large rectangular containers. To the left, towards the narrower and more tapering end, were what appeared to be searchlights and long slender remote-control grabs housed in spring clips along the side.

I took a good long look at all of this, then

straightened. 'Sorry.' I shook my head. 'Never seen it in my life.'

I needn't have bothered straightening for next moment I was lying on the deck: maybe five seconds later I had pushed myself to my knees and was shaking my head from side to side in an attempt to clear it. I looked up, groaned with the pain just behind my ear, and tried to focus my eyes. I focused one of them, at any rate, for I made out Vyland standing above me, his pistol held by the barrel.

'I kind of thought you might say that, Talbot.' A nice quiet controlled voice, we were sitting at the vicar's afternoon tea-table and he was asking me to pass along the muffins. 'Your memory, Talbot. Perhaps you would like to jog it again a little, eh?'

'Is all this really necessary?' General Ruthven sounded distressed. He looked distressed. 'Surely, Vyland, we –'

'Shut up!' Vyland snapped. We were no longer calling on the vicar. He turned to me as I climbed to my feet. 'Well?'

'What's the good of beating me over the head?' I said savagely. 'How will that make me remember something I never –?'

This time I saw it coming, got the palm of my hand up to the side of my head and was riding the blow, going fast away from it, when it connected. I staggered and hit the bulkhead. It was nearly all show and to complete the effect I slid down to the deck. Nobody said anything. Vyland and his two hoodlums were looking at me with a detached interest, the general was white and he had his lower lip caught in his teeth; Larry's face was a mask of unholy glee.

'Remember anything now?'

I called him an unprintable name and rose shakily to my feet.

'Very well.' Vyland shrugged. 'I think Larry here would like to persuade you.'

'Can I? Can I really?' The eagerness on Larry's face was revolting, frightening. 'Want that I make him talk?'

Vyland smiled and nodded. 'Remember he's got to work for us when you're finished.'

'I'll remember.' This was Larry's big moment. To be in the centre of the stage, to get his own back for my sneers and gibes, above all to indulge a sadistic streak wide as a barn door – this was going to be one of the high spots of his existence. He advanced towards me, big gun wavering slightly, wetting his lips continuously and giggling in a high and horrible falsetto. 'The inside of the right thigh, high up. He'll scream like – like a pig going under the knife. Then the left. And he'll still be able to work.' The eyes were wide and staring and mad, and for the first time in my life I was confronted by a human being drooling at the mouth.

Vyland was a good psychologist; he knew I would be ten times more scared of Larry's viciousness, his neurotic instability, than of any coldly calculated brutality he or his two thugs would have brought to bear. I was scared all right. Besides, I'd put up a good enough front, it would have been expected of me, but there was no point in overdoing it.

'It's a development of the early French bathy-scaphes,' I said rapidly. 'This model is a combined British and French naval project, designed to reach only about twenty per cent of the depths of its pre-decessors – it's good for about 2,500 feet – but it's faster, more manoeuvrable and it's equipped for actual underwater salvage which its predecessors weren't.'

Nobody ever hated anyone more than Larry hated me at that moment. He was a little boy, I was a promised toy, the most wonderful he had ever seen, and he was being robbed of it just as it came within his grasp. He could have wept with rage and frustration and the sheer bitterness of his disappointment. He was still prancing in front of me and waving the gun around.

'He's lying!' His voice was shrill, almost a scream. 'He's just trying –'

'He's not lying,' Vyland interrupted coldly. No triumph, no satisfaction in his voice, the end had been achieved and the past was done with. 'Put that gun away.'

'But I tell you—' Larry broke off in an excla-mation of pain as one of the two big silent men caught his wrist and forced the gun down till it was pointing at the floor.

'Put that heater away, punk,' the man growled, 'or I'll take it off you.'

Vyland glanced at them, then ignored the by-play. 'And you not only know what this is, Talbot, but you've actually worked on it. The general has impeccable sources in Europe and we got the word this morning.' He bent forward and went on softly: 'And you also worked on it later on. Recently. Our sources in Cuba are even better than those in Europe.'

'I didn't work on it recently.' I held up my hand as Vyland tightened his mouth. 'When this bathyscaphe was brought out in a freighter to do its preliminary unmanned dives in the sheltered waters off Nassau, the British and French thought it would be cheaper and more sensible to hire a local vessel suitable for the job instead of bringing one out from Europe. I was working with a salvage firm in Havana at the time and they had a ship with a heavy crane and boom right aft. It was ideal for the job. I was aboard it, but I didn't work on the bathyscaphe itself. What would be the point in denying it if it wasn't so?' I smiled faintly. 'Besides, I was only aboard the salvage ship for a week or so. They got wind that I was there, I knew they were after me and I had to leave in a hurry.'

'They?' Vyland's eyebrow was still working as smoothly as ever.

'What does it matter now?' Even to myself I sounded tired, defeated.

'True, true,' Vyland smiled. 'From what we know of your record it might have been any one of the police forces of half a dozen countries. Anyway, General, it explains one thing that has been worrying us – where we saw Talbot's face before.'

General Ruthven said nothing. If ever I'd needed conviction that he was a tool, a pawn of Vyland's I needed it no longer. He was miserable, unhappy and clearly wished to have no part whatever in what was going on.

I said, as if a great light had suddenly dawned upon me: 'Have you – were *you* the people responsible for the loss of this bathyscaphe? My God, it *was* you! How in the –'

'You didn't think we brought you here just to discuss the diagrammatic layout of this vessel?' Vyland permitted himself a small pleased smile. 'Of course it was us. It was easy. The fools moored it on a wire hawser in ten fathoms of water. We unhitched it, substituted a frayed hawser so that they would think that it had broken its moorings and that the tide had carried it out to deep water, then we towed it away. We made most of the trip in darkness, and the few ships we saw we just slowed down, pulled the bathyscaphe up on the side remote from the approaching vessel and towed it like that.' He smiled again – he was spoiling himself this morning. 'It wasn't difficult. People do not expect to see a bathyscaphe being towed by a private yacht.'

'A private yacht. You mean the –?' I could feel the hairs on the back of my neck prickling, I'd almost made the blunder that would have finished everything. It had been on the tip of my tongue to say the *Temptress* – but no one knew I'd ever heard that name, except Mary Ruthven, who'd told me. 'You mean the general's private yacht? He has one?'

'Larry and I certainly haven't one,' he grinned. 'Larry and I' – an off-beat phrase, but there was nothing in it for me, so I let it pass. 'Of course it's the general's yacht.'

I nodded. 'And equally of course you have the bathyscaphe somewhere near here. Would you mind telling me what in the world you want a bathyscaphe for?'

'Certainly not. You'll have to know anyhow. We are – ah – treasure-hunting, Talbot.'

'Don't tell me you believe this Captain Kidd and Blackbeard nonsense,' I sneered.

'Recovering your courage, eh, Talbot? No, it's rather more recent than that and very close to here.'

'How did you find it?'

'How did we find it?' Vyland seemed to have forgotten his urgency; like every criminal who ever lived he had a streak of the ham in him and wouldn't pass up the chance of basking in the glow of his own glory. 'We had a vague idea where it was. We tried trawling for it – in the days before I met the general, that was – but had no success. Then we met the general. As you may not know, the general provides his yacht for his geologists when they plod around setting off their little bombs on the bottom of the ocean tuning in with their seismographic instruments to find out where the oil strata are. And while they were doing this we were plotting the ocean bed with an extremely sensitive depth recorder. We found it all right.'

'Near here?'

'Very near.'

'Then why haven't you recovered it?' Talbot giving his impression of a salvage specialist so engrossed in a problem that he has forgotten his own circumstances.

'How would *you* recover it, Talbot?'

'Diving for it, of course. Should be easy in those waters. After all, there's a huge continental shelf here, you have to go a hundred miles out from any point off the west coast of Florida before you even reach five hundred feet. We're close inshore here. Hundred feet, hundred fifty?'

'The X 13 is standing in how much, General?'

'One-thirty feet low tide,' Ruthven said mechanically.

I shrugged. 'There you are then.'

'There we are not.' Vyland shook his head. 'What's the greatest depth at which you can expect divers to perform really useful work, Talbot?'

'Perhaps three hundred feet.' I thought a moment. 'The deepest I know was by US divers off Honolulu.

221

Two hundred and seventy-five feet. US Submarine F4.'

'You really are a specialist, aren't you, Talbot?'

'Every diver and salvage man worth his salt knows that.'

'Two hundred and seventy-five feet, eh? Unfortunately, what we're after is in the bottom of a big hole, a deep chasm in the sea bed. The general's geologists were very interested indeed when we located this hole. Said it was just like – what was it, General?'

'The Hurd Deep.'

'That's it. The Hurd Deep. In the English Channel. Deep valley in the sea-bed where the Limeys dump all their old explosives. This one here is four hundred and eighty feet in depth.'

'That makes a difference,' I said slowly.

'Doesn't it now? And how would you get at that?'

'All depends how difficult it is to reach. The newest Neufeldt-Kuhnke rigid diving-suit, armour-plated in cast steel, could just about make it. I doubt if any diver could accomplish anything at that depth. He'd be under a pressure of two hundred pounds to the square inch and any movement would be like a barrel of heavy tar. Anything except the simplest manoeuvre would be beyond him. The way to do it would be with observation turrets – Galeazzi and my old firm, Siebe-Gorman, produce the best – and use those. They can go down about one thousand five hundred feet. You get inside

222

one of these and use a phone to guide laying of explosives or dredgers or grapnels or power grabs. That's the way they took over ten million dollars' worth of gold from the *Niagara*, from about the same depth, off New Zealand, and about four million dollars' worth of gold from the *Egypt*, lying four hundred feet off Ushant. Those are the two classic cases of modern times and that's how I would do it.'

'And of course that would require at least a couple of surface vessels and much specialized equipment,' Vyland said softly. 'Do you think we can go around buying up observation turrets – if there are any available in this country – and dredgers and then sit anchored in the same spot for weeks without exciting suspicion?'

'You have a point,' I admitted.

'So the bathyscaphe,' Vyland smiled. 'The valley in the sea floor is less than six hundred yards from here. We take with us grabs and hooks attached to wires on drums fastened to the outside of the scaphe, fix them on – you can do some very fancy work with those extension arms and graphs fitted in front – then come back here, unreeling the wire as we go. Then we haul the wire in from the X 13.'

'As easy as that, eh?'

'Just as easy as that, Talbot. Clever, you would say?'

'Very.' I didn't think it clever at all, I didn't think Vyland had even begun to appreciate the

223

difficulties involved, the endless slow-motion try, try, try again frustration of underwater salvage, the scope of the initial preparation, the skill and experience of years required. I tried to remember how long it had taken to salvage two and a half million dollars' worth of gold and silver from the *Laurentic*, sunk in only just over a hundred feet of water – something like six years if I remembered rightly. And Vyland spoke as if he was going to do it in an afternoon. 'And where exactly is the scaphe?' I asked.

Vyland pointed at the semi-circular trunking. 'That's one of the support legs of this rig – but it happens to be raised twenty feet above the sea bed. The bathyscaphe is moored below that.'

'Moored below it?' I stared at him. 'What do you mean? It's beneath the bottom of that leg? How did you get it there? How do you get into it? How in the world –?'

'Simple,' he interrupted. 'I am not, as you may have gathered, much of an engineer but I do have an – ah – professional friend who is. He devised the simple expedient of fitting a reinforced and completely waterproof steel floor of great strength across the bottom of this leg – about six feet from the bottom, actually – and letting into this a tapering steel cylinder about six feet long and not quite three feet in diameter, projecting downwards, open top and bottom, but the top capable of being sealed off flush with the waterproof floor by a screwed hatch. In a recession about two

224

feet from the top of this cylinder is a reinforced rubber tube . . . You begin to see daylight, I think, Talbot?'

'I see daylight.' They were an ingenious bunch, if nothing else. 'Somehow – almost certainly at night – you got the rig's engineer's to co-operate with you in the lowering of this leg – I suppose you told them the yarn about top secret research, so secret that no one was allowed to see what was going on. You had the bathyscaphe on the surface, unbolted its bridge cover, lowered the leg slowly until this cylinder fitted over the bathyscaphe's entrance hatch, pumped this rubber ring full of compressed air to make a perfect seal, then lowered the leg into the water, pushing the bathyscaphe down before it while someone inside the bathyscaphe, probably your engineering friend, adjusted the hydrostatic valve for one of the adjacent flooding chambers enough to let it sink easily but not so much as to rob it of its slight positive buoyancy necessary to keep the top of the entrance chamber jammed into the cylinder at the foot of the leg. And when you want to take off you just climb into the bathyscaphe, seal both the cylinder and the bathyscaphe hatches, have someone on the rig blow the air from the rubber seal gripping the entrance chamber of the bathyscaphe, flood your tanks to get enough negative buoyancy to drop clear of the leg and there you are. Reverse process when you come back except that you'll need a suction pump to clear the water that's accumulated in the cylinder. Right?'

'In every detail.' Vyland permitted himself one of his rare smiles. 'Brilliant, you might call it?'

'No. The only brilliant thing was stealing the bathyscaphe. The rest is within the scope of any moderately competent underwater operator. Just an application of the double-chambered submarine rescue diving bell which can fit in much the same way over the escape hatch of practically any submarine. And a fairly similar principle has been used for caisson work – sinking underwater piers for bridges and the like. But smart enough for all that. Your engineer friend was no fool. A pity about him, wasn't it?'

'A pity?' Vyland was no longer smiling.

'Yes. He's dead, isn't he?'

The room became very still. After perhaps ten seconds Vyland said very quietly: 'What did you say?'

'I said he was dead. When anyone in your employ dies suddenly, Vyland, I would say it was because he had outlived his usefulness. But with your treasure unrecovered, he obviously hadn't. There was an accident.'

Another long pause. 'What makes you think there was an accident?'

'And he was an elderly man, wasn't he, Vyland?'

'What makes you think there was an accident?' A soft menace in every word. Larry was licking his lips again.

'The waterproof floor you had put in in the bottom of the pillar was not quite as waterproof as you had thought. It leaked, didn't it, Vyland? Only a very small hole, possibly, and in the perimeter of the floor where it joined the side of the leg. Bad welding. But you were lucky. Somewhere above where we're standing there must be another transverse seal in the leg – to give structural strength, no doubt. So you used this machine here' – I pointed to one of the generators bolted to the deck – 'to drive in compressed air after you'd sent someone inside the leg and sealed this door off. When you'd driven in enough compressed air the accumulated water was driven out the bottom and then the man – or men – inside were able to repair the hole. Right, Vyland?'

'Right,' He was on balance again, and there was no harm in admitting something to a person who would never live to repeat it to anyone. 'How do you know all this, Talbot?'

'That footman up in the general's house. I've seen many cases. He's suffering from what used to be called caisson disease – and he'll never recover from it. The diver's bends, Vyland. When people are working under a high air or sea pressure and that pressure is released too quickly they get nitrogen bubbles in the blood. Those men in the leg were working in about four atmospheres, about sixty pounds to the square inch. If they'd been down there more than half an hour they should have spent at least half an hour decompressing, but

227

as it was some criminal idiot released the built-up pressure far too fast – as fast as it could escape, probably. At the best of times caisson work, or its equivalent, is only for fit young men. Your engineer friend was no longer a fit young man. And you had, of course, no decompressor. So he died. The footman may live long enough but he'll never again know what a pain-free existence is. But I don't suppose that troubles you, does it, Vyland?'

'We're wasting time.' I could see the relief on Vyland's face, for a moment there he'd suspected that I – and possibly others as well – knew too much about the happenings on the X 13. But he was satisfied now – and very relieved. But I wasn't interested in his expression, only in the general's.

General Ruthven was regarding me in a very peculiar fashion indeed: there was puzzlement in his face, some thought that was troubling him, but worse than that there were the beginnings of the first faint incredulous stirrings of understanding.

I didn't like that, I didn't like that at all. Swiftly I reviewed everything I'd said, everything I'd implied, and in those matters I have an almost total recall, but I couldn't think of a single word that might have been responsible for that expression on his face. And if he'd noticed something, then perhaps Vyland had also. But Vyland's face showed no sign of any knowledge or suspicion of anything untoward and it didn't necessarily follow that any off-beat word or circumstance noted by the general would also be noted by Vyland. The general was a very clever man indeed: fools don't start from scratch and accumulate close on 300 million dollars in a single lifetime.

But I wasn't going to give Vyland time to look at and read the expression on the general's face – he might be smart enough for that. I said: 'So your engineer is dead and now you need a driver, shall we say, for your bathyscaphe?'

'Wrong. We know how to operate it ourselves: You don't think we'd be so everlastingly stupid as to steal a scaphe without at the same time knowing what to do with it. From an office in Nassau we had obtained a complete set of maintenance and operation instructions in both French and English. Don't worry, we know how to operate it.'

'Indeed? This is most interesting.' I sat down on a bench without as much as a by-your-leave and lit a cigarette. Some such gesture would be expected from me. 'Then what precisely do you want with me?'

For the first time in our brief acquaintance Vyland looked embarrassed. After a few seconds he scowled and said harshly: 'We can't get the damned engines to start.'

I took a deep draw on my cigarette and tried to blow a smoke-ring. It didn't come off – with me it never came off.

'Well, well, well,' I murmured. 'How most inconvenient. For you, that is. For me, it couldn't be more convenient. All you've got to do is to start those two little engines and hey presto! you pick up a fortune for the asking. I assume that you aren't playing for peanuts – not operating on this scale. And you can't start them up without me. As I said, how convenient – for me.'

'You know how to make that machine run?' he asked coldly.

'I might. Should be simple enough – they're just battery-powered electric motors.' I smiled. 'But the electric circuits and switches and fuse boxes are pretty complicated. Surely they're listed in the maintenance instructions?'

'They are.' The smooth polished veneer was showing a distinct crack and his voice was almost a snarl. 'They're coded for a key. We haven't got a key.'

'Wonderful, just wonderful.' I rose leisurely to my feet and stood in front of Vyland. 'Without me you're lost, is that it?'

He made no answer.

'Then I have my price, Vyland. A guarantee of my life.' This angle didn't worry me at all but I knew I had to make the play or he'd have been as suspicious as hell. 'What guarantee do you offer, Vyland?'

'Good God, man, you don't need any guarantee.' The general was indignant, astonished. 'Why would anyone want to kill you?'

'Look, General,' I said patiently. 'You may be a big, big tiger when you're prowling along the jungles of Wall Street, but as far as the other side of the legal divide is concerned you're not even in the kitten class. Anyone not in your friend Vyland's employ who knows too much will always come to the same sticky end – when he can no longer be of any use to him, of course. Vyland likes his money's worth, even when it costs him nothing.'

'You're suggesting, by inference, that *I* might also come to the same end?' Ruthven inquired.

'Not you, General. You're safe. I don't know what the stinking tie-up between you and Vyland is and I don't care. He may have a hold on you and you may be up to the ears in cahoots with him but either way it makes no difference. You're safe. The disappearance of the richest man in the country would touch off the biggest man-hunt of the decade. Sorry to appear cynical, General, but there it is. An awful lot of money buys an awful lot of police activity. There would be an awful lot of pressure, General, and snowbirds like our hopped-up young friend here' – I jerked a finger over my shoulder in the general direction of Larry – 'are very apt indeed to talk under pressure. Vyland knows it. You're safe, and when it's all over, if you're not really Vyland's ever-loving partner, he'll find ways to ensure your silence. There would be nothing you could prove against him, it would only be your word against his and many others and I don't suppose even your own daughter knows what's going on. And then, of course, there's Royale – the knowledge that Royale is prowling around on the loose waiting for a man

231

to make just one slip is enough to guarantee that man putting on an act that would make a clam seem positively garrulous.' I turned from him and smiled at Vyland. 'But I'm expandable, am I not?' I snapped my fingers. 'The guarantee, Vyland, the guarantee.'

'I'll guarantee it, Talbot,' General Ruthven said quietly. 'I know who you are. I know you're a killer. But I won't have even a killer murdered out of hand. If anything happens to you I'll talk, regardless of the consequences. Vyland is first and foremost a business man. Killing you wouldn't even begin to be compensation for the millions he'd lose. You need have no fear.'

Millions. It was the first time there had been any mention of the amounts involved. Millions. And I was to get it for them.

'Thanks, General, that puts you on the side of the angels,' I murmured. I stubbed out my cigarette, turned and smiled at Vyland. 'Bring along the bag of tools, friend, and we'll go and have a look at your new toy.'

NINE

It isn't the fashion to design tombs in the form of two-hundred-foot-high metal cylinders, but if it were that pillar on the X 13 would have been a sensation. As a tomb, I mean. It had everything. It was cold and dank and dark, the gloom not so much relieved as accentuated by three tiny glow-worms of light at top, middle and bottom: it was eerie and sinister and terrifying and the hollow, reverberating echoing boom of a voice in those black and cavernous confines held all the dark resonance, the doom-filled apocalyptic finality of the dark angel calling your name on the day of judgement. It should have been, I thought bleakly, a place you went through after you died, not just before you died. Not that the question of precedence mattered at the end of the day.

As a tomb, fine: as a means of getting anywhere, terrible. The only connection between top and bottom lay in a succession of iron ladders welded on to the riveted sides of the pillar. There were twelve of those ladders, each with fifteen rungs, not one break or resting place between top and bottom. What with the weight of a heavy circuit-testing bridge Megger hanging down my back and the fact that the rungs were so wet and slippery that I had to grip them with considerable force to keep myself from falling off the ladder, the strain on forearm and shoulder muscles was severe; twice that distance and I wouldn't have made it.

It is customary for the host to lead the way in strange surroundings but Vyland passed up his privilege. Maybe he was frightened that if he preceded me down the ladder I'd take the opportunity of kicking his head off and sending him a hundred and more feet to his death on the iron platform below. However it was, I went first, with Vyland and the two cold-eyed men we'd found waiting in the little steel room following close behind. That left Larry and the general up above, and no one was under the impression that Larry was fit to guard anyone. The general was free to move around as he wished, yet Vyland appeared to have no fears that the general might use his freedom to queer his pitch. This I had found inexplicable: but I knew the answer to it now. Or I thought I knew: if I were wrong, innocent people would surely die. I put the thought out of my mind.

'Right, open it up, Cibatti,' Vyland ordered.

The larger of the two men bent down and unscrewed the hatch, swinging it up and back on its hinges to lock into a standing catch. I peered down the narrow steel cylinder that led to the steel cabin beneath the bathyscaphe and said to Vyland: 'I suppose you know you'll have to flood this entrance chamber when you go looking for your Blackbeard's treasure?'

'What's that?' He looked at me narrowly, suspiciously. 'Why?'

'Were you thinking of leaving it unflooded?' I asked incredulously. 'This entrance chamber is usually flooded the minute you start descending – and that's normally surface level, not a hundred and thirty feet down as you are here. Sure, sure, I know it looks solid, it might even hold at double this depth, I don't know. But what I do know is that it is completely surrounded by your gasoline buoyancy tanks, about eight thousand gallons of it, and those are open to the sea at the bottom. The pressure inside those tanks corresponds exactly to the sea pressure outside – which is why only the thinnest sheet metal is required to hold the gasoline. But with only air inside your entrance chamber you're going to have at least two hundred pounds to the square inch pressing on the outside of this entrance chamber. And it won't stand that. It'll burst inwards, your gasoline will escape, your positive buoyancy will be gone for ever and there you are, four hundred and eighty feet below the surface of the sea. And there you would remain until the end of time.'

It was hard to be positive in that thinly-lit gloom,

but I could have sworn that the colour had drained from Vyland's face.

'Bryson never told me this.' Vyland's voice was a vicious whisper and there was a shake in it.

'Bryson? Your engineering friend?' There was no answer, so I went on: 'No, I don't suppose he would. He was no friend, was he, Vyland: he had a gun in his back, didn't he, and he knew that when his usefulness was over someone was going to pull the trigger of that gun? Why the hell should he tell you?' I looked away from him and shouldered the bridge Megger again. 'No need for anyone to come down with me – it'll only make me nervous.'

'Think I'm going to let you go down there on your own?' he asked coldly. 'To get up to your tricks?'

'Don't be stupid,' I said wearily. 'I could stand there in front of an electrical switchboard or fuse-box and sabotage the bathyscaphe so that it would never move again, and neither you nor your friends would ever know anything about it. It's in my own interests to get this machine going and have the whole thing over as soon as possible. The quicker the better for me.' I glanced at my watch. 'Twenty to eleven. It'll take me three hours to find out what's wrong. At least. I'll have a break at two. I'll knock on the hatch so that you can let me out.'

'No need.' Vyland wasn't happy, but as long as he couldn't put his finger on any possibility of treachery he wasn't going to deny me – he

236

wasn't in any position to. 'There's a microphone in the cabin, with its extension cable wound round a drum on the outside and a lead through a gland in the side of the leg that's carried up to that room where we were. There's a button call-up. Let us know when you're ready.'

I nodded and started down the rungs welded into the side of the cylinder, unscrewed the upper hatch of the bathyscaphe's flooding and entrance chamber, managed to wriggle down past it – the downward projecting cylinder which encompassed the top of the entrance chamber was only a few inches wider and didn't give enough room to open the hatch fully – felt for the rungs below, pulled down the hatch, clamped it shut and then worked my way down the constricting narrowness of that chamber to the cabin below. The last few feet involved an almost right-angle bend, but I managed to ease myself and the Megger round it. I opened the heavy steel door to the cabin, wriggled through the tiny entrance, then closed and locked the door behind me.

Nothing had changed, it was as I had remembered it. The cabin was considerably bigger than that of the earlier FRNS from which it had been developed, and slightly oval in shape instead of round: but what was lost in structural power was more than compensated for in the scope and ease of movement inside, and as it was only intended for salvage operations up to about 2,500 feet, the relative loss in strength was unimportant.

There were three windows, one set in the floor, cone-shaped inwards as was the entrance door, so that sea pressure only tightened them in their seats: they looked fragile, those windows, but I knew that the specially constructed Plexiglas in the largest of them – and that was no more than a foot in its external diameter – could take a pressure of 250 tons without fracturing, many times the strain it would ever be required to withstand in the depths in which that bathyscaphe would operate.

The cabin itself was a masterpiece of design. One wall – if approximately one-sixth on the surface area of the inside of a sphere could be called a wall – was covered with instruments, dial, fuse-boxes, switchboards and a variety of scientific equipment which we would not be called upon to use: set to one side were the controls for engine starting, engine speed, advance and reverse, for the searchlights, remote-controlled grabs, the dangling guiderope which could hold the bathyscaphe stable near the bottom by resting part of its length on the sea-bed and so relieving the scaphe of that tiny percentage of weight which was sufficient to hold it in perfect equilibrium; and, finally, there were the fine adjustments for the device for absorbing exhaled carbon dioxide and regenerating oxygen.

One control there was that I hadn't seen before, and it puzzled me for some time. It was a rheostat with advance and retard positions graded on either side of the central knob and below this was the brass legend 'Tow-rope control'. I had no idea what this could be for, but after a couple of minutes I could make a pretty sure guess. Vyland – or rather, Bryson on Vyland's orders – must have fitted a power-operated drum to the top, and almost certainly the rear, of the bathyscaphe, the wire of which would have been attached, before the leg had been lowered into the water, to some heavy bolt or ring secured near the base of the leg. The idea, I now saw, was not that they could thereby haul the bathyscaphe back to the rig if anything went wrong – it would have required many more times the power that was available in the bathyscaphe's engines to haul that big machine along the ocean bed – but purely to overcome the very tricky navigational problem of finding their way back to the leg. I switched on a searchlight, adjusted the beam and stared down through the window at my feet. The deep circular ring in the ocean floor where the leg had originally been bedded was still there, a trench over a foot in depth: with that to guide, re-engaging the top of the entrance chamber in the cylinder inside leg shouldn't be too difficult.

At least I understood now why Vyland hadn't objected too strongly to my being left by myself inside the scaphe: by flooding the entrance chamber and rocking the scaphe to and fro if and when I got the engines started, I might easily have managed to tear clear of the rubber seal and sail the bathyscaphe away to freedom and safety: but I wouldn't get very far with a heavy cable attaching me to the leg of the

X 13. Vyland might be a phoney in the ways of dress, mannerisms and speech, but that didn't alter the fact that he was a very smart boy indeed.

Apart from the instruments on that one wall, the rest of the cabin was practically bare except for three small canvas seats that hinged on the outer wall and a rack where there was stored a variety of cameras and photo-flood equipment.

My initial comprehensive look round the interior didn't take long. The first thing that called for attention was the control box of the hand microphone by one of the canvas seats. Vyland was just the sort of person who would want to check whether I really was working, and I wouldn't have put it past him to change over wires in the control box so that when the switch was in the off position the microphone would be continuously live and so let him know that I was at least working, even if he didn't know what kind of work it was. But I'd misjudged or over-rated him, the wiring was as it should have been.

In the next five minutes or so I tested every item of equipment inside that cabin except the engine controls – should I have been able to start them anyone still waiting on the bottom floor of that leg would have been sure to feel the vibration.

After that I unscrewed the cover of the largest of the circuit boxes, removed almost twenty coloured wires from their sockets and let them hang down in the wildest confusion and disorder. I attached a lead from the Megger to one of those wires, opened the covers of another two circuits and fuse-boxes and emptied most of my tools on to the small work-bench beneath. The impression of honest toil was highly convincing.

So small was the floor area of that steel cabin that there was no room for me to stretch out my length on the narrow mesh duckboard but I didn't care. I hadn't slept at all the previous night, I'd been through a great deal in the past twelve hours and I felt very tired indeed. I'd sleep all right.

I slept. My last impression before drifting off was that the wind and the seas must be really acting up. At depths of a hundred feet or over, wave-motion is rarely or never felt: but the rocking of that bathyscaphe was unmistakable, though very gentle indeed. It rocked me to sleep.

My watch said half-past two when I awoke. For me, this was most unusual: I'd normally the ability to set a mental alarm-clock and wake up almost to the pre-selected moment. This time I'd slipped, but I was hardly surprised. My head ached fiercely, the air in that tiny cabin was foul. It was my own fault, I'd been careless. I reached for the switch controlling carbon dioxide absorption and turned it up to maximum. After five minutes, when my head began to clear, I switched on the microphone and asked for someone to loosen the hatch-cover set into the floor of the leg. The man they called Cibatti came down and let me out and three minutes later I was up again in that little steel room.

'Late, aren't you?' Vyland snapped. He and Royale – the helicopter must have made the double trip safely – were the only people there, apart from Cibatti who had just closed the trunking door behind me.

'You want the damn thing to go sometime, don't you?' I said irritably. 'I'm not in this for the fun of the thing, Vyland.'

'That's so.' The top executive criminal, he wasn't going to antagonize anyone unnecessarily. He peered closely at me. 'Anything the matter with you?'

'Working for hours on end in a cramped coffin is the matter with me,' I said sourly. 'That and the fact that the air purifier was maladjusted. But it's OK now.'

'Progress?'

'Damn little.' I lifted my hand as the eyebrow went up and the face began to darken in a scowl. 'It's not for want of trying. I've tested every single contact and circuit in the scaphe and it's only in the past twenty minutes that I began to find out what's the matter with it.'

'Well, what *was* the matter with it?'

'Your late engineer friend Bryson was the matter with it, that's what.' I looked at him speculatively. 'Had you intended taking Bryson with you when you were going to recover this stuff? Or were you going to go it alone?'

'Just Royale and myself. We thought –'

'Yes, I know. Not much point in taking him

242

along with you. A dead man can't accomplish much. Either you dropped a hint that he wouldn't be coming along and he knew *why* he wouldn't be coming along so he'd fixed it so that he'd get a nice little posthumous revenge, or he hated you so much that if he had to go along he was determined that he was going to take you with him. Out of this world, I mean. Your friend had made a very clever little fix indeed, only he hadn't quite time to finish it before the bends knocked him off – which is why the engines are still out of commission. He'd fixed it so that the bathyscaphe would have operated perfectly; would have gone backwards and forwards, up and down, anything you liked – until you had taken it down to a depth of just over three hundred feet. Then he had fixed that certain hydro-static cut-outs would come into operation. A beautiful job.' I wasn't gambling much, I knew their ignorance of those matters was profound.

'And then what?' Vyland asked tightly.

'Then nothing. The bathyscaphe would never have been able to get above three hundred feet again. When either the batteries had been exhausted or the oxygen regenerating unit had failed, as it would have to in a few hours – well, you'd have died of suffocation.' I looked at him consideringly. 'After, that is, you had screamed your way into madness.'

On a previous occasion I had thought I had seen Vyland losing some colour from his rather ruddy cheeks, but on this occasion there was no doubt: he turned white and to conceal his agitation fumbled a pack of cigarettes out of his pocket and lit a cigarette with hands whose tremor he could not conceal. Royale, sitting on the table, just smiled his little secret smile and went on unconcernedly swinging his foot. That didn't make Royale any braver than Vyland, maybe it only meant he was less imaginative. The last thing a professional killer could ever afford was imagination; he had to live with himself and the ghosts of all his victims. I looked at Royale again. I swore to myself that one day I would see that face the mask and mirror of fear, as Royale himself had seen so many other faces the masks and mirrors of fear in that last second of awareness and knowingness before he pulled the trigger of his deadly little gun.

'Neat, eh?' Vyland said harshly. He had regained a measure of composure.

'It wasn't bad,' I admitted. 'At least I sympathize with his outlook, the object he had in mind.'

'Funny. Very funny indeed.' There were times when Vyland forgot that the well-bred business tycoon never snarls. He looked at me with sudden speculation in his eyes. 'You wouldn't be thinking along the same lines yourself, Talbot? Of pulling a fast one like Bryson tried to pull?'

'It's an attractive idea,' I grinned at him, 'but you insult my intelligence. In the first place, had I had any ideas along those lines do you think I would have given you any hint of them? Besides,

I intend to go along with you on this little trip. At least, hope to.'

'You do, eh?' Vyland was back on balance, his shrewd quick self again. 'Getting suspiciously co-operative all of a sudden, aren't you, Talbot?'

'You can't win,' I sighed. 'If I said I *didn't* want to go, you'd think that a damn sight more suspicious. Be your age, Vyland. Things aren't as they were a few hours ago. Remember the general's speech about ensuring my continued well-being? He meant it all right, he meant every word of it. Try seeing me off and he'll see you off. And you're too much of a business man to make a bad deal like that. Royale here is going to be deprived of the pleasure of killing me.'

'Killing gives me no pleasure,' Royale put in softly. It was a simple statement of fact and I stared at him, temporarily off-balance by the preposterousness of it.

'Did I hear what I thought I heard?' I asked slowly.

'Ever hear of a ditch-digger digging ditches for pleasure, Talbot?'

'I think I see your point.' I stared at him for a long moment, he was even more inhuman than I had ever imagined. 'Anyway, Vyland, now that I'm going to live I have a different outlook on things. The sooner this business is over, the sooner I'll be away from you and your cosy little pals. And then, I think, I could put the touch on the general for a few thousand. I hardly think he would like it known that he had been aiding and abetting criminal activities on a grand scale.'

'You mean – you mean, you'd put the black on the man who saved your life?' Apparently some things were still capable of astonishing Vyland. 'God, you're as bad as any of us. Worse.'

'I never said I wasn't,' I said indifferently. 'These are hard times, Vyland. A man must live. And I'm in a hurry. That's why I suggest I come along. Oh, I admit a child could steer and lower and raise the bathyscaphe once he'd read the instructions, but salvage is no job for amateurs. Believe me, Vyland, I know, and it's not. You're amateurs. I'm an expert. It's the one thing I'm really good at. So I come, eh?'

Vyland looked at me long and consideringly, then he said softly: 'I just wouldn't dream of going along without you, Talbot.'

He turned, opened the door and gestured to me to precede him. He and Royale came out behind me and as we walked along the passage we could hear Cibatti slamming home a heavy bolt and turning a key in the lock. Which made it as safe as the Bank of England, except for one thing: in the Bank of England a code knock does not automatically open the door to the vaults. But it opened doors here, and I had remembered it: and even had I forgotten it, it would have come back there and then for Vyland was using it again on a door about fifteen yards along the passage.

The door was opened by Cibatti's opposite

number. The compartment beyond wasn't as bleakly furnished as the one we had just left, but it was a near thing. It had no wall coverings, no floor coverings, it didn't even have a table: but it did have a padded bench along one wall, and on this the general and Mary were sitting. Kennedy was sitting very straight on a wooden chair in a corner and Larry, his big pistol out, his eyes twitching away feverishly as ever, was pacing up and down, doing his big watch-dog act. I scowled at them all impartially.

The general was his usual erect, impassive self, all his thoughts and emotions under the usual impeccable control; but there were dark half-moons under his eyes that hadn't been there a couple of days ago. His daughter's eyes, too, were smudged with blue, her face was pale and though it was composed enough she didn't have the iron in her that her father had: the droop of the slender shoulders, slight though it was, was there for all to see. Myself, I didn't go much for iron women at any time; there was nothing I would have liked better than to put an arm round those self-same shoulders, but the time and the place were wrong, the reactions anyway unpredictable. Kennedy was just Kennedy, his good-looking hard face a smooth brown mask, and he wasn't worried about anything: I noticed that his maroon uniform fitted him better than ever; it wasn't that he had been to see his tailor, someone had taken his gun from him and now there wasn't even the suspicion of a bulge to mar the smooth perfection of the uniform.

As the door closed behind us, Mary Ruthven rose to her feet. There was an angry glint in her eye, maybe there was more iron to her than I had supposed. She gestured towards Larry without looking at him.

'Is all this really necessary, Mr Vyland?' she asked coldly. 'Am I to assume that we have now arrived at the stage of being treated like criminals – like criminals under an armed guard?'

'You don't want to pay any attention to our little pal here,' I put in soothingly. 'The heater in his hand doesn't mean a thing. He's just whistling in the dark. All those snow-birds are as jittery and nervous as this, just looking at the gun gives him confidence: his next shot's overdue, but when he gets it he'll be ten feet tall.'

Larry took a couple of quick steps forward and jammed the gun into my stomach. He wasn't any too gentle about it. His eyes were glazed, there were a couple of burning spots high up in the dead-white cheeks and his breath was a harsh and hissing half-whistle through bared and clenched teeth.

'I told you, Talbot,' he whispered. 'I told you not to ride me any more. That's the last time –'

I glanced over his shoulder then smiled at him.

'Look behind you, sucker,' I said softly. As I spoke I again shifted my gaze over his shoulder and nodded slightly.

He was too hopped up and unbalanced not to fall for it. So sure was I that he would fall for it that my right hand was reaching for his gun as he started to turn and by the time his head was twisted all the way round I had my hand locked over his and the gun pointing sideways and downwards where it would do no harm to anybody if it went off. No direct harm, that was: I couldn't speak for the power and direction of the ricochet off steel decks and bulkheads.

Larry swung round, his face an ugly and contorted mask of fury and hate, swearing softly, vilely, continuously. He reached down with his free hand to try to wrench the pistol clear, but the hardest work Larry had ever done was pushing down the plunger of a hypodermic syringe and he was just wasting his time. I wrenched the gun away, stepped back, stiff-armed him joltingly with the heel of my palm as he tried to come after me, broke open the automatic, ejected the magazine and sent it clattering into one corner while the gun went into another. Larry half-stood, half-crouched against the far wall where my push had sent him, blood trickling from his nose and tears of rage and frustration and pain running down both cheeks. Just to look at him made me sick and cold.

'All right, Royale,' I said without turning my head. 'You can put your gun away. The show's over.'

But the show wasn't over. A hard voice said: 'Go

pick up that gun, Talbot. And the clip. Put the clip in the gun and give it back to Larry.'

I turned round slowly. Vyland had a gun in his hand and I didn't care very much for the whiteness of the knuckle of the trigger finger. He looked his usual polished urbane self, but the rigidity of his gun hand and the ever so slightly too fast rate of breathing gave him away. It didn't make sense. Men like Vyland never allowed themselves to become emotionally involved, far less so concerned over what happened to a punk like Larry.

'How would you like to go up top and take a walk over the side?' I asked.

'I'll give you till I count five.'

'And then what?'

'Then I'll shoot.'

'You wouldn't dare,' I said contemptuously. 'You're not the type to pull triggers, Vyland. That's why you employ this big bad hatchetman here. Besides, who would fix up the bathyscaphe then?'

'I'm counting, Talbot.' As far as I was concerned he'd gone nuts. 'One . . . two –'

'OK, OK,' I interrupted, 'so you can count. You're a swell counter. I bet you can count up to ten. But I bet you can't count up to all those millions you're going to lose just because I don't feel like picking up a gun.'

'I can get other people to fix up that bathyscaphe.'

'Not this side of the Atlantic, you won't. And you haven't got all that much time to play around with, have you, Vyland? What's the betting a planeload of the FBI aren't already on the way to Marble Springs to investigate that curious telegram Jablonsky sent? What's the betting they aren't already there? What's the betting they aren't knocking on the door of the general's villa right now, saying, "Where's the general?" and the butler saying, "Why the general's just gone out to the rig gentlemen," and then the FBI saying, "We must call upon the general immediately. We have important things to discuss with him." And they will call, Vyland, just as soon as this storm blows over.'

'I'm afraid he's right, Mr Vyland.' The unexpected help came from Royale. 'We haven't all that much time.'

For a long moment Vyland said nothing. Then he lowered his gun, turned and walked out of the room.

Royale, as always, showed no sign of strain or emotion whatever. He smiled and said: 'Mr Vyland has gone to eat over on the other side. Lunch is ready for all of us,' and stood to one side to let us out through the door.

It had been a strange off-beat episode. It didn't make sense, it didn't even begin to make any kind of sense at all. I pondered it, I tried to find a shadow of an explanation while Larry collected his gun and ammunition clip, but it was no good, I couldn't find an explanation to fit the facts. Besides, I'd suddenly realized that I was very hungry indeed. I stood to one side to let all the others except Royale precede

251

me, not so much out of courtesy as to ensure that Larry didn't shoot me in the back, then hurried, without seeming to, to catch up on Mary and Kennedy.

To get to the other side of the rig we had to cross the hundred-foot width of the well-deck where I'd talked to Joe Curran, the roustabout foreman, in the early hours of that morning. It was by all odds the longest, wettest and windiest hundred feet that I'd ever walked.

They'd rigged up a couple of wire life-lines clear across to the other side. We could have done with a couple of dozen. The power of that wind was fantastic, it seemed to have redoubled in strength since we had arrived on the rig four hours previously and I knew now that we could expect no boat or helicopter to approach the rig until the storm had passed. We were completely cut off from the outer world.

At half-past two in the afternoon it was dark as twilight and out of the great black wall of cumulo-nimbus that all but surrounded us the wind flung itself upon the X 13, as if it were going to uproot it from its thirteen-leg foundation, topple it and drown it in the depths of the sea. It roared and howled across the deck of the oil rig in a maniacal fury of sound, and even at the distance of a couple of hundred feet we could plainly hear above the deep thunder of the storm the cacophonous obbligato, the screaming satanic music as the great wind whistled and shrieked its falsetto way through the hundreds of steel girders that went to make up the towering structure of the drilling derrick. We had to lean at an angle of almost forty-five degrees against the wind to keep our balance and at the same time hang on grimly to one of the life-lines. If you fell and started rolling along that deck you wouldn't stop until the wind had pushed you clear over the side: it was as strong as that. It sucked the breath from your lungs and under its knife-edged hurricane lash the rain flailed and stung the exposed skin like an endless storm of tiny lead shot.

Mary led the way across this exposed storm-filled working platform, and right behind her came Kennedy, one hand sliding along the wire, his free arm tightly round the girl in front. At another time I might have been disposed to dwell on the subject of luck and how some people seemed to have all of it, but I had other much more urgent things on my mind. I came close up to him, actually treading on his heels, put my head close to his and shouted above the storm: 'Any word come through yet?'

He was smart, all right, this chauffeur. He neither broke step nor turned round, but merely shook his head slightly.

'Damn!' I said, and meant it. This was awkward. 'Have you phoned?'

Again the shake of the head. An impatient shake, this time, it looked like, and when I thought about it I couldn't blame him. Much chance he'd had of either hearing or finding out anything with Larry dancing around flourishing his pistol, probably ever since he had come out to the rig.

'I've got to talk to you, Kennedy.' I shouted.

He heard me this time too; the nod was almost imperceptible but I caught it.

We reached the other side, passed through a heavy clipped door and at once found ourselves in another world. It wasn't the sudden quiet, the warmth, the absence of wind and rain that caused the transformation, though those helped: compared to the other side of the rig from which we had just come, this side resembled a sumptuous hotel.

Instead of bleak steel bulkheads there was some form of polythene or Formica panelling painted in pleasing pastel shades. The floor was sheathed in deep sound-absorbing rubber and a strip of carpeting covered the length of the passageway stretching in front of us. Instead of harsh unshaded lighting falling from occasional overhead lamps, there was a warm diffused glow from concealed strip lighting. Doors lined the passage and the one or two that were open looked into rooms as finely furnished as the cabins you might find in the senior officer's quarters aboard a battleship. Oil drilling might be a tough life, but the drillers obviously believed in doing themselves well in their off-duty hours. To find this comfort, luxury almost, in the Martian metal structure standing miles out to sea was somehow weird and altogether incongruous.

But what pleased me more than all those evidences of comfort was the fact that there were concealed loudspeakers at intervals along the passage. Those were playing music, soft music, but perhaps loud enough for my purpose. When the last of us had passed through the doorway, Kennedy turned and looked at Royale.

'Where are we going, sir?' The perfect chauffeur to the end, anyone who called Royale 'sir' deserved a medal.

'The general's stateroom. Lead the way.'

'I usually eat in the drillers' mess, sir,' Kennedy said stiffly.

'Not today. Hurry up, now.'

Kennedy took him at his word. Soon he had left most of them ten feet behind – all except me. And I knew I had very little time. I kept my voice low, head bent and talked without looking at him.

'Can we put a phone call through to land?'

'No. Not without clearance. One of Vyland's men is with the switchboard operator. Checks everything, in and out.'

'See the sheriff?'

'A deputy. He got the message.'

'How are they going to let us know if they had any success?'

'A message. To the general. Saying that you – or a man like you – had been arrested at Jacksonville, travelling north.'

I should have loved to curse out loud but I contented myself with cursing inwardly. Maybe

255

it had been the best they could think up at short notice, but it was weak, with a big chance of failure. The regular switchboard operator might indeed have passed the message on to the general and there would be no chance that I might be in the vicinity at the time: but Vyland's creature supervising the operator would know the message to be false and wouldn't bother passing it on, except perhaps hours later, by way of a joke: nor was there any certainty that even then the news would reach my ears. Everything, just everything could fail and men might die because I couldn't get the news I wanted. It was galling. The frustration I felt, and the chagrin, were as deep as the urgency was desperate.

The music suddenly stopped, but we were rounding a corner which cuts off momentarily from the others, and I took a long chance.

'The short-wave radio operator. Is he on constant duty?'

Kennedy hesitated. 'Don't know. Call-up bell, I think.'

I knew what he meant. Where, for various reasons, a radio post can't be continuously manned, there is a device that triggers a distant alarm bell when a call comes through on the post's listening frequency.

'Can you operate a short-wave transmitter?' I murmured.

He shook his head.

'You've got to help me. It's essential that –'

'Talbot!'

It was Royale's voice. He'd heard me, I was sure he'd heard me, and this was it, if he'd the slightest suspicion, then I knew Kennedy and I had exchanged our last words and that I was through. But I passed up the guilty starts and breaking of steps in mid-stride, instead I slowed down gradually, looked round mildly and inquiringly. Royale was about eight feet behind and there were no signs of suspicion or hostility in his face. But then there never were. Royale had given up using expressions years ago.

'Wait here,' he said curtly. He moved ahead of us, opened a door, peered in, had a good look round, then beckoned. 'All right. In.'

We went in. The room was big, over twenty feet long, and luxuriously furnished. Red carpet from wall to wall, red drapes framing square rain-blurred windows, green and red chintz-covered armchairs, a cocktail bar lined with red leather-covered stools in one corner, a Formica-topped table to seat eight near the door: in the corner opposite the bar, a curtained-off alcove. The dining-room of the suite – internal doors opened off right- and left-hand walls – where the general roughed it when he came out to the oil rig.

Vyland was there, waiting for us. He seemed to have recovered his equanimity, and I had to admit that that smooth urbane face with its neatly trimmed moustache and distinguished sprinkling of iron-grey at the temples belonged right there in that room.

'Close the door,' he said to Larry, then turned to me and nodded towards the curtained alcove. 'You eat there, Talbot.'

'Sure,' I agreed. 'The hired help. I eat in the kitchen.'

'You eat there for the same reason that you saw no one on your way through the corridors coming here. Think we want the drilling-rig crew running around shouting that they've just seen Talbot, the wanted murderer? Don't forget they have radios here and the chopper delivers papers every day . . . I think we might have the steward in now, General, don't you?'

I went quickly to my seat at the tiny table behind the curtain and sat down. I felt shaken. I should have felt relieved to know that Royale had not been suspicious, that he'd merely been checking to see that the coast was clear before we went into the general's room, but I was more concerned about my own slip-up. My attention was so taken up with immediate problems that I had forgotten that I was playing the part of a murderer. Had I been a genuine and wanted killer, I'd have kept my face hidden, walked in the middle of the group and peered fearfully round every corner we'd come to. I had done none of those things. How long would it be before it occurred to Royale to wonder why I had done none of those things?

The outside door opened and someone, a steward, I assumed, entered. Once again it was the general who was the host, the man in charge, with Vyland his employee and guest: the general's ability to switch roles, his unfailing command of himself in all circumstances, impressed me more every time I noticed it. I was beginning to hope that perhaps it might be a good thing to let the general in on something of what was happening, to seek his help in a certain matter, I was certain now he could carry off any deception, any duplicity where the situation demanded it. But he might as well have been a thousand miles away for any hope I had of contacting him.

The general finished giving his orders for lunch, the door closed behind the departing steward and for perhaps a minute there was complete silence. Then someone rose to his feet and crossed the room and the next I heard was the sound of bottles and glasses clinking. Trifles like murder and forcible coercion and underwater recovery of millions weren't going to get in the way of the observance of the customs of the old Southern hospitality. I would have taken long odds that it was the general himself who was acting as barman, and I was right: I would have taken even longer odds that he would pass up Talbot the murderer, and I was wrong. The alcove curtain was pushed back and the general himself set down a glass before me: he remained bent over my tiny table for a couple of seconds, and the look he gave me wasn't the look you give a known murderer who has at one time kidnapped your daughter and threatened her with death. It was a long, slow, considering, speculative look: and then incredibly, but unmistakably, the corner of his mouth twitched in a smile and his eye closed in a wink. Next moment he was gone, the curtain falling into place and shutting me off from the company.

I hadn't imagined it, I knew I hadn't imagined it. The general was on to me. How much he was on to me I couldn't guess, any more than I could guess at the reasons that had led to the discovery of what he knew or suspected. One thing I was sure of, he hadn't learned from his daughter, I'd impressed her enough with the necessity for complete secrecy.

There was a rumble of conversation in the room and I became aware that it was General Ruthven himself who held the floor.

'It's damnably insulting and utterly ridiculous,' he was saying in a voice that I'd never heard before. A dry, icy voice that I could just see being brought to bear for maximum effect in quelling an unruly board of directors. 'I don't blame Talbot, murderer though he is. This gun-waving, this guarding has got to stop. I insist on it, Vyland. Good God, man, it's so utterly unnecessary and I don't think a man like you would go in for cheaply melodramatic stuff like this.' The general was warming to his theme of making a stand against being shepherded around at pistol point, or at least against constant

260

surveillance. 'Look at the weather, man – no one can move from here in the next twelve hours at least. We're not in the position to make any trouble – and you know I'm the last man in the world to want to. I can vouch personally for my daughter and Kennedy.'

The general was sharp, sharp as a needle, sharper than either Vyland or Royale. He was a bit late in the day in making his stand against surveillance, I guessed what he was really after was the power of freedom of movement – possibly for himself, even more possibly for his chauffeur. And, what was more, he was getting it. Vyland was agreeing, with the reservation that when he and Royale went in the bathyscaphe the general, his chauffeur and Mary should remain in the room above the pillar along with the rest of Vyland's men. I still had no idea how many men Vyland actually had aboard the rig, but it seemed likely that apart from Larry, Cibatti and his friend there were at least three others. And they would be men in the mould of Cibatti.

Conversation broke off short as a knock came again to the door. A steward – or stewards – set down covers, made to serve but were told by the general to go. As the door closed he said: 'Mary, I wonder if you would take something to Talbot?'

There came the soft sound of the rubbing of chair legs on the carpet, then Kennedy's voice, saying: 'If I might be permitted, sir?'

'Thank you, Kennedy. Just a minute while my

daughter serves it out.' By and by the curtain was pushed to one side and Kennedy carefully laid a plate in front of me. Beside the plate he laid a small blue leather-covered book, straightened, looked at me expressionlessly and left.

He was gone before I had realized the significance of what he had done. He knew very well that whatever concessions in freedom of movement the general had gained did not apply to me, I was going to be under eye and gun for sixty seconds every minute, sixty minutes every hour and that our last chance for talking was gone. But not our last chance for communication, not with that little book lying around.

It wasn't strictly a book, it was that cross between a diary and an account book, with a tiny pencil stuck in the loop of leather, which garages and car-dealers dole out in hundreds of thousands, usually at Christmas time, to the more solvent of their customers. Nearly all chauffeurs carried one for entering up in the appropriate spaces the cost of petrol, oil, services, repairs, mileage and fuel consumption. None of those things interested me: all that interested me was the empty spaces in the diary pages and the little blue pencil.

With one eye on the book and one on the curtain and both ears attuned to the voices and sounds beyond that curtain I wrote steadily for the better part of five minutes, feeding myself blindly with fork in the left hand while with my right I tried to set down in the briefest time and the shortest compass everything I wanted to tell Kennedy. When I was finished I felt reasonably satisfied: there was still a great deal left to chance but it was the best I could do. Accepting of chances was the essence of this game.

Perhaps ten minutes after I had finished writing Kennedy brought me in a cup of coffee. The book was nowhere to be seen, but he didn't hesitate, his hand went straight under the crumpled napkin in front of me, closed over the little book and slid it smoothly inside his tunic. I was beginning to have a great deal of confidence indeed in Simon Kennedy.

Five minutes later Vyland and Royale marched me back to the other side of the rig. Negotiating the hurricane blast that swept across the open well-deck was no easier this time than it had been the last, and in the intervening half-hour the darkness had deepened until it was almost as black as night.

At twenty past three I dropped once more down into the bathyscaphe and pulled the hatch cover tight behind me.

TEN

At half-past six I left the bathyscaphe. I was glad
to leave. If you have no work to occupy you –
and apart from a task lasting exactly one minute I
hadn't done a stroke that afternoon – the interior
of a bathyscaphe has singularly little to offer in the
way of entertainment and relaxation. I left Cibatti
to screw down the hatch in the floor of the pillar
and climbed alone up the hundred and eighty iron
rungs to the compartment at the top. Royale was
there, alone.

'Finished, Talbot?' he asked.

'All I can do down there. I need paper, pencil,
the book of instructions and if I'm right – and I
think I am – I can have those engines going within
five minutes of getting down there again. Where's
Vyland?'

'The general called for him five minutes ago.'
Good old general, dead on the dot. 'They've gone
off somewhere – I don't know where.'

It doesn't matter. This'll only take me half an

hour at the most. You can tell him we'll be ready to go shortly after seven. Now I want some paper and peace and quiet for my calculations. Where's the nearest place?'

'Won't this do?' Royale asked mildly. 'I'll get Cibatti to fetch some paper.'

'If you imagine I'm going to work with Cibatti giving me the cold cod eye all the time you're mistaken.' I thought a moment. 'We passed a regular office a few yards along the passage on the way back here. It was open. Proper desk and everything, all the paper and rules I need.'

'What's the harm?' Royale shrugged and stood aside to let me pass. As I went out Cibatti emerged through the trunking from the pillar and before we'd gone ten feet along the passage I heard the solid thudding home of a bolt, the turning of a key in the lock behind us. Cibatti took his keeper of the castle duties very seriously indeed.

Halfway along the passage an opened door led into a small, fairly comfortable room. I looked over my shoulder at Royale, saw his nod and went in. The room looked as if it had been used as an architect's office, for there were a couple of large drawing boards on easels topped by strip lighting. I passed those up in favour of a big leather-covered desk with a comfortable armchair behind it.

Royale looked round the room the way Royale would always look round a room. It was impossible to imagine Royale sitting down anywhere with his back to a door, overlooked by a window or with light in his eyes. He would have behaved the same in a children's nursery. In this case, however, he seemed to be examining the room more with an eye to its qualification as a prison, and what he saw must have satisfied him: apart from the doorway through which he had just entered, the only other point of egress from the room was through the plate-glass window that overlooked the sea. He picked a chair directly under the central overhead light, lit a cigarette and sat there quietly, the lamplight gleaming off his dark blond slick hair, his expressionless face in shadow. He was no more than six feet from me and he had nothing in his hands and could have had that little black gun out and two little holes drilled through me before I covered half the distance towards his chair. Besides, violence wasn't on the cards just then: not, at least, for me.

I spent ten minutes in scribbling down figures on a sheet of paper, fiddling with a slide rule, consulting a wiring diagram and getting nowhere at all. I didn't conceal the fact that I was getting nowhere at all. I clicked my tongue in impatience, scratched my head with the end of my pencil, compressed my lips and looked with mounting irritation at the walls, the door, the window. But mostly I looked in irritation at Royale. Eventually he got it – he would have been hard pressed not to get it.

'My presence here bothering you, Talbot?'

'What? Well no, not exactly – I just don't seem to be getting –'

'Not working out as easily as you thought it would, eh?'

I stared at him in irritable silence. If he wasn't going to suggest it I would have to, but he saved me the trouble.

'Maybe I'm just as anxious as you to get this thing over. I guess you're one of those characters who don't like distraction. And I seem to be distracting you.' He rose easily to his feet, glanced at the paper in front of me, picked up his chair with one hand and made for the door. 'I'll wait outside.'

I said nothing, just nodded briefly. He took the key from the inside of the door, went out into the passage, shut the door and locked it. I got up, crossed to the door on cat feet and waited.

I didn't have to wait long. Within a minute I heard the sound of feet walking briskly along the passage outside, the sound of somebody saying, 'Sorry, Mac' in a pronounced and unmistakably American accent and then, almost in the same instant, the solid, faintly hollow sounding impact of a heavy blow that had me wincing in vicarious suffering. A moment later the key turned in the lock, the door opened and I helped drag a heavy load into the room.

The load was Royale and he was out, cold as a flounder. I hauled him inside while the oilskinned figure who'd lifted him through the door reversed the key and turned it in the lock. At once he started throwing off sou'wester, coat and leggings, and beneath everything his maroon uniform was as immaculate as ever.

'Not at all bad,' I murmured. 'Both the sap and the American accent. You'd have fooled me.'

'It fooled Royale.' Kennedy bent and looked at the already purpling bruise above Royale's temple. 'Maybe I hit him too hard.' He was as deeply concerned as I would have been had I accidentally trodden on a passing tarantula. 'He'll live.'

'He'll live. It must have been a long deferred pleasure for you.' I had shed my own coat and was struggling into the oilskin rig-out as fast as I could. 'Everything fixed? Get the stuff in the workshop?'

'Look, Mr Talbot,' he said reproachfully, 'I had three whole hours.'

'Fair enough. And if our friend here shows any sign of coming to?'

'I'll just kind of lean on him again,' Kennedy said dreamily.

I grinned and left. I'd no idea how long the general could detain Vyland on whatever spurious errand he'd called him away, but I suspected it wouldn't be very long; Vyland was beginning to become just that little bit anxious about the time factor. Maybe I hadn't done myself any good by pointing out that the government agents might only be waiting for the weather to moderate before coming out to question the general, but with Vyland pointing his gun at me and threatening to kill me I had to reach out and grasp the biggest straw I could find.

The wind on the open well-deck shrieked and gusted as powerfully as ever, but its direction had changed and I had to fight my way almost directly against it. It came from the north now and I knew then that the centre of the hurricane must have passed somewhere also to the north of us, curving in on Tampa. It looked as if the wind and the seas might begin to moderate within a few hours. But, right then, the wind was as strong as it had ever been and on my way across I had my head and shoulders so far hunched into the wind that I was looking back the way I came. I fancied, in the near darkness, that I saw a figure clawing its way along the life-line behind me, but I paid no attention. People were probably using that line all day long.

The time for circumspection, for the careful reconnoitring of every potential danger in my path, was past. It was all or nothing now. Arrived at the other side I strode down the long corridor where I had whispered to Kennedy earlier in the afternoon, turned right at its end instead of left as we had done before, stopped to orientate myself and headed in the direction of the broad companionway which, Mary had said, led up to the actual drilling deck itself. There were several people wandering around, one of the open doors I passed gave on to a recreation room full of blue smoke and crowded with men: obviously all work on drilling and the upper deck was completely stopped. It didn't worry the drillers, their ten-day tour of duty was paid from the time they left shore till they set foot on it again, and it didn't worry me for it was to the working deck I was going and the absence of all traffic that I'd find up there would make my task all the easier.

Rounding another corner I all but cannoned into a couple of people who seemed to be arguing rather vehemently about something or other: Vyland and the general. Vyland was the man who was doing the talking but he broke off to give me a glare as I apologized for bumping him and continued down the passage. I was certain he could not have recognized me, my sou'wester had been pulled right down to my eyes, the high flyaway collar of my oilskin was up to my nose and, best disguise of all, I had dispensed with my limp, but for all that I had the most uncomfortable sensation between the shoulder blades until I had rounded another corner and was lost to their sight. I wasn't sure whether this obvious argument between the general and Vyland was a good thing or not. If the general had managed to get him deeply interested in some controversial subject of immediate and personal importance to them both, then well and good; but if Vyland had been expostulating over what he regarded as some unnecessary delay, things might get very rough indeed. If he got back to the other side of the rig before I did, I didn't like to think what the consequences would be. So I didn't think about them. Instead, I broke into a run, regardless of the astonished looks from

270

passers-by at a complete loss to understand the reason for this violent activity on what was in effect a well-paid holiday; reached the companion way and went up two steps at a time.

Mary, tightly wrapped in a hooded plastic raincoat, was waiting behind the closed doors at the top of the steps. She shrank back and gave a little gasp as I stopped abruptly in front of her and pulled down the collar of my oilskin for a moment to identify myself.

'You!' She stared at me. 'You – your bad leg – what's happened to your limp?'

'Never had one. Local colour. Guaranteed to fool the most suspicious. Kennedy told you what I wanted you for?'

'A – a watchdog. To keep guard.'

'That's it. I don't want a bullet or a knife in my back in that radio shack. Sorry it had to be you, but there was no one else. Where's the shack?'

'Through the door.' She pointed. 'About fifty feet that way.'

'Come on.' I grabbed the door handle, incautiously twisted it open, and if I hadn't had a strong grip on it I'd have been catapulted head over heels to the foot of the stairs. As it was, the hammerblow blast of that shrieking wind smashed both door and myself back against the bulkhead with a force that drove all the breath out of my lungs in an explosive gasp and would possibly have stunned me if the sou'wester hadn't cushioned the impact as the back of my head struck painfully against the steel. For a moment I hung there, my head a kaleidoscopic whirl of shooting colour, bent double against the hurricane force of the wind, whooping painfully as I fought to overcome the shock of the blow and the sucking effect of the wind and to draw some breath into my aching lungs: then I straightened up and lurched out through the door, pulling Mary behind me. Twice I tried to heave the door close, but against the sustained pressure of that wind I couldn't even pull it halfway to. I gave it up. They could, and no doubt very shortly would, send up a platoon from below and heave it shut: I had more urgent things to attend to.

It was a nightmare of a night. A dark howling nightmare. I screwed my eye almost shut against the hurricane-driven knife-lash of the rain and stared up into the black sky. Two hundred feet above my head I could just distinguish the inter-mittent flicker of the derrick-top aircraft warning lights, utterly unnecessary on a night such as this unless there were some lunatic pilots around, and quite useless as far as giving any illumination at deck-level was concerned. The absence of light was a mixed blessing but on the whole, I felt, favour-able: I might run into dangerous, even crippling obstacles because I couldn't see where I was going but on the other hand no one else could see where I was going either.

Arm in arm we lurched and staggered across the deck like a couple of drunks, heading for a square patch of light shining on the deck from a concealed window. We reached a door on the south side, on the near corner and sheltered from the wind, and I was on the point of bending down and having a squint through the keyhole when Mary caught the handle, pushed the door and walked into a small unlit corridor. Feeling rather foolish, I straightened and followed. She pulled the door softly to.

'The entrance door is on the far end on the right,' she whispered. She'd reached both arms up round my neck to murmur in my ear, her voice couldn't have been heard a foot away. 'I think there's someone inside.'

I stood stock still and listened, with her arms still round my neck. Given a more favourable time I could have stayed there all night, but the time wasn't favourable. I said: 'Couldn't it be that they just leave that light on to guide the operator to the shack when his call-up bell rings?'

'I thought I heard a movement,' she whispered.

'No time to play it safe. Stay out in the passage,' I murmured. 'It'll be all right.' I gave her hands a reassuring squeeze as I disengaged them from my neck, reflecting bitterly that Talbot luck was running typically true to form, padded up the passage, opened the door and walked into the radio room.

For a moment I stood there blinking in the brightness of the light, but not blinking so fast that I couldn't see a big burly character sitting at the radio table whirling round in his seat as the door opened. And even if I couldn't have seen him I'd

273

still have heard him a split second later as he sent his seat toppling backward with a crash and leapt to his feet, spinning so as to face me, with a speed so remarkable in so big a man. In so very big a man. He was taller than I was, a good bit wider, heavier and younger: he had that blue-jowled, black-eyed, black-haired very tough face that you occasionally see in first or second generation Italian-Americans and if he was a genuine radio-man I was the Queen of Sheba.

'What's all the panic about?' I demanded shortly. It was my best American accent and it was terrible. 'The boss has a message for you.'

'What boss?' he asked softly. A build like a heavy-weight champion and a face to match doesn't necessarily mean a mind like a moron and this boy was no moron.

'Let's have a look at your face, Mac.'

'What the hell's bitin' you?' I demanded. I turned down the collar of my coat. 'Is that what you want?'

'Now the hat,' he said quietly.

I took off the hat and flung it in his face just as I heard him spit out the solitary word 'Talbot!' I was into a dive even as I threw the hat and I hit him fair and square in the middle with the point of my left shoulder. It was like hitting the trunk of a tree, but he wasn't as well anchored as a tree and he went over.

His head and shoulders crashed against the far wall with a crash that shook the radio shack to its metal foundations. That should have been that, but it wasn't, I would have sworn that boy didn't even blink. He brought up one knee in a vicious jab that would have been a sad farewell for me had it landed where it had been intended to land. It didn't, it caught me on the chest and upper arm, but even so it had sufficient power behind it to knock me over on one side and the next moment we were rolling across the floor together, punching, kicking, clawing, and gouging. The Marquess of Queensberry wouldn't have liked it at all.

I was under two big disadvantages. The heavy oilskins hampered my movements, and although they helped absorb some of the impact of his jolting short-arm jabs they also, because of their constricting effect, robbed my own blows of much of their power, and while he was obviously more than willing to turn the entire radio shack into a shambles of broken furniture and fittings, that was the last thing I wanted: everything, literally everything, depended on my keeping that radio intact. And we both rolled against the radio table now, myself underneath, where I could have a good view of one of the legs splintering and caving in under the combined weight of our bodies against it.

I wasn't feeling any too good by this time. I had just the evidence of my own eyes to show me that this lad was only equipped with arms and fists just like anyone else and not a couple of flexible sledge-hammers which was what it felt like, but the sight of that tottering radio table made me desperate. A particularly vicious clubbing blow to the lower ribs didn't make it at all hard for me to gasp out in pain and fall back limply on the floor, and while he was taking advantage of my co-operation and time off to wind up his right sledge-hammer to drive me through the floor I brought up my knee and simultaneously chopped him across the exposed neck with the edge of my right hand and all the power those hampering oilskins would permit.

By all the rules he should have gone out like a light, only he had never read any of the rules. But I had hurt him, though: the grunt of agony was as genuine as mine had been faked, and he was momentarily dazed – just long enough to let me squirm out from under and roll over and over until I brought up against the half-open doorway through which I had entered. I might have nailed him then, back where we had been, but I wasn't going to take even the chance of touching the few splintered pieces of table leg which were all that kept the transmitter from crashing on to the steel deck.

He was tough, all right. By the time I was on my feet he was on his, shaken, but still on his feet. For a moment I thought he had lost all taste for the hand to hand stuff, the heavy wooden chair he had picked up and was bringing whistling over his shoulder certainly made it seem so, but when I ducked and heard the chair smash to pieces on the door jamb behind, it turned out that this was only his long-range artillery bombardment and that the assault troops were moving in later. Later, in this case, was almost right away, but I managed to avoid his wild flailing bull-rush and whirled round to meet his next charge.

It never came. He was crouching there, facing me, teeth showing and his eyes a couple of wicked slits in his dark Latin face, hands pressed against the wall behind him ready to help him in his take-off, when I saw a slender wrist appearing in the doorway behind him, high up. At the end of the wrist was a white-gloved hand and gripped in the hand was a broken chair-leg.

Mary Ruthven hit him as I would have taken long odds that she would hit him – a hesitant experimental tap on the head that wouldn't have dazed a cockroach – but for all that it had the galvanic effect of an electric shock. He whipped his head round to locate the source of this fresh threat and as he did I moved in with two long steps and hit him with everything I had on the neck, just below the ear, my knuckles socketing solidly into the hollow behind the back of his left jawbone.

One of the most deadly blows in boxing, it could easily have dislocated his jaw or broken his neck, and with any normal man might well have done just that. But he was phenomenally tough. He crashed back against the steel bulkhead and started to slide down towards the floor, eyes unfocused in his head, but even as he slid he made a last despairing effort to fling himself at me and wrap his arms around my legs to bring me down. But his co-ordination, his timing were gone. I had time to step back as his face came down near my right foot. I saw no reason why I shouldn't bring the two into contact and every reason why I should, so I did.

He lay spread-eagled face downwards on the floor, silent and still. I was far from silent myself, my breath was coming in great heaving gasps as if I had just run a mile, and I hadn't even run a hundred yards in years. My arms, my hands, my face were wet with sweat, and it was this that made me think to get out a handkerchief and rub it all over my face. But there was no blood there, and I couldn't feel any bruise. It would have been very difficult indeed to explain away a black eye or a bleeding nose to Vyland when I met him later. I tucked the handkerchief away and looked at the girl in the doorway. The hand that still held the chair-leg was trembling slightly, her eyes wide, her lips pale and what little expression there was on her face couldn't easily have been misconstrued as the beginnings of a worshipping admiration.

'Did you – did you have to use your boot?' she asked shakily.

'What did you expect me to use?' I asked savagely. 'The palm of my hand to smooth his fevered brow? Be your age, lady. That guy never heard of little Lord Fauntleroy, he'd have chopped me into

278

bits and fed me to the barracuda if he'd had half the chance. Now, just you stand by with your shillelagh there and clout him if he bats an eyelid – but hard, this time. Not,' I added hastily, lest she suspect me of being thought ungracious, 'that I'm not grateful for what you've already done.'

I turned round, already a precious minute had been lost since I had come into the shack, and found what I was looking for right away. Several pegs on the walls were festooned with tightly-rolled coils of wire and flex, material for antenna leads and radio repairs. I picked a nice flexible roll of flex and within one minute I had the radio operator trussed like a chicken ready for the broiler, passed a slip knot round his neck and tied the end of it to a cupboard handle. There could only be some bells or pushes or phones he might try to reach but he'd soon give up when he found that all he was doing was strangling himself. I gave the matter of a gag only a passing thought: there may be those who know how to draw a happy median line between suffocating a man and making a gag loose enough to permit breathing without at the same time letting the victim be heard a hundred miles away, but I'm not one of them. Besides, with that great hurricane howling outside he could holler away till he got laryngitis and nobody below deck would ever hear him.

I reached for the only other chair in the shack and sat down before the radio. It was a standard aircraft-type transmitter, I knew it well and I knew how to operate it. I switched on, tuned it on the wavelength the sheriff had given me through Kennedy and clamped on a pair of headphones. I wouldn't have long to wait, I knew that: the police were keeping a twenty-four hour watch on their short-wave receivers. Within three seconds of the end of my call-up sign the headphones crackled in my ears.

'Police headquarters. Sheriff Prendergast here. Please go ahead.'

I threw the transmitter switch from manual to microphone.

'Car Nineteen reporting.' The agreed subterfuge wasn't necessary for identification, every police car in the county had been warned to stay off the air and the sheriff knew it could only be me: but in these days of enthusiastic radio hams airwave eavesdroppers abound and I wouldn't have put it past Vyland's organization to maintain a perma-nent listening watch on the police wavelengths. I continued: 'Suspect answering to description detained near Ventura crossroads. Shall we bring him in?'

'Negative,' the voice crackled. A pause. 'We've found our man. Please release suspect.'

I felt as if someone had given me a million dol-lars. Almost without realizing it I relaxed heavily against the back-rest of the chair, the strain of the keyed-up tension of the past forty-eight hours had been far greater than I had realized. The sheer mental relief, the depth of satisfaction I experienced then surpassed anything I had ever known.

'Car Nineteen,' I said again. Even to myself my voice didn't sound quite steady. 'Would you repeat that, please?'

'Release your suspect,' Prendergast said slowly and distinctly. 'We have found our man. Repeat, we have found –'

The transmitter leapt backwards about two inches, a great jagged hole appeared in the centre of the tuning band and the radio shack seemed to explode about my ears so deafening, so shattering was the effect of a heavy gun being fired in that confined space.

I didn't jump more than a couple of feet and after I came down I got to my feet the normal way, but slowly, carefully. I didn't want anyone getting too nervous, and whoever had pulled that stupid trick, unnecessarily smashing the set and tipping off the cops that something had gone wrong, was very nervous indeed. Almost as nervous as I felt as I turned slowly round and saw who my guest was.

It was Larry and the smoking Colt in his hand was lined up, as nearly as his shaking hand would permit, on a spot somewhere between my eyes. It looked as large as a howitzer. His lank black hair was plastered wetly over his forehead, and the coal-black eye behind that wavering barrel was jerking and burning and crazy as a loon's. One eye. I couldn't see the other, I couldn't see any part of him except half his face, his gun-hand and a left forearm crooked round Mary Ruthven's neck. The rest of him was completely hidden behind the girl. I looked at her reproachfully.

'Fine watchdog you are,' I said mildly.

'Shut up!' Larry snarled. 'A cop, eh? A john. A dirty crawling double-crossing screw!' He called me several names, all unprintable, his voice a venomous hiss of hate.

'There's a young lady here, friend,' I murmured.

'Lady? A – tramp.' He tightened his grip around her neck as if it gave him pleasure and I guessed he had at some time mistakenly tried to make time with her and the roof had fallen in on him. 'Thought you were clever, Talbot didn't you? You thought you knew all the answers, you thought you had us all fooled, didn't you, cop? But you didn't have me fooled, Talbot. I've been watching you, I've been following you every second since we came out to the rig.' He was jazzed up to the eyebrows, shaking and jumping as if he had the St Vitus's Dance, and his voice held all the venomous and vindictive triumph of the consistently ignored and derided nonentity who has been proved right in the end while all those who despise him have been proved wrong. It was Larry's night to sing, and he wasn't going to miss out on a single note. But I had listened to pleasanter voices.

'Didn't know that *I* knew that you were in cahoots with Kennedy, did you, cop?' he went ranting on. 'And with this tramp. I was watching you when you came up from the bathyscaphe ten minutes ago, I saw that smooth-talking chauffeur give it to Royale on the head and –'

'How did you know it was Kennedy?' I interrupted. 'He was dressed up –'

'I listened outside the door, mug! I could have finished you off there and then, but I wanted to see what you were up to. Think *I* care if Royale gets sapped down?' He broke off suddenly and swore as the girl went limp on him. He tried to hold her up but heroin is no substitute for protein when it comes to building muscle and even her slight weight was too much for him. He could have lowered her gently, but he didn't: he stood back abruptly and let her collapse heavily on the floor.

I took half a step forward, fists clenched till they hurt, murder in my heart. Larry bared his teeth and grinned at me like a wolf.

'Come and get it, copper. Come and get it,' he whispered. I looked from him to the floor and back again and my hands slowly unclenched. 'Scared, aren't you, copper? Yellow, aren't you, copper? Sweet on her, aren't you, copper? Just like that pansy Kennedy is sweet on her.' He laughed, a high falsetto giggle carrying the overtones of madness. 'I'm afraid a little accident is going to happen to Kennedy when I get back over to the other side. Who's going to blame me for gunning him down when I see him sapping Royale?'

'All right,' I said wearily. 'You're a hero and a great detective. Let's go see Vyland and get it over with.'

'We're going to get it over with,' he nodded. His voice was suddenly very quiet and I think I liked it even less that way. 'But you're not going to see Vyland, copper, you're never going to see anyone again. I'm going to kill you, Talbot. I'm letting you have it now.'

My mouth felt as if someone had gone over it with a roll of high-absorbency blotting-paper. I could feel the slow heavy beat of my heart and the sweat coming on the palms of my hands. He meant every word he said. He was going to squeeze the trigger of that heavy Colt and if he lived to be a hundred nothing would ever give him half so much pleasure again. Finish. But I managed to keep my voice steady.

'So you're going to kill me,' I said slowly. 'Why?'

'Because I hate your lousy rotten stinking guts, Talbot, that's why,' he whispered, a whisper with a shake in it, a horrible sound. 'Because you've ridden me and laughed at me from the moment we met, hophead this, junky that, always asking about my syringe. Because you're sweet on this dame here and if I can't get her no one will. And because I hate cops.'

He didn't like me, I could see that. Even when he wasn't talking his mouth was working and twitching like an epileptic's. He just told me things that I knew he'd never tell another, and I knew why. Dead men tell no tales. And that's what I'd be any second now. Dead. Dead as Herman Jablonsky. Jablonsky in two feet of earth, Talbot in 130 feet of water, not that it made any difference where you slept when it was all over. And it made things no better to reflect that the end was going to come at the hands of a quivering mass of doped-up neuroses disguised as a human being.

'You're going to let me have it now?' My eye never lifted off that jumping trigger finger.

'That's it.' He giggled. 'In the guts, low down, so I can watch you flop around for a while. You'll scream and you'll scream and you'll scream and no one will ever hear it. How do you like it, copper?'

'Hophead,' I said softly. I'd nothing to lose.

'What?' His face was a mask of disbelief. He went into a crouch over his gun that would have been laughable in different circumstances. It wasn't any strain at all not to laugh. 'What did you say, copper?'

'Junky,' I said distinctly. 'You're all doped up so that you don't know what you're doing. What are you going to do with the body?' It was the first time I'd ever thought of myself as a corpse and I didn't care for the feeling very much. 'Two of you couldn't lift me out of here and if they find me shot in this cabin they'll know it was you who did it and than you'll be in for the high jump, because they still need my services very badly, more than ever. You won't be popular, Larry boy.'

He nodded cunningly as if he had just thought up all this himself.

'That's right, copper,' he murmured. 'I can't

shoot you in here, can I? We'll have to go outside, won't we, copper? Near the edge, where I can shoot you and shove you into the sea.'

'That's it,' I agreed. This was macabre, this arrangement for my own tidy disposal, but I wasn't going as crazy as Larry, I was gambling on my last hope. But the gamble was crazy enough.

'And then they'll be running around and looking for you,' Larry said dreamily. 'And I'll be running around and looking for you too and all the time I'll be laughing to myself and thinking about you and the barracuda down among the seaweed there and knowing that I'm smarter than any one of them.'

'You have a charming mind,' I said.

'Haven't I now?' Again that high falsetto giggle and I could feel the hairs rise on the back of my neck. He poked at Mary with his foot, but she didn't stir. 'The dame will keep till I come back. I won't be long, will I, copper? Come on. You first. And don't forget I have a torch and a gun.'

'I'm not likely to forget.'

Neither Mary nor the radio operator had stirred. I was pretty sure that the operator wouldn't stir for a long time, I could still feel the ache in my fist and foot. But I wasn't at all sure about Mary, I wasn't even sure that she wasn't faking, her breathing seemed much too quick and irregular for an unconscious person.

'Come on, now,' Larry said impatiently. He thrust the gun painfully into the small of my back. 'Out.'

I went out, through the door, along the passage and through the outer door on to the wind- and rain-swept deck beyond. The outer door had opened on the sheltered side of the radio shack but in a moment we would be exposed to the pile-driving blast of that wind and I knew that when that moment came it would be then or never.

It was then. Urged on by the revolver in my back I moved round the corner of the shack, crouched low and barrelling forward into that great wind as soon as it struck me. Larry wasn't so prepared, not only was he slightly built but he was standing upright, and the sudden wavering and jerking of the torch beam on the deck by my feet was intimation enough to me that the wind had caught him off-balance, perhaps sent him staggering several feet backward. I lowered my head still farther until I was in the position of a hundred yards sprinter in the first two steps of the race and lurched forward into the wind.

Almost at once I realized that I had miscalculated. I had miscalculated the strength of the wind, running into that hurricane was like running through a barrel of molasses. And I had also forgotten that while a seventy-mile-an-hour wind offers an almost insuperable resistance to a human being it offers relatively none to a heavy slug from a Colt with a muzzle velocity of 600 mph.

I'd got maybe eight yards when the frantically searching torch beam picked me up and steadied on me, and managed to cover perhaps another two before Larry fired.

Gangsters and hoodlums are notoriously the world's worst marksmen, their usual method being to come within a couple of yards before firing or spraying the landscape with a sufficient hail of bullets to make the law of averages work for them and I had heard a hundred times that those boys couldn't hit a barn door at ten paces. But maybe Larry had never heard of this, or maybe the rule applied only to barn doors.

A mule-kick is nothing compared to the slamming stopping power of a forty-five. It caught me high up on the left shoulder and spun me round in a complete circle before dropping me in my tracks. But it was this that saved my life, even as I fell I felt the sharp tug on my oilskin collar as another slug passed through it. Those weren't warning shots that Larry was firing: he was out to kill.

And kill he would if I had remained another couple of seconds on that deck. Again I heard the muffled boom of the Colt – even at ten yards I could hardly hear it over the howling power of that wind – and saw sparks strike off the deck inches from my face and heard the screaming whirr of the spent bullets ricocheting off into the darkness of the night. But the sparks gave me hope, it meant that Larry was using full metal-jacketed slugs, the kind cops use for firing through car bodies and locked doors, and that made an awful sight cleaner wound than a mushrooming soft-nose. Maybe it had passed clear through the shoulder.

I was on my feet and running again. I couldn't see where I was running to and I didn't care, all that mattered was running from. A blinding, bulleting gust of rain whistled across the deck and made me shut both eyes tight and I loved it. If I had my eyes shut so had Larry.

Still with my eyes shut I bumped into a metal ladder. I grabbed it to steady myself and before I properly realized what I was doing I was ten feet off the ground and climbing steadily. Maybe it was just man's age-old instinct to climb high to get out of danger that started me off but it was the realization that this ladder must lead to some sort of platform where I might fend off Larry that kept me going.

It was a wicked, exhausting climb. Normally, even in that giant wind, it wouldn't have given me so much trouble, but, as it was, I was climbing completely one-handed. My left shoulder didn't hurt much, it was still too numb for that, the real pain would come later, but for the moment the entire arm seemed paralysed, and every time I released a rung with my right hand and grabbed for the one above, the wind pushed me out from the ladder so that my fingers hooked round the next rung usually at the full extent of my arm. Then I had to pull myself close with my one good arm and start the process all over again. After I'd climbed about forty rungs my right arm and shoulder were beginning to feel as if they were on fire.

I took a breather, hooked my forearm over a rung and looked down. One look was enough. I forgot about the pain and weariness and started climbing faster than ever, hunching my way upwards like a giant koala bear. Larry was down there at the foot of the ladder, flickering his torch in all directions and even with that bird-brain of his it was only going to be a matter of time until it occurred to him to shine that torch upwards.

It was the longest ladder I had ever climbed. It seemed endless, and I knew now that it must be some part of the drilling derrick, the ladder, I was now almost sure, that led up to the 'monkey board,' that narrow shelf where a man guided the half-ton sections of the drill pipe, as it came from the ground, into the storage-racks behind. The only thing I could remember about the monkey was the cheerless fact that it was devoid of hand-rails – those would only get in the way of the man guiding the heavy drill sections into place.

A jarring vibrating clang as if the iron ladder had been struck by a sledge-hammer was Larry's way of announcing that he had caught sight of me. The bullet had struck the rung on which my foot rested and for one bad moment I thought it had gone through my foot. When I realized it hadn't I took another quick look down.

Larry was coming up after me. I couldn't see him, but I could see the torch clutched in one hand making regularly erratic movements as he swarmed his way up the ladder making about three times the speed I was. It wasn't in character this, Larry could never have been accused of having an excess of courage: either he was loaded to the eyes or he was driven by fear – fear that I should escape and Vyland find out that he had been trying to murder me. And there was the further possibility, and a very strong one, that Larry had only one or two shells left in his gun: he couldn't afford not to make those count.

I became gradually aware of lightness above and around me. I thought at first that this must be a glow cast from the aircraft warning lights in the top of the derrick, but in the same instant as the thought occurred I knew it to be wrong: the top of the derrick was still over a hundred feet above where I was. I took another breather, screwed my eyes almost shut against the stinging lash of the rain and peered upwards into the murky gloom.

There was a platform not ten feet above my head, with a light shining off feebly to the right. It wasn't much of a light, but enough to let me see something of the dark maze of girders that was the derrick, enough to let me see a dark shadow above and also to the right which looked like some tiny cabin. And then Larry's torch steadied and shone vertically upwards and I saw something that made me feel slightly sick: the platform above was not solid sheet-metal but open grille-work through which a person's every move could be

291

seen: gone were my hopes of waiting till Larry's head appeared above the level of the platform and then kicking it off his shoulders.

I glanced downwards. Larry was no more than ten feet below, and both his gun and torch were levelled on me, I could see the dull glint of light in the barrel and the dark hole in the middle where death hid. One little pull on the trigger finger and that dark hole would be a streaking tongue of fire in the darkness of the night. Curtains for Talbot. I wondered vaguely, stupidly, if my eyes would have time to register the bright flame before the bullet and the oblivion it carried with it closed my eyes for ever . . . And then, slowly, I realized that Larry wasn't going to fire, not even Larry was crazy enough to fire, not then. The 185-pound deadweight of my falling body would have brushed him off that ladder like a fly and from that ten-storey height neither of us would have bounced off that steel deck enough so that anyone would notice.

I kept on climbing and reached the top. Had it been a solid platform there and I don't think I would have managed to pull myself on to it against that wind, my one good hand would just have scrabbled about on the smooth metal surface until exhaustion took me and I fell back off the ladder: but as it was I managed to hook my fingers in the openwork steel grille and drag myself on to the platform.

Larry was close behind. He gestured with his

292

torch and I got his meaning. I moved to one side, past the little cabin at the corner where a lamp on a recessed shelf threw a faint light that was cut off abruptly at waist level, and waited.

Slowly, carefully, his eyes never leaving my face, Larry came over the top and straightened to his feet. I moved farther along the monkey-board, slowly, backwards, with my face to Larry. On my right I could dimly make out the big pipe storage racks, on my left the edge of the monkey board, no handrail, just a sheer drop of a hundred feet. Then I stopped. The gallery of the monkey-board seemed to run all the way round the outside of the derrick and it would have suited Larry just fine to have me out on the northern edge where, wind or no wind, a good shove – or a .45 slug – might have sent me tumbling direct into the sea a hundred and fifty feet below.

Larry came close to me. He'd switched off his torch now. The fixed light on the cabin side might leave the lowermost three feet in darkness, but it was enough for him and he wouldn't want to take even the remote chance of anyone spotting a flickering torchlight and wondering what any crazy person should be doing up on the monkey-board in that hurricane wind and with all the work stopped.

He halted three feet away. He was panting heavily and he had his wolf grin on again.

'Keep going, Talbot,' he shouted.

I shook my head. 'This is as far as I'm going.' I

hadn't really heard him, the response was purely automatic, I had just seen something that made me feel ice-cold, colder by far than the biting lash of that rain. I had thought, down in the radio shack, that Mary Ruthven had been playing possum, and now I knew I had been right. She had been conscious, she must have taken off after us immediately we had left. There was no mistaking at all that gleaming dark-blonde head, those heavily plaited braids that appeared over the top of the ladder and moved into the night.

You fool, I thought savagely, you crazy, crazy little fool. I had no thought for the courage it must have taken to make that climb, for the exhausting nightmare it must have been, even for the hope it held out for myself. I could feel nothing but bitterness and resentment and despair and behind all of those the dim and steadily growing conviction that I'd count the world well lost for Mary Ruthven.

'Get going,' Larry shouted again.

'So you can shove me into the sea? No.'

'Turn round.'

'So you can sap me with that gun and they find me lying on the deck beneath, no suspicion of foul play.' She was only two yards away now. 'Won't do, Larry boy. Shine your torch on my shoulder. My left shoulder.'

The flash clicked on and I heard again that maniac giggle.

'So I did get you, hey, Talbot?'

'You got me.' She was right behind him now,

that great wind had swept away any incautious sound she might have made. I had been watching her out of the corner of my eye, but now I suddenly looked straight at her over Larry's shoulder, my eyes widening in hope.

'Try again, copper,' Larry giggled. 'Can't catch me twice that way.'

Throw your arms round his neck or his legs, I prayed. Or throw your coat over his head. But don't, don't, don't go for his gun-hand.

She went for his gun-hand. She reached round his right side and I plainly heard the smack as her right hand closed over his right wrist.

For a moment Larry stood stock-still. Had he jumped or twisted or moved, I would have been on to him like an express train, but he didn't, the very unexpectedness of the shock temporarily petrified his gun hand too – it was still pointing straight at me.

And it was still levelled at my heart when he made a violent grab for Mary's right wrist with his left hand. A jerk up with his left hand, a jerk down with his right and his gun-hand was free. Then he moved a little to his left, jerked her forward a foot, pinned her against the storage racks to the right and started to twist her wrist away from him. He knew who he had now and the wolf grin was back on his face and those coal-black eyes and the gun were levelled on me all the time.

For five, maybe ten seconds, they stood there straining. Fear and desperation gave the girl strength she would never normally have had, but Larry too was desperate and he could bring far more leverage to bear. There was a half-stifled sob of pain and despair and she was on her knees before him, then on her side, Larry still holding her wrist. I couldn't see her now, only the faint sheen of her hair, she was below the level of the faint light cast by the lamp. All I could see was the madness in the face of the man opposite me, and the light shining from the shelf of the little cabin a few feet behind him. I lifted the heel of my right shoe off the ground and started to work my foot out of it with the help of my left foot. It wasn't even a chance.

'Come here, cop,' Larry said stonily. 'Come here or I'll give the girl friend's wrist just another little turn and then you can wave her goodbye.' He meant it, it would make no difference now, he knew he would have to kill her anyway. She knew too much. I moved two steps closer. My heel was out of the right shoe. He thrust the barrel of the Colt hard against my mouth, I felt a tooth break and the salt taste of blood from a gashed upper lip, on the inside. I twisted my face away, spat blood and he thrust the revolver deep into my throat.

'Scared, cop?' he said softly. His voice was no more than a whisper, but I heard it above the voice of that great wind, maybe it was true enough, this business of the abnormally heightened sensitivity of those about to die. And I was about to die. I was scared all right, I was scared right to the depths as I had never been scared before. My shoulder was beginning to hurt, and hurt badly, and I wanted to be sick, that damned revolver grinding into my throat was sending waves of nausea flooding through me. I drew my right foot back as far as I could without upsetting my balance. My right toe was hooked over the tongue of the shoe.

'You can't do it, Larry,' I croaked. The pressure on my larynx was agonizing, the gun-sight jabbing cruelly into the underside of my chin. 'Kill me and they'll never get the treasure.'

'I'm laughing.' He was, too, a horrible maniacal cackle. 'See me, cop, I'm laughing. I'd never see any of it anyway. Larry the junky never does. The white stuff, that's all my old man ever gives his ever-loving son.'

'Vyland?' I'd known for hours.

'My father. God damn his soul.' The gun shifted, pointed at my lower stomach. 'So long, cop.'

My right foot was already swinging forward, smoothly, accelerating, but unseen to Larry in the darkness.

'I'll tell him goodbye from you,' I said. The shoe clattered against the corrugated iron of the little hut even as I spoke.

Larry jerked his head to look over his right shoulder to locate the source of this fresh menace. For a split second of time, before he started to swing round again, the back of his left jawbone was exposed to me just as that of the radio operator had been only a few minutes before.

I hit him. I hit him as if he were a satellite and I

was going to send him into orbit round the moon. I hit him as if the lives of every last man, woman and child in the world depended on it. I hit him as I had never hit anyone in my life before, as I knew even as I did it that I could never hit anyone again.

There came a dull muffled snapping noise and the Colt fell from his hands and struck the grille at my feet. For two or three seconds Larry seemed to stand there poised, then, with the unbelievably slow, irrevocable finality of a toppling factory chimney, he fell out into space.

There was no terror-stricken screaming, no wild flailing of arms and legs as he fell to the steel deck a hundred feet below: Larry had been dead, his neck broken, even before he had started to fall.

ELEVEN

Eight minutes after Larry had died and exactly twenty minutes after I had left Kennedy and Royale in the cabin I was back there, giving the hurriedly prearranged knock. The door was unlocked, and I passed quickly inside. Kennedy immediately turned the key again while I looked down at Royale, spread-eagled and unconscious on the deck.

'How's the patient been?' I inquired. My breath was coming in heaving gasps, the exertions of the past twenty minutes and the fact that I'd run all the way back there hadn't helped my respiration any.

'Restive.' Kennedy grinned. 'I had to give him another sedative.' Then his eyes took me in and the smile slowly faded as he looked first at the blood trickling from my mouth then at the hole in the shoulder of the oilskin.

'You look bad. You're hurt. Trouble?'

I nodded. 'But it's all over now, all taken care of.' I was wriggling out of my oilskins as fast as I could

299

and I wasn't liking it at all. 'I got through on the radio. Everything is going fine. So far, that is.'

'Fine, that's wonderful.' The words were automatic, Kennedy was pleased enough to hear my news but he was far from pleased with the looks of me. Carefully, gently, he was helping me out of the oilskins and I heard the quick indrawing of breath as he saw where I'd torn my shirt-sleeve off at the shoulder, the red-stained wads of gauze with which Mary had plugged both sides of the wound – the bullet had passed straight through, missing the bone but tearing half the deltoid muscle away – in the brief minute we'd stopped in the radio shack after we'd come down that ladder again. 'My God, that must hurt.'

'Not much.' Not much it didn't there were a couple of little men, working on piece-time rates, perched on either side of my shoulder and sawing away with a crosscut as if their lives depended on it, and my mouth didn't feel very much better: the broken tooth had left an exposed nerve that sent violent jolts of pain stabbing up through my face and head every other second. Normally the combination would have had me climbing the walls: but today wasn't a normal day.

'You can't carry on like this,' Kennedy persisted. 'You're losing blood and –'

'Can anyone see that I've been hit in the teeth?' I asked abruptly.

He crossed to a wash-basin, wet a handkerchief and wiped my face clear of blood.

'I don't think so,' he said consideringly. 'Tomorrow your upper lip will be double size but it hasn't started coming up yet.' He smiled with humour. 'And as long as the wound in your shoulder doesn't make you laugh out loud no one can see that one of your teeth is broken.'

'Fine. That's all I need. You know I've got to do this.' I was slipping off the oilskin leggings and had to reposition the gun in my waistband. Kennedy, beginning to dress up in the oilskins himself, saw it.

'Larry's?'

I nodded.

'He did the damage?'

Another nod.

'And Larry?'

'He won't need any more heroin where he's gone.' I struggled painfully into my coat, more than ever grateful that I'd left it off before going. 'I broke his neck.'

Kennedy regarded me long and thoughtfully. 'You play kind of rough, don't you, Talbot?'

'Not half as rough as you'd have been,' I said grimly. 'He'd Mary on her hands and knees on the monkey-board of the derrick, a hundred feet above the deck, and he was proposing that she go down again without benefit of the ladder.'

He stopped in the middle of tying the last button on his oilskin, crossed in two quick strides, grabbed me by the shoulders then released them again at my quick exclamation of pain.

'Sorry, Talbot. Damn foolish of me.' His face wasn't as brown as usual, eyes and mouth were creased with worry. 'How – is she all right?'

'She's all right,' I said wearily. 'She'll be across here in ten minutes' time and you'll see for yourself. You'd better get going, Kennedy. They'll be back any minute.'

'That's right,' he murmured. 'Half an hour, the general said – it's nearly up. You – you're sure she's all right?'

'Sure I'm sure,' I said irritably, then at once regretted the irritation. This man I could get to like very much. I grinned at him. 'Never yet saw a chauffeur so worried about his employer.'

'I'm off,' he said. He didn't feel like smiling. He reached for a leather note-case lying beside my papers on the desk and thrust it into an inside pocket. 'Mustn't forget this. Unlock the door, will you, and see if the coast is clear?'

I opened the door, saw that it was clear and gave him the nod. He got his hands under Royale's armpits, dragged him through the doorway and dumped him unceremoniously in the passageway outside, beside the overturned chair. Royale was stirring and moaning: he would be coming to any moment now. Kennedy looked at me for a few moments, as if searching for something to say, then he reached out and tapped me lightly on the shoulder.

'Good luck, Talbot,' he murmured. 'I wish to God I was coming with you.'

302

'I wish you were,' I said feelingly. 'Don't worry, it's just about over now.' I wasn't even kidding myself, and Kennedy knew it. I nodded to him, went inside and closed the door. I heard Kennedy turn the key in the lock and leave it there. I listened, but I didn't even hear his footsteps as he left: for so big a man he was as silent as he was fast.

Now that I was alone, with nothing to do, the pain struck with redoubled force. The pain and the nausea came at me in alternate waves, I could feel the shore of consciousness advancing and receding, it would have been so easy just to let go. But I couldn't let go, not now. It was too late now. I would have given anything for some injection to kill the pain, something to see me through the next hour or so. I was almost glad when, less than two minutes after Kennedy had left, I heard the sound of approaching footsteps. We had cut things pretty fine. I heard an exclamation, the footsteps broke into a run and I went and sat behind my desk and picked up a pencil. The overhead light I had switched off and now I adjusted the angle extension lamp on the wall so that it shone directly overhead, throwing my face in deep shadow. Maybe, as Kennedy had said, my mouth didn't show that it had been hit but it certainly felt as if it showed and I didn't want to take any chances.

The key scraped harshly in the lock, the door crashed open and bounced off the bulkhead and a thug I'd never seen before, built along the same lines as Cibatti, jumped into the room. Hollywood had taught him all about opening doors in situations like this. If you damaged the panels or hinges or plaster on the wall it didn't matter, it was the unfortunate proprietor who had to pay up. In this case, as the door was made of steel, all he had damaged was his toe and it didn't require a very close student of human nature to see that there was nothing he would have liked better than to fire off that automatic he was waving in his hand. But all he saw was me, with a pencil in my hand and a mildly inquiring expression on my face. He scowled at me anyway, then turned and nodded to someone in the passageway.

Vyland and the general came in half-carrying a now conscious Royale. It did my heart good just to look at him as he sat heavily in a chair. Between myself a couple of nights ago and Kennedy tonight we had done a splendid job on him; it promised to be the biggest facial bruise I had ever seen. Already it was certainly the most colourful. I sat there and wondered with a kind of detached interest – for I could no longer afford to think of Royale with anything except detachment – whether the bruise would still be there when he went to the electric chair. I rather thought it would.

'You been out of this room this evening, Talbot?' Vyland was rattled and edgy and he was giving his urban top executive's voice a rest.

'Sure I dematerialized myself and oozed out

through the keyhole.' I gazed at Royale with interest. 'What's happened to the boyfriend? Derrick fall on him?'

'It wasn't Talbot.' Royale pushed away Vyland's supporting hand, fumbling under his coat and brought out his gun. His tiny deadly little gun, that would always be the first thought in Royale's mind. He was about to shove it back when a thought occurred to him and he broke open the magazine. Intact, all the deadly little cupro-nickel shells there. He replaced the magazine in the automatic and the gun in his holster and then, almost as an afterthought, felt in his inside breast pocket. There was a couple of flickers of his one good eye that a highly imaginative character might have interpreted as emotions of dismay, then relief, as he said to Vyland: 'My wallet. It's gone.'

'Your wallet?' There was no mistaking Vyland's feeling, it was one of pure relief. 'A hit-and-run thief!'

'Your wallet! On my rig? An outrage, a damnable outrage!' The old boy's moustache was waffling to and fro, he had the Method school whacked any day. 'God knows I hold no brief for you, Royale, but on my rig! I'll have a search instituted right away and the culprit –'

'You can save yourself the trouble, General,' I interrupted dryly. 'The culprit's got the money safely in his pants pocket and the wallet's at the bottom of the sea. Besides, anyone who takes money away from Royale deserves a medal.'

'You talk too much, friend,' Vyland said coldly. He looked at me in a thoughtful way I didn't like at all and went on softly: 'It could have been a cover-up, a red herring, maybe Royale was knocked out for some other reason altogether. A reason *you* might know something about, Talbot.'

I felt cold. Vyland was nobody's fool and I hadn't looked for this. If they got suspicious and started searching me and found either Larry's gun or the wound – and they would be bound to find both – then this was definitely Talbot's farewell appearance. Next moment I felt colder still. Royale said: 'Maybe it *was* a plant,' rose groggily to his feet, crossed over to my desk and stared down at the papers in front of me.

This was it. I remembered now the far too carefully casual glance Royale had given the papers as he had left the room. I'd covered maybe half a sheet with letters and figures before he had gone and hadn't added a single letter or figure since. It would be all the proof that Royale would ever want. I kept looking at his face, not daring to glance down at the papers, wondering how many bullets Royale could pump into me before I could even start dragging Larry's cannon from my waistband. And then, incredulously, I heard Royale speak.

'We're barking up the wrong tree. Talbot's in the clear, he's been working, Mr Vyland. Pretty well nonstop, I should say.'

I glanced at the papers in front of me. Where I'd left half a page of scribbled figures and letters there were now two and a half pages. They had been written with the same pen and it would have taken a pretty close look to see that they hadn't been written by the same hand – and it was upside down to Royale. The scribbled nonsense was as meaningless as my own had been, but it was enough, it was more than enough, it was my passport to life, given me by Kennedy, whose acute foresight in this case had far outstripped my own. I wished I had met Kennedy months ago.

'OK. So it's somebody short of cash.' Vyland was satisfied, the matter dismissed from his mind. 'How did you make out, Talbot? We're getting pushed for time.'

'No worry,' I assured him. 'All worked out. Guaranteed. Five minutes buttoning-up down in the scaphe and we're set to go.'

'Excellent.' Vyland looked pleased but that was only because he didn't know what I knew. He turned to the thug who had kicked the door open. 'The general's daughter and his chauffeur – you'll find them in the general's stateroom. They're to come here at once. Ready, Talbot?'

'Ready.' I got to my feet, a bit shakily, but compared to Royale I looked positively healthy and nobody noticed. 'I've had a long hard day, Vyland. I could do with something to fortify me before we go below.'

'I'll be surprised if Cibatti and his friends haven't enough supplies to stock a bar.' Vyland was seeing the end of the road, he was all good humour now. 'Come along.'

We trooped out into the corridor and along to the door of the room that gave access to the caisson. Vyland gave his secret knock – I was glad to note that it was still the same – and we went inside.

Vyland had been right, Cibatti and his friend did indeed do themselves well in the liquor line and by the time I had three stiff fingers of Scotch inside me the two little men sawing with the crosscut on my shoulder had given up the piece-work and were back on time rates and I no longer felt like banging my head against the wall. It seemed logical to expect that the improvement might be maintained if I poured myself another shot of anaesthetic and I'd just done this when the door opened and the thug Vyland had sent to the other side of the rig appeared, ushering in Mary and Kennedy. My heart had been through a lot that night, heavy overtime stuff to which it wasn't accustomed, but it only required one look at Mary and it started doing its handsprings again. My mind wasn't doing handsprings, though, I looked at her face and my mind was filled with all sorts of pleasant thoughts about what I'd like to do to Vyland and Royale. There were big bluish-dark patches under her eyes, and she looked white and strained and more than a little sick. I'd have taken any odds that that last half-hour with me had scared and shaken her as she'd never been scared and shaken before. It had certainly scared and shaken me enough. But neither Vyland nor Royale seemed to notice anything amiss, people forced to associate with them and not scared and shaken would be the exception rather than the rule.

Kennedy didn't look scared and shaken, he didn't look anything at all except the perfect chauffeur. But Royale wasn't any more fooled than I was. He turned to Cibatti and his side-kick and said: 'Just go over this bird here, will you, and see that he's not wearing anything that he shouldn't be wearing.'

Vyland gave him a questioning look.

'He may be as harmless as he looks – but I doubt it,' Royale explained. 'He's had the run of the rig this afternoon. He might just possibly have picked up a gun and if he has he might just possibly get the drop on Cibatti and the others when they weren't looking.' Royale nodded to the door in the convex wall. 'I just wouldn't fancy climbing a hundred feet up an iron ladder with Kennedy pointing a gun down the way all the time.'

They searched Kennedy and found nothing. Royale was smart all right, you could have put in your eye all the bits he missed. But he just wasn't smart enough. He should have searched me.

'We don't want to hurry you, Talbot,' Vyland said with elaborate sarcasm.

'Right away,' I said. I sent down the last of the anaesthetic, frowned owlishly at the notes in my hand, folded them away in a pocket and turned towards the entrance door to the pillar. I carefully avoided looking at Mary, the general or Kennedy.

Vyland touched me on my bad shoulder and if it hadn't been for the anaesthetic I'd have gone through the deckhead. As it was I jumped a couple of inches and the two lumberjacks on my shoulder started up again, sawing away more industriously than ever.

'Getting nervous, aren't we?' Vyland sneered. He nodded at a mechanism on the table, a simple solenoid switch that I'd brought up from the scaphe. 'Forgotten something, haven't you?'

'No. We won't be needing that any more.'

'Right, on your way. You first . . . Watch them real close, Cibatti, won't you?'

'I'll watch them, boss,' Cibatti assured him. He would, too, he'd bend his gun over the head of the first person to breathe too deeply. The general and Kennedy weren't going to pull any fast ones when Vyland and Royale were down there with me in the bathyscaphe, they'd stay there under gun-point until we returned. I was sure that Vyland would even have preferred to have the general with us in the bathyscaphe as extra security, but apart from the fact that the scaphe held only three in comfort and Vyland would never move into the least danger without his hatchetman by his side, that 180-rung descent was far too much for the old general to look at.

It almost proved too much for me, too. Before

I was halfway down, my shoulder, arm and neck felt as if they were bathed in a mould of molten lead, and the waves of fiery pain were shooting up into my head and there the fire turned to darkness, and down into my chest and stomach and there they turned to nausea. Several times the pain and the darkness and the nausea all but engulfed me. I had to cling on desperately with my good hand until the waves subsided and full consciousness returned. With every rung descended the periods of darkness grew longer and awareness shorter, and I must have descended the last thirty or forty rungs like an automaton, from instinct and memory and some strange sort of subconscious willpower. The only point in my favour was that, courteous as ever, they had sent me down first so that I wouldn't have to fight the temptation of dropping something heavy on their heads, and so they weren't able to see how I was suffering. By the time I had reached the platform at the bottom and the last of them – Cibatti's friend, who was to close the platform hatch – had arrived, I was at least able to stand up without swaying. My face, I think, must have been the colour of paper and it was bathed in sweat, but the illumination from the tiny lamp at the foot of the cylindrical tomb was so faint, that there was little danger of Vyland or Royale detecting anything unusual. I suspected that Royale wouldn't be feeling so good after the trip either, any man who has sustained a blow or blows sufficient to put him away for half an hour

311

isn't going to be feeling on top of his form a mere fifteen minutes after he recovers. As for Vyland, I had a faint suspicion that he was more than a little scared and that his primary concern, at the moment, would be himself and the journey that lay ahead of us.

The platform hatch was opened and we clambered down through the entrance flooding chamber of the bathyscaphe into the steel ball below. I took the greatest care to favour my bad shoulder when I was negotiating the sharp, almost right-angle bend into the observation chamber and the journey wasn't any more than agonizing. I switched on the overhead light and made for the circuit boxes leaving Vyland to secure the flooding-chamber hatch. Half a minute later he wriggled into the observation chamber and shut the heavy wedge-shaped circular door behind him.

They were both suitably impressed by the profusion and confusion of the wires dangling from the circuit boxes and if they weren't equally impressed by the speed and efficiency with which, barely consulting my notes, I buttoned them all back in place again, they ought to have been. Fortunately, the circuit boxes were no higher than waist level, my left arm was now so far gone that I could use it only from the elbow downwards.

I screwed home the last lead, shut the box covers and started to test all the circuits. Vyland watched me impatiently; Royale was watching me with a face, which, in its expressionlessness and battered appearance, was a fair match for the great Sphinx of Giza; but I remained unmoved by Vyland's anxiety for haste – I was in this bathyscaphe too and I was in no mind to take chances. Then I turned on the control rheostats for the two battery-powered engines, turned to Vyland and pointed at a pair of flickering dials.

'The engines. You can hardly hear them in here but they're running just as they should. Ready to go?'

'Yes.' He licked his lips. 'Ready when you are.'

I nodded, turned the valve control to flood the entrance chamber, pointed to the microphone which rested on a bracket at the head-height between Royale and myself and turned the wall-switch to the 'on' position. 'Maybe you'd like to give the word to blow the air from the retaining rubber ring?'

He nodded, gave the necessary order and replaced the microphone. I switched it off and waited.

The bathyscaphe had been rocking gently, through maybe a three- or four-degree arc in a fore-and-aft line when suddenly the movement ceased altogether. I glanced at the depth gauge. It had been registering erratically, we were close enough to the surface for it to be affected by the great deep-troughed waves rolling by overhead, but even so there could be no doubt that the average depths of the readings had perceptibly increased.

'We've dropped clear of the leg,' I told Vyland. I switched on the vertical searchlight and pointed through the Plexiglas window at our feet. The sandy bottom was now only a fathom away. 'What direction, quick – I don't want to settle in that.'

'Straight ahead, just how you're pointing.'

I made the interlock switch for the two engines, advanced to half-speed and adjusted the planes to give us the maximum forward lift. It was little enough, not more than two degrees: unlike the lateral rudder the depth planes on the bathyscaphe gave the bare minimum of control, being quite secondary for the purpose of surfacing and diving. I slowly advanced the engines to maximum.

'Almost due south-west.' Vyland was consulting a slip of paper he had brought from his pocket. 'Course 222°.'

'True?'

'What do you mean "true", he snapped angrily. Now that he had his wishes answered and the bathyscaphe a going concern Vyland didn't like it at all. Claustrophobic, at a guess.

'Is that the true direction or is it for this compass?' I asked patiently.

'For this compass.'

'Has it been corrected for deviation?'

He consulted his slip of paper again. 'Yes. And Bryson said that as long as we took off straight in this direction the metal in the rig's legs wouldn't affect us.'

I said nothing. Bryson, the engineer who had died from the bends, where was he now? Not a couple of hundred feet away, I felt pretty certain.

To drill an oil well maybe two and a half miles deep they'd have needed at least six thousand bags of cement and the two bucketsful of that needed to ensure that Bryson would remain at the bottom of the ocean until long after he was an unidentifiable skeleton wouldn't even have been missed.

'Five hundred and twenty metres,' Vyland was saying. 'From the leg we've left to the plane.' The first mention ever of a plane. 'Horizontal distance, that is. Allowing for the drop to the bottom of the deep, about six hundred and twenty metres. Or so Bryson said.'

'Where does this deep begin?'

'About two-thirds of the distance from here. At a hundred and forty feet – almost the same depth as the rig is standing in. Then it goes down about thirty degrees to four hundred and eighty feet.'

I nodded, but said nothing. I had always heard that you couldn't feel two major sources of pain at the same time but people were wrong. You could. My arm, shoulder and back were a wide sea of pain, a pain punctuated by jolting stabbing spear-points of agony from my upper jaw. I didn't feel like conversation, I didn't feel like anything at all. I tried to forget the pain by concentrating on the job on hand.

The tow-rope attaching us to the pillar was, I had discovered, wound round an electrically driven power drum. But the power was unidirectional only, for reeling in the wire on the return journey. As we were moving just then it was being paid out against a weak spring carrying with it the insulated phone cable which ran through the centre of the wire, and the number of revolutions made by the drum showed on a counter inside the observation chamber, giving us a fairly accurate idea of the distance covered. It also gave us an idea of our speed. The maximum the bathyscaphe could do was two knots, but even the slight drag offered by the tow-cable paying out behind reduced this to one knot. But it was fast enough. We hadn't far to go.

Vyland seemed more than content to leave the running of the bathyscaphe to me. He spent most of his time peering rather apprehensively out of a side window. Royale's one good cold unwinking eye never left me; he watched every separate tiny movement and adjustment I made but it was only pure habit; I think his ignorance of the principles and controls of the bathyscaphe were pretty well complete. They must have been: even when I turned the intake control of the carbon dioxide absorption apparatus right down to its minimum operating figure it meant nothing to him.

We were drifting slowly along about ten feet above the floor of the sea, nose tilted slightly upwards by the drag of the wire, our guide-rope dangling down below the observation chamber and just brushing the rock and the coral formations or dragging over a sponge-bar. The darkness of the water was absolute, but our two searchlights and the light streaming out through the Plexiglas windows gave us light enough to see by. One or two groupers loafed lazily by the windows, absentmindedly intent on their own business; a snake-bodied barracuda writhed its lean grey body towards us, thrust its evil head against a side window and stared in unblinkingly for almost a minute; a school of what looked like Spanish mackerel kept us company for some time, then abruptly vanished in an exploding flurry of motion as a bottle-nosed shark cruised majestically into view, propelling itself along with a barely perceptible motion of its long powerful tail. But, for the most part, the sea floor seemed deserted; perhaps the storm raging above had sent most fish off to seek deeper waters.

Exactly ten minutes after we had left, the sea-floor abruptly dropped away beneath us in what seemed, in the sudden yawning darkness that our searchlight could not penetrate, an almost vertical cliff-face. I knew this to be only illusion; Vyland would have surveyed the ocean bed a dozen times and if he said the angle was only 30° it was almost certainly so, but nevertheless the impression of a sudden bottomless chasm was overwhelming.

'This is it,' Vyland said in a low voice. On his smooth polished face I could make out the faint sheen of sweat. 'Take her down, Talbot.'

'Later.' I shook my head. 'If we start descending now that tow-rope we're trailing is going to pull our tail right up. Our searchlights can't shine ahead, only vertically downwards. Want that we should crash our nose into some outcrop of rock that we can't see? Want to rupture the for'ard gasoline tank? – don't forget the shell of those tanks is only thin sheet metal. It only needs one split tank and we'll have so much negative buoyancy that we can never rise again. You appreciate that, don't you, Vyland?'

His face gleamed with sweat. He wet his lips again and said: 'Do it your way, Talbot.'

I did it my way. I kept on course 222° until the tow-wire recorder showed 600 metres, stopped the engine and let our slight preponderance of negative buoyancy, which our forward movement and angled planes had so far overcome, take over. We settled gradually, in a maddeningly deliberate slow motion, the fathometer needle hardly appearing to move. The hanging weight of the tow-wire aft tended to pull us astern, and at every ten fathoms, between thirty and seventy, I had to ease ahead on the motors and pay out a little more wire.

At exactly seventy-six fathoms our searchlights picked up the bed of the sea. No rock or coral or sponge bars here, just little patches of greyish sand and long black stretches of mud. I started the two motors again, advanced them almost to half speed, trimmed the planes and began to creep forward very slowly indeed. We had to move only five yards. Bryson's estimate had been almost exactly right; with 625 metres showing on the tow-wire indicator I caught a glimpse of something

318

thrusting up from the bed of the sea, almost out of our line of vision to the left. It was the tail-plane of an aircraft, we had overshot our target to the right, the nose of the plane was point-ing back in the direction from which we had come . . . I put the motors in reverse, started up the tow-wire drum, backed about twenty yards then came forward again, angling to the left. Arrived at what I judged to be the right spot, I put the motors momentarily into reverse, then cut them out altogether. Slowly, surely, the bathyscaphe began to sink: the dangling guide rope touched bottom, but this lessening of weight failed to over-come the slight degree of negative buoyancy as it should have done, and the base of the observation chamber sank heavily into the black mud of the ocean floor.

Only fifteen minutes had elapsed since I'd turned down the intake control of the carbon monoxide absorption unit but already the air in the cabin was growing foul. Neither Vyland nor Royale seemed to be affected; maybe they thought that that was the normal atmospheric condition, but they probably didn't even notice it. Both of them were com-pletely absorbed in what could be seen, brightly illuminated by the for'ard searchlight, through our for'ard observation window.

I was absorbed in it myself, God only knew. A hundred times I had wondered how I'd feel, how I'd react when I finally saw, if ever I saw, what was lying half-buried in the mud outside.

Anger I had expected, anger and fury and horror and heartbreak and maybe more than a little of fear. But there was none of those things in me, not any more. I was aware only of pity and sadness, of the most abysmal melancholy I had ever known. Maybe my reactions were not what I had expected because my mind was befogged by the swirling mists of pain, but I knew it wasn't that: and it made things no better to know that the pity and the melancholy were no longer for others but for myself, melancholy for the memories that were all I would ever have, the pity a self-pity of a man irretrievably lost in his loneliness.

The plane had sunk about four feet into the mud. The right wing had vanished – it must have broken off on impact with the water. The left wing-tip was gone, but the tail unit and fuselage were still completely intact except for the riddled nose, the starred and broken glass that showed how the DC had died. We were close up to the fuselage, the bow of the bathyscaphe was overhanging the sunken cabin of the plane and the observation chamber no more than six feet distant from those shattered windows and almost on the same level. Behind the smashed windscreens I could see two skeletons: the one in the captain's seat was still upright, leaning against the broken side window and held in position by the seat belt, the one in the co-pilot's seat was bent far over forward and almost out of sight.

'Wonderful, eh, Talbot? Isn't that just something?' Vyland, his claustrophobic fear in momentary abeyance, was actually rubbing his hands together. 'After all this time – but it's been worth it, it's been worth it! And intact, too! I was scared it might have been scattered all over the floor of the sea. Should be no bother for an experienced salvage man like yourself, eh, Talbot?' He didn't wait for an answer but turned away immediately to stare out of the window and gloat. 'Wonderful,' he repeated again. 'Just wonderful.'

'It's wonderful,' I agreed. I was surprised at the steadiness, the indifference in my own voice. 'With the exception of the British frigate *De Braak*, sunk in a storm off the Delaware coast in 1798, it's probably the biggest underwater treasure in the western hemisphere. Ten million, two hundred and fifty thousand dollars in gold specie, emeralds and uncut diamonds.'

'Yes, sir.' Vyland had forgotten he was an urbane top executive and he was back at the hand-washing again. 'Ten million, two hundred and—' His voice trailed off slowly, faltered to a stop. 'How – how did *you* know that, Talbot?' he whispered.

'I knew it before you ever heard of it, Vyland,' I said quietly. Both of them had turned away from the window and were staring at me, Vyland with a mixture of puzzlement, suspicion and the beginnings of fear, Royale with his one good, cold, flat, marbled eye wider than I had ever seen it. 'You're not quite so smart as the general, I'm afraid, Vyland. Neither am I for that matter. He caught on to me this morning, Vyland. I've worked out why. Do *you* know why, Vyland? Do you want to know why?'

'What are you talking about?' he demanded hoarsely.

'He's smart, is the general.' I went on as if I hadn't heard the interruption. 'He saw when we landed on the rig this morning that I only hid my face until I was certain that a certain person wasn't among the reception committee and that then I didn't bother any longer. Careless of me, I admit. But that tipped him off to the fact that I wasn't a murderer – if I were I'd have hidden my face from everybody – and it also tipped him off to the fact that I had been out on the rig before and was frightened someone there would recognize me. He was right on both counts – I wasn't a murderer, and I had been out on the rig before. In the early hours of this morning.'

Vyland had nothing to say, the shattering effect of my words, the limitless avenues of dark possibilities they were opening up had him completely off balance, too confused even to begin to put his conflicting thoughts into words.

'And the general noticed something else,' I went on. 'He noticed that when you were telling me about this salvage job that I never once asked the first, the most obvious question in the world – what was the treasure to be salvaged, what kind of vessel or aircraft the treasure was in, if any. I never once asked one of those questions, did I, Vyland? Again careless of me, wasn't it, Vyland? But you never noticed. But General Ruthven noticed, and he knew there could only be one answer – I already knew.'

There was a pause of perhaps ten seconds, then Vyland whispered: 'Who are you, Talbot?'

'No friend of yours, Vyland.' I smiled at him, as near as my aching upper jaw would allow. 'You're going to die, Vyland, you're going to die in agony and you're going to use your last breath on earth cursing my name and the day you ever met me.'

Another silence, deeper even than the one that had gone before. I wished I could smoke, but it was impossible inside that cabin, and heaven only knew the air there was foul enough already, our breathing was already unnaturally quickened, and sweat was beginning to trickle down our faces.

'Let me tell you a little story,' I went on. 'It's not a fairy story but we'll start it with "Once upon a time" for all that.

'Once upon a time there was a certain country with a very small navy – a couple of destroyers, a frigate, a gunboat. Not much of a navy, is it, Vyland? So the rulers decided to double it. They were doing pretty well in the petroleum and coffee export markets, and they thought they could afford it. Mind you, they could have spent the money in a hundred more profitable ways but this was a country much given to revolution and the strength of any current government largely depended on the strength of the armed forces under their control. Let's double our navy, they said. *Who* said, Vyland?'

He tried to speak, but only a croak came out. He wet his lips and said: 'Colombia.'

'However did you know, I wonder? That's it, Colombia. They arranged to get a couple of second-hand destroyers from Britain, some frigates, mine sweepers and gunboats from the United States. Considering that those second-hand ships were almost brand new, they got them dead cheap: 10,250,000 dollars. But then the snag: Colombia was in a state of threatened revolution, civil war and anarchy, the value of the peso was tumbling abroad and Britain and the United States, to whom a combined payment was to be made, refused to deliver against the peso. No international bank would look at Colombia. So it was agreed that the payment be made in kind. Some previous government had imported, for industrial purposes, two million dollars' worth of uncut Brazilian diamonds which had never been used. To that was added about two and a half million dollars' worth of Colombian gold, near enough two tons in 28-lb ingots: the bulk of the payment, however, was in cut emeralds – I need hardly remind you, Vyland, that the Muzo mines in the Eastern Andes are the most famous and important source of emeralds in the world. Or perhaps you know?'

Vyland said nothing. He pulled out his display handkerchief and mopped his face. He looked sick.

'No matter. And then came the question of transport. It was supposed to have been flown out to Tampa on its first leg, by an Avianca or Lansa freighter but all the domestic national airlines were temporarily grounded at the beginning of May, 1958, when the new elections were coming up. Some members of the permanent civil service were desperately anxious to get rid of this money in case it fell into the wrong hands, so they looked around for a foreign-owned freight airline operating only external flights. They picked on the Trans-Carib Air Charter Co. Lloyd's agreed to transfer the insurance. The Trans-Carib freighter filed a false flight plan and took off from Barranquilla, heading for Tampa via the Yucatan Strait.

'There were only four people in that plane, Vyland. There was the pilot, a twin brother of the owner of the Trans-Carib Line. There was the co-pilot, who also doubled as navigator, and a woman and a small child whom it was thought wiser not to leave behind in case things went wrong at the elections and it was found out the part played by the Trans-Carib in getting the money out of the country.

'They filed a false flight plan, Vyland, but that didn't do them any good at all for one of those noble and high-minded civil servants who had been so anxious to pay the debt to Britain and

325

America was as crooked as they come and a creature of yours, Vyland. He knew of the true flight plan, and radioed you. You were in Havana, and you'd everything laid on, hadn't you, Vyland?'

'How do you know all this?' Vyland croaked.

'Because I am – I was – the owner of the Trans-Carib Air Charter Co.' I felt unutterably tired, I don't know whether it was because of the pain or the foul air or just because of the overwhelming sense of the emptiness of living. 'I was grounded at Belize, in British Honduras, at the time, but I managed to pick them up on the radio – after they had repaired it. They told me then that someone had tried to blow up the plane, but I know now that wasn't quite true, all they had tried to do was to wreck the radio, to cut the DC off from the outer world. They almost succeeded – but not quite. You never knew, did you, Vyland, that someone was in radio contact with that plane just before it was shot out of the sky. But I was. Just for two minutes, Vyland.' I looked at him slowly, consideringly, emptily. 'Two little minutes that mean you die tonight.'

Vyland stared at me with sick terror in his eyes. He knew what was coming all right, or thought he knew: he knew now who I was, he knew now what it was to meet a man who had lost everything, a man to whom pity and compassion were no longer even words. Slowly, as if at the expense of great effort and pain, he twisted his head to look at Royale, but, for the first time ever, there was no comfort, no security, no knowledge of safety to be found there, for the incredible was happening at last: Royale was afraid.

I half-turned and pointed at the shattered cabin of the DC.

'Take a good look, Vyland,' I said quietly. 'Take a good look at what you've done and feel proud of yourself. In the captain's seat – that skeleton was once Peter Talbot, my twin brother. The other is Elizabeth Talbot – she was my wife, Vyland. In the back of the plane will be all that's left of a very little boy. John Talbot, my son. He was three and a half years old. I've thought a thousand times about how my little boy died, Vyland. The bullets that killed my wife and brother wouldn't have got him, he'd have been alive till the plane hit the water. Maybe two or three minutes, the plane tumbling and falling through the sky, Vyland, and the little boy sobbing and screaming and terrified out of his mind, and his mother not coming when he called her name. When he called her name over and over again. But she couldn't come, could she, Vyland? She was sitting in her seat, dead. And then the plane hit the water and even then, perhaps, Johny was still alive. Maybe the fuselage took time to sink – it happens that way often, you know, Vyland – or had it air trapped inside it when it sank. I wonder how long it was before the waters closed over him. Can't you see it, Vyland, three years old, screaming and struggling and dying and no one near him? And then the screaming and struggling stopped and my little boy was drowned.'

I looked out at the smashed plane cabin for a long time, or what seemed like a long time, and when I turned away Vyland caught my right arm. I pushed him off and he fell on the duckboard floor, staring up at me with wide, panic-stricken eyes. His mouth was open, his breathing coming in quick, harsh gasps, and his entire body was trembling. Royale was still in control of himself, but only just: ivory knuckled hands rested on his knees and his eyes were moving constantly about the observation chamber, a hunted animal seeking a way to escape.

'I've waited a long time for this, Vyland,' I went on. 'I've waited two years and four months and I don't believe I've ever thought for five minutes about anything else in all that time.

'I've nothing left to live for, Vyland, you can understand that. I've had enough. I suppose it's macabre, but I'd kind of like to stay here beside them. I've stopped kidding myself about the point in carrying on living. There's none, not any more, so I might as well stay here. There's no point now, because all that's kept me going was the promise I made myself on the third of May, 1958, that I'd never rest again till I'd sought out and destroyed the man who had destroyed life for me. That I've done, and there's no more now. It should spoil it for me, I suppose, the thought that you'll be here also, but on the other hand I suppose it's kind of fitting. The killers and their victims, all together in the end.'

'You're mad,' Vyland whispered. 'You're mad. What are you saying?'

'Only this. Remember that electrical switch that was left on the table? The one you asked about and I said "We won't be needing that any more"? Well we won't. Not any more. That was the master control for the ballast release switches and without it the ballast release is completely jinxed. And without releasing ballast we can never rise again. Here we are, Vyland, and here we stay. For ever.'

TWELVE

The sweat poured down our faces in rivulets. The temperature had risen to almost 120° Fahrenheit, the air was humid and now almost indescribably foul. Our hoarse rasping gasps as we fought for oxygen was the only sound in that tiny steel ball resting on the floor of the Gulf of Mexico, 480 feet below the level of the sea.

'You jinxed it?' Vyland's voice was a weak incredulous whisper, his eyes near-crazed with fear. 'We're – we're stuck here? Here, in this—' His voice faded away as he turned his head and started looking around with all the terror-stricken desperation of a cornered rat about to die. Which was all he was.

'There's no way out, Vyland,' I assured him grimly. 'Only through that entrance hatch. Maybe you want to try opening it? – at this depth there can only be a pressure of fifty tons or so on the outside of it. And if you could open it – well, you'd be flattened half an inch thick against the opposite

330

bulkhead. Don't take it too badly, Vyland – the last few minutes will be agony such as you've never believed man could know, you'll be able to see your hands and your face turning blue and purple in the last few seconds before all the major blood vessels in your lungs start to rupture, but soon after that you'll –'

'Stop it, stop it!' Vyland screamed. 'For God's sake stop it! Get us out of here, Talbot, get us out of here! I'll give you anything you like, one million, two millions, five millions. You can have it all, Talbot, you can have it all!' His mouth and face worked like a maniac's, his eyes were staring out of his head.

'You make me sick,' I said dispassionately. 'I wouldn't get you out if I could, Vyland. And it was just in case that I might be tempted that I left the control switch up in the rig. We've got fifteen, maybe twenty minutes to live, if you can call the screaming agony we'll know living. Or, rather, the agony you'll know.' I put my hand to my coat, ripped off the central button and thrust it into my mouth. 'I won't know a thing, I've been prepared for this for months. That's no button, Vyland, it's a concentrated cyanide capsule. One bite on that and I'll be dead before I know I'm dying.'

That got him. Dribbling from a corner of his mouth and babbling incoherently, he flung himself on me, with what purpose in mind I don't know. He was too crazed to know. He was too crazed to know himself. But I had been expecting it, a heavy spanner lay to hand and he'd picked it up and swung it before he even touched me. It wasn't much of a blow, but it was enough: he reeled backwards, struck his head against the casing and collapsed heavily on the floor.

That left Royale. He was half-sitting, half-crouched on his little canvas stool, his sphinx-like control had completely snapped, he knew he had only minutes to live and his face was working overtime making up for all those expressions it hadn't used in those many years. He saw closing in on himself what he had meted out to so many victims over so long a time and the talons of fear were squeezing deep, reaching for the innermost corners of his mind. He wasn't panic-stricken yet, not completely out of control as Vyland had gone, but his capacity for reason, for thought, was gone. All he could think to do was what he always thought to do in an emergency and that was of using his deadly little black gun. He had it out now and it was pointing at me, but I knew it meant nothing, it was purely a reflex action and he had no intention of using it. For the first time Royale had met a problem that couldn't be solved by a squeeze of the trigger finger.

'You're scared, Royale, aren't you?' I said softly. It was an effort now even to speak, my normal breathing rate of about sixteen was now up to fifty, and it was difficult to get the time to force out a word.

He said nothing, just looked at me, and all the

devils in hell were in the depth of those black eyes. For a second time in forty-eight hours, and this time in spite of the humidity, the foul and evil-smelling air in that cabin, I could have sworn I caught the smell of new-turned, moist, fresh earth. The smell you get from an open grave.

'The big bad hatchet-man,' I whispered huskily. 'Royale. Royale the killer. Think of all the people who used to tremble, who still do tremble, whenever they hear the breath of your name? Don't you wish they could see you now? Don't you, Royale? Don't you wish they could see you trembling? You are trembling, Royale, aren't you? You're terrified as you've never been terrified in your life. Aren't you, Royale?'

Again he said nothing. The devils were still in his eyes, but they weren't watching me any more, they were riding hard on Royale, they were digging deep into the dark recesses of that dark mind, the shift and play of expression on his contorted face was evidence enough that they were pulling him every which way but the overall pull was towards the dark precipice of complete breakdown, of that overmastering fear that wears the cloak of insanity.

'Like it, Royale?' I said hoarsely. 'Can't you feel your throat, your lungs starting to hurt? I can feel mine – and I can see your face starting to turn blue. Not much, yet, just starting under the eyes. The eyes and the nose, they always show up first.' I thrust my hand into my display pocket, brought out a little rectangle of polished chrome. 'A mirror, Royale. Don't you want to look in it? Don't you want to look in it? Don't you want to see –?'

'Damn you to hell, Talbot!' He knocked the mirror flying out of my hand, his voice was halfway between a sob and a scream. 'I don't want to die! I don't want to die!'

'But your victims did, didn't they, Royale?' I could no longer speak intelligibly, it took me four or five breaths to pant out that one sentence. 'They all had their minds bent on suicide and you just helped them out of the depths of the kindness of your heart. Isn't that it, Royale?'

'You're going to die, Talbot.' His voice was a frenzied croak, the shaking gun was lined up on my heart. 'It's coming to you now.'

'I'm laughing. I'm laughing out loud. I've got a Cyanide tablet between my teeth.' My chest was hurting, the inside of the observation chamber was beginning to swim before my eyes. I knew I couldn't last out much longer. 'Go ahead,' I gasped. 'Go ahead and pull the trigger.'

He looked at me with crazy unfocused eyes that had hardly any contact left with reality and fumbled the little black gun into its holster. The beating he'd taken over his head was now beginning to take its toll, he was in an even worse state than I was. He began to sway in his seat, and suddenly fell forward on to his hands and knees, shaking his head from side to side as if to clear away a fog. I leaned across him, barely conscious myself, closed my fingers over the control knob of the carbon dioxide absorption unit and turned it from minimum all the way up to maximum. It would take two minutes, perhaps three, before there would be any noticeable improvement, maybe the best part of ten minutes before the atmosphere inside that chamber was anything like back to normal. Right then, it made no difference at all. I bent over Royale.

'You're dying, Royale,' I gasped out. 'How does it feel to die, Royale? Tell me, please, how does it feel? How does it feel to be buried in a tomb five hundred feet beneath the surface of the sea? How does it feel to know that you'll never breathe that wonderful, clean, fresh air of the world above again? How does it feel to know that you'll never see the sun again? How does it feel to die? Tell me, Royale, how does it feel?' I bent still closer to him. 'Tell me, Royale, how would you like to live?'

He didn't get it, he was that far gone.

'How would you like to live, Royale?' I almost had to shout the words.

'I want to live.' His voice was a harsh moan of pain, his clenched right fist was beating weakly on the deck of the chamber. 'Oh, God, I want to live.'

'Maybe I can give you life yet. Maybe. You're down on your hands and knees, aren't you, Royale? You're begging for your life, aren't you, Royale? I've sworn I'd see the day when you were on your hands and knees begging for your life and now you're doing just that, aren't you, Royale?'

'Damn you, Talbot!' His voice was a hoarse, despairing, agonized shout, he was swaying on his hands and knees now, his head turning from side to side, his eyes screwed shut. Down there on the floor the air must have been foul and contaminated to a degree, almost completely without oxygen, and his face was really beginning to show the first tinges of blue. He was breathing with the rapidity of a panting dog, each brief indrawn breath a whoop of agony. 'Get me out of here! For God's sake get me out of here.'

'You're not dead yet, Royale,' I said in his ear. 'Maybe you will see the sun again. But maybe you won't. I lied to Vyland, Royale. The master switch for the ballast release is still in position – I just altered a couple of wires, that's all. It would take you hours to find out which two. I could fix it in thirty seconds.'

He stopped swaying his head, looked up at me with a blue-tinged sweat-sheened face, with bloodshot fear-darkened eyes that carried far back in them the faintest flicker of hope. 'Get me out of here, Talbot,' he whispered. He didn't know whether there was any hope or whether this was just a further refinement of torture.

'I could do it, Royale, couldn't I? See, I've got the screwdriver right here.' I showed it to him, smiled down without any compassion. 'But I've still got this cyanide tablet in my mouth, Royale.'

I showed him the button, gripped between my teeth.

'Don't!' A hoarse cry. 'Don't bite on that! You're mad, Talbot, mad. God, you're not human.' Coming from Royale that was good.

'Who killed Jablonsky?' I asked quietly. It was becoming easier to breathe now, but not down where Royale was.

'I did. I killed him,' Royale moaned.

'How?'

'I shot him. Through the head. He was asleep.'

'And then?'

'We buried him in the kitchen garden.' Royale was still moaning and swaying, but he was putting everything he could muster into his reeling thoughts to try to express them coherently: his nerve, for the moment, was gone beyond recall, he was talking for his life and he knew it.

'Who's behind Vyland?'

'Nobody.'

'Who's behind Vyland?' I repeated implacably.

'Nobody.' His voice was almost a scream he was so desperate to convince me. 'There were two men, a Cuban minister in the government, and Houras, a permanent civil servant in Colombia. But not now.'

'What happened to them?'

'They were – they were eliminated,' Royale said wearily. 'I did it.'

'Who else did you eliminate since you've been working for Vyland?'

'Nobody.'

I showed him the button between my teeth and he shuddered.

'The pilot. The pilot flying the fighter that shot down this plane. He – he knew too much.'

'That's why we could never find that pilot,' I nodded. 'My God, you're a sweet bunch. But you made a mistake Royale, didn't you? You shot him too soon. Before he'd told you exactly where the DC had crashed . . . Vyland give you orders for all this?'

He nodded.

'Did you hear my question?' I demanded.

'Vyland gave me orders for all of that.'

There was a brief silence. I stared out of the window, saw some strange shark-like creature swim into sight, stare incuriously at both bathyscaphe and plane, then vanish into the stygian blackness beyond with a lazy flick of its tail. I turned and tapped Royale on the shoulder.

'Vyland,' I said. 'Try to bring him round.'

While Royale stooped over his employer I reached above him for the oxygen regenerating switch. I didn't want the air getting too fresh too soon.

After maybe a minute or so Royale managed to bring Vyland to. Vyland's breathing was very distressed, he was pretty far gone in the first stages of anoxia, but for all that he still had some breath left, for when he opened his eyes, stared wildly around and saw me with the button still between my teeth he started screaming, time and again, a horrible nerve-drilling sound in that tiny confined metal space. I reached forward to smack his face to jolt him out of his panic-stricken hysteria, but Royale got there first. Royale had had his tiny fleeting glimpse of hope and he meant to play that hope to the end of the way. He lifted his hand and he wasn't any too gentle with Vyland.

'Stop it!' Royale shook him violently. 'Stop it, stop it, stop it! Talbot says he can fix this machine. Do you hear me? Talbot says he can fix it!'

Slowly the screaming died away and Vyland stared at Royale with eyes where the first faint flicker of comprehension was beginning to edge in on the fear and the madness.

'What did you say?' he whimpered hoarsely. 'What was that, Royale?'

'Talbot says he can fix this machine,' Royale repeated urgently. 'He says he lied to us, he says that the switch he left up top wasn't important. He can fix it!'

'You – you can fix it, Talbot?' Vyland's eyes widened until I could see a ring of white all round the irises, his shaking voice was a prayer, the whole curve of his body a gesture of supplication. He wasn't even daring to hope yet, his mind had gone too deeply into the shadow of the valley of death to glimpse the light above: or rather he didn't dare to look, in case there was no light there. 'You can get us out of this? Now – even now you –'

'Maybe I will, maybe I won't.' My voice, for all its rasping hoarseness, had just the right shade of indifference. 'I've said I'd rather stay down here, I mean I'd rather stay down here. It all depends. Come here, Vyland.'

He rose trembling to his feet and crossed to where I was standing. His legs, his whole body were shaking so violently that he could barely support himself. I caught him by the lapels with my good hand and pulled him close.

'There's maybe five minutes' air left; Vyland. Perhaps less. Just tell me, and tell me quickly, the part you played in this business up until the time you met the general. Hurry it up!'

'Get us out of here,' he moaned. 'There's no air, no air! My lungs are going, I can't – I can't breathe.' He was hardly exaggerating at that, the foul air was rasping in and out his throat with the frequency of a normal heartbeat. 'I can't talk. 'I can't!'

'Talk, damn you, talk!' Royale had him round the throat from behind, was shaking him to and fro till Vyland's head bounced backwards and forwards like that of a broken doll. 'Talk! Do you want to die, Vyland? Do you think I want to die because of you? Talk!'

Vyland talked. In less than three gasping, coughing, choking minutes he'd told me all I ever wanted to know – how he had struck a deal with a Cuban service minister and had a plane standing by for weeks, how he had suborned the officer in charge of a radar tracking station in Western Cuba, how he suborned a very senior civil servant in Colombia, how the plane had been tracked, intercepted and shot down and how he had had Royale dispose of those who had served his purposes. He started to talk of the general, but I held up my hand.

'OK, that'll do, Vyland. Get back to your seat.' I reached for the carbon dioxide switch and turned it up to maximum.

'What's that you're doing?' Vyland whispered.

'Bringing a little fresh air into the place. Getting rather stuffy down here, don't you think?'

They stared at each other, then at me, but remained silent. Fury I would have expected, chagrin and violence, but there was nothing of any of those. Fear was still the single predominating emotion in their minds: and they knew that they were still completely at my mercy.

'Who – who are you, Talbot?' Vyland croaked.

'I suppose you might call me a cop.' I sat down on a canvas chair, I didn't want to start the delicate job of taking the bathyscaphe up till the air – and my mind – was completely clear. 'I used to be a bona fide salvage man, working with my brother. The man – or what's left of the man – out there in the captain's seat, Vyland. We were a good team, we struck gold off the Tunisian coast and used the capital to start our own airline – we were both wartime bomber pilots, we both had civilian licences. We were doing very well, Vyland – until we met you.

'After you'd done this' – I jerked a thumb in

341

the direction of the broken, weed- and barnacle-encrusted plane – 'I went back to London. I was arrested, they thought I'd something to do with this. It didn't take long to clear that up and have Lloyd's of London – who'd lost the whole insurance packet – take me over as a special investigator. They were willing to spend an unlimited sum to get even a percentage of their money back. And because state money was involved both the British and American governments were behind me. Solidly behind me. Nobody ever had a better backing, the Americans even went to the length of assigning a top-flight cop whole-time to the job. The cop was Jablonsky,'

That jolted them, badly. They had lost sufficient of their immediate terror of death, they had come far enough back into the world of reality to appreciate what I was saying, and what that meant. They stared at each other, then at me; I couldn't have asked for a more attentive audience.

'That was a mistake, wasn't it, gentlemen?' I went on. 'Shooting Jablonsky. That's enough to send you both to the chair; judges don't like people who murder cops. It may not be complete justice, but it's true. Murder an ordinary citizen and you may get off with it: murder a cop, and you never do. Not that that matters. We know enough to send you to the chair six times over.'

I told them how Jablonsky and I had spent well over a year, mostly in Cuba, looking for traces of the bullion, how we had come to the conclusion that it still hadn't been recovered – not one of the cut emeralds had appeared anywhere in the world's markets. Interpol would have known in days.

'And we were pretty certain,' I continued, *why* the money hadn't been recovered. Why? Only one reason – it had been lost in the sea and someone had been a mite hasty in killing off the only person who knew exactly where it was – the pilot of the fighter plane.

'Our inquiries had narrowed down to the west coast of Florida. Somebody was looking for money sunk in the water. For that they needed a ship. The general's *Temptress* did just fine. But for that you also needed an extremely sensitive depth recorder, and there is where you made your one and fatal mistake, Vyland. We had requested every major marine equipment supplier in Europe and North America to notify us immediately they sold any special depth-finding equipment to any vessels other than naval, mercantile or fishing. You are following me, I trust?'

They were following me all right. They were three parts back to normal now and there was murder in their eyes.

'In the four-month period concerned no fewer than six of those ultra-sensitive recorders had been sold privately. All to owners of very large yachts. Two of those yachts were on a round-the-world cruise. One was in Rio, one was in Long Island

343

Sound, one on the Pacific coast – and the sixth was plodding up and down the west of Florida. General Blair Ruthven's *Temptress*.

'It was brilliant. I admit it. What better cover could you ever have had for quartering every square yard of sea off the Florida Coast without arousing suspicion? While the general's geologists were busy setting off their little bombs and making seismological maps of the under-sea rock strata, you were busy mapping every tiniest contour of the ocean floor with the depth recorder. It took you almost six weeks, because you started operating too far to the north – we were watching your every move even then and had fitted out a special boat for night prowling – that was the boat I came out on early this morning. Well, you found the plane. You even spent three nights dragging for it with grapples but all you could drag up was a small section of the left wing-tip.' I gestured through the window. 'You can see how comparatively recent that break is.'

'How do you know all this?' Vyland whispered.

'Because I had secured a job as a replacement engineer aboard the *Temptress*.' I ignored the startled oath, the involuntary clenching of Vyland's hands. 'You and the general thought you had seen me aboard that Havana salvage vessel, but you hadn't, though I had been with the firm. I was five weeks on the *Temptress* and it wasn't till I left that I dyed my hair this hellish colour, had a plastic surgeon fix up this scar and affected a

344

limp. Even so, you weren't very observant, were you, Vyland? You should have cottoned on.

'So there you were. You knew where the treasure was, but you couldn't get your hands on it – anyone who started using diving bells and all the complicated recovery gear necessary for a job like this would have been putting a noose round his own neck. But then someone had another brilliant idea – this one, I'd wager anything, came from the mind of our deceased engineer friend, Bryson. He'd read all about those bathyscaphe trials that were being carried out in the West Indies and came up with the idea of using it in conjunction with this rig.'

The air was almost back to normal inside the observation chamber and though the atmosphere was still stuffy and far too warm for comfort there was plenty of oxygen in the air and breathing was no longer any problem. Royale and Vyland were getting their meanness and courage back with the passing of every moment.

'So, you see, everyone was having brilliant ideas,' I continued. 'But the real beauty, the one that's brought you two to the end of the road, was Jablonsky's. It was Jablonsky who thought that it would be real kind and helpful of us if we could provide a bathyscaphe for you to do the job.'

Vyland swore, softly and vilely, looked slowly at Royale then back to me. 'You mean –?' he began.

'It was all laid on,' I said tiredly. I was taking no pleasure in any of this. 'The French and British

Navies were carrying out tests with it in the Gulf of Lions, but they readily agreed to continue those tests out here. We made sure that it got terrific publicity, we made sure that its advantages were pointed out time and time again, that not even the biggest moron could fail to understand how good it was for stealthy underwater salvage and recovery of buried treasure. We knew it would be a matter of time before the *Temptress* turned up, and she did. So we left it in a nice lonely place. But before we left it I jinxed it so thoroughly that no one apart from the electrician who'd wired it in the first place and myself could ever have got it going again. You had to have someone to unjinx it, didn't you, Vyland? Wasn't it a fortunate coincidence that I happened to turn up at the right time? Incidentally, I wonder what our friends the field foreman and petroleum engineer are going to say when they find that they've spent the better part of three months drilling a couple of miles away from where the geologists told them to: I suppose it was you and Bryson who altered the reference navigation marks on the charts to bring you within shouting distance of the treasure and miles away from where the oil strata lie. At the present rate they'll end up with the pipe in the Indian Ocean and still no oil.'

'You're not going to get off with this,' Vyland said savagely. 'By God, you're not –'

'Shut up!' I interrupted contemptuously. 'Shut up or I'll turn a knob here, pull a switch there and have the two of you grovelling on your hands and knees and begging for your lives as you were doing not five minutes ago.'

They could have killed me there and then, they could have watched me die in screaming agony and the tears of joy would have rolled down their cheeks. Nobody had ever talked like this to them before, and they had just no idea what to say, what to do about it: for their lives were still in my hands. Then, after a long moment, Vyland leaned back in his stool and smiled. His mind was working again.

'I suppose, Talbot, that you were entertaining some idea of turning us over to the authorities. Is that it?' He waited for a reply, but when none came he went on: 'If you were, I'd change my mind about it. For such a clever cop, Talbot, you've been very blind in one spot. I'm sure you wouldn't want to be responsible for the deaths of two innocent people, would you now, Talbot?'

'What are you talking about?' I asked slowly.

'I'm talking about the general.' Vyland flicked a glance at Royale, a glance for the first time empty of fear, a look of triumph. 'General Blair Ruthven. The general, his wife, and his younger daughter. Do you know what I'm talking about, Talbot?'

'What's the general's wife got to do –?'

'My God! And for a moment I thought you had us!' The relief in Vyland's face was almost tangible quality. 'You fool, Talbot. You blind fool! The general – did it never occur to you to think how we got him to come in with us? Did it never occur to you to wonder *why* a man like that would let us use his yacht, his rig and anything else we wanted to? Didn't it, Talbot? Didn't it?'

'Well, I thought –'

'You thought!' he sneered. 'You poor fool, old Ruthven had to help us whether he wanted to or not. He helped us because he knew the lives of his wife and young daughter depended on us.'

'His wife and young daughter? But – but they've had a legal separation, haven't they – the general and his wife, I mean. I read all about it –'

'Sure. Sure you read all about it.' Vyland, his terror forgotten, was almost jovial now. 'So did a hundred million others. The general made good and sure that the story got around. It would have been just too bad if the story hadn't got around. They're hostages, Talbot. We've got them in a place of safety where they'll stay till we're finished here. Or else.'

'You – you kidnapped them?'

'At last the penny drops,' Vyland sneered. 'Sure we kidnapped them.'

'You and Royale?'

'Me and Royale.'

'You admit it? A federal and capital offence – kidnapping – you freely and openly admit it. Is that it?'

'That's it. Why shouldn't we admit it?' Vyland blustered. But he had become suddenly uneasy. 'So you'd better forget about the cops and any ideas

348

you have about delivering us to them. Besides, how do you think you're going to get us up the caisson and off the rig without being chopped into little pieces? I reckon you're mad, Talbot.'

'The general's wife and daughter,' I mused, as if I hadn't heard him. 'It wasn't a bad idea. You'd have let them go in the end, you couldn't afford not to, it would have been the Lindbergh case ten times over had you tried anything. On the other hand you knew the general wouldn't start anything afterwards: it would only be his word against yours, and up your sleeve you always carried the trump card – Royale. As long as Royale walked the face of America the general would never speak. This whole operation probably cost him a cool million – for the general a bagatelle compared to the value of wife and children. A sweet set-up.'

'Correct. I hold the trumps, Talbot.'

'Yes,' I said absently. 'And every day, just on noon, you sent a coded telegram – in the general's company code – to your watchdogs who kept an eye on Mrs Ruthven and Jean. You see, Vyland, I even know the daughter's name. And if the coded telegram didn't arrive in twenty-four hours they had instructions to shift them to another place, a safer hide-out. Atlanta wasn't too safe, I'm afraid.'

'Vyland's face was grey, his hands beginning to shake again. His voice came as a strained whisper. 'What are you saying?'

'I only caught on twenty-four hours ago.' I

replied. 'We'd been blind – we'd been check-ing every outgoing cable from Marble Springs for weeks, but forgot all about the inland telegrams. When I did catch on, a message to Judge Mollison from me – through Kennedy, remember that fight we had, I slipped it to him then – started off what must have been the most concentrated and ruthless man hunt for years. The FBI would stop at nothing, not since Jablonsky got his, and obviously they stopped at nothing. Mrs Ruthven and Jean are safe and well – your friends, Vyland, are under lock and key and talking their heads off to beat the rap.' This last bit was guesswork, but I thought my guess wouldn't be so far out.

'You're making this up,' Vyland said huskily. Fear was back in his face and he was clutching at straws. 'You've been under guard all day and –'

'If you were up in the radio shack and could see the state of that creature of yours who tried to stop me from putting through a radio call to the sheriff, you wouldn't say that. It was Kennedy who gave Royale here his sore head. It was Kennedy who dragged him inside the room and kept on making those calculations on the papers on my desk while I went up to attend to things. You see, I didn't dare move till they were free. But they are free.'

I looked at the grey and stricken and hunted face and looked away again. It wasn't a pretty sight. The time had come to get back, I had found out all I wanted to know, got all the evidence I would ever want. I opened up a circuit box, unbuttoned

350

and repositioned four wires, closed the box again and pulled the first of the four electro-magnetic releases for the lead shot ballast.

It worked. Two clouds of grey pellets showered mistily by the side observation windows and disappeared into the black mud on the seabed. It worked, but the lightening of the weight made no difference, the bathyscaphe didn't budge.

I pulled the second switch, emptied the second pair of containers: still we remained immovable. We were sunk pretty deep into that mud, how deep I didn't know, but this had never happened before on tests. I sat down to work out if there was any factor I had forgotten, and now that the strain was over the pain was back in my shoulder and mouth and I wasn't thinking so well any more. I removed the button from between my teeth and absent-mindedly placed it in a pocket.

'Was – was that cyanide?' Vyland's face was still grey.

'Don't be silly. Antler-horn, best quality.' I rose, pulled the other two switches simultaneously. They worked – but again nothing happened. I looked at Vyland and Royale, and saw reflected in their faces the fear that was beginning to touch in my own mind. God, I thought, how ironic it would be if, after all I had said and done, we were to die down here. There was no point in putting off the moment of decision. I started up both motors, inclined the planes to the maximum upwards elevation, started up the tow-rope motor and at the same moment pressed the switch that jettisoned the two big electric batteries mounted on the outside of the scaphe. They fell simultaneously with a thud that jarred the bathyscaphe, sending up a dark spreading cloud of black viscous-looking mud: for two moments of eternity nothing happened, the bolt was shot, the last hope was gone, when, all in a second, the scaphe trembled, broke suction aft and started to rise. I heard Vyland sobbing with relief and terror.

I switched off the engines and we rose steadily, smoothly, on an even keel, now and again starting the tow-rope motor to take in some slack. We were about a hundred feet up when Royale spoke.

'So it was all a plant, Talbot. You never had any intention of keeping us down there.' His voice was an evil whisper, the one good side of his face back to its expressionless normal again.

'That's it,' I agreed.

'Why, Talbot?'

'To find out exactly where the treasure was. But that was really secondary, I knew it wasn't far away, a government survey ship could have found it in a day.'

'Why, Talbot?' he repeated in the same monotone.

'Because I had to have evidence. I had to have evidence to send you both to the chair. Up till now we had no evidence whatsoever, all along the way your back trail was divided into a series of water-tight compartments with locked doors. Royale locked the doors by killing everybody and anybody who might talk. Incredibly, there wasn't a single solitary thing we could pin on you, there wasn't a person who could split on you for the sufficient reason that all those who could were dead. The locked doors. But you opened them all today. Fear was the key to all the doors.'

'You've got no evidence, Talbot,' Royale said. 'It's only your word against ours – and you won't live to give your word.'

'I expected something like that,' I nodded. We were at a depth of about 250 feet now. 'Getting your courage back, Royale, aren't you? But you don't dare do anything. You can't get this scaphe back to the rig without me, and you know it. Besides, I have some concrete evidence. Taped under my toes is the bullet that killed Jablonsky.' They exchanged quick startled looks. 'Shakes you, doesn't it? I know it all, I even dug Jablonsky's body up in the kitchen garden. That bullet will match up with your automatic, Royale. That alone would send you to the chair.'

'Give it to me, Talbot. Give it to me now.' The flat marbled eyes were glistening, his hand sliding for his gun.

'Don't be stupid. What are you going to do with it – throw it out the window? You can't get rid of it, you know it. And even if you could, there's something else that you can never get rid of. The real reason for our trip today, the reason that means you both die.'

There was something in my tone that got them. Royale was very still, Vyland still grey, still shaking. They knew, without knowing why, that the end had come.

'The tow-rope,' I said. 'The wire with the microphone cable leading back to the speaker in the rig. You see the microphone switch here, you see it's at "Off"? I jinxed it, I fixed it this afternoon so that the microphone was always live. That's why I made you speak up, made you repeat most things, that's why I dragged you, Vyland, close up to me so that you were right against the mike when you were making your confession. Every word that's been spoken down here today, every word we're speaking now is going through live to that speaker. And every word is being taken down three times: by tape-recorder, by a civil stenographer and by a police stenographer from Miami. I phoned the police on the way back from the rig this morning, they were aboard the rig before daylight – which probably accounts for the field foreman and the petroleum engineer looking so nervous when we came aboard today. They've been hidden for twelve hours – but Kennedy knew where they were. And at lunchtime, Vyland, I gave Kennedy your secret knock. Cibatti and his men would have fallen for it, they were bound to. And it's all over now.'

They said nothing. There was nothing they could say, at least not yet, not until the full significance of what I had said had become irrevocably clear to them.

'And don't worry about the tape recording,' I went on. 'They're not normally acceptable as court evidence but those will be. Every statement you made was volunteered by yourselves – think back and you'll see that: and there'll be at least ten witnesses inside the caisson who can swear to the genuineness of the recordings, who will swear that they could not have come from any source other than the bathyscaphe. Any prosecutor in the Union will call for and get a verdict of guilty without the jury leaving the box. You know what that means.'

'So.' Royale had his gun out, he must have had some crazy notion of trying to snap the tow-rope and sailing the scaphe off to safety. 'So we were all wrong about you, Talbot, so you were smarter than we were. All right, I admit it. You have what it takes – but you'll never live to hear the jury give their verdict. As well hung for a sheep as a lamb.' His trigger finger began to tighten. 'So long, Talbot.'

'I wouldn't,' I said. 'Not if I were you. Wouldn't you like to be able to grip the arm-rests of the electric chair with *both* hands when the time comes?'

'It's no good talking, Talbot, I said –'

'Look down the barrel,' I advised him. 'If you

want to blow your hand off, you know what to do. When you were unconscious this evening Kennedy used a hammer and punch to jam a lead cylinder right down the barrel. Do you think I'd be so crazy as to come down here and you with a loaded gun in your hand? Don't take my word for it, Royale – just pull the trigger.'

He squinted down the barrel and his face twisted into a malevolent mask of hate. He was using up ten years' quota of expressions in one day – and he was telegraphing his signals. I knew that gun was coming before he did. I managed to dodge, the gun struck the Plexiglas behind me and fell harmlessly to the floor at my feet.

'No one tampered with my gun,' Vyland said hoarsely. He was almost unrecognizable as the smooth urbane slightly florid top executive he'd been, his face was haggard now, curiously aged and covered in a greyish sheen of sweat. 'Made a mistake at last, haven't you, Talbot?' His breath was coming in brief shallow gasps. 'You're not going –'

He broke off, hand halfway inside his coat, and stared down into the muzzle of the heavy Colt pointing in between his eyes.

'Where – where did you get that? It – it's Larry's gun?'

'Was. You should have searched me, shouldn't you – not Kennedy? Fools. Sure it's Larry's gun – that dope-headed junky who claimed he was your son.' I looked steadily at him, I didn't want

356

any gunfire 150 feet below sea level. I didn't know what might happen. 'I took it off him this evening, Vyland, just about an hour ago. Just before I killed him.'

'Just – just before –?'

'Just before I killed him. I broke his neck.'

With something between a sob and a moan Vyland flung himself at me across the width of the chamber. But his reactions were slow, his movements even slower and he collapsed soundlessly to the floor as the barrel of Larry's Colt caught him across the temple.

'Tie him up,' I said to Royale. There was plenty of spare flex lying around and Royale wasn't fool enough to get tough about it. He tied him up, while I was blowing gasoline through a valve and slowing our ascent about 120 feet, and just as he finished and before he could straighten I let him have it behind the ear with the butt of Larry's Colt. If ever there had been a time for playing it like a gentleman, that time was long gone, I was now so weak, so lost in that flooding sea of pain, that I knew it would be impossible for me to bring that scaphe back to the rig and watch Royale at the same time. I doubted whether I could even make it at all.

I made it, but only just. I remember easing the hatch of the bathyscaphe up inside the caisson, asking through the mike, in a slurred stumbling voice that wasn't mine, for the annular rubber ring to be inflated and then lurching across to

357

twist open the handle of the entrance door. I don't remember any more. I am told they found the three of us lying unconscious on the floor of the bathyscaphe.

EPILOGUE

I walked down the court-house steps out into the still, warm October sunshine. They'd just sentenced Royale to death and everybody knew there would be no appeal, no reversal of the decision. The jury, as I had prophesied, had convicted without leaving the box. The trial had lasted only one day and during the entire day Royale had sat as though carved from stone, his eyes fixed on the same spot for hour after interminable hour. That spot had been me. Those blank, flat, marbled eyes had been as expressionless as ever, they hadn't even altered a fraction when the prosecution had played the recording of Royale begging for his life on his hands and knees in the scaphe at the bottom of the sea, they hadn't altered when the death sentence had come but for all the lack of expression a blind man could have read his message. 'Eternity's a long time, Talbot,' his eyes had said. 'Eternity is forever. But I'll be waiting.'

Let him wait: eternity was too long for me to worry about.

They hadn't sentenced Vyland, for they never even had the chance to try him. On the way up the caisson from the bathyscaphe, 170 steps from the bottom, Vyland had simply let go his grip on the ladder and leaned back into space: he hadn't even screamed on the long way down.

I passed the general and his wife on the steps. I had met Mrs Ruthven for the first time on my first day out of hospital, which had been yesterday. She had been very charming and gracious and endlessly grateful. They had offered me everything, from a job at the top of the tree in Ruthven's oil companies to enough money to last any man half a dozen lifetimes, but I just smiled and thanked them and turned them all down. There was nothing in them for me, all the fancy directorships and money in the world couldn't buy me back the days that were gone. And money couldn't buy the only thing I wanted out of the world today.

Mary Ruthven was standing on the sidewalk beside her father's sand and beige Rolls-Royce. She was dressed in a plain white, simple one-piece dress that couldn't have cost more than a thousand bucks, her braided wheat-coloured hair was piled high on her head and I had never seen her looking so lovely. Behind her was Kennedy. For the first time I saw him dressed in a lounge suit, dark blue and immaculately cut, and when you saw him like that it was impossible to imagine him any other way. His chauffeuring days were over: the general knew how much the Ruthven family owed him and you couldn't pay a debt like that with chauffeur's wages. I wished him all the luck in the world: he was a nice guy.

I halted at the foot of the steps. A little wind was blowing in from the blue sparkling shimmer that was the Gulf of Mexico, sending tiny little dust devils and small pieces of paper dancing across the street.

Mary saw me, hesitated a moment, then came across the sidewalk to where I was standing. Her eyes seemed dark and curiously blurred but maybe I was imagining it. She murmured something, I couldn't make out what it was, then suddenly, careful not to hurt my left arm still in its sling, she put her two arms round my neck, pulled down my head and kissed me. Next moment she was gone, making her way back to the Rolls like a person who couldn't see too well. Kennedy looked at her coming towards him, then lifted his eyes to mine, his face still and empty of all expression. I smiled at him and he smiled back. A nice guy.

I walked down the street, along towards the shore, and turned into a bar. I hadn't intended to, I didn't really need a drink, but the bar was there so I went in anyway. I had a couple of drinks, double Scotches, but it was just a waste of good liquor; I left and made my way down to a bench by the shore.

An hour, two hours, I don't know how long I

sat there. The sun sank down close to the rim of the ocean, the sea and the sky turned to orange and gold, and I could see, faintly on the horizon and weirdly silhouetted against this flaming backdrop, the massively grotesque angularity of the oil rig X 13.

X 13. I suppose that would always be a part of me now, that and the broken-winged DC that lay 580 yards to its south-west, buried under 480 feet of water. For better or for worse, it would always be part of me. For worse, I thought, for worse. It was all over and done with and empty now and it meant nothing, for that was all that was left.

The sun was on the rim of the sea now and the western world a great red flame, a flame that would soon be extinguished and vanish as if it had never been. And so it had been with my red rose, before it had turned to white.

The sun was gone and the night rushed across the sea. With the dark came the cold so I rose stiffly to my feet and walked back to the hotel.

The Guns of Navarone

'The most successful British novelist
of his time' Jack Higgins

The guns of Navarone, huge and catastrophically accurate,
embedded atop an impregnable iron fortress in the
Mediterranean Sea.

Twelve hundred British soldiers trapped on a nearby island,
with no hope of rescue from Allied ships, waiting to die.

Keith Mallory, world-famous mountaineer, skilled saboteur.
His mission: to lead a small team of misfits and silence
the German guns forever.

'Could hardly be bettered'
Sunday Times

'Its strength comes from the speed of its narrative,
its vivid creation of tensions and its power in
handling descriptions of action'
Evening Standard

HMS Ulysses

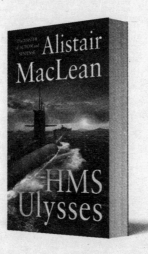

'The most successful British novelist
of his time' Jack Higgins

Already pushed beyond the limits of endurance, *HMS Ulysses* and
her crew must put to sea again, to escort a vital supply convoy
heading for Murmansk.

Surging deep into the frozen Arctic waters, they must battle not
only the fierce weather, but German attacks from the air, the sea, and
beneath the waves, as the feared U-boats close in on their prey.

With each day bringing greater destruction, and increasing hardships
aboard the frozen cruiser, it soon becomes a tense and deadly game of
cat and mouse between the crippled *Ulysses* and her silent pursuers.

'A brilliant, overwhelming piece of descriptive writing'
Observer

'It deserves an honourable place among twentieth-century war books'
Daily Mail

'*HMS Ulysses* is in the same class as *The Cruel Sea*'
Evening Standard

Ice Station Zebra

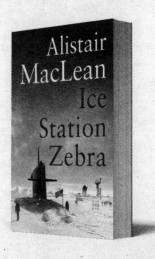

'The most successful British novelist
of his time' Jack Higgins

With America and the Soviet Union on the brink of global war,
a US atomic submarine sprints under the Arctic ice cap on a top-
secret race to Ice Station Zebra.

Its crew believe they go to rescue survivors of the burned-out
weather station. What they don't know it that they are on a
suicide mission: to beat the Soviets to a falling Russian satellite –
containing information that could tip the balance of power.

With bad weather grounding American, British and Soviet jets,
the submarine may reach the satellite crash site first – but the
Russians have a plan...

'Tense, terrifying, moves at a breathless pace'
Daily Express

The Satan Bug

'The most successful British novelist
of his time' Jack Higgins

Mordon Chemical Research Centre: an ultra top secret facility
hidden in the English countryside and one of the most secure
places in the world. But now it has been broken into and the
Satan Bug, the deadliest toxin in the world, has been stolen.

Private detective Pierre Cavell is recruited by the British Secret
Service to investigate, and it soon becomes clear that not
everyone is who they seem.

And then a letter is sent giving the authorities just 72 hours to
meet the thief's outrageous demands. There is no way they can
pay the ransom, but if they refuse he will release the virus…

'Utterly compelling'
Punch

Where Eagles Dare

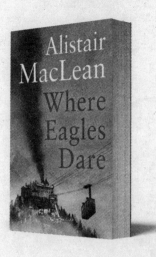

'The most successful British novelist
of his time' Jack Higgins

Winter 1943, and US General Carnaby has been captured
by the Nazis. He is being held in a fortress high in the Bavarian
Alps. headquarters of the German Secret Service, and in his head
are plans for the invasion of Normandy.

A special team of British commandos, a US Army ranger and
a female secret agent is hurriedly assembled. Their mission:
parachute into the area, break in to the alpine Castle, and rescue
General Carnaby before the Germans can interrogate him.

But unknown to all, there is another mission,
and someone in the group is a traitor...

'A real dazzler of a thriller, with vivid action, fine set pieces of
suspense, and a virtuoso display of startling plot twists'
New York Times